IT CANNOT BE STORMED

Translated from the German by M. S. Stephens
First English edition published 1935 by Jonathan Cape Ltd.
Second English Edition published in 2011 by Arktos Media Ltd.

© 2011 Arktos Media Ltd.

No part of this book may be reproduced or utilised in any form or by any means (whether electronic or mechanical), including photocopying, recording or by any information storage and retrieval system, without permission in writing from the publisher.

Printed in the United Kingdom

ISBN 978-1-907166-12-9

BIC classification: Historical fiction (FV),
Classic fiction (FC) & Germany (1DFG)

Editor: Martin Häggkvist
Cover Design: Andreas Nilsson
Layout: Daniel Friberg
Proofreader: Michael J. Brooks

Back cover photos: left and centre, scenes of street-fighting in Weimar-era Germany; on the right, Ernst von Salomon.

ARKTOS MEDIA LTD.
www.arktos.com

IT CANNOT BE STORMED

BY

ERNST VON SALOMON

ARKTOS
MMXI

EDITOR'S FOREWORD

ERNST VON SALOMON (1902-1972) was one of the most enigmatic individuals who have come to be classified as a part of the Conservative Revolution, a school of thought which flourished in the days of the German Weimar Republic up until the National Socialist Party (N.S.D.A.P.) came to power in 1933. He is today often, when at all, remembered for his 1951 book *Der Fragebogen*. This lengthy, sarcastic treatise based on the Allied denazification questionnaire prompted *Time Magazine* to condemn the author's 'moral colour blindness' and 'self-pity mixed with arrogant self-righteousness' as expressions of the prime motors behind Nazism.* There are, however, many other (and less puerile) things to say about von Salomon, his life and his work.

After training as a military cadet from the age of eleven, while inadvertently avoiding serving in the First World War on account of his youth, von Salomon joined the Freikorps in 1919 to fight Bolshevism in the Baltics, later combating Polish insurgents in Upper Silesia. His involvement in the paramilitary group grew, until he was arrested in 1922 for providing the car used in the assassination of the German Foreign Minister, Walther Rathenau. Later, during the Second World War, this would work to his advantage, as he was excused from military service; upon being asked by the examining officer whether he was a Jew, von Salomon replied 'No, but a murderer.'**

From his release in 1927 onwards von Salomon developed his skills as a writer. In *Die Geächteten* (1930, translated into English as *The Outlaws*) he drew on his earlier experiences to create a fictionalised account of the Freikorps, and in the following years he published a number of works, including the present one (published as *Die Stadt* [The City] in 1932). When Hitler came to power, a prospect towards which von Salomon had been ambivalent for years, he turned to writing movie scripts, while living a relatively apolitical life with his Jewish wife until the end of the war. With the fall of the Third Reich he and his wife were imprisoned due to the U.S. policy of automatic arrest of

---

* 'It just happened,' in *Time Magazine*, www.time.com/time/magazine/article/0,9171,861117,00.html. Accessed February 2011.
** *Ibid.*

anyone associated with the former regime, and allegedly abused by Allied forces, but they were released after being classed as 'erroneous arrestees.'*

For the remainder of his life von Salomon wrote a number of other books, as well as numerous screenplays (including a series of semi-exploitation films centred upon the character of Liane, a blonde, partially nude woman ruling a primitive African tribe).

The present book is a peculiar one. Written in the early 1930s, *It Cannot Be Stormed* has few equals when it comes to transmitting the ambiance and sentiments of the Weimar Republic era: the frustration with the draconian reparations, the incompetence of public officials, and the seething popular dissatisfaction with the general state of affairs. The book's protagonist makes his way through a bleak, volatile city landscape and tries to form alliances in order to further the cause of a national farmers' movement. He interacts with all sorts of political and cultural radicals, and is sometimes disappointed, sometimes hopeful, while he almost always maintains a detached, sceptical attitude that keeps him at a certain distance from the centre of events.

It is highly likely that parts of *It Cannot Be Stormed* drew inspiration from the actions of von Salomon's brother Bruno, who abandoned the N.S.D.A.P. for the section of the German Communist Party directed at the German peasantry.** However, it also seems to be deeply coloured by the author's own sentiments and orientations, as is suggested by the distanced tone — it is truly the work of an activist turned observer (the latter being a term used on numerous occasions by von Salomon to define himself). In the book's many long discourses on politics, revolution and the German condition, one clearly sees both the strengths and the weaknesses of the Conservative Revolutionary position. Intellectual flexibility, spiritual depth and a vision both realistic and romantic — all these positive traits are partly undone by inconsistency and an unwillingness (or inability) to take a concrete position in a real, political context. This is probably the key to understanding why the Conservative Revolution not only dissipated during the Third Reich, with the efforts of certain of its representatives to 'work from within the system' more or less wasted, but also why it was later condemned by the victorious Allies as proto-Nazi. The effort to remain spiritually and intellectually precise, nuanced and honest made the path of many

---

* Markus Josef Klein, *Ernst von Salomon. Eine politische Biographie. Mit einer vollständigen Bibliographie* (San Casiano: Limburg an der Lahn, 1994) p 260.

** Klemens Von Klemperer, *Germany's New Conservatives: Its History and Dilemma in the Twentieth Century* (London: Oxford University Press, 1990), p 148, n 32.

of the Conservative Revolutionaries, Ernst von Salomon included, a harsh and unrewarding one.

Upon editing this book I have altered little of M. S. Steven's 1935 translation. Certain words have been modernised, a few blatant errors in translation corrected and the often cumbersome dialogue structure reorganised. It is my belief that the book will be of great value to the reader—whether he wishes to understand the circumstances of inter-war Germany or reflect upon some of the more difficult issues facing man as a social and political being.

Martin Häggkvist
Mumbai, India, February 2011

'The spiritual capital of a kingdom lies not
behind fortresses and cannot be stormed.'
—NOVALIS (FRIEDRICH FREIHERR VON HARDENBERG)

TO
MARTHA DODD

I

BEHIND the sheltering dykes of the west coast of Schleswig-Holstein from Niebüll to Glückstadt stretches an expanse of pleasant green country. As far as the gentle range of the Geest there is hardly an undulation to break the wide curving line of the horizon. Narrow clinker-roads wind like reddish ribbons through the plain connecting the farmhouses which lie scattered over the countryside, each in its cluster of trees. Very rarely the farms are grouped to form an established settlement, and it is difficult for the eye to distinguish one community from another. These farms dominate the country, the clean little hamlets and market-towns appearing as hardly more than bright spots in the grey-green landscape. The low brick farmhouses with their heavy thatched roofs and small windows, the entrance doors spreading almost across the whole front, stand in the middle of the narrow rectangle of pasture-land cut off by the dykes of the marshland. The grass of the pasture grows luxuriantly, enriched by the black earth and close cropped by the grazing cattle. As a rule, cow-shed and dwelling-house are united under one gigantic roof, and the warm pungent smell of the tethered animals pervades the whole house. The cattle are the wealth of the country, and the farmers of the Geest say, probably with a touch of envy, that the only work the Marsh farmers need do is to pinch the tails of their oxen occasionally to see if they are fat enough. Actually there was always plenty to do on the farms, and if the Geest had to reap the ripe corn under a burning sun, the Marsh had to stand knee-deep in the thick oozing water of the dykes, perpetually clearing them out; if the Geest had to suffer loss from thunderstorms and hail, the Marsh had to pay its toll in epidemics and fevers. In the Geest, the owner of thirty acres of land and five head of cattle could not be considered a big farmer, whereas in the marshland the owner of ten acres could keep thirty head of cattle and yet not be considered a big farmer. But they were all independent, and St. Annen-Klosterfelde, the farm owned by Claus Heim, had been in his family for four centuries—a family of independent farmers, who could always claim equality with any nobleman. The oak trees, too, which surround the farm to this day, had stood there for four hundred years.

There were many such farmsteads and such families in the country. The eldest son inherited the farm, and the others went out as labourers, or, if opportunity offered, to sea, or to the town, or, if the farm were prosperous, they might study to be lawyers or parsons. For property regulated everything, and property was something more than money and stock; it was inheritance and race, family and tradition, and honour, past, present and future. If a man lost his farm, he lost more than a possession, and he lost it because he had been a bad manager. Bad management meant faulty thinking about the farm, and to lose the farm was more of a misdemeanour than a misfortune. Whatever the farm required had to be supplied, even if it meant breaking away from old traditional methods. Thus the farmer and cattle breeder had to turn dealer when the times demanded it, and, while the Geest had to watch the market prices and store or sell off its wheat accordingly, the Marsh had to be no less vigilant to choose the most favourable moment in autumn to drive the summer-fattened cattle to the sales. But the Marsh was the first to feel bad times, for the cattle had to be marketed at any price when they were ready for slaughtering.

Throughout the Great War things were kept going, for the old men and women could manage the farms at a pinch. The period of inflation, too, passed and even did the farmers a certain amount of good: old debts disappeared and new machines were introduced, and here and there a farmer managed to buy a motor car, which was useful for speeding up business. So later, when a large part of the burden of stabilisation fell on them, the farmers considered it only just. They were prepared to live and let live, and even if they kept a sharp hold on what was theirs, they did not hesitate to make sacrifices when necessary, and always paid their taxes punctually. But this question of taxes became more and more curious. All this business from the town was anything but pleasant; it meant endless reckoning and letter-writing, and an official letter always meant bother. But now there were more and more of these official documents, and the parish magistrate was kept busy giving advice and answering letters. When the young men from the farms were at home—many of them were in the town at agricultural schools and at the newfangled farmers' colleges, where they learnt all sorts of things which could not be taught to them on the farms—they had lots to say about breed and the soil, and mythology and primitive forces, and the farmers listened and were delighted at the nice things said about them in the towns. But then maybe, when the wife was clearing away the supper things, the farmer at his fireside would ask:

'What's this about a landed property tax?'

For there was no end to these taxes, property tax, land tax, landed property tax, income tax, tax on profits—and, Lord help us! Weren't they one and the same thing, land and property and income and profits! Wasn't it all just the farm? And the farmer was expected to pay twice and three times over, and then on top of that the local taxes and the dyke duties and the civil dues, and they kept increasing, and before you could turn round the results of your work had been subtracted away to nothing on a little scrap of paper until you didn't know where you were. And then again there was the bank interest and the roads and improvements dues, not to mention subscriptions to the various societies and the Land League and the other agricultural associations. But why not mention all these; for if one went to the officials, and in the end one had to go to them, then there would be regrets and head-shakings, and a mountain of promises and a dungheap of advice, and finally a meeting to deal with the emergency and bring up special points, and a resolution would be passed unanimously; and there it ended.

So it meant a visit to the Treasury-office. And frequently the farmers set out on this mission, even though it meant the loss of a whole day, all for nothing. For the people at the Treasury-office were not the same as they used to be, when it was possible to exchange a few sensible words with one another, and the District Presidents, who used to rule like good kings, were no longer there. They had understood the farmers, and used to ask after their wives and their cattle. There were no more District Presidents to be seen going round in their green caps with their stout sticks and high boots. The men who sat behind the desks now were serious gentlemen with pince-nez and dispatch-cases. They were no longer men from the district; they came from the Rhineland or from the province of Saxony or some other Godforsaken hole.

'Well, well,' said the farmers, 'work is work; I have my job and he has his, but we used to be able to work together, and we can't any more. And we used not to have to ask for help, and now we have to. And we used to get things done when it was necessary, and now if we succeed in getting something done it is regarded as a favour. But we don't want favours, we want our rights.'

So they went to the Board of Agriculture. And there it was yet another story. If it had been nothing but the taxes! But now there was something wrong with the cattle trade.

'Rationalisation,' said the gentlemen of the Board of Agriculture to the farmers' deputations. 'Rationalisation' was the great cry. But, said the farmers, what was there to be rationalised when everything had been worked out to the minutest detail?

'Conversion,' said the gentlemen of the Board of Agriculture. 'Conversion' was the great cry. It was no use trading in oxen any more on account of the Commercial Treaty with Denmark. 'Conversion.'

Krupp had converted his factories—from cannons to mattresses. You must convert your oxen into pigs. Many of the farmers did convert. But it was a slow process. Machines work quickly, but live-stock needs time to grow and fatten, and a farm is not a factory. And when the time came, and the farm had been converted, and, after much trouble and many failures, the pigs were ready for slaughter, then they had to be sold at a loss on account of the Commercial Treaty with Serbia. They had worked at a loss, but the conversion had been accomplished, and the tax-collectors wanted their money.

'This won't do,' said the farmers, 'we are paying out of capital.'

The tax-collectors did not care.

'We will not pay out of capital,' said the farmers, and put their solid heads together and the word capital became a word of great significance. Then the bailiffs came. And the farmers went to the Treasury-office.

At first it was only two or three who were always going to the Treasury-office.

'You have managed badly,' said the others.

At first it was only two or three who had to leave their farms.

'You have managed badly,' said the others. But then there were more. Then some who were known far and wide as good managers had to leave their farms, some who were known to be men who thoroughly understood their business. The passages of the Treasury office were crowded and the building had to be enlarged. And the bailiffs were kept busy. First oxen were seized. That had a bad effect on credit. Then still more oxen were seized. And credit was suspended altogether. Then the farm was put up for auction, and nobody said any longer 'You have managed badly.'

'What are we to do?' said the farmers one to another. 'What are we to do?' they said in unison.

They went to Claus Heim, who had always taken the lead among his fellows.

Claus Heim said, 'You must help yourselves.'

'Help yourselves,' said Hamkens too, and Heim and Hamkens had a meeting.

Claus Heim was a man of about fifty at the time. He was a tall fellow, as strong as one of his own oxen, with bristling fair hair going grey on his square red head. Anybody observing his hands would scarcely have dared to offer him much opposition. And it was known that he had travelled, and had knocked about with all sorts and conditions in many parts of the world. But Hamkens was short and inclined to be thin, a quiet man in his thirties, pale and unassuming. He had gone to the Great War as an officer's orderly and returned home as adjutant, and, like Heim, he had passed the ten years since the war quietly on his farm without taking any particular interest in politics.

'Help yourselves,' they said, and that was the great cry.

'We cannot help you,' said the others, the gentlemen in the offices, the gentlemen at the green tables. 'We should like to, but we cannot.'

'Why not?' asked the farmers, as they went from one to the other.

They went from one office to another, from one association to another, and from one party to another.

'We have lost the war,' they said in the offices and at the party headquarters.

'Well?' said the farmers.

'We are paying reparations,' they said.

That might be so—losers have to suffer the consequences.

'How can we pay without collecting the money from the taxes? How can we rehabilitate ourselves unless sacrifices are made?' asked the gentlemen, and the farmers said they didn't know, and, of course, they were very glad to make sacrifices, as they had already proved time and again, but one thing they did know, that they had to pay their taxes out of capital—and who would be such a fool as to kill his best milk cow?

'It is unjust,' said the farmers, 'that we should have to pay twice and three times over, and it won't do. And what is all this about commercial treaties?'

The gentlemen shrugged their shoulders and referred them to other gentlemen, and they, too, shrugged their shoulders and referred them further, and finally the farmers left in a rage. There were still the other parties to be tried, the radicals, the opposition parties. But there they found nothing but empty talk and the farmers wouldn't stand for that.

'Help yourselves,' said Hamkens and Heim, and took the matter in hand.

They called a meeting of farmers at Rendsburg. And fifty thousand turned up. The bailiffs had already visited many houses and there were rumours of this one and that one having to leave his farm, and there were highly respected names among them, men from North and South Dithmarsch, from the neighbourhood of Itzehoe and Rendsburg, from Wilster and Heide; even from Preetz and Flensburg the bad news came, and for some time past it had been not only the west coast where the farmers were feeling the pinch and were rising up against it. Fifty thousand farmers at one meeting!

'Well, what of it?' said the workers of Kiel, 'we can produce fifty thousand of our men any day you like.'

But these were farmers who had assembled, and from Schleswig-Holstein moreover. And the farmer up there was not one to leave his farm. If he has anything to say he calls on his neighbour, or at most at the beer-house which is kept by the baker or the butcher nearby, or he goes for a drink after his business in the market-town. And merely for a question of politics! Before the war they had voted National-Liberal, because they did not want to vote for the Old Prussian conservatives. They were, moreover, a stronghold, as they read in the newspapers, but that did not concern them, for since 1864 they had had no use for politics. And now? Fifty thousand! And in the offices and party headquarters they began to prick up their ears. There was not much for them to hear in Rendsburg. But it was enough. For the last time we demand... and then, things have come to a climax! And the refrain began to be heard: 'Better dead than slaves, sea-girt Schleswig-Holstein.'

When the farmers returned home, however, they knew considerably more than they had known before, more even than the anxiously listening ears in the offices had been able to discover. In every community emergency committees were formed, and only the best men were considered good enough to be eligible for these.

'Is that all?' asked the gentlemen in the offices.

It was not all.

Then the officers of the law came to distrain, and they found a great crowd of farm labourers on all the roads round about the village; they allowed the officers to pass through unmolested, greeting them with friendly grins; but afterwards the bailiffs had to sit idle all the afternoon in the sun, for there was not a soul to be seen, and there was no question of holding a sale. There was another distraint. This time the auction room was packed full, and there were a certain number of strangers present, who were probably anxious to pick up a bargain; but all round the strangers stood the farmers, casually contemplating their fists, and not a single bid was made. Another time, in the Treasury-office at Husum, the passages were full of farmers. There was no room for the busy officials to get through.

'Make room, you people,' they said. 'What do you want?'

'We're just waiting,' said the farmers, 'don't shove,' and they laughed, and some of them began to sing softly.

'This won't do,' said the officials, and they said a lot more.

And one thing led to another, and the farmers went on just waiting. Then the police came and there were blows and broken windows and a preliminary enquiry, at which next to nothing came out, for the farmers had only been waiting for Hamkens who was inside giving a long explanation as to why he could not pay his taxes out of capital.

'This won't do,' muttered the minor officials.

'This will not do at all,' said the higher officials.

'Stringent measures must be taken,' said the highest authorities, and the Minister declared in the Landstag: 'Stringent measures will be taken.'

The emergency committees became very busy. For the whole machinery of administration began to creak into movement. 'Machinery of administration,' that was the great cry.

'Who is to blame for everything? Whom did we warn after quietly stating what we wanted? Who is putting on great airs now that the damage has been done? The machinery of administration. They could not help us. They could not act for us. But they can act against us. Up to now everything had been peaceful in the country.'

The womenfolk were not greatly in favour of the new attitude.

'Leave it alone,' they, said to the men, 'it'll change all in good time—don't get mixed up in these things.'

Then the machinery of administration began to confiscate the milk-money. Now, the milk-money is the daily money, and it is in the hands of the farmer's wife, who with it keeps the daily life of the farm-house going.

'What, the milk-money? What are we to live on? How are we to buy the dinner and pay the cobbler?'

The milk-money—that settled it. They resorted to stringent measures.

'Stringent measures,' that was the great cry.

Every policeman knew what it meant, and what had to be done. But when the policeman on his round happened to go into the bar to have a quick nip of brandy, the farmers, who were there in crowds, stood up without a word and left the room, and the innkeeper didn't like to see a lot of good customers leaving for the sake of one good customer. The policeman didn't fancy his brandy any more, and at home his wife, herself a farmer's daughter, pestered him because, since they had recently confiscated the milk-money in the next village, she couldn't get any of the farmers' wives to oblige her if she happened to run out of butter.

'Go over to Mrs. Petersen, she's not like that,' advised her husband. But Mrs Petersen was like that too. For suddenly there was great solidarity and there was a rumour from the town that Farmer Heim, after much quiet deliberation, had stood up at a meeting and had said—no more than that—that, as he knew there were many who did not want to be loyal to the cause, all he had to say was that in Schleswig-Holstein the farms were at a great distance from one another and for the most part they had thatched roofs. But, however that might be, the young men were more zealous in riding from place to place to rouse the farmers, and they visited the parish magistrates and told them, with the compliments of the emergency committee, that if any new taxation demands turned up they could just send the rubbish back where it came from.

There was a dangerous atmosphere in the country, and it was not surprising that many wanted to cook their gruel on the same fire and helped to fan the flames. The parties prepared for action, and in the little towns there was great unrest. The numerous agricultural associations anticipated a great haul of new members, and, if they had not been greatly united before, they were still less so now. They all agreed in wanting to present a united front, and the more united the front, the green front, became, the greater grew the internal dissensions. The farmers did not bother their heads much about this, for their movement was not an organisation, and the meetings of their emergency committees were not board meetings. And the authorities did not negotiate with them, they merely adopted stringent measures. The authorities would gladly have called a halt, but there was prestige to be considered. Had not the farmers' recently gone so far as to threaten a parish magistrate who was loyal to the Government?

'Above all, don't weaken. We have the powerful hand of the State behind us!'

Farmer Kock from Beidenfleth went three times to the District President in Itzehoe, who promised to intervene to prevent his distrained oxen from being fetched away, if he would pay off his arrears of tax within a given period. But before the appointed period had elapsed the zealous district officer had sent the bailiff to collect the oxen, and with him he sent a couple of unemployed men, since no one else could be found to undertake the job.

The three men arrived at the farm and proceeded to take the oxen. The farmer made no difficulties, but when they came out on to the road they suddenly encountered a number of farm labourers in their blue caps and with their sticks in their hands. They stood there and said nothing. Some of them piled bundles of straw on the narrow road, a few bundles in one place and then a few bundles a bit further on. And when the three men had dragged the oxen a little way along the road, suddenly tongues of flame shot up out of the straw and smoke rose. The oxen smelt the fire and stopped short. Why fire? From time immemorial fire has blazed in the land in time of trouble. And Farmer Kock was in trouble. The fire-horn was sounded because there was fire on the road, and the people gathered together because the fire-horn had sounded. Unfortunately, the oxen did not know this: they wrenched themselves loose and rushed back to the stable.

The District President in Itzehoe was a sensible man. On the one hand he felt sympathetic towards the farmers, and on the other hand he had superior officials to deal with. The district officer had acted too precipitately, he thought, and the words 'stringent measures, stringent measures' echoed in his ears. I am responsible for my district, he thought to himself; to whom am I responsible? My official superiors. The District President of Itzehoe was a thoughtful man. Whatever he decided to do was sure to be wrong. So, he said firmly, I will do my duty. And in the grey morning hours the police surrounded the house of Farmer Kock and forced their way into the farm-yard. There stood the oxen. They stared stupidly at the blue-and-white seal with the Prussian eagle on the boards of the loose-box. They were loaded into the motor-lorry and rumbled away with their brilliant escort. The driver of the lorry glanced along the road. Right across his path stood a barricade of carts. The police got down from the lorry and removed the obstacles. The next village was dead and empty. The bells were ringing. They were sounding an alarm. The fire-horn was tooting. The noise resounded hollowly in the deserted streets. And here again carts were placed across the road. The driver of the lorry was a townsman of Itzehoe, he knew a lot about farmers. Farmers were strange beings. The driver of the lorry had a breakdown half-way. It was impossible, he said, to drive any further. And the police had to lead the oxen into the town. The District President of Itzehoe was a wise man. The very next morning the oxen were up for sale in the cattle-market at Hamburg. But in the afternoon three farmers visited the director of the cattle-market. These oxen, they told him, were not ordinary oxen. They were distraint oxen.

'And if the oxen are not released from the market-pens and returned within twenty-four hours, you can find some other place to get your oxen, but you won't get any from Schleswig-Holstein.'

The director of the cattle-market was also a wise man. And he was sympathetic towards the farmers. If he could get no more oxen from Schleswig-Holstein he might as well let the grass grow in his pens. He put his hand in his own purse and paid Farmer Kock the amount of the tax.

The story of Beidenfleth flamed through the countryside. Stringent measures must be taken now or never. The police issued summonses and held trials. Fifty-two farmers were accused of a breach of the peace. Two hundred farmers gave themselves up to the court and said they also were involved, and it was only right and just that they too should come up for trial. Farmer Claus Heim knew that matters had come to a climax. The country people were united. Incessantly and everywhere the farmers were holding meetings. The young men on their horses were perpetually on the road. Their case had to be prepared; the farmers had to be made firmer and still firmer in their solidarity. In the provincial newspapers the emergency committees invited attendance at meetings, published resolutions and proclamations. But the provincial newspapers were also district and official organs, and they also contained official announcements. They had always been careful not to express themselves unequivocally on the side of the country people, and now they made difficulties even about announcing their meetings.

The farmers asked, 'What does this mean? You will not write for us? You think we have turned to you because we have no paper of our own, because we are not an association or a party? We will have a paper.'

'We will and we must have our own paper,' said Claus Heim.

The farmers clubbed together. At the worst, they said, it will be better to have thrown away our good money for our paper than for the taxes. They bought a little printing-office in Itzehoe. Claus Heim had happened to read some article about the battle of the country people in the *Iron Front*, a small Hamburg weekly. They were signed 'Ive' and they were the only ones which seemed to him to be clear, good, and to the point. He went to Hamburg to find this Ive.

Hans Karl August Iversen, called simply Ive by his friends, was still a soldier during the disturbed post-war period three years after the Armistice. The last roll-call of his unit found him the possessor of brand-new lieutenant's stripes, his demobilisation papers, and an indomitable determination to seize every chance that came his way. Apart from slashing, shooting and stabbing, he had no experience of any kind of work, but he could adapt himself to any situation. He had nothing to regret the loss of, for he had never possessed anything. When he began to observe the world consciously he found himself in a dirty-grey, devastated landscape in which an unceasing hail of iron poured down from the sky. He crouched down into a cavity half-filled with mud, and discovered that the most practical method of progress was, almost blinded and yet with his attention strained to the utmost, to jump from hole to hole. Of the great works of literature he knew best the 'Introduction to the Use of the Weapons of Close Combat,' and his handwriting, large, clear and round, could easily be read by the light of a glowing cigarette. The front was his home and the company his family. The post-war period hardly made any difference to this. It is true complications of an ideological nature arose, which he investigated from beneath the rim of his steel helmet, as though they were the particularly involved contours of the enemy's trench system. On the whole, the impression he got was that he had been transferred to another battle-sector, to the different conditions and duties of which he had to adapt himself. Many of his companions had had the same experience, and as they were unconvinced by any governmental pronouncements that made it unnecessary to believe that they might be called up again as a fighting unit, they decided to remain together and to start a settlement. They took possession, therefore, of a plot of land which had been put at their disposal on apparently favourable conditions, and began at once to dig and hew. But the authorities found the presence of these restless men in the wood a nuisance. They believed them—not without good reason—to be in secret possession of firearms, and they resorted to what the settlers considered to be underhand methods against the undertaking. Promised materials were not delivered—credit which had been guaranteed, and which was needed in the first place for the bare necessities of life, was not forthcoming. The housing inspectors refused to give their sanction to the hastily erected mud-huts, and when, finally, the forester of the district reported a terrifying increase in the number, of poachers, and the police reported the extraordinary insubordination of this almost communistic society of demobilised soldiers, the government abruptly withdrew all support and the grumbling men gradually disappeared, and no one knew where they had gone.

Ive had taken up a post as a night watchman and field guard on a manor estate in Pomerania. In his spare time he collected the youth of the whole district and drilled them. At first this was not much more than a game, but the game was not looked on with disfavour, and so Ive very soon established a band of young volunteers, which spread over the whole of Pomerania and met together for strenuous drilling and grand parades, rousing the Labour press of the small country towns to violent comment. Ive answered these comments in the papers of the National Party, and the quick wit which characterised his answers drew the attention of the lord of the manor even more than hitherto to the modest young night watchman, and he even invited him to dine at his table. The lord of the manor did yet more. He gave Ive a considerable sum of money, which had been placed at his disposal by the National Party, and enabled him to found the *Battle-Cry*, a weekly paper, the object of which was to defend the old ideals against an inimical world. *The Battle-Cry* appeared and, by its rough but straightforward language, won for itself many friends and opponents. But this language was not always pleasing in the ears of his employer, for it became clear, in the course of time, that Ive had an uncomfortable conception of ideals, as, for example, when no amount of instruction in political economy could prevent him from referring to the mass importation of Polish reapers as a gross scandal. When Ive was sentenced to three months' imprisonment or a fine of sixty thousand marks on account of an unbecoming remark about the President of the Reich, the gentlemen of the Party Committee informed him regretfully that unfortunately they could not pay his fine. At the same time, they suspended the appearance of the paper, a measure which was easily justified by the fall of the mark in the period of inflation. For since the postal subscriptions were paid monthly in advance, but the papermaker had to be paid as soon as the paper was delivered, the *Battle-Cry*'s burden of debt grew in direct proportion to the increase in the number of subscribers.

Ive would not have minded spending a short time in prison. He knew that the other patriotic associations were only waiting to swallow up his young volunteers as a fat morsel. But since at this juncture young men of his type in the Ruhr territory were transforming their passive resistance into a despairing attack, he resigned his position as leader of the volunteers, scratched together all the money he could find in his drawers, sold all his belongings except what he absolutely needed, paid his fine, which was now worth no more than a pound, and set off to answer the call of his blood. But when he got to the Ruhr he soon found himself in prison again, and indeed he brought this upon himself by deliberately playing with fire. At the end of the Ruhr campaign he was released and, somewhat pale but without any trace of a persecution complex, he tried his hand at being an insurance agent. He gave up his activities in this field when a charitable person, whom he had been canvassing for a long time, instead of shutting the door in his face, pressed the insurance premium into his hand and advised him to seek another profession. Minimax and Electrolux in turn failed to fulfil his hopes of social improvement; however, he won the third prize of five hundred marks in the Veedol oil competition with a couplet:

'O'er sea and land Graf Zeppelin chooses.
To fly and only Veedol uses.'

This sum of money, which was the largest he had ever possessed in his life, had cost him only five seconds' work, and he decided to expend it prudently. He provided himself with a smoking-jacket and a cello—which he played deplorably badly—and became a member of a restaurant band which spent the summer months making music in the seaside resorts of the Baltic coast. During the winter he subsisted by means of a variety of odd jobs. But before the second season was over the conductor of the band had decided that he would have to replace his cellist by a nimble Negro who was an expert on his instrument. When they parted, the conductor tried to box Ive's ears, and the latter, scorning the intervention of the civil authorities, wreaked his vengeance on the manly beauty of his director, sold his smoking-jacket to the second violin and decided, in order to complete the exchange, to set sail for Africa.

At the docks he could find no employment either as a stoker or a sailor, nor could he find the money for his passage. So he took on a job in the Hamburg wool-combing factory, a thing, as he told himself, that he should have done long ago. He remained there for a year. He lodged with and shared the bed of a buxom widow, and morning after morning he went off with his tin-can to the factory. On Sundays he went dancing. His fellow-workers called him simply 'the lieutenant,' and tried to induce him to join their party and the trades union. But he had an insurmountable horror of co-operative societies and trades union secretaries, and his attitude was much more akin to that of the communists and syndicalists than he was himself aware. He was attracted to them temperamentally; but he differed from them in his absolute belief in other than economic values. He wanted to get on himself. For him Germany at that time consisted of six million people who had a feeling that they were in the wrong place, and of the balance who actually were in the wrong place. He wanted to be in the right place. He wanted to get on, in order to take up his rightful position.

At the moment his prospects seemed very meagre. He wrote articles. In his dinner hour he wrote 'The Dinner Hour,' and after work he wrote 'After Work. Provincial papers with a strong social conscience were glad to accept his little contributions, and, in view of his circumstances, paid him at the rate of four pfennigs a line. On one of his visits to an editorial office, he heard that a small national weekly had gone bankrupt and was now the property of a book-printer. He immediately sought this man out and offered his services to carry on the paper. The publisher, although he had made up his mind on the spot, kept him on tenterhooks for a month; he then appointed him as editor at a salary of two hundred marks and fifty marks editorial expenses. Ive was enthusiastic. He was enchanted with his work. The *Iron Front*, as the paper was called, had no front, nor could there be said to be any iron about it. The list of subscribers was lamentable. The Letters to the Editor were mostly in connection with the Puzzle Corner and the supplement 'The German Woodland,' which provided a regular stereotyped correspondence. Ive made a general clearance. He abolished the Puzzle-Corner and 'The German Woodland.' The supplement 'Arms and Defence' he transformed into the 'School of Politics.' The heading 'Our Colonies' experienced a change which drew from an old subscriber, a retired major, a postcard headed 'The National Traitors.' The previous editorial staff were offended and resigned. It was difficult to find a new staff who were ready to submit to Ive's dictatorial direction. At times he wrote the whole number from the first to the last line. He could write what he liked. Sometimes his publisher grumbled, but the number of subscribers grew. Ive made contacts all over the country, hunted out small and directionless groups of young people, as well as individuals, who seemed to be of his opinions. There were plenty of them who were anxious to express themselves but against whom all editorial doors were closed. He organised little lecture evenings, which ended in serious discussions, and he continued the discussions in the paper. Frequently what he printed was nonsense, but it was always nonsense which had an attraction of its own. The *Iron Front* became a paper which had something individual to say and this it said, Ive saw to it, in unequivocal language.

Ive was happy. Even at the most dismal moments he had always found life pleasant, but now he found it quite indescribably pleasant. He knew he would always land on his feet, and the word 'adventure' could have no meaning for him that was not attractive. He could take a firm stand about everything in his life, because he always had the courage to take a plunge into the unknown. He had taken the plunge and he stood firmly on his two feet in front of his editorial table. When he surveyed the field of his opportunities from this spot, however much work the short day might pile on him, he could confidently believe that he had found his *métier*. Until one day Farmer Claus Heim called on him.

'We need a man who can write,' said Claus Heim, 'Will you come to us?'

Ive looked round his editorial office for a few moments.

Then, flushing, he said: 'Yes.'

II

GRAFENSTOLZ owned a printing works in Itzehoe. Despite all his efforts he had never been successful. He panted after orders like a terrier after rabbits; wherever he scented a customer he was on the spot. The little grey man was well known in the town, trotting industriously along the streets, or sitting on the edge of his chair, over a glass of beer, gesticulating vehemently in his endeavour to persuade his unwilling partner to close the deal. But the printing business went from bad to worse. Whatever Grafenstolz might do everything went awry, and he became more and more convinced that his failure was due solely to the machinations of the Jews, Jesuits and Freemasons. He felt that the evil must be attacked at the roots and henceforward devoted himself entirely to his crusade against these super-national powers. He left off buying his underwear at Salomon Steinbach's, the leading house for that commodity in the Square, and he was never again seen in consultation with Lawyer Haffich, who wore a strange amulet on his watch-chain; he did not know any Jesuits: there were none in Itzehoe. But this he took for a further proof of the uncanny power of his opponents. He knew that his shots could not misfire, for the invisible enemy was on every side. Even the smiles of his friends sometimes betrayed the cloven hoof, for were they not the smiles of the initiated, or at least of those in the pay of the enemy? Sometimes too, when he was lying curled up in his bed, his thin body broke out in a sweat at the thought of the omnipotent forces against which he, Grafenstolz, was engaged. But nothing could deter him from throwing himself into the breach for his convictions. Heedless of danger, he published a pamphlet which directed a merciless searchlight on the criminal activities of Germany's destroyers. Thereupon the authorities withdrew their printing orders—particularly the publication of official announcements. Grafenstolz went bankrupt. He fell, but his very fall tore the veil from the secret understanding, between the super-national powers and the machinery of administration.

No one welcomed the farmers' struggle as much as he did, and it was he who gave the farmers the opportunity to buy the printing business. He suggested that the new paper should be called *Balmung*, but the farmers were against that; one of them wanted *The Alarm Bell*, another *Pidder Lyng*, but Ive decided to call the paper simply *The Peasant*. So the name was settled, but it was the only thing that was settled. For when Ive followed Grafenstolz into the printing works for the first time, he found that the back premises consisted of a derelict courtyard and a large dirty room, of which the windows were either broken or boarded up, furnished with a miscellaneous collection of scrap iron. This was the composing room. The type was lying in muddled heaps in the cases, the rotary press—an antiquated model—-appeared to be completely in ruins, the two composing machines were as useless as the hand press. Silently Ive mounted the rickety stairs which led to the editorial office, still accompanied by Grafenstolz, who, without displaying the slightest interest in his former business premises, was pointing out eagerly the more than extraordinary circumstance that the minister of the Centre, Trimborn, was in the habit of dining frequently with the banker, Oppenheimer.

The editorial office consisted of four bare walls and a floor of cracked flagstones on which boxes, barrels and shelves were lying about. Ive took off his coat and began to knock together his editorial table from the boxes and shelves. Out of the planks and iron bars he erected a structure nor unlike a bedstead. He carefully put the Rotary machine in order and oiled and cleaned the handpress. He whitewashed the walls and put in new window panes. He installed the big wireless set which Claus Heim had sent him, he engaged compositors and a lay-out man, and negotiated with the post office and the paper merchant. Even Grafenstolz, whose activities were enlivened by all sorts of disclosures about the Zionist protocols, was allotted a task. Ive sent him into the town to look for any wall space that might be suitable for posters.

Ive slept in the editorial office; he lived on cigarettes and tea and the liberal gifts which Claus Heim sent him from his farm. After a fortnight's uninterrupted work, he published the first number. The gentlemen of the *Itzehoe Advertiser* shrugged their shoulders. That rag wasn't a newspaper. There wasn't a scrap of local news. There was no mention of the collapse of the scaffolding at the cement works, nor the jubilee in celebration of the twenty-five years' service of the Chief Secretary of the District Savings Bank of Lower Saxony—not even a line about the great Hilde Scheller murder trial; on the other hand the news from the Telegraphen Union and Wolff's Bureau was given startling headlines and comments which, at any rate, showed an original point of view. The leading article was an outburst from Herr Hamkens, whose efforts had several times already provoked the authorities to drastic interference. There were observations on the nature and uses of the boycott; an obviously fabricated report of the Reichstag proceedings, which gibed at everyone in office and, instead of a feuilleton, an article entitled 'My Reactions as Prisoner in the Dock,' the point of which was to indicate in advance the attitude to be adopted towards the Beidenfleth oxen-case. The whole thing was written in the unbridled language of one who had little tolerance for law and order. Apart from this the issue was full of printer's errors; for instance the name of the Minister of Public Safety, Gresczinsky, which occurred five times, was written differently each time until at last it was nothing but a string of consonants.

'Pure demagogy,' said the editor of the old-established *Itzehoe Advertiser*. 'We must ignore them; simply ignore them, especially as they have no advertisements.'

Ive himself was not satisfied.

'We're not cutting any ice,' he said to Heim. 'What I want is the voice of the farmers.'

But the farmers still held back. The emergency committees brought in a number of useful reports, and a few of the young farmers tried their hands at the unaccustomed work—indeed they were Ive's main support. His colleagues of the *Iron Front* were still hesitant, so Ive had to write nearly the whole paper himself. As a rule he dictated straight on to the composing machine, and if he got stuck, the compositor, who wore a Redfront Star in his button-hole, egged him on with obscene comments. After the first week the paper was banned. Ive changed the title and brought out *The West Coast*. The President of the Province, Kürbis, banned this too; and he banned *The Farmers' Front* and *The Country Herald*, and any version of the paper that dealt with politics. Then Ive called the paper *The Pumpkin,** *A Technical Journal of Agriculture*. The first article began with the words: 'The pumpkin thrives best on a dung-heap...'

The farmers laughed, the farmers bought the paper, and subscriptions rolled in. A professor at the College of Agriculture contributed a supplement, 'Harrow and Plough, ' and was summarily dismissed by the authorities of the college. This put the paper on its feet. It was able to appear once more as *The Peasant*, and at the farmers' meetings resolutions were passed that they should buy no other paper than *The Peasant*. Advertisements came in and very soon there was hardly a farmhouse in the Schleswig-Holstein where the paper was not read.

The *Itzehoe Advertiser* said: 'An evil spirit has now entered the portals of our peaceful town.'

Ive resolved that when the oxen case came up for trial the paper should appear twice daily, one edition when the court rose at twelve o'clock, and another in the evening.

Ive needed help. It came to him in the form of a young man who turned up in his editorial office one day out of the blue. No one knew

---

*   The name of the President of the Province, Kürbis, means pumpkin.

where he came from. All that was known was that he now called himself Hinnerk, but that in Bavaria he had gone by the name of Seppl, and in the Rhineland he had been known as Jupp. If he was questioned closely he would say thoughtfully that he was the salt of the earth, and as old as the earth. Anyway, he knew everything and could do anything and during the trial he proved his worth. The very first time he came into the editorial office he said sorrowfully that, according to the inscrutable decree of God, there had to be organisation. And he organised! By the time the trial began he not only had a battalion of young farmers at his disposal, there were not merely fleets of cyclists, motor-cyclists and motorists, but actually an aeroplane landed in the fields outside the town, ready to drop the paper punctually in the remotest spots of the province.

Both farmers and authorities realised the significance of the trial, that it was a test case, the outcome of which must be of the greatest importance in determining the future course of the struggle. Over two thousand farmers assembled in the town; representatives from all the emergency committees and deputations from other provinces, from Hannover, East Prussia, Silesia and Oldenburg. The big papers sent their reporters and the *Berliner Tageblatt*, for the first time, devoted a leading article to the happenings in Schleswig-Holstein, written not by their Hamburg correspondent, but by a member of the editorial staff. The heads of the administration were present in the courtroom (Frau Bebacke, the wife of the President of the Government Board, in a simple afternoon frock of plain wool alpaca fitting close to the figure) and, of course, Police-Commissioner Müllschippe from Berlin, Division I. A. A force of two hundred police marched into the little town, and Ive had good reason to ask himself: 'What is this costing the State?'

He sat in the court-room of the Town Hall, where the trial was held, at the foot of Charles the Great, the founder of the town. During the war the worthy townsmen had ingeniously studded this gigantic statue with black, silver and gold nails, possibly because Charles, in his day, had had twenty thousand Lower Saxons put to death. Ive by no means forgot to allude to this. He sat between Dr. Lütgebrune, the counsel for the defence, and the shorthand-writer, who was taking a verbatim report of the proceedings. While the gentlemen who were reporting for the big papers sat round looking bored—for the fifty-two defendants all had exactly the same story, all explained how it was that the farm was in debt, how it was that trouble had come to the rich marshland—Ive sat and wrote and wrote. Once he bent over to speak to counsel; once he looked at the shorthand note; Heim whispered to him; the President of the court looked up disapprovingly as the young farmers kept pushing their way through to Ive to collect his sheets of copy for the printer.

At the press Hinnerk was in command, sending his messengers tearing about the town, where the farmers were standing about in idle groups, telephoning and answering calls, and every now and again pouring himself out a stiff drink. Hardly had the President adjourned the sitting at twelve o'clock when the damp sheets were pouring into the court-room, the farmers in the streets and squares and in the public houses already had the paper in their hands, and the defendants could not only read an exact account of all they had said, but they could learn what they had yet to say. A descriptive story, a verbatim report, comments from the point of view of politics and criminal law—every sentence a dig at the Public Prosecutor—telegrams of sympathy from all the farming provinces of the country, a word of censure for the President of the court, reassuring comments for housewives—with reference, of course, to the milk money—anecdotes which the farmers were retailing to one another about the trial. The trial monopolised the paper and the paper monopolised the trial.

'The inaccurate reports in a certain newspaper...' wrote the *Itzehoe Advertiser.*

'The determined faces of the farmers must be causing the authorities...' Ive dictated to the compositor in the evening. Then the rotary machine gave a crack and stood stock still. For three hours they hammered away at it—but where was Hinnerk? The young farmers plunged into the night life of Itzehoe, into the 'Blue Grotto,' and there he was sitting completely drunk, embracing three police constables, whom he had forced to drink three 'pumpkins,' a decoction invented and named by himself, made up of the most potent spirits well flavoured with pepper. There he sat hobnobbing with the governmental bailiffs, and they were all singing 'Sea-girt Schleswig-Holstein,' an event which resulted in disgrace and transfer for the worthy officials, and for Hinnerk three days' incapacity for work. So the young farmers took turns at the hand-press, but Ive had to be satisfied with a supplement instead of the evening edition.

The trial ended with a sentence of six months' imprisonment for all the defendants, with a period of remand which gave the sentence the significance of an acquittal. The farmers rightly regarded this as a sign of the half-heartedness of the System and they celebrated a victory. But Ive was uneasy; he sensed a deadlock. He not only sensed it in regard to the farmers' struggle, he suspected it applied to himself as well. Actually nothing had been decided either by the trial or by the events which had led up to it. All that had occurred so far was no more than the merest reflex action. The only thing was that this Movement had been carried through with a degree of determination which gave it importance and left a feeling of hope which persisted. Claus Heim and Hamkens, who were now the uncontested leaders of the

Movement, had sacrificed their farms to save their farms. The whole force of the Movement, which was beginning to spread to all parts of the province, was directed towards preserving their property in the face of a System that was threatening it for some unknown reason. In this struggle it seemed to Ive that there was too great a time-lag between effort and result. The value of this period lay in the energy which had produced it. Time and again Heim, Hamkens and Ive had referred to the solidarity of the farmers, had compared it with the solidarity of the workers, but at that time solidarity had only been a hypothesis. It was a good thing that this hypothesis had been realised, had become once more a matter of course, after having been submerged for so long.

But this was not enough. Everyone felt that this could not be enough. All along, even while the farmers were still only protesting against the exorbitant taxes, what the authorities had feared more than the Movement itself had been the dangers that they knew must arise from it, and they had armed themselves against these dangers, in whatever form they might appear. Now farmers from all over the country were looking towards the province, anxious to discover what signs there were which might apply to themselves.

The parties and political organisations were asking: 'What do you really want?' and they were prepared, should they get an unsatisfactory reply, to provide guild programmes.

The farmers, too, came to Hamkens and Heim and Ive and asked: 'What now?'

Hitherto it had been more or less a joke, a clumsy, mad, bucolic joke, with a quite calm purpose in the forefront. Ive enjoyed a joke of this kind. The farmers felt that their existence, the very kernel of their existence—the farm—was threatened, and they protected themselves with the means offered them, the means nearest to hand, against a System that was inimical to them, not merely seemed to be, but actually was, since it was governed by interests which were anything but the interests of the farmers. Yet it claimed the right to manage their affairs. Hitherto it had all been clear and simple. The farmers spoke of the System, they did not speak of the State; there must be a State, they said, and what then? The power in the hands of the people! Who were the people if not themselves? The farmers did not bother themselves much as to whether the Constitution was good or bad. But: what is decreed is decreed!

And then there was Article 64 which read: 'Particularly to protect commerce, agriculture and industry.' It was concise and clear. We farmers are in the right, and the System is in the wrong, it is corrupting the Constitution (whether it be good or bad). They had never been particularly good Christians, the farmers up in the north, but they had always been able clearly to differentiate between God and Satan. God signified the real essence of everything, Satan stood for corruption. The System belonged to Satan.

'Our cause is a good one,' said the farmers, 'a good cause is the concern of all; therefore we are fighting for all, and all must fight for us.'

This was the point that gave Ive hope.

'There are two ways,' said Ive. 'Either we must strengthen our position; we must carry the Movement into the whole country, with the single object of preserving the status of the farmers, come what may...'

'Yes,' said Hamkens, 'we farmers want no more than that'

'Or, ' continued Ive, 'we must act from the outset as the advance guard of a new reality, we must aim at a complete transformation of the German position. We must not stand as the country against the town; we must be the germ of a new State, revolutionary, if you will, and we must leave no stone unturned.'

'That,' said Claus Heim, 'is what we should aim at.'

Old Reimann, the representative from the emergency committee of South Dithmarsch, looked at Hamkens and Heim: 'These two ways are one way,' he said, 'and what I think is that a talent has been put into our hands and we must not hide it in a napkin.'

Ive turned to him: 'What we have before us is no longer a joke. You must know the extent of your strength and whether your confidence is not too great for your strength. You wanted solidarity, now you have it. The workers could find no other means of liberation than solidarity. Today we can see what they have won. We know what a temptation it is to dig oneself more comfortably into the System instead of destroying it. If you give way to it, you will change nothing. Do you want to give way or to change things?'

'To change things,' said Heim and old Reimann at once, and Hamkens too said, 'Change things.'

So the farmers' struggle continued; the machinery of administration saw to that. But the struggle had taken on a different aspect. Claus Heim saw to that, and Ive, and all who were of their way of thinking, and there were many of them. Almost imperceptibly the centre of gravity was shifting. Ive realised that it was impossible to force an issue which had not its roots in the cause from the outset. Revolutions are not made by a wave of the hand. But in this Movement something was rooted which was striving for wider, deeper and more emphatic expression. One thing developed out of another, the time had come to indicate direction and tempo. The farmers were making a stand against the impenetrable cover of the System, and already behind the cover of the farmers' front was developing the germ of the new growth which was destined to replace the System. It was a spontaneous development, the inevitable outcome of the struggle; it was not the result of a considered programme. The whole province was in the hands of the farmers' leaders. All business that concerned the farmers—and very soon more than this—was being withdrawn from official hands.

Claus Heim had more decisions to make than the President of the Province, and the emergency committee more than the Parish Council. The community took on a new meaning for the farmers—that of the closest comradeship in need; instead of being grouped in districts they formed battle zones, to which the characteristic features of the landscape gave natural boundaries; and were not the hamlets and little market towns dependent on the country?

The summons went out to them to join up and the summons was to become more urgent—to be changed into a threat.

'Self-government,' that was the cry.

'Self-government?' questioned the reporters, who came from the town to interview the farmers, raising their eyebrows, 'surely that is a democratic idea!'

'Whether it is democratic or not,' said the farmers, raising their eyebrows, 'is all one to us. We thought that your System was democratic?'

'Give it good to the Land League!' said the reporters, who suddenly discovered that they had always been sympathetic towards the farmers.

'You do not understand us, ' said the farmers, 'your battle is not our battle.'

'The farmers of the whole country,' wrote Ive, 'must be welded together, not into societies and unions—they can go on and attend to their own business, and the individual farmer can keep up his membership, if he has always been a member. But what we have accomplished in Schleswig-Holstein must become the aim of all the provinces: unconditional solidarity of the farmers. Self-government of the farming communities, and elimination of the direction of the System, which is inimical to the farmers, in matters concerning the farmers. We are a member of the State and not the least important; we form, just as do the organised workers, as it were, a State within the State, acting as an equal among equals, from strength to strength. We have made a beginning; we have set out on this path because it is the only one possible for us. We have been assigned the task of setting an example, and our goal is still before us, the reorganisation of German affairs.'

But Ive was divided in his mind as he wrote. He felt that there was something thin and immature about this. He had let the idea fall, as it were a shaving from his work. But he was soon to win popularity. For the authorities took action. Police surrounded the building, searched the printing and editorial offices, snatched up any papers they could find and, before Ive knew where he was, he found himself involved in legal proceedings.

'Treason against the State and the Reich,' said the judge at the Enquiry.

Against the State, because Ive was obviously planning to overthrow the Constitution, and against the Reich because this obviously could only be accomplished by the separation of the province from Germany.

'Can it be possible,' said Ive to himself, 'that they think that more dangerous than my attempts at incitement?'

The Judge of the Enquiry also seemed to find the story rather a thin one—he hurriedly handed the documents over to the prosecution, with a friendly 'I leave it to you.' But the public prosecutor turned over the pages of *The Peasant*, from the first to the last number, red pencil in hand, and before Ive knew where he was again, he had twenty-seven libel actions round his neck.

This happened at a propitious moment, for the spring was urging the farmers to sow their fields and the summer was before them with all its work and, if they attended meetings punctually when required in order to ward off the encroachments of the machinery of administration, they did not go out of their way to do so. So that everything was comparatively quiet in the country and yet nobody could interpret this as a sign of submission. Then something happened. Hamkens was arrested; demands for payment poured into the houses—the distraints began once more.

'So you are at it again?' asked the farmers. 'This is sheer arrogance. But do as you like!'

Hamkens was silenced now, and Heim was the great man.

III

THE District Officer of Beidenfleth was a strictly just man who never failed to observe the letter of the law. He, therefore, knew nothing of conflicts of conscience. The farmers' struggle was a constant thorn in his side, but he never swerved from his duty. He appeared as a witness in the oxen case, and the evidence he gave, as he stood broad-shouldered and unmoved before the statue of Charles the Great, weighed heavily against the farmers in the eye of the law. He testified to the same facts as the defendants, using the same expressions, the only difference being that he regarded the things that had happened as unlawful, whereas the defendants considered them justifiable. Coming between him and the defendants, the second witness for the prosecution, the District President of Itzehoe—a thin, nervous man, perpetually at pains to bring about a settlement—produced an almost comic effect. The farmers had no grudge against the District President. They regarded him merely as the tiresome representative of a tiresome system. But the District Officer of Beidenfleth, though himself of farmer's stock and tradition, did not range himself with the farmers, and took no part in their solidarity. Nor did he change his attitude later on; he never hesitated to carry out a boycott or a threat. When the second wave of oppressive official measures swept the countryside, he carried out his duties with his usual inflexibility, regardless of the fact that his instructions frequently fell on deaf ears.

One night, just as he was going to bed, a terrific report was heard outside his house. A window-pane was broken. The District Officer came out to see what was happening. All he could discover was the burnt remains of some fire works. In accordance with his duty, he reported the incident in detail to his superiors in the office of the District President, without attempting to offer any explanation. The President was greatly agitated. He informed the Press that a bomb had destroyed the house of the District Officer; and the newspapers printed this item of news with prominent headlines.

'Loyal subjects,' they wrote, 'recoil with horror from such methods of political conflict.'

And again: 'We hope that the authorities will redouble their precautions for the safety of the country.'

The account went on to say that a commission of enquiry had immediately been sent to the scene of the criminal attack, but its findings could not yet be published. They were never published.

The farmers shook their heads—'But it can't have done the District Officer any harm.'

Hinnerk, too, shook his head:—'A bomb?' That was news to him. All the same it gave him something to think about.

'A bomb,' said the President, shocked. Whatever were things coming to in his district? He at least was not to blame; he had done all he could to mitigate the trouble in his district, everything that he could possibly do. And that was all the thanks he got! No, it was not worth while to continue the regime of tolerance.

One night, just as he was going to bed, a terrific report was heard outside his house. Several window-panes were broken. The district messenger came out to see what was happening. All he could discover was the burnt remains of a bomb. Without doubt this was no firework—it was an explosive that had torn the coping from the front of the house.

'An attempt to blow up the house,' declared the police, and the newspapers reported it with prominent headlines.

'It is time that an end is put to this criminal behaviour,' they wrote. And again, 'We challenge the authorities to take the most stringent measures to ensure for the peaceful citizen the safety to which he has a right.'

The farmers shook their heads—'But it can't have done the District President any harm.'

Hinnerk, too, shook his head—'An explosion?' He bent down over the coping stone, surrounded by the curious crowd that had collected in front of the President's house.

'In my judgment,' he said, 'that is not gunpowder, it is black powder, common or garden black powder, wrapped up in this integument,' and he held up a bit of blackened sticking-plaster.

'But at any rate,' he said to the sergeant, who was ordering the crowd to disperse, 'the fellow must have had some experience.'

'An explosion,' said the President of the Government Board in Schleswig, when he heard the news. He paid very little attention to the Farmers' Movement, regarding it as a sporadic outburst stirred up by professional agitators. He regarded with disapproval the inefficiency of the subordinate administrative departments. Was not he himself on excellent terms with the heads of the agricultural organisations? Were not his negotiations with the leading gentlemen of the Green Front carried on peaceably and with propriety? An example must be made to frighten these bomb-throwers.

One night, just as he was going to bed, a terrific report was heard outside his house. All the window-panes were smashed. The porter went out to see what was happening. All he could discover was the burnt remains of a bomb and a few pieces of broken iron. The whole facade of the governmental building from top to bottom was damaged. 'An infernal machine,' said the expert who was called in immediately. The newspapers reported it with prominent headlines.

'There was fortunately no loss of life,' they wrote, 'but undoubtedly this was only a lucky chance.' And again, 'All this preposterous fooling with infernal machines is an insult to the authority of the State.'

The farmers no longer shook their heads. 'Well,' they said, 'it won't have done the chief Bumble any harm.'

But Hamkens, who had completed his month's imprisonment for opposition to distraint, said:

'We farmers don't want this sort of thing. This has nothing to do with the farmers,' he said, 'alien elements...'

'What's that?' asked Ive. 'I know that expression "alien elements." That's what is always said when one's own cause begins to stink in the nostrils.'

And Hinnerk sneered: 'Since when has the mite been alien to the cheese?'

'We farmers don't want this sort of thing,' said Hamkens.

'Am I an alien?' asked Claus Heim. Hamkens was silent.

Ive did not want a breach and he decided to hold Hinnerk in a bit. But Hamkens was not long out of humour: for the farmers after all did want that sort of thing, and soon explosions were heard all over the place; not only in Holstein but in Oldenburg and in Lüneburg as well. The newspapers had published photographs of the pieces of iron that were found, together with detailed instructions for making the infernal machine. Ive too printed the police reports in full.

In his editorial he wrote:

'Bomb outrages have nothing to do with the Farmers' Movement as such. We are not an organisation: we have no power to limit the activities of the individual so long as they are not directed against the Movement itself. It is for the police, and not for us, to quell bomb outrages.'

'Nonetheless,' wrote the *Itzehoe Advertiser*, 'we know who is morally responsible for these criminal attacks.'

Ive made great fun of the word 'moral.' It seemed to him somewhat foolish to demand any but revolutionary morality from a revolutionary. Of course, he knew that his manner of writing and acting was demagogic, but he was taking part in a battle, and from time immemorial battles had not been waged by methods of gentle persuasion, and in time of war grenades had never been filled with sugar. What mattered to him was, not whether demagogy was morally irreproachable or not, but whether it served its end well or ill. He differentiated between primitive and artistic demagogy and was inclined to use either as occasion demanded.

The Communist deputy, who had come from the town to observe the Movement, raised his eyebrows and said, 'This is pure Communism.'

'Whether it is Communism or not,' said Ive, raising his eyebrows, 'is all one to us; I thought it was communistic to repudiate individual terrorism?'

'Give it to the capitalist system for all you're worth,' said the deputy, who suddenly discovered that he had always been in sympathy with the farmers.

'You do not understand us,' said Ive, 'your battle is not our battle.'

Moreover, Ive was realising that artistic demagogy—demagogy with a superstructure of ideology, as it were—must be a more effective means of propaganda. But at this stage of the battle propaganda was not the important point. It might even be harmful. For although all their hopes were centred in the Movement, it was also full of dangers. The Movement must not develop into a party. Its energies must be directed, not restrained. Actually the ideological aspect had had its basis from the outset in the actions of the farmers, although it was not the decisive issue (it did not become that until later). For it was not only their farms, not only their property, which had to be preserved, the entire farmer class, as a representative part of the whole nation, must be saved from extinction. Stability must not be sacrificed for the ephemeral. Work could not be regarded as a commodity in this case, for all their work was for the farm—how could it then be regarded as a commodity? In fact what might be applicable in the town and for workers and masters, did not apply in this case. The farmer was worker and master in one, and at the same time he was neither—he was a farmer. But wasn't business on a large scale said to be more profitable than business on a small scale? That too did not apply—none of these things applied.

At Grafenecke von Eckernförde, the district where there were large estates, things were even worse than in the rest of the farming province. Grafenecke was taking no part in the farmers' battle. It was not against it, certainly, but it simply could not take one side or the other. Possibly, large estates were too closely entangled in the capitalist mesh; their troubles were not the farmers' troubles, at least not completely.

'You are thinking on capitalist lines,' said the workers of the small towns to the farmers.

The farmers said: 'We used to put all our profits into the farm. It gave us a proportionate return. Today we are putting more than our profits into the farm; we work all the year round, and at the end we are left with a loss. We might as well have taken the money to the bank and spent the whole year looking out of the window; we should have been no worse off. Why don't we do that? Why don't we sell our farms and live on the proceeds? That would be thinking on capitalist lines, we are thinking of the farm. The farm is not a factory, and our work is not a commodity.'

The gentleman at the Treasury-office had said: 'You do not think on economic lines.'

The farmers said: 'Even before the war we made no more than two percent profit: that just enabled us to keep the farm going. Today we are throwing away our capital. Why are we doing it? We can live without selling or buying; shall we prove it to you? But we sell and we buy. Because we cannot separate the farm from the people. We do not want to live on an island; we live with the people; we are ourselves the people, we ourselves represent political economy. But what are you doing with our money?'

The gentleman at the Treasury-office had replied: 'Reparations.' That was understandable, losers have to pay the cost.

'And what are the French doing with the reparations?' asked the farmers.

'They are paying their debt to America.

'And what is America doing with the money?'

'She is giving us credits.'

'But that is nonsense,' said the farmers, 'what if we paid no reparations?'

'Then they would cut off our credits, and would not take our goods.'

'And when we pay, we pay in goods, and we glut the market.'

'That is the problem of transfer.'

'What does that mean?'

And the gentleman at the Treasury-office explained to them.

'So our learned professors are sitting there and racking their brains to find a way for us to pay out our capital without using up other people's capital? And they are being paid for that? Out of the money you are taking from us?'

'Revision of the Treaties!'

'Meanwhile our farms are ruined and your political economy as well. It's all madness,' said the farmers. 'You always said that the war was madness; is what's going on today any less mad? We're not going to risk our skins for madness. But perhaps you would like to? But of course your machinery of administration was always well behind the lines!'

'What actually do you want?' asked the gentleman at the Treasury-office.

'We don't want you,' said the farmers, and departed. And shortly afterwards a bomb exploded.

'Bombs are not arguments,' wrote the *Berliner Tageblatt*. But events proved that bombs were arguments. Ive observed this with delight. He observed the remarkable, spiral progress of the Movement, of all movements. In this case it began with the farm, went through the whole gamut of thought, reason and passion, to end again with the farm. Frequently, when he was writing, he would stop with a smile, realising that he had thought in the very same way a long time ago, had had the same idea and rejected it; now it was taking possession of him again, equipped with a wealth of chaotic experience, matured, clarified, tested, and firmly established. Yet it was still the same simple idea, only carrying greater weight. Epochs are built up in this way; this process is the foundation of life itself. The farm represented life, the continuity of life, subject to every phase. There came a time when the farmer no longer wanted to be a farmer: he called himself a landowner, or an agriculturist. Something entered into his life which was not of the essence of the farm, not of the essence of his work, and yet was both profitable to the farm and pleasant. The temptation was small at first and insignificant and yet it expressed the whole situation. Prosperity meant cheapness, that was clear. It was ridiculous to waste hard work on preserving objects that could be replaced cheaply. Old chests decayed, old cupboards, which had served for hundreds of years, gave way at the hinges. Then one day there was a bright green carpet in the house, a linen cupboard and an expanding bookcase; a stiff, grand drawing-room with an upholstered sofa and a plate-glass mirror. There was a lustre scintillating with hundreds of cut-glass pendants, a precious possession which the wife at once swathed in a dust-sheet, for the labour of keeping it free from dust and cobwebs would have been robbed from the farm. Then there was electric light; and the telephone and the suction cleaner and the milk-separator, and later the wireless. Did the farmer regret all this? He did not, because the farmer had become a landowner, he was modern, he had to be modern. He had his club and his union and his banking account, and all this he had won for himself, and it was useful and pleasant.

'A stupid farmer,' a good landowner would say of a bad landowner, and he would talk of international markets and take his money to the bank. Poetry was forgotten; the old costumes, the old festivals, dances, and songs disappeared; the girls no longer sat at their spinning-wheels in the evenings, chatting with the boys; they went to the establishment decorated with paper, garlands, down the street, and danced to the music of the gramophone.

Poetry was forgotten, and the townspeople regretted it deeply. The townspeople wrote affecting books about it and founded societies for the preservation of the national costume. The movement was patronised by a titled lady, and the schoolmaster introduced it into the village. There was a grand carnival, but the next day the costumes were hung up in the wardrobe, for no girl could stand at a chaff-cutting machine in those wide skirts? When the young people of the town rose in revolt against bourgeois customs, groups of them would go to the village—for, if they would had nothing to do with bourgeois customs, they were all for rural customs—to play and sing to the farmpeople to the music of their fiddles—not violins, mark you. That was very nice but it was not rural. All this talk about back to the land that the townspeople were indulging in was right. The landowner, or the farmer, if you like, knew exactly how his land was constituted, where there was gravel in the soil, or marl or lime, that was important in deciding what manure to use, and indeed was only to be learnt by long experience; he knew exactly from what direction the storm came and where it would end; knew where it was a good thing to regulate the stream and where not. He left the undergrowth in the wood, although it prevented the trees from growing straight; for singing birds nested in the undergrowth and caught the insects, and the finest timber forest with the smoothest tree trunks is ruined if it harbours bark-beetles or tree-hoppers.

Poetry was forgotten (if it had ever existed); but was it nothing that the owner of the farm stood at the threshing machine and let the golden corn run through his fingers? Was it nothing that the ninehundredweight sow won the first prize at the agricultural show in Neumünster? The farm flourished, and one could consider building, buying machinery, or a new cart, or—for one moved with the times—reorganising the pigsties, hygienically, with tiles and shining metal rails, if that proved a good plan (but it did not prove a good plan; a pig that is a pig doesn't like hygiene). The farm prospered and everything was clear and simple and good. All the talk of the flight from the land was rubbish, up here at any rate. How is the farm to subsist if the sons divide their patrimony? The younger sons did not flee from the land, they helped to support it. They became for the most part proletarians, which was unfortunate; but what old Bismarck had done for agriculture, the young Kaiser was probably doing for the workers and, for the rest, let each one look out for himself. The landowner too, has his troubles, his misfortunes, his hard times, when the harvest is spoiled by hailstorms, or drought burns up the corn, or there is disease among the cattle. Prosperity means cheapness, and when the international markets are bad we still have the tariffs. It was a good thing to have a big and widespread organisation on which one could depend when interests clashed. The bourgeoisie, industry, trade, each had constructed its apparatus, and now agriculture had done the same, and all were interdependent. The farmer realised that he was an important member of the State and that his production was the basis of economy. On every side he saw the same reasoned order founded on standards of utility, developing nearer and nearer to perfection. Everyone had a direct participation in this order and in everything that was created within it; everyone came under the direct influence of the wholesome impulse to share in the task. If ideas were lacking, the human mind strove perpetually to create new and more complicated images, and wherever there was injustice it was soon replaced by progress, a single, forward impetus. The hand of order reached to the furthest corners of the world; a powerful, inspiring spirit had conquered the earth, had erected the great and glorious edifice, and pervaded it from its foundations to its dizzy heights. Unceasing progress seemed to be the essence of this spirit and perpetual change its medium. Inexhaustible energies were transforming the towns into towering citadels, were attacking the atom and using all their scientific skill to disintegrate it. The rich treasure-house of the elements was sending its rays flashing to the darkest recesses, a stupendous, transfigured squandering of strength, which could only be curbed at an ever further receding point. The earth seemed to have become a plaything of the creative spirit, and the great task was to discover the rules of the game. Every form of energy was producing to excess, so that it was more important to study the laws of production than to produce, necessary check was to be kept on the flood of overproduction. It seemed as if the released energies were reacting against themselves; more and more violent shocks shaking the scales, and over-weighting first one side and then the other.

On the one hand the dynamic forces tossed events into a dense entanglement, while on the other they laid bare an expanse of empty chambers in which gases assembled and smouldered; here and there destructive explosions tore at the steels walls, and the sparks from one ignited yet another. The same mysterious power which winged this great period to victory or to defeat, repeated the process in powerfully concentrated form with all its cruelty and splendour in the Great War. The campaign, which began with beating of drums and armies marching forward to fulfil themselves in glorious victories, led at last through uncontrolled dissipation of energy to complete exhaustion. Those who had thought they could control the war were now controlled by the war. The values, which seemed to have been created for eternity, failed when oppressed by bloodshed and faced with death, and the simple question as to the meaning of it all remained unanswered. If the individual was reminded of the futility of his industry, the certainty grew nonetheless of a fuller and maturer strength, developing with all the miracles of growth, directing the mind to the invisible, teaching men to see every phenomenon with new, as it were, spiritual eyes. The old order was still there, but the energy which had directed it was no longer subject to its laws. Life in its manifold forms, imprisoned within this order, fettered by the gigantic, wasteful machine, might attempt to master fate, but every attempt failed. Thus it seemed that the only thing to do was to complete the circle, to grope one's way back to the starting-point, to the indestructible basis, which once had been the beginning and was to be the beginning again.

Prosperity had vanished, and the only cheap things were the explanations of the professors and politicians, cheap and mass produced, but not good; one is entitled to require of an explanation that it be comprehensible, but for a long time now science had consisted of mysteries, and politics of secrets, inaccessible to the ordinary intelligence. Masses of figures and incomprehensible words gave an air of importance to the problem, but nobody could check the result to see whether it was right or wrong. This atmosphere begat a wild empiricism and there were few buildings that did not house laboratories with retorts and test tubes. The mixed brew bubbled away in the vessels, spreading its fumes in thick clouds over the country.

'Seek knowledge and make changes,' said some, bustling about with their pots and crucibles, and melting down Marx and Hegel to produce the philosopher's stone. Others stirred up the blackened remains, mixing them according to a new recipe, and set fire to the powder, fancying in the magic illumination of the Bengal light that they had produced a conservative-revolutionary compound.

This was undoubtedly a great period for our valiant Grafenstolz; for him the world was completely veiled by the powers of good and evil which swayed it, and if this was all a figment it was one that did not daunt his fiery spirit. Leave me alone,' cried a voice within him, and he made a stand against the super-national powers and against the democracy, which was a fiction of the newspapers, and against the fiction of the Constitution, the free Republic.

'How should I know, I am only a stupid farmer,' said Hamkens, when the gentlemen of the Board of Agriculture, asked him what he thought of the effect of the great rye subsidy. 'I cannot know that, you can ask Privy Councillor Sering, for he doesn't know either.'

Actually the privy councillor did know, for he wasn't a stupid farmer. Privy councillors always knew, and if what they said was not done, then of course they had been in the right, and, if it was done, then it had been done in the wrong way. It was always wrong, not only for the privy councillors but for the farmers.

At first the farmer decided that one thing was not right and had to be altered, then more and more, and for every hole that was mended two new ones appeared; for everything was interdependent, and what had once proved to be a blessing proved now to be a curse.

'Everything must be changed,' said the farmers.

They said: 'We have tried everything, barter, intensive production, speculative production: we have tried associations and federations, they have all in their turn served the farm, but they are no use to the farm any more. We must begin at the beginning again!'

The farm was the only thing that remained, the permanent centre of their thoughts.

'You must leave us alone,' said the farmers, 'for if you destroy the farm, you destroy us with it.'

This happened just when the bright green carpet had lost its shiny pile, and the grey foundation of sackcloth was showing through the worn patches; when the children were using the glittering glass pendants from the lustre as playthings, when the linen-cupboard was standing in the shed, to be used as a store-place for the food-sacks. Once more it was worth while to put hard work into a good piece of furniture, everything was worth while again that was done for the ultimate good of the farm.

'You must leave us alone,' said the farmers, and for a long time it had been not only the taxes, not the dues, not the failure of the commercial treaties, which made them say this. It was the knowledge that they were in the right in making a stand against a seething, stinking, rapacious tide; it was the desire to begin afresh, starting from the eternal farm, at the end of an era, a wonderful era, a powerful era, but past and over now! Away with the rubbish and the lumber that blocks the way, and away with those who would preserve it, not even themselves knowing why. Who would preserve an order which no longer has any sense in it except those who are too timid to risk a new order? It had been proved that bombs were arguments: all the worse for those who did not understand their language. Farmers, stolid figures, for whom life meant hard, obvious labour, whose minds turned naturally to natural things, like Claus Heim, were now playing about with dangerous grey powder, were critically weighing concentrated destruction in their rough hands.

They were hob-nobbing together in the exciting atmosphere of conspiracy, and their low-toned, quiet words dealt with explosive-power and fuses. In the no-man's-land of night-time they crept like patrols through the deserted streets of the enemy town; and if one of them ran away, like the young farm-owner, of whom Hinnerk made such fun, it was not because he was afraid, but because a message had been brought to him that the cow was calving. There were explosions all over the place, not only in Holstein; and it was farmers who were causing the explosions, who were meeting together without the summons of a leader, who visited each other and helped each other. Certainly there were people from the town too, people of the type of Hinnerk, who could smell powder fifteen streets away and who started explosions because they enjoyed explosions (and considered themselves lucky into the bargain that they were furthering a good cause thereby).

But what about the machinery of administration; was it asleep? It was not asleep. It repeatedly took action, and repeatedly arrested anybody it could get hold of—for instance Farmer Hamkens, who was travelling about the country making speeches. The fact that he never mentioned the bombs seemed all the more suspicious, and since they could not find much to bring up against him in regard to the bombs, Hamkens had to go into quod for a month to serve an old sentence. But the farmers marched up and down in front of his prison and caused a public disturbance in the town. So they removed Hamkens to another prison in another town, and other farmers marched up and down, and Hamkens wandered from one cell to another and quite enjoyed himself. But the farmers decided to hold a great demonstration on the day of his release. Not so much to celebrate the release of Farmer Hamkens, as to show the townspeople their power and their unity and to state their demands on the spot; for though the townspeople knew a lot about the farmers' struggle, they did not know the truth, and they still did not grasp how much they were involved in the struggle.

On the day of his release Hamkens was to have been in Neumünster, which was the most important fair-sized town of the province, was of some industrial standing and had an excellent burgomaster. The excellent burgomaster wanted to have peace and order and, as he understood the farmers and also understood the machinery of administration, he did three things: he arranged for Hamkens to be removed on the last night to the prison at Rendsburg, he gave his sanction to the farmers' demonstration, and he kept the company of State police, which had been sent to him, outside the town. He thought that thus, in the interests, of the town, he had played a trick on everyone. The burgomaster of Neumünster was an excellent man. But he did not know what had long since become evident to the farmers: namely, that every measure, prompted by the spirit of a declining era, must of necessity have a completely contrary reaction to that intended. This was to be proved by the incident of the flag.

For the farmers the elastic, almost anonymous Movement represented a political weapon, and the intangible boycott an economic one, and the bomb an inarticulate argument, but they still lacked a visible sign, a pictorial and emotional symbol. Here as usual Hinnerk, with his natural and uninhibited delight in inspiring effects, immediately struck the right note. A flag! A marching movement must have a flag, which would head the procession, which could be waved, which could be hoisted, and—not least important--for which one could, with complete justification, do battle. The flag was black, with a white plough and a red sword; the great undulating sheet was not attached to a simple pole, but to a scythe which had been hammered straight! The scythe-flag had been the battle-standard of the Dithmarsch men in the Danish wars; it flew in the old colours, black white, red, which still meant so much to many of them, but with new symbols: everything was there. And Hinnerk bore it in front of the procession.

'Well, well, a flag,' said the farmers, and smiled a little, as they saw it fluttering—it was nothing but a piece of coloured bunting, but, quite pretty.

For the police-superintendent in Neumünster, too, it was only a piece of coloured bunting; but when two people think the same thing, they do not necessarily mean the same thing. The police-superintendent of Neumünster regarded the flag with disfavour; it did not bear the colours of the republic. The procession began to move towards the prison, where Hamkens no longer was; the farmers set out, a solid mass of big, strong figures, each of whom had his tough stick in his hand (for a farmer never leaves the house without his stick); the close-formed column threaded its way through the almost empty streets. From the windows of the houses the heads of the townspeople were peering curiously, and the townspeople were calling jokes to each other across the streets, and even saying spiteful things, for Neumünster was a stronghold of social democracy. Suddenly the police-superintendent of Neumünster bethought himself, of the by-law of 1842, which laid down that it was unlawful to carry an unprotected scythe through the streets of the town, and the by-law in the Defence of the Republic Act prohibiting the carrying of arms, and the by-law of the Prussian Ministry of the Interior by which in demonstrations, walking-sticks were to be regarded as arms, and a whole lot of other by-laws, and the Article of the Service Regulations concerning the behaviour of the police in cases of provocation. Then the police-superintendent of Neumünster pushed his way through the farmers' procession and seized Hinnerk by the sleeve:

'The flag,' he gasped, 'the flag!'

Hinnerk did not even look at the man; with a simple movement of his arm, he shook himself free. The farmers shoved aside the uniformed obstacle to their march, and the police-superintendent discovered himself several ranks behind the wide-spreading black flag, pressed up against the walls of a house. That was resisting the executive power of the State. It was no longer merely the breach of a by-law;

it was an offence against the law! He trotted along the procession to the front; he took a deep breath, for there, a little way off in front of the marching column, stood his superior officers.

'The flag,' he cried out to them and, drawing his sword, advanced, a body of constables behind him, towards Hinnerk.

Hinnerk was proudly bearing the flag, holding it aloft with both hands, his chest thrown out, blinking up beneath his fair hair to the windows where the pretty girls were to be seen. When the police-superintendent tried to seize the flag, he refused to let go, shaking the staff vigorously to rid himself of the useless appendage. A sword flashed and gave him a deep gash in the hand. The farmers in the rear, who had not seen what was going on in front, pressed forward with their even, steady tread. They pushed the front ranks against the body of police and, while Hinnerk was struggling with the superintendent, tenaciously clutching the flag-staff with his bleeding hands, the farmers' sticks were raised and directed against the constables. Hinnerk clung to the flagstaff, blows fell on his head, shoulders and arms, he stumbled, fell, still clinging to the flag, staggered up again, biting and kicking; swords flashed up and down, the flag-staff was broken, arms seized hold of Hinnerk, blows rattled down on him, feet trampled him. Enveloped in the black cloth, Hinnerk reeled, was thrown on one side, staggered to his feet and, after being knocked down again and again, lost consciousness, but not the flag. The whole street resounded with the noise, swords clashed against sticks, a blinding flash clapped Farmer Helmann in the face and sliced off his nose, solid wood thudded heavily on the skull of the policeman, cries re-echoed along the ranks of farmers:

'What has happened in front?' and 'Halt—the police.'

Claus Heim shouted a command:

'To the Agricultural Show!'

Slowly the procession broke up. Hinnerk lay, under arrest and still unconscious, the flag at his side, in the entrance hall of a house; the echoes of the slowly ebbing fight resounded in the neighbouring streets. Singly and in groups, the farmers advanced on their new objective; but the superintendent had given the alarm to the police waiting outside the town and, as the farmers arrived, they found the armed force; drawn up in line, before the entrance to the Agricultural Show. As the farmers entered one after another, their sticks were taken from them.

In the immense hall the farmers seethed up and down:

'What's this about the flag?' they shouted.

'They have taken our flag!' and 'Hinnerk stuck to the flag!'

The thing that lay beside Hinnerk in the passage was no longer a piece of coloured bunting: the very honour and self-respect of the farmers, consecrated by their blood, lay there, stained and torn by shameless, desecrating hands. From now on the name of Neumünster would be used as a curse in the farmhouses. Suddenly the word went round that Hamkens was no longer in the prison, and that the burgomaster had provoked the police against the farmers, after enticing them into the town with a hypocritical sanction of their demonstration. For this there could only be one answer! In the midst of the confusion Claus Heim formulated the terms of expiation. The flag must be returned to the farmers by the foremost of the town authorities with solemn ceremony and apologies. The guilty superintendent must be dismissed immediately. The town was to undertake to pay to every one of the farmers injured by this breach of hospitality, an adequate compensation, the amount to be decided by the farmers in each case.

'The meeting is dismissed,' cried the police-officer to the seething mob, and the farmers left the town, not to set foot in it again for over a year. The excellent burgomaster of Neumünster was an astute man; but all his clever foresight had failed; the very thing he most wanted to avoid had occurred; not only the farmers, but also the machinery of administration, and the loyal citizens of the town, believed it to have been a preconcerted plot. Everything that he had done strengthened the ugly suspicion and, since there had to be one, he was selected as the scapegoat. He did, whatever might be thought, the only thing that he could do as an upright man: he defended the superintendent's action, in spite of the fact that it was contrary to his own intentions. That was the second great mistake that the burgomaster of Neumünster made (if he hadn't defended the superintendent it would equally have been a mistake); he refused to accede to the demands of the farmers. And the farmers boycotted the town! Neumünster, a fair-sized town of some industrial standing, was not entirely dependent on the country and, although in hard times, in every budget, public or private, every penny counted, it was nevertheless the town which stood the better chance of holding out in the struggle. The burgomaster relied on his town, and he relied on all the help which must be afforded him by the authorities, and he relied on the eventual good sense of the farmers, whom he knew to be quiet people of apt intelligence who believed in guarding their own interests. What point was there in this petty revenge for the sake of a torn flag, for the sake of a stupid incident, which was likely to occur at any time if I there was a clash between an excited crowd and disconcerted officials? But the farmers were not concerned with revenge; they were concerned with their cause, which was at a critical juncture. No farmer was to set foot in the town where the desecrated flag lay; not so much as a button was to be bought in the town; not even a glass of beer to be drunk: the young farmers left the Agricultural College, the market was deserted, no more cattle shows, no more gymkhanas! The town was despised and everything that came out of it; the friend in the town was no longer a friend, the girls in the town no longer found sweethearts among the young farmers. Not a single egg, nor a pound of butter for the wives in the town; no petrol or help for a car bearing a town number.

The town was wiped out and existed only as a dirty blot on the landscape. And woe betide the farmer who should dare to break the boycott!,

But who was it who broke the boycott? Who crept into the town like a thief in the night? Grafenstolz broke the boycott. Grafenstolz crept into the town like a thief in the night. Trembling he stole from shadow to shadow, his back bent and damp with sweat. The package under his arm was a heavy burden. He peered cautiously round every corner, gliding like a fish past the light of the street lamps to dive as quickly as possible into the safety of darkness. The town; was full of enemies; every possible danger gaped out of the dark jaws of the street. Secret dens of the powers of destruction! The work of the devil and his minions come to lure mankind into their sinister realm! But Grafenstolz was on the watch; the stars had foretold victory for him. A leap, a fling, a flash, a report, a rumble and a thunderous din...

Ive sat alone at his desk in the editorial office. The greenish glare of the lamplight gave depth to the large bare room, whose windows looked now like sheets of lead; shed a pale light on the papers lying scattered and in piles all over the room, illuminated brilliantly and with quivering shadows the typewriter on which Ive was morosely thumping away. From the composing room rose the pungent smell of printer's ink mingled with the sweetish mouldy smell of the glue pot. Ive hated these night vigils, waiting for the last news over the wireless. These hours, which were always filled with the most disagreeable tasks, instead of acting as a preliminary to refreshing sleep after the lively excitements of the day, only led to confused dreams, which eluded memory, and blocked him at the moment of awakening, confusing again the sentences which came rushing into his mind and for the period of a second seemed to be so happily phrased. He rummaged peevishly among the files, which he never succeeded in keeping tidy. One file only was neatly arranged and labelled—the bomb file, which Hinnerk had organised and which contained all the reports and articles, annotated with humorous underlinings and expressive exclamation marks from Hinnerk's red pencil. Ive turned over the papers in this file, wrote a few sentences, stopped to think, wrote again. It seemed as if in the public mind the Farmers' Movement had developed into a regular bomb-throwing organisation. This must not be. Hinnerk ought to look for some civil position, thought

Ive, but immediately dismissed the absurd idea. Why should this well-constructed piece of care-free life be allowed to dry up? Moreover all the developments which had resulted from Hinnerk's always disinterested actions had in the end proved useful. It seemed almost as though the complete lack of prejudice is his character had communicated itself to his actions: what ever he did established itself as an expression of the will of the farmers, whose battle he fought, without being in the least concerned in it. But with Grafenstolz it was a different matter. Government buildings and Treasury-offices were not particularly in favour with anyone. But now it was a private individual, Doctor Israel, specialist in internal diseases, half the front of whose house had been blown up. That the public indignation of the citizens should have turned immediately, with unexpected vehemence against the farmers, did not seem particularly worthy of note; what was more dangerous was that this incident had provided much grist to the mills of undesirable friends. Ive of course was an anti-Semite; but only because it was too much trouble to be anything else. In all his activities he had found only enemies among the Jews. This was remarkable, but did not worry him. For him their inferiority was a fact learned from experience. He found them alien to the spirit of the times in their attitude and unprogressive in their point of view like, say, the French. In the course of many conversations he had discovered that they had no understanding of certain things, no grasp of certain straightforward and material issues; thus, however much he tried, he had never been able to get them to understand the simple problem of the farm; they found it completely incomprehensible. Of course, their undeniable supremacy in certain fields, particularly in business, the arts and journalism, was almost intolerable. But it seemed to him that this was the result of the present order, and it was, therefore, necessary to replace this by a new order which, if it was to be national, by its intrinsic character, must, of necessity, put an end to this unpopular supremacy. For it would be founded on values at any rate completely foreign to the Jewish mentality, values which were making themselves everywhere evident, most particularly in the farmers' struggle. The case of Israel had not only roused a storm of indignation among the citizens, it had also roused the chattering activity of the mountebank preachers. Up and down the countryside, in every village, the itinerant apostles were to be found expounding the Talmud. Ive had no doubts as to the steady instincts of the farmers, but he did fear disintegration of the front. The Movement was exposed to every kind of ideological attack. In that lay both its strength and its weakness. Competition for the support of the farmers and their votes had been rife for a long time among the parties and federations. The existence of the Movement was enough to make the parties radical in their promises. And they could certainly, if they belonged to the opposition, count on a big increase of votes at the next elections. This state of affairs held no dangers for the Movement until, perhaps, the insistent attitude of the parties forced individuals to take a decisive position. The agricultural federations too had worked strenuously. A peasants' party had been formed, whose object was to establish its political position purely on the economic interests of the peasants. There was in fact an actual need for independent representation of their interests in the parliaments, and the federations knew this. It might well prove successful to play a double game, and to set the peasants against the peasants. But if Hamkens and Heim and all the leaders of the Movement were proof against snobbery it would be easy enough for the bureaucrats to act in the name of the Movement, manoeuvre the Movement itself into dependence on them and to set themselves up as dictators! Already the influence of all kinds of different activities was being felt throughout the province, and it was not always easy to distinguish by whose hand and in whose interests the wires were being pulled. The bomb outrages cleared the air: they were a test, just as the boycott of Neumünster had been a test. Not only the farmers, but more particularly the good people who approached the Movement with helpful smiles and always knew best about everything, were faced with the stern task of making a decision. All at once the farmers found themselves alone; in place of the parties the Conventicle hoisted its banner: prophets and quacks came in masses and Grafenstolz was a great man.

The farmers laughed at Grafenstolz, but they did not interfere with him. Bombs were arguments, but the things which were seeking expression in the province were not to be formulated by the Grafenstolzes. And the Grafenstolzes must not throw bombs, especially if they could not keep their tongues still afterwards. Ive was angry; for the first time since his activities on *The Peasant* he was faced with a conflict, a stupid ridiculous one, but still a conflict. In the battle against the System he could spring any mine; but how were these asses to be dealt with, especially as they were asses loaded with a world philosophy? To enter into any sort of discussion with them was ridiculous, and if he used the weapons of irony and satire he would be putting himself in the wrong, placing himself in a line with the common enemy. Anyway, Ive had asked Grafenstolz to come and see him, but Grafenstolz was a great man and kept Ive waiting. If he brings our solidarity into disrepute I will break all his bones, thought Ive. He thought: the bomb-throwing must be put an end to. A joke should not be carried too far. The bombs had done their work: they had put the administration in a fluster, they had shown that the farmers were not to be played with, they had at least drawn a clear line of demarcation between the farmers and the townspeople, between friend and foe. There had been no loss of life in any of the many outrages, which was all to the good. Ive was acquainted with the magic effect of bloodshed, but in this case there was no truth in the hypothesis on which the effect was based. Hinnerk had once, in one of his very rare moments of reflection, drawn a comparison between this Movement and that of the Russian Social-Revolutionaries before the revolution. But this comparison was not apt. The System was not Czarism and the farmers were not an oppressed serfdom. The thing that characterised the farmers' battle was the absence of any brutal opposition. They were not fighting against a mighty, tyrannical and pitiless master-class but against a senseless, wasteful machine, whose driving oil was already growing rancid. In the struggle there were no ideal-ridden intellectuals, no desperate outlaws, no explosive bundles of nerves, hut men who had to fight for their very life in the stench of putrefying disintegration, men who were not taking action or a theory for a distant exhilarating and glittering goal, but in their homes were steadily carrying out, one by one, the tasks that lay nearest to hand, in the full knowledge that they were doing this for the sake of posterity. Sometimes Ive felt bitter about this; he wished it had been otherwise; but wherever he looked, it seemed to him that the Farmers' Movement had really reached the highest degree of revolutionary activity possible in Germany at that time.

The crash of bombs had not served as a wide-resounding signal, had not even carried the message of liberation to the far-spread masses of the people—who were being suffocated under the same oppression—the message that they were not standing alone, that it was time for them to rise and to join forces. Its only echo was in the excited headlines of the papers, and in terror-striking police reports.

'What repeatedly causes us astonishment,' Ive rattled out on the typewriter,' is the complete failure to take action, the inactivity of the police, which can only be explained by the absolute lack of initiative... One might have imagined,' he wrote, 'that the attack on the Reichstag, on the noble house of the elected and honourable representatives—we cannot say of the people, but of the System—would at last have sufficiently provoked the authorities to put a stop to the bombing attacks on governmental window-panes...'

He heard steps on the stairs. He suspected it was Grafenstolz and put on a severe expression. But it was not Grafenstolz, it was Hinnerk—Hinnerk with his arm in a sling, Hinnerk whom Ive had thought was still in the Neumünster hospital under police supervision.

'The ways of God are miraculous,' said Hinnerk, 'and so are mine. No, no, not from Neumünster,' he said, 'from Berlin. No, no, not what

you are thinking; that was only three windows of the Reichstag. I guarantee you better work than that.'
'What's up?' asked Ive, and Hinnerk replied:
'Tomorrow morning at six o'clock you are all to be arrested.'
Ive sat down slowly. He considered for a moment, then took up the telephone.
'The others?' he asked.
Hinnerk put his hand on the receiver.
'That will be attended to,' he said, and Ive flushed. 'I am just going to tell the others; afterwards I am going to see Heim. Are you coming?'
'I shall stay here,' said Ive. 'Send up the first young farmer you see, to help me clear away the stuff.'
'Extremely silly,' said Hinnerk, 'but as you like.'
And then—'Good luck!' and he clattered down the stairs.
Ive remained seated for a while. I must get the article about our arrest written tonight, he thought. Then he began to collect the important papers. There was not much. Ive had had the place searched a number of times before. According to the Explosives Act the minimum sentence was five years' imprisonment. He wondered whether Heim would stand his ground. He would. Heim would at once realise how important it was not to run away, to let himself be taken. Ive tied the papers into a bundle. The young farmer arrived. Hinnerk had fetched him out of a bar—a young fellow with a broad, smiling face. He took the packet with an eagerness which proved that he knew what was up. Ive gave him a few lines to take to old Reimann, who was to see that a successor was found to take on the work as soon as the editorial rooms were vacated by the police. The door banged; Ive was alone. He walked up and down for a while. What next? he thought. He wouldn't have much trouble with the President of the Enquiry. Presidents of Enquiries always know much less than the accused imagines. Ive was almost enjoying the thought of the sharp intellectual battle in front of him. The prospect of an incalculable period in prison did not alarm him; wherever he went, or wherever he had to be, he had always discovered secret interests and excitements that were the heart-beats of fate for him. Imprisonment, with its greater hardships, only meant for him richer results. But the others, the Movement, the farmers and Claus Heim? Claus Heim, to whom he felt most strongly attached? Ive was not a farmer, but Claus Heim was so much a farmer that he could give up being a farmer—just as a man who truly loves life has no desire to avoid the thought of death. The tall, dark, reticent man had sacrificed security, had found the way to that militant readiness which had always been Ive's attitude, which enabled him to regard reality as a mad whirlpool of dangers, a deliberate, inexorable chain of trials. But what for Ive was the natural

course, the only conceivable state of events, had become for Claus Heim a fanatical passion. The more the Movement threatened to become encrusted, the more he allowed himself to indulge in wild dreams, which, fed by his indomitable will and transformed by his short, slow phrases into glowing images, could carry Ive away and give an impetus to his activities as though they had been ignited by a sudden flame. Ive would then see the clumsy farmer beside him enlarging his field of action until it burst all bounds, and the art of the possible transformed into an art to which everything must be possible. Hamkens *Cunctator* seemed to urge the necessity of carefully preserving what had been achieved, keeping the Movement straightforward and pure and always comprehensible to his simple mind; but Heim had cut the cords which bound him to the farm; he had set out to sea, like a pirate, knowing that this was demanded of him for the sake of the farm. Between the two stood Ive, who had once and for all anchored himself to the farmers' cause, more because the 'how' rather than the 'what' of the farmers' struggle appeared to him significant. At heart Ive was a barbarian; he knew this and made no bones about it. It did not occur to him to pretend that necessity was a virtue, but he regarded it as unvirtuous to try to avoid it. The unconcern with which he began every enterprise, with which he tried to adapt himself to everything which presented itself as a manifestation of the period or of life, may have had some sort of an explanation, but it never occurred to him to search for reasons. As a son of the war he found himself placed among circumstances and events with which his natural gifts enabled him to deal perfectly adequately. Since he had no troubles and no memories to burden him, he never regarded himself or his position as a problem in any society. He belonged neither to the townspeople nor to the farmers, nor to the workers, and meanwhile he felt no urge to range himself with any particular class or profession. He knew that an infinite number of people in the country were in the same boat and, if here and there they went under, this could only be for the time being. Ive did not need to go under, for he could find subsistence wherever he was. Certainly he had a longing for attachments—the only one which he was firmly and inalienably aware of arose from the fact that he was a German. This attachment was his only reservation; it amazed him that the uncompromising character which resulted from this was regarded in all the circles into which his activities brought him, apparently not only as exceptional, but even as dangerous and intolerable. He did not stand for the opposition on principle, but everything he thought or said or did declared him an oppositionist; he found from the very beginning that he was shut out from every established system and he did not mind this; what hurt him was the discovery that actually the standards of every system were not fully respected or administered by those who upheld them; the anonymity of the systems and the timid subservience of those who had dug themselves into them, seemed to him insupportable. Thus he was anti-bourgeois, not from the sociological point of view, but because of his attitude of mind. He examined this attitude and, using it as a basis, he sought for attachments and comradeship; and its uncompromisingness was for him the sine qua non of every kind of politics. This caused him to regard all political theories with fierce mistrust; the masses collected round their dry bones and clothed them with the flesh of their most intimate hopes, and when it was established that every theory, or, if it took an imaginative form, every ideal only ended in corruption, he was unable to see why so much spirit, blood, and devotion need be expended on it. He was often told that this kind of thought was anarchistic, and he would have had nothing against this if Anarchism had not delighted in hair-splitting theories. His fellow workers in the woolcombing factory had quickly found an epithet for him: they called him 'declassed,' and that in a tone which plainly betrayed mistrust. He sought for the reason of this mistrust, and found it in the supposition that he had had an academic education. As this did not happen to be the case, and as he thought to himself that Marx and Lenin must without doubt have been under the same suspicion, he contented himself with admitting that he possessed no class-consciousness, and he could the more easily dissociate himself from the solidarity of the workers, as this, in fact, did not exist. Ive was not quite clear whether class-solidarity was regarded as an essential factor or merely as an expedient. In any case solidarity remained the chief slogan for seventy years. It seemed to him that the study of this phenomenon, investigation into its causes, and the possibilities of modifying it would prove a more fruitful revolutionary task than to acquire and continually propagate the economic doctrine, a doctrine in which everything worked out too pat to be true. So he occupied himself with the living body of the proletariat, which had more to tell him than the learned theses over which professors and bureaucrats disputed, a dispute the jangling echo of which in the various trades was far more likely to confuse and divide the proletariat than to consolidate it. In fact, independent solidarity, in an illuminating and fruitful form, was to be found only in that section of the proletariat where they were concerned with militant action, that is where the importance of what they had staked in common was felt so strongly that they were no longer united merely by interest but where, on the contrary, the network of hidden interests was being forced into the light of day. When Ive threw in his lot with Claus Heim and the farmers, the chief attraction for him had been the existence of a militant partnership, the first and most natural form of solidarity, which from the very first displayed a fundamentally different character from that which the workers announced as their aim. After the failure of the unions as an expression of solidarity, and their increasing absorption into the capitalist system, it was clear that class-organisation could only be possible when individual interests had been disentangled and when the whole body had been disintegrated with the object of educating it and subjecting it to the discipline of realising some theory—or of refuting some theory—whatever it might be. But the militant partnership of the farmers had stood from the outset under the discipline of the farm. The farm was the law-giver—set the boundaries and enlarged them. It presented itself as the superior will which the proletariat had to seek in a leader, had so far not found, and would only with difficulty ever find; for the task of a leader of the proletariat could only be one of instruction. Claus Heim and Hamkens knew why they were so unwilling to be called leaders, why they perpetually drew attention to the spontaneity of the farmers' campaign; it was the farm which regulated and gave form to their emotional reactions—the farm, which no longer belonged to the farmer if he reckoned up his accumulation of debts. True, the events which had taken place in the province could only be regarded as raw material, but they already contained the germ of a complete development as well as the laws of a new order. Thus no single action of the Movement could be lost; it crystallised immediately into a new motive-force, and, if the growth of the Movement was strictly limited as regards numbers, this was not the case as regards the far-reaching influence of its impetus. The resistance to the encroachments of the System, the battle of Neumünster, united to build up the preliminary structure of self-government; showed the difficulties and, through them, the prospect, and through the prospect, the plan of the complete revolution.

'What we have to do,' said Claus Heim, 'is, starting as it were with the farmers, to enrol the whole country. And why should that not be possible? The town is against us,' said Claus Heim. 'It must not be, but today it is, because it has not got as far as we have. Our task was easier; we must attack the town in order to help it. It must find itself, as we have found ourselves. Then we can see a step further.'

Claus Heim said: 'All the misery comes from the town. It was not always so, but it is so now. The town is sick and its breath is foul. Are we too to be destroyed by its pestilential vapours? How does one protect oneself against a plague-stricken man? By isolating him. Let us isolate the town. How does one cure a fever-ridden man? By bringing him to a crisis. Let us bring the town to a crisis. Neumünster,' said Claus Heim, 'is a beginning. What is possible in Neumünster is also possible in Berlin. Let us declare a boycott against Berlin. Once the whole of the country-people are united, Berlin will be in our power.

The town needs us, because we feed it. The town thought that our troubles were not its troubles; we must show it that our troubles are its troubles. What is the world coming to when corn is rotting in the barns, and the people in the towns are starving? They will change things when they have starved a bit longer. They will learn to divide equally, so that the farm which feeds them may live, and that they who are starving may also live. They will not be able to import food, either by sea or by land, for farmers live near all the railways and near all the canals.'

'As soon as the whole of the country-people are united...' said Ive, and indeed that was his concern.

'Forty-five percent of the farmers' children in Schleswig are undernourished,' said the Schleswig farmers to Hamkens. 'We live on potatoes with dripping.'

'What are you going to do?' asked Hamkens.

The farmers said, 'We shall have to eat potatoes with linseed oil now.'

'And the farm?' asked Hamkens. The farmers shrugged their shoulders sheepishly and said, 'Well, a railway porter is all right—he has everything he needs and a regular salary as well.'

'Very well, become railway porters,' said Hamkens, 'but don't complain, if you are not prepared to fight.'

'We want to, but we can't,' said the Schleswig farmers, and they hoisted the black flag; but that didn't help them and next to nothing was changed.

'How are we to exist?' said the landowners in East Prussia to Hamkens. 'We have forests and fields and machines and labourers, and we have nothing. How are we to get rid of our timber when the Polish rafts are coming down the Vistula; how are we to sell our corn at prices which will not even bring in enough for wages and rates and taxes?'

'How is it,' said Hamkens, 'that at one time it used to be said that it was a crime against the Fatherland to feed wheat to the cattle, and now you are being suffocated by it? What are you going to do?'

The landowners said, 'Corn duties.'

'Nonsense,' said Hamkens. 'Are you going to hinder cultivation by putting up the prices of foodstuffs?'

The landowners shrugged their shoulders.

'The System is to blame,' they said, and hung the black flag out of their front windows, and sat behind them discussing the duties and the removal of the land-tax. And the position was the same everywhere. In the Rhineland the trouble took a different form from that in Thuringia; and in Hessen different from that in Württemberg. Everywhere the associations were worming their way in; if it was not the peasants' party, it was the farmers' party; if it was not the National Land Association, it was the District Land Association; solidarity was their one cry, and each one challenged the other to amalgamate; the whole farmer-class consisted of a tangle of groups, and the groups of a mad conglomeration of smaller groups, all fighting with each other and all with the proud watchword, 'Unity.' What was possible in Schleswig-Holstein and was still possible in North Hanover and could gradually be extended to the whole of North-west Germany, was difficult in Pomerania and in Mecklenburg and in East Prussia, and desperately difficult in Schleswig or the Gretizmark, and everywhere it meant a long, bitter, tough task.

'The System,' they repeated throughout the country with grim hatred.

But some were for the System, and some were against the System, but most of all were both for and against. Claus Heim never lost sight of the goal, nor Hamkens, nor Ive. But whereas Claus Heim urged and pressed for action, Hamkens was for waiting. While Claus Heim wanted to make use of every opportunity—and what numbers offered themselves daily!—while he wanted to form an alliance with anyone who came whirling to the forefront even for a moment—were it the devil himself—wanted to hurl the weapon of the boycott against every form of opposition (and when he uttered the word 'System' it sounded as though he was speaking of murder and arson and bombs and farmers armed with scythes), Hamkens' idea was carefully to hoard the resources of the Movement, to use it prudently, to begin in a small way and feel his way slowly step by step, to be prepared, not for the moment, but for the day on which he must be the victor who could act at once with solid support behind him. Now Heim was to be arrested and the Movement was left entirely in Hamkens' hands.

Perhaps that is a good thing for the moment, thought Ive, as he paced anxiously up and down. Even in prison Claus Heim would serve the cause, better, at any rate, than as though he took to flight. The flag in Neumünster, the free farmer offered as a sacrifice to the System, imprisoned as a martyr of the country-people's war; that might be a perpetual incentive to the farmers not to give way, at least not to give way. If the method of Heim was right, because it was ruled by the laws of hazard, the method of Hamkens' was equally right because it followed the laws of experience. What now? thought Ive. In the most fortunate circumstances it would be months before he was free again. He could not foresee what changes might have occurred in the Movement by that time, but, in any case, he would have to rush, into the ranks again, to renew the conflict and to introduce the Heimian line of attack. For, even if it had come to pass that every single farmer in the province was concerned not only in safeguarding the position but in revolution—and actually the safeguarding of the position in the form desired by the farmers was not conceivable without revolution—Ive's concern went further in requiring that the revolution must be initiated by the farmers, and by no one else. Revolution had been attempted by workers and by soldiers without success, and yet it was the hope of almost half the nation and the aim of every active group. But the farmers, with their securist position at stake, so thought Ive, would of all revolutionary groups not only have the best prospects of success, but would also be able to strike the strongest blow. For whatever power was to be won by the farmers, even in the event of victory, undoubtedly could not—and this was not to be said of any other group—cause any great disturbance in any other revolutionary field however extensive. It must, therefore, be possible, thought Ive, for the first time to recapture the dissipated energies, to unite and direct the forces with a common aim, to organise them into an allied army, and to launch the attack. The first task must be to make preparations for this, and form the alliance, and the best co-operator in this was time. Ive had for a long time been making preliminary investigations, putting out feelers in all directions; Claus Heim had been to the capital and had knocked at many doors and found ready listeners (if the response was noncommittal), and the admirable Hinnerk, who was ready for anything, kept in continual contact. But this was not enough. Ive, accustomed to suck honey from any blossom, suddenly found hope and resolution in the fact that he was to be arrested on the following day.

He went up to the table and looked meditatively at the chaotic mass of papers. I must write the article about our arrest, he thought. No, it would not suffice to be an outpost of the farmers' front. What had to be done, could, as things were turning out, only be done by himself. Perhaps it was all madness; but at least there should be method in the madness. Heim wanted to conquer the town. But was the town to be conquered except from within? This was an original idea:—from within. He must go into the town. In the interest of the farmers, in Heim's interest, in his own interest. The machinery of administration, he thought grimly, will give me free transit. He took the typed page out of the machine and put in a fresh sheet of paper. Let us see what importance the town has, he thought. He examined himself and was filled with great happiness. He wrote until the officers of the law arrived on the following morning.

IV

POLICE-COMMISSIONER MÜLLSCHIPPE of Division I. A. had been given very wide powers. He was a young man with small, alert, dark eyes and a fresh complexion, and did not hesitate to make full use of the great opportunity which his task offered him. His interviews with the Under-Prefect of Police and with the representatives of the Ministry of the Interior had made clear to him what the State expected of him, and smoothed the way for the exercise of his talents. It was not petty ambition which fired this admirable officer, but the delightful prospect of for once being able to give full play to the many-sided brilliance of his intellect. At one blow—a blow which resounded with a thunderclap of sensation and the echoes of which reverberated in the newspapers for weeks to come—he arrested anyone who was in the least degree suspicious, or who, in his opinion, might be considered in the least capable of throwing a bomb: in all, one hundred and twenty men. He made short shrift of the old prejudice that one should make enquiries before arresting; he arrested before making enquiries. The room which he occupied in his official capacity was no longer an ordinary office of the political police, but a headquarters. Day and night he was on duty in the barely furnished room, with its air of Spartan militariness. He stood in his shirt-sleeves, sweating, his nerves vibrating under the strain, the telephone receiver at his ear—the untiring central figure. In the passages and ante-rooms newspaper reporters and photographers thronged, anxious to catch a momentary glimpse of the important man, to snatch up the morsels of news he hastily threw to them. The officers of his staff hurried hither and thither following his agitated directions, telephones buzzed, typewriters rattled, the dust rose in clouds and settled on the bundles of documents. He stood there in the dim light of the flickering lamps, in the dawning gleam of the morning sun rising over the dark courtyards; he stood, with his tie unloosened, in the fierce midday heat, and in the cooling shadows of the evening sunlight when a day of unceasing activity was sinking into a night crowded with work. He was never seen to slacken, and if he himself had not once, between two dramatic examinations, expressed a humorous and kindly concern for his anxiously waiting wife and his dinner most certainly long since stone cold, it would have occurred to no one that this inflexible machine of duty, this noble example of sacrifice in the service of his office, had any connection with human weaknesses.

As a trained criminal psychologist, he could adopt any attitude, from the tyrannical severity of the man of iron upholding the law to the benevolent friendliness of the man who understands and forgives all. He never failed to offer a cigarette to the accused, nor to rebuff him with cold calculation. He was always ready to refute the crafty tissue of lies of the notorious lawbreaker with just as much ingenuity as it had been fabricated, the depth of his design veiled by deliberately ambiguous phraseology. His arm reached far, but still farther the rays from his indefatigable intellect.

This unpleasant business of the bombs had long been enveloped in a paralysing silence, but with his intervention blow after blow fell, striking with ever-increasing violence, and with repeatedly demonstrated justification. He stepped up to Ive threateningly, accumulated energy in his expression.

'Do you know Claus Heim?' he asked, and the officers in the room stopped working and held their breath.

'I am his best friend,' said Ive, astonished.

A murmur arose in room, expressive glances were exchanged, and rested expectantly and in silent admiration on Müllschippe's face, stood upright. He went close to Ive, who was sitting humped up on his stool. The Police-Commissioner raised his voice again, every one of his words disclosing the result of a concentrated and intricate calculation, the absolute certainty of victory, the tension of a cunningly laid trap.

'Have you taken part in the Farmers' Movement?' he asked, fixing Ive with a penetrating glance.

'For the past year I have been accepting responsibility for it in the farmers' paper,' said Ive in astonishment.

A whisper went round the room.

'Good,' said Müllschippe, and he seemed to increase in stature. 'Very good,' he said hoarsely, and left the room with rapid strides.

The door was ajar and Ive could hear what the Commissioner was reporting over the telephone to the Press Bureau of the Ministry of the Interior.

'Double confession of the bomb-thrower Iversen. After an exhaustive examination by Police-Commissioner Müllschippe, the accused Iversen broke down and made a double confession.'

Ive listened in silent admiration. He had always been attracted by demagogic talents and he understood the art of creating atmosphere. He could scarcely feel indignant, and so when Müllschippe returned to him, mopping the sweat from his crimson forehead, he merely said that he would prefer to be examined by a legal official. He did not make this request because the Commissioner struck him as dangerous, or even because he expected impartiality from a lawyer; he understood that the significance of justice was no more than a moral fiction. But he wanted his request to be incorporated in the evidence, so that from the outset there should be a little point of friction between the Police and the Court.

Police-Commissioner Müllschippe was not to be put off so easily, however. He proved to be an affable man, socially inclined, and Ive spent a pleasant hour in conversation with him.

'This isn't meant to be an examination,' said the friendly Commissioner, and in fact Ive had no difficulty in parrying all questions which seemed to him too personal by making even more personal disclosures.

'But you must have heard that!' said Müllschippe, referring to a remark of Heim's disclosing complicity in a bombing plot.

'I am a man, who uses his eyes more than his ears,' explained Ive, and expatiated for half an hour on his theory about this.

He knew that there were no set rules for a defence, every one had his own. The important point was to stick to the method you had chosen through thick and thin. Ive decided to talk, to talk a lot, to talk so much that in the end no one would be able to remember or question anything he had said. In such an indulgent atmosphere he thought he might well ask to dictate his own statement. He dictated half a page and ruled a thick diagonal line across the space left between the statement and his signature, politely asking for a ruler in order to do so. Herr Müllschippe seemed a little hurt by this lack of confidence. He dismissed Ive to his cell, and called for Claus Heim.

The two men met in the doorway. Claus Heim srniled faintly and gave Ive his hand. Müllschippe looked curiously at the big man who stood there, three heads taller than himself. Side doors opened, official spectacles gleamed, and heads were lifted from musty documents. So this was Claus Heim. (On the table lay the documents in the Grafenstolz case.)

'What is your name?' asked Police-Commissioner Müllschippe, with hesitating severity. Claus Heim took a chair and sat down. He laid his enormous hands on the table and said nothing.

'You are Claus Heim?' asked Herr Müllschippe; he repeated it; he tried gentleness, he gave his voice a metallic sharpness; Claus Heim sat immobile, looking scornfully at the excited little man and saying nothing.

'So you refuse to speak?' said the Commissioner.

The Commissioner said a lot more. Claus Heim said nothing. He had not prepared any defence, and had never even thought about methods of defence. But he had declared a boycott of the System. He did not speak to representatives of the System and would be silent for the rest of his life, if necessary. All this buzz around him did not interest him. He looked straight in front of him, but in his eyes gleamed implacable, cold, eternal hatred.

'I have never had anyone like Heim before,' said Warder Scholz II that evening to his wife 'He squats at the table all day without moving. He does not go out for recreation, he never answers when spoken to, he doesn't touch his hot dinner, just eats the bread. You could almost think he didn't see you go into his cell. He's a strange fellow and no mistake. I have never had one like him before.'

Police-Commissioner Müllschippe reported to the Press Bureau of the Ministry of the Interior:

'Claus Heim convicted. The enquiries of Police-Commissioner Müllschippe have proved without doubt that Claus Heim must be regarded as the instigator of the bomb outrages.'

Police-Commissioner Müllschippe was indefatigable. Day after day he hurled the results of his enquiries into the office. The reverberations of his activities penetrated to the prison cells. They were Ive's first impression of the town. Crouched on his narrow bed he listened for the sound of rapid, shuffling footsteps, for the rattle of the key, for the muffled cries: 'To the Court.'

The whole place was full of political prisoners. In September there were still Communists there, left over from the May disturbances, who had not yet been finally examined. Every day National Socialists were brought in. At exercise-time some called out 'Red Front' and others 'Heil,' looking furiously at each other, while the warders, armed with pistols, swords, and rifles, stood about quite indifferent. There were very few criminal prisoners in the building, and most of them were working at the furnaces. One of them came up to Ive and whispered to him eagerly, offering to carry clandestine notes. Ive prepared notes for all his comrades, which he gave to the prisoner, and which contained only two words:

'Beware—Müll-spy.'

Late into the night the activities in the building continued —Müllschippe was conducting examinations. Only the distant murmur of the town penetrated to the cells, the multitudinous cries of the pavements, which mingled together in one dull, vibrating roar, containing all the excitement and danger of life. It seemed impossible that the prison walls could stand against the perpetual tumult of the thousands of agitations which the town was continually spewing out. Every night Ive stood on the end of his bed clinging to the iron bars of the window, all his senses riveted on the distant world, the life, the danger surging in bondage down there outside, colouring the dirty sky with greyish-red tints, sending up their exhalations to penetrate even the miserable isolation of his cell. Leavened by the metallic breath of the town he went in the morning to his examination. The gigantic red building of the Police Court vibrated with activity, the long, echoing corridors teemed with important people, who, even as they waited, snorted like machines on the brake, the uninterrupted rhythm of perpetual, driving activity swept him into the grey room with its dirty carpets, its stained, scratched tables, its dark cupboards and the zealous, sweating Herr Müllschippe.

'How long do you imagine you're going to keep this up?' asked Ive after a fruitless exchange of questions and answers.

'What?' asked the Commissioner sharply.

'All this business,' said Ive, and he continued reflectively, 'I suppose that from this room life looks quite different.'

Müllschippe started. —'What do you mean?' he asked, and then said curtly: 'I am doing my duty.'

'Of course,' said Ive, and once more requested that a legal officer... He was removed to the big house of detention in the Moabit district.

The Judge of the County Court, Dr. Fuchs, was none of your shirt-sleeved hail-fellow-well-mets. He was a serious official in a high position, an elegant man of the world, worthy of becoming a judge of the Supreme Court.

'You know,' he said deliberately, in a sonorous, courteous voice, 'I entirely understand your action.'

He held up his hand reassuringly.

'But I consider it a point of honour to accept the consequences of one's actions. I too am a nationalist,' he said.

'I am not,' said Ive, paused a moment, and then continued: 'I don't particularly want to be landed in gaol, even with the help of Herr Müllschippe.'

Dr. Fuchs frowned and turned over the pages of the documents, then handed them to the Assessor, Matz, a young man who did not appear to be quite grown up, which was the more astonishing as he was unusually tall. When Ive entered the room he folded up in a polite bow. Ive was more and more disappointed every time he went to be examined. Instead of opponents, the machinery of administration was facing him with bombastic upstarts, *causeurs*, and young puppies, and there must have been plenty of evidence to make the situation dangerous for him. The evidence was clear enough, but these people did not know how to handle it.

'Only a confession can improve your position,' said Judge Fuchs.

'Where are your proofs?' asked Ive, and continued, 'you want to put the burden of proof on me? Good, all three of the incriminating statements are contradictory. Each one contains contradictions within itself. The only statement you can use as a basis for the proceedings is the one which contains no contradictions, and that is my own.'

'The witness Luck,' said the Judge, 'saw you.'

'The witness Luck,' said Ive, 'saw me at the time of the act in the vicinity of the scene of action, with a package, which, only after the act, of course, he thought suspicious, and he identified me again after three weeks. What does the witness Luck say in his statement? "I identify Iversen as the perpetrator." His statement contains circumstantial evidence, not facts.'

Ive played with the disjointed pieces of a bomb, which had been found on Grafenstolz, and were now lying on the table as an exhibit in the case. He fitted them together absent-mindedly.

'You know how to deal with bombs,' said the Judge.

'Is this a bomb?' asked Ive. 'I thought it was a wireless set.'

And he said: 'You know as well as I do how much reliance can be placed on the statements of witnesses. You know just as well as I do that every witness can be corrupted. Why do you want a confession from me? Because you know as well as I do that you have no evidence beyond what I can give you; I shall give you no evidence.'

'You have, just as I have,' said Dr. Fuchs, 'an interest in having the case settled. As matters stand I am convinced of your guilt; convince me to the contrary.'

Ive said: 'Since you are convinced of my guilt, why do you want a confession? What do you want of me? My manly pride to be roused at the bar of Justice? But I fear I might violate your conception of justice thereby; you would be justified in considering it as presumptuous.'

The Judge said: 'That is your theory.'

'That is my theory,' said Ive, 'and you must admit that I am acting in accordance with it. I demand evidence because I know that you have forgotten how to produce evidence. Not that I consider evidence as conclusive in all circumstances, but I will not play your game. I will not play your cute game with a confession as trump card, relieving you of risk and responsibility. You stand for the law, and I against it.'

'You admit guilt, then?' asked the Judge quickly.

'I admit nothing whatever,' said Ive, leaning forward, 'but at least I expect to be questioned about what I was responsible for. And you are not able to put such questions. That is where I have the advantage, and I am making use of it. Even supposing I made a confession, it might be the result of despair, it might be merely to escape your interrogation. You have had plenty of such instances in your practice! You know as well as I do that every confession, whether it has been extracted by psychological tactics or by force, or whether it has been made voluntarily, immediately encumbers the facts of the case with a flood of irrelevances. You yourself, since you are an enlightened, liberal, humane and patriotic judge with modern ideas,' Ive rolled out the words with relish, 'have brought psychology to bear on the case. But the historical task of psychology, namely to crush the conceptions and standards of centuries, has probably been fulfilled by the very result which it has been the means of developing. It negatives itself. I will not speak of the Müllschippes, but you, you and the Public Prosecutor, and Counsel, and experts, what have you left of your own functions, what have you left of the accused, what have you left of the law? The Medical Officer of Health has superseded the Judge, the Commissioner the Public Prosecutor, and in your proceedings the culprit has neither a favourable nor an unfavourable position; he has no position at all.

The Judge opened his eyes wide.

'You are here in the position of prisoner at the bar,' he said. 'All that you can prove,' said Ive, 'destroys the evidence; the relation of the culprit to the crime, guilt or innocence, for your psychological method deprives this relationship of its former validity. What the accused has done or not done, anybody else might have done or not done. Therefore you demand a confession. Your method has nullified the proceedings, and the proceedings have made the law ridiculous. I assure you that this delights me.'

The Judge looked at the bomb and then gave Ive a cautious sidelong glance.

'So you are an anarchist?' he asked.

Ive drew himself up a little.

'No,' he said indifferently, 'I merely want to reform the criminal code. It is quite simple. You only need to add a rider to Article 51..."is punishable with death."'

The Judge meditated for a long time whether he should not ask the medical officer to report on Ive's mental condition. But he desisted. At the end of the trial he did all in his power to prevent Ive's release, and he succeeded, although the incriminating evidence was very meagre. He realised that Ive held the key to the whole mystery of the bomb outrages, and Ive realised that he realised it. The Judge had officiated at a number of political trials, and was accustomed to one prisoner incriminating another. Of the hundred and twenty prisoners that Herr Müllschippe had brought up before him, he had to dismiss a hundred (and as a result exposed himself to a good deal of unpleasantness at the Ministry of Internal Affairs) and the material produced by Division I.A. had been by no means adequate. They were not all as silent as the gloomy Claus Heim, but they were on the whole a taciturn set of men, and his adroitly turned surprise questions simply had no effect on these farmers. They had such an odd way of looking at him when he had lured them to the very edge of a trap. He had the feeling all the time that they were secretly laughing at him. At every turn there was a hitch in the proceedings. His superiors were urging speed, for voices were making themselves heard on every side, pointing out that the proceedings were illegal. Actually Dr. Fuchs knew as well as the government that Altona and not Berlin was the competent tribunal; it was only the attack on the Reichstag which could justify the concentration of the trial in the capital, but that was the one crime which was never cleared up. This Iversen, thought the County Court Judge.

But Iversen had said, 'Show me a contradiction in my statement, and if you do show me one, then the devil would be in it if I couldn't make it plausible.'

Ive not only dragged out all his examinations interminably, but he made them ridiculous. He denied nothing, he admitted nothing; he left everything open.

'You are on the wrong track,' he said to Dr. Fuchs. 'The longer you follow it, the further you will get from the right one.'

But the Judge did not believe this; he was unfortunate in these proceedings, for whenever the truth did emerge he refused to believe it. He stuck obstinately, to individual points, as stubbornly as the farmers themselves, and he made no progress. One by one as they appeared in the Court his witnesses fell down on their evidence; and Police-Comissioner Müllschippe had every reason to refer to justice with an expressive gesture and to throw himself with enthusiasm into a new case.

Six months after his arrest, although not acquitted, Ive was released, and simultaneously the proceedings were referred to Altona. Claus Heim remained in custody. Claus Heim was to be sentenced, and according to the Explosives Act the minimum sentence was five years' imprisonment. Old Reimann, who had come to visit his son in prison, waited for Ive at the gates. A tall, motionless figure, his blue cap on his straggling white hair, his stick in his hand, he stood in front of the small iron gate, looking along the shining grey pavement. The point of his stick burrowed into a square of slimy dirty-black earth between the paving-stones, which provided meagre nourishment for a tree whose bare, damp branches made it look as though it had been corroded by acids.

'Well, there you are,' said old Reimann simply, as Ive came out of the gate.

He relieved him of a few of the ridiculous cardboard boxes, full to bursting point and clumsily tied up, which contained all Ive's possessions. They walked along beside the tall, gloomy houses, with quiet, deliberate steps as though they were walking on the clinker roads of the Marsh. To Ive, whose eyes were still focused to the grey walls of his cell, the people who pushed by him, the trees, the cars and omnibuses looked like shadows, or the flat figures of a film; to his ear, still under the strain of listening to the significant sounds of the prison house, the noises of the street seemed like a hard, cold rumble through which the hooting of motor horns shot like bright flames. He was not numbed, as he had pictured himself in the long night meditations of his cell, but rather dangerously and excitedly empty, ready to absorb impressions through every pore. He lifted his head and sniffed up the pungent odour of the town and unconsciously fell into the same quick, firm steps as the girl with the clicking heels, who brushed by them, slender and impersonal in her plain grey coat. He looked at his companion, and suddenly in the town; in the chilly light of the early spring sun, the Marsh seemed to him to be distant, strange and remote; the voice of old Reimann, too, sounded distant as, in his characteristic quiet manner, he gave the news of the Movement.

'I have spoken to Hamkens about you,' he said—for they had had to release Hamkens after a few weeks—'and we have a job for you. There is nothing more to be done with bombs, I suppose,' he said, rapping his stick on the pavement. 'I don't mean, of course, that they did no good. If you want a big thing, you must risk big things, and I have never in my life been afraid of taking a risk. My lad and Heim and the others aren't a lot of silly schoolboys who didn't know what they were doing. It helped, but now it can't help any more. There is the trial in Neumünster, I'm not anxious about that, and if things don't go well in Altona, we have it in our power to put the matter right in the long run. In East Prussia things seem to be going ahead now; it is all very promising, and the paper as it is at present answers the purpose.'

'The make-up is shocking,' said Ive angrily.

'I know,' said old Reimann, 'everything is not as it should be and there is a lot of back-biting, but there always is back-biting. But the Movement is sticking it, and now it is a question of who can hold out longest. They have been coming to us with their quack cures and that is the greatest danger, but as long as we are there, Hamkens and the others and I, they won't be able to corrupt us. We need you, Ive,' said old Reimann, suddenly digging him with a cardboard box, and Ive said dryly: 'Claus Heim.'

Reimann turned his face full on Ive and looked at him with his bright eyes.

'What are you going to do? I have spoken to Claus Heim. He is not a man to run away, and he is not a man to ask for mercy.'

'No, not that,' said Ive, 'we must put up a fight for him. What the Communists were able to do for their Max Hölz we should be able to do also.'

He pulled himself together and said: 'I am staying in the town.'

He went on talking rapidly.

'First of all the solicitors must be consulted, then I will work the press; I shall get help wherever I can. Of course, Heim will say that he is innocent, and the worst of it is that they have in him a hostage with which to tempt us. That must not be, and he won't want that either. It must be worked differently. And then there is another thing...'

'One thing leads to another,' said old Reimann, 'we know that; I won't say that we need a lot of friends but the more pressure there is from the other side the quicker we shall gain our ends.'

'That's it,' said Ive, and explained his plan.

They spoke quietly, as was their habit, but Ive grew excited, for he realised what the farmers wanted of him, and he realised also that they had feared he might misconstrue them, and so he exerted himself to make it clear to old Reimann, by his attitude and by what he said, that he did understand, and that for him, too, the separation was not really a separation.

'I am not a farmer,' he said, 'and you know why I have been on your side; nothing has been changed.'

'There is no change,' said the farmer at once, and then again, 'we need you, Ive, and from whatever direction you come to us, when you come, we shall know you, and certainly of all there is to do you have chosen the bitterest portion. I tell you frankly there have been gossip-mongers who have let their tongues rattle about you, and Hamkens even thought it would be better for you to take over a paper in Schleswig, but that's really all nonsense, you are more useful to us over there as things are at present. You are more useful to us if you are your own master.'

But the present position was that the Movement had become a kind of organisation, not a registered association with secretary and treasurer, but a kind of organisation, with restricted aims and definite limits, for there was no other way of saving the Movement.

'We miss Claus Heim,' said old Reimann, 'but it can't be helped, everything will come right.'

They walked on in silence, through noisy, narrow, streets, by crumbling house-fronts and dirty courtyards, over bare, clumsy, rough bridges, under blackened railway arches that shook and groaned when the trains thundered across them. Reimann looked neither to the left nor to the right, he went stolidly on his way.

'Oho,' he said to a motor car that rushed past him, almost touching his sleeve, and when they stood in front of the house in which he lived—he was staying with one of his sons-in-law, a professor at the University in Berlin—a large new block of flats with rows of straight, flat windows and jutting balconies, he rapped with his stick against one of the cornices.

'Dead,' he said, 'cement—not living stone that breathes,' and he looked at Ive reproachfully. On the following morning they parted.

It was the first of April, and the porter at the Town Hall thought he was being made a fool of when a young man walked into his lodge and asked for work.

'There's no work here,' he said gruffly, and hurried the fellow out of the door; he walked a few steps in front of the gate to look after the retreating figure, then the telephone rang, he was wanted in the building. He went off, and when he came back to his lodge, which in his haste he had omitted to lock, he found a longish packet behind the door. He picked it up, shook it a little, turned it over, and was about to open it when he heard a strange ticking. He started, listened, and put his ear to the side of the box. Suddenly his heart began to beat violently; the blood rushed as though driven by electric currents into his finger-tips and set his whole quaking body aglow. He held his breath and placed the package on the table, seized it again and ran, rushing, the packet in his outstretched arms in front of him, out of the lodge, out of the gate into the street, into the middle of the road. There he laid it down. Five minutes later the flying-squad was on the spot, police cars rattled along, the fire brigade engines ringing their bells and tooting their horns. The street was already thick with people.

'What's up?' asked the people as they came up. The police jumped from their cars and unhooked their rubber truncheons.

'A bomb,' was the cry. The firemen circled round the largish black object that lay there alone in the middle of the square.

'Move on!' said the police, and barricaded the street so that no one could move on.

Herr Müllschippe, too, had arrived. Herr Müllschippe waited for the experts.

'A bomb,' he said to the newspaper men.

Trams, motor cars put on their brakes. Lieutenant Brodermann of the police force telephoned for reinforcements.

'Stand back!' was the cry, and a hard black hat collapsed under a blow from a rubber truncheon.

'A bomb!' shouted the Berliners, and played football with the hat. Then the car of the Assistant Commissioner of Police arrived, on its bonnet the white flag with the police star.

'Stand back!'

The expert approached, his coat flying open. For a while silence reigned in the Square. All eyes were turned on the man who was bending over the object. Then the man stood upright again. A happy murmur of relief passed through the rows of people.

'Gentlemen,' said the Police-Commissioner to the reporters, 'the examination of the police expert, who has just rendered the bomb innocuous, has proved without a doubt that the explosive is made up of the same constituents as those used for the bombs in the outrages in Schleswig-Holstein.'

The reporters wrote rapidly, and the newspapers printed the news with startling headlines.

The civil expert came too late. The crowd had long since dispersed; the police and the fire-brigade had driven off. So Herr Müllschippe telephoned to the Ministry of the Interior when the civil expert declared that the explosive material in the bomb consisted of garden soil, nothing but black rich garden soil which it would be difficult to prove as being of Schleswig-Holstein origin.

On the following evening Ive read the correction, printed in small type, as he stood in front of the kiosk where he had bought his paper. The vendor of rolls, who was crying his wares in a hoarse voice beside him, tapped him lightly on the shoulder.

'Hinnerk!' exclaimed Ive in astonishment.

'Emil is my name,' said Hinnerk.

He pointed to the report in the paper.

'That'll teach them to forget about bombs,' he said. 'That's the way of the world; from the sublime to the ridiculous, from dynamite to garden soil.'

V

I VE came to the town to conquer it. This happened in those remarkable years which have left little trace of their character in our memories. Not that it was a time of peace; violent convulsions shook the world, throwing the nations into confusion. Nor indeed was there any lack of effort to make things tolerable. Serious and responsible men were unceasingly active in the interests of public welfare. But although everyone realised the insupportable state of affairs, although every one was directly affected by it, and therefore strove in his own way to change it, it seemed as though every endeavour was doomed to failure. We were living in a whirl of industry and stimulating activity; every short day was filled with events and yet it passed without impressing its importance on our consciousness. Looking back we can recall how pointless all this activity seemed to us, how it only increased our anxiety. No event, no personality stood out to give a name to this period. We can only regard it as one of those lulls which occur in history between two epochs. Yet it would be a mistake to speak lightly of those years. With all their tumult they were mute, with all their variety they registered no images, but the very lack of positive manifestations led men to probe beneath the surface, which offered so bare an answer to their questionings, and to seek deeper issues—issues which lay hidden like the unconscious potions masked by the death-like features of a sleeper tortured by wild dreams. When the sleeper awakes he knows nothing of the work which was fulfilled in his rigid body, of the vibrations whose lightest movement was registered in his quivering brain and transformed into nightmare. So hidden in the dream-world lay the presage of what the day had in store for us, and those who had the courage to search discovered the possibilities awaiting them, and found the chambers thrown open which despair had so carefully closed on them. And the paramount reason which makes us inclined to regard even these years of unrest as significant is the fact that in them, all at once, so many were driven by their dissatisfaction to tear down the bars from every bolted door.

Once we are clear in our minds that everything that happened during that time was necessary, we must not seek the explanation by turning our minds to the leading spirits, to the prominent men who, with flourish of trumpets, were perpetually unfolding before our eyes the immense scroll of propaganda, nor yet to those who observed the trend of events with cold detachment and accurately reported what they saw, which was merely the surface, nor to all those who were considered the representatives of their age, and, indeed, were worthy representatives of that age; we must turn rather to those whom we met in our daily life, the men who held no office, and had no opinions, but who set out to find both, and to discover moreover what it was that alone could make office and opinion worthy of pursuit. It was they who prepared the way, and they prepared the way because they fulfilled in themselves what the period demanded of them. They were able to do this because, with the receptiveness of dreamers, they were influenced by every swing of the pendulum, their minds were open to every intellectual reaction, they plunged forward and upward, and, strong in the assurance of being indomitable they possessed themselves of that intrinsic quality which is the germ of life itself and by which alone it can be measured and judged. At the time it appeared to us that these men were more menaced than menacing. Certainly they did not know how to adjust themselves, to make use of all the salutary guarantees which an order-loving society had prudently created for the preservation of their well-being.

How could it have been otherwise, since to them every guarantee must have seemed like evasion? Moreover, who was to know when every guarantee would not be called into question? The machine still functioned and, even if its laws were no longer adequate for the reasoning mind, it was still in the interest of all to keep it running smoothly. Thus anyone who refused to take part in this effort must needs have appeared to be suspect. Isolated instances, however, settled themselves, and in those cases it was scarcely necessary even to use the means they had to repulse a tiresome demand when it became crystallised into a claim. But when this incomprehensible attitude became apparent in an ever-increasing degree and in ever wider circles, public attention began to busy itself with the problem. What had previously been merely a personal difficulty unworthy of particular attention in the confusion of events had become a problem. The fanatics of cause and effect had explanations at their finger-tips. Some said that a new sociological stratum was developing, and they made a fierce attack on its elements, although they never doubted that it was, in any case, doomed to destruction. Clippings from the aspiring proletariat, they said, and the declining middle-class, and found the cause in the overcrowding of the universities, the reduction of the standing army and the increasing lack of opportunity for social climbers, and various other phenomena of this kind. The people in this new class could see themselves variously described in newspapers of every political colour. Learned articles described them as victims of the class-struggle, or of capitalism or of the lost; but in the political leaders they became fascist hirelings, work-shy louts, or emasculated dilettanti. Others again spread themselves on the subject of the experiences at the front, which they said had undoubtedly changed men's whole characters; from this it was not far to the well-known theory of the generation destroyed by the war, even though it escaped shell-fire, and through that to the effort to describe the difficult material in one trenchant phrase as a 'problem of the age.'

Thus it could not fail to happen that a number of representatives of this class succumbed to the magic of public interest, sinking into a prolonged contemplation of their own navels and bewailing their tragic fate; whereas, among these again were some who were able to transmute their deep meditations into printable manuscripts, and it was no longer unusual for them to find some publishing house sufficiently interested to provide them with a living, if of a somewhat insecure kind. For the majority, however, another fate was decreed. The System, after its ineffectual outcry, probably never seriously meant, against the younger generation, again bethought itself of the old solution, which was, quite simply, to abandon to the social misery which they presumably themselves desired the erring creatures who were, by their very nature, injurious to the process of production. For in the long run, naturally, only that special and specialised efficiency could be of ultimate importance which was dependent neither on epoch nor origins, and whose essential characteristic was its resignation to its appointed sphere. The machine produced for itself all it needed in the way of intellect, and everything beyond that must perforce peter out in fruitless sophistry. The best means of averting an immediate danger, of whatever kind it might be, was to manoeuvre it out of its menacing proximity and to appoint to it a sufficiently remote field of operation. Actually this was easy to accomplish, for since the representatives of unrest were scattered among all camps there was no fear of united action. Even within the different camps they were isolated, so that the individuals were unassailable, and yet seemingly without hope of uniting the outpourings of their discontent in one mighty stream and approaching a positive political objective. Whenever two or three discovered themselves to be in even the most superficial agreement they immediately declared a front, and very soon there were so many fronts that the real battle was lost sight of. Then the prophets of cross-union arose, an attempt not only to bring about for the first time an organised consolidation of this hitherto elusive class, but also, by this means, to effect its gradual absorption into the machine and to produce a reformation from within, an attempt which certainly did not suffer from lack of grandiose slogans and, in due course, came to a disastrous end.

Actually the only bond of union in this class, the only common ground, was their mental attitude—their mental attitude, but by no means the results which this produced. Ideas were as cheap as blackberries and could be gathered on every hedge, whether they connoted racial regeneration, socialistic economic planning, or a central revolution. But, in any case, it was not the objective significance of these astonishingly original contributions to the problems of the day which took our attention so much as the manner of their expression. A new mind seemed to be speaking in a new tongue. Their literary manifestations, for instance, appeared in a sort of code, the essence of which lay in the fact that old and familiar conceptions were used in quite a new sense only to be understood by those who from the outset were more or less of the same mind. This language acted as a sort of sieve, and it was owing to this useful circumstance, probably, that a special encyclopaedia was not prodded with each work, There was of course no accord about definitions; the process of thought seemed rather to begin with critical examination of the most fundamental hypotheses, and the only point in common was their unutterable seriousness and the obvious effort they were making to get the root of even the tritest and most banal phenomena and from the new significance thus attached to them to derive new developments. Thus the centre of gravity of every phenomenon shifted from the bare fact to the experience of the fact, and from the bare experience to the sublimisation of it; which showed very plainly the innate relationship of this political manifestation with every act of artistic creation—political manifestation, for these people were obsessed by politics, which appeared to them not as the simple administration of public affairs, with all its obstinate bandying to and fro, but as the great spirit embracing all life, whose movements are history and whose essence is power. The town as a spiritual image, the centre of every volition, the arena of every interest and effort, seemed for this species of men to be particularly favourable ground, and it might have been likened to a mountain within which an immense army of moles was at work, boring through rock and earth in every direction, invisibly undermining the mountain with their network of passages—an activity which did not spring from any particular infamy—they could not help themselves. And Ive bored merrily with them.

It was only natural that he, in his search for the active forces which were directing themselves against the common enemy, the 'System,' should in the first place encounter those men who had no firm, assured, and recognised position, but were to be found on all sides. Moreover, Ive probably realised that his whole nature and attitude made him one of them. But, as the farmers' ambassador, he possessed a certain amount of power, and this made him mistrust the predominantly intellectual attitude of his new friends and, although he shared their freedom from prejudice, it seemed to him that this all too alert mental activity was a sign of lack of firmness; but in any case firmness was not of very great importance in that scene of action, and so he was inclined to agree with the statement which was frequently made to him: that every one would be prepared to stand on the barricades if it were demanded of him; but no one demanded it. Ive still had a naive belief in the efficacy of the barricades; at any rate as a stimulus to imagination. But he had not been long in the town when he realised, and every experience taught him anew, that his natural simplicity of attitude was quite sufficient to enable him to exist there, but if he were to live, that is, to make himself felt and bring the town to subjection, then he would require a very different equipment. He was not inimical to the town as such, he was prepared to accept it as a reality; but a few walks in the streets were enough to destroy his preconceptions, and very soon he could no longer remember what these conceptions had been except that they were of something quite different. At first he resisted the force which was overwhelming him, the uninterrupted flow of thoughts and images, each one of which by its strangeness held such a high degree of allurement; but he was accustomed to investigate men, things and opinions, first to discover their innate strength and then to classify them, and in the town, in the phenomenon of the town, he encountered the powerful executor of an indomitable will and he realised that to hold his own against this daemonic force would be a hard test and a glorious victory. It would not do to withdraw; if he were to shut himself off from pain he would have to set about investigating new values, and it must not be from lack of confidence that he sought a new equipment, but from the knowledge that with it he would be preparing himself for the greatest possible development. Of course, of this he was firmly convinced, at the root things must be quite simple, but what a maze had to be threaded in order to reach it! Ive lived the life of the town. And he did not hesitate, in order to do this, to begin at the very beginning. At first he tried to use his memories as a guide.

But the town gave him no clue. It seemed as though it would accept no responsibility that was not of the moment, therefore, no personal relation that was not intimately bound up with its own peculiar character. Ive learned, as it were, to understand himself as an individual for whom past and future were united in the present, and who could experience nothing for which the reason was not to be found within himself. To know the town, therefore, required a degree of self-renunciation which increased as results were obtained. This meant that the town must be apprehended in its totality if one were to be assured of one's own totality. Face to face with the town he realised why this, the apprehension of totality, had never been possible to him with the farmers; the farmers had been under the influence of the town (even in their battle for freedom), and though the fight might be fiercest at the circumference it was regulated by the centre. The farmers had identified the town with the System, the crystallisation of the material with the material itself. But the System was everywhere, and every one who felt any responsibility towards life had settled down under its wing. And from this standpoint only could the attack be launched which for the farmers meant the preservation of their status, but for the town the fulfilment of its purpose.

VI

I've had never feared loneliness, but even on sentry-duty during the Great War, or in his prison cell, he had never felt its brutal and bewildering character so much as in the town. It overpowered him wherever he went. In the war, after all, he had always had a warm circle of comrades to return to; the silent marshes were peopled with gods, or, when they were enveloped by sea-mists, with ghosts; in his cell he had himself and the companionship of his fellow prisoners knocking on the walls. But the town offered him nothing but desolate oppression. It began in his lodging on the fifth floor of a town tenement, where the top landing bore no relation to the marble-and-plaster splendour of the grand staircase down below. He lived in a furnished room which seemed merely to tolerate its occupant as though he were some alien body—not that Ive could be called an occupant, he was only a camper. He had not taken up his abode in the town, he had pitched his camp, and he refused to regard it in any other way. The significance of that camp was that you could depart at any moment, and he felt that the town dwellings were no better than entrenchments in which camp-followers and women might live, but for men they were only a place in which to snatch a brief rest.

On the front door of his lodging-house there were, besides the landlady's brass plate, seven visiting-cards attached with drawing-pins, and occasionally in the dark passage Ive would run into a figure slipping by him with a silent greeting. In the street he would not have recognised one of the people who lived in the adjoining rooms, separated only by two inches of wall, and he never felt the slightest desire to make their acquaintance. Thicker than the walls of the room was the barrier of mistrust which there seemed no point in breaking down; what was to be would be, and if there was no special motive to stimulate association it was not worth while pursuing it. Ive took for granted that it was mistrust that shut off each individual in his own atmosphere; it hardly affected him personally; he was conscious of his own invulnerability, by virtue of which every new trouble enriched him. Serious harm could only come to him through himself, and he was amazed that this simple truth could not be accepted as a general maxim.

Ive hardly knew himself how he lived. He possessed nothing that he could pawn, and he filled up the income-tax declaration form with a certain amount of scornful satisfaction. He did not work, because any work he could do would have been useless. He occasionally wrote a few articles for the farmers, because he was convinced that they ought to be written, but they brought him in next to nothing. And he wrote nothing that was not absolutely necessary; to do so would have seemed to him a sort of literary charlatanry. Moreover, he found the league of respectable poverty was widespread, and he made the acquaintance of men who would have considered the possession of a dinner-jacket a form of social charlatanry, men whose minds were filled with new and extremely odd ideas, some even who introduced their revolutionary gospel with a plan for the reform of male clothing.

Frequently when he was walking through the neighbouring streets at night, he would stand in front of the houses, reading the innumerable plates on the front doors which announced the names and professions of the inmates. He discovered that there was hardly any condition of life in which one had no more to lose; poverty always managed to hide itself behind a trade. How, otherwise, could whole asylums of misery have been filled to the roof with people who lived, fortified by the mad illusion that they had a calling; lived, worked, ate, and produced children; lived by an occupation which they had chanced upon and to which they clung, knowing that it was the only thing left which assured them the status of a citizen? Astrologers and rat-catchers, agents for everything and nothing, barbers and shampooers of dogs, professional singers and hawkers, honest people out of luck, who ran no risks because they had nothing to lose except the passionate belief in their own usefulness, a belief that they shared with every one else whom Ive met in the town, sharing with them also the conviction that they were really destined for better things. Even Ive found himself indulging in foolish dreams from time to time and asking himself: What would you do if you were suddenly very rich? He examined himself conscientiously and discovered that he would certainly find such a position very pleasant, but that fundamentally there was nothing in his manner of life that he would change. At any rate he guarded himself against speculating on poverty as a stimulating factor; its strength, in any circumstances, was more sentimental than heroic. It was not the poorest, but the richest farmers in the country who had begun to rebel, and it was a complete fallacy that the workers' revolution had benefited by the deterioration of their economic position; the very increase in numbers acted as a check on radicalism. Nowhere in the town was Ive able to observe what he had expected to find, namely, the stimulating aggravation of contrasts; it seemed much more as though, as distress increased, people strove to shuffle their positions and settle down into a state of pleasant and dull mediocrity, a phenomenon described by the newspapers, with complacent satisfaction, as a democratic achievement. It was not only the behaviour and clothing of the people in the streets; the modern dwellings, the shops and warehouses all followed the same line of modest display, and he who had eyes to see might notice the same mood of indifference in the nativities of the populace and in social life.

The town, which was great as a phenomenon, forced one also to recognize the greatness of its deception; its sensationalism in film and festival, in advertisement and trade, all pointed to the same underlying process as did its persistent industry, an inexorable process dragging everything with it in its course, Ive too was forced by the town to ignore the personal problem of his poverty; he was merely cut off from the most fascinating side of town life, always supposing he had wished to have any part in it. Up to a point one was forced to share in its deception in order to understand its nature. Thus, day after day, Ive felt himself more and more involved in a tangle of odious contradictions, and his attempts to reconcile them, however reasonable, only entangled them the more. The fact was that he was far too much interested to wish to cut the Gordian knot with the sword of ideological construction, and his hopes were centred on the discovery not so much of absolute truth as of the path which led to it. He adopted an attitude of detached but keen interest towards the endeavours of mankind as well as towards his own state of utter confusion, and he was neither astonished nor dismayed to find himself falling victim to the same passionate intellectualism which, when he was working for the farmers, he had scorned as the most despicable type; of pavement-civilisation. Yet this seemed to be the only form of inspiration which the town could tolerate. In this dangerous state of mind he began his task of furthering the farmers cause, but his critical attitude acted as a perpetual check and limited the number of friends he was able to make. He did not find these where he had expected to find them, in the offices of the national parties, of the agricultural associations, nor on the editorial staffs of newspapers, where he solicited in vain for understanding of the farmers' struggle. He found them in none of the places where they would have been most useful. He had been rash enough to believe that the aims and individual character of the Farmers' Movement would give it value as a new political factor and would prevent it from being received with the usual intolerance and mud-slinging, but he found he had made a big mistake. The only place where he found his hopes realised, and received the welcome he had anticipated, was among people who, no matter under what flag they happened to be gathered, were really in the same position as himself; people he met at night—for it seemed as though their day only began at nightfall—in obscure bars, where they sat leaning their elbows on rough battered tables with strong drinks in front of them, in the warm smoky atmosphere of underground haunts whose low entries reminded him of the trenches in the Great War, or again in little modern cafés where serious men and intense women assembled every evening round low tables to discuss every conceivable subject over tea and cakes. For them the farmers' cause was interesting enough, but only a problem among hundreds of other problems, none of which could be solved independently. So Ive had to be content to pluck a rose here and there from the thorny bushes. He carried on slow, tiresome and humiliating negotiations with officials in connection with Claus Heim—after first attempting to induce them at least to take a more decisive step to escape from their anomalous position with regard to the 'System,' which they were perpetually grumbling at, and finding himself confronted from the very outset with an amazing obstinacy. Or he would indulge in fantastic debates, picking up a miscellaneous collection of information, which gave cohesion to his disconnected experiences and consolidated his own mental position. He was honest enough to admit to himself that his knowledge of the things with which he had to deal was completely inadequate, even though he was familiar enough with the axioms which were common currency in the homes the Marsh farmers, and whose wisdom, translated into the picturesque language of proverb, could be summed up in such phrases as 'people are the same all the world over' or 'aptness comes with the office.' Thus he was only too glad to make use of the opportunities offered on every side by the town of becoming acquainted with actual facts, and what he learnt from these found a natural place in his new attitude.

As a completely useless member of human society, more or less forced to stand outside the processes of production, he was not able, it is true, to derive his knowledge from his own experience. Still, by making personal contacts with all sorts of people, he managed to get all the information he wanted. All over the town there were discussion circles, whose pleasant task appeared to be to act as an outlet for the energies released after the strain of the day's work. For since family life had become discredited by the almost complete destruction of individualism, some social substitute was needed, and this was provided by these unofficial gatherings of those who had interests in common. A circle which Ive found particularly instructive was that of Dr. Schaffer. This was a formal gathering, but by no means exclusive. Every member of it could have delivered a lecture on some learned subject, and the general effect was rather like having access to a living encyclopaedia.

Dr. Schaffer was a man of about the same age as Ive. On the completion of his economic studies—the subject of his thesis had been *The Tin-mining Industry in Southern Siam*—he had had the exceptional good fortune to find a post as assistant-wharfinger in the Hamburg docks, and Ive had got to know him slightly when he himself was working in the wool-combing factory. Inspired by an indomitable ambition, Schaffer had succeeded in rising gradually to the position of assistant-correspondent in the office of the firm of shippers which employed him. On the strength of this position he got married immediately, and by thrift and ingenuity managed to furnish a home with a remarkable collection of objects picked up in the Hamburg market. In his spare time, amongst other things, he drew up a plan for the formation of the Orient-Trust, a project of great mercantile importance, which caused a considerable sensation in interested circles. But the interested parties; cool, calculating merchants, feared the risk of Schaffer's bold plan, and preferred to carry out the project according to their own ideas. The Orient-Trust went bankrupt soon after its formation, an event which gave Dr. Schaffer, who meanwhile had lost his post in the office, no small amount of malicious satisfaction. The young man had, as he used to say himself, a happy fund of ideas. He tried his hand as a reporter for a domestic-economy journal, which soon ceased publication; as advertisement manager for a motor firm, which was swallowed up in an amalgamation scheme; as sales manager of a radio firm, whose patents were prohibited by America—in fact, he tried everything that came his way, and if he did not succeed in striking luck he never lost heart. One day, once more out of work, he took the advice of his friends and wrote down the fairy tales he used to invent and tell to his little daughter every evening. They were simple stories, gay and fanciful, which delighted the child. It was, in fact, the child who led him to the ingenious idea which was to be the foundation of his success.

Since the little girl's birthday was very near Christmas, she felt the injustice of getting fewer presents during the year than other children. She would much rather have had her birthday in the middle of the year. In fact, meditated Schaffer, the curse of the toy industry is that it has a seasonal trade. There is far too long a period without festivals between Easter and Christmas. On this particular evening he was telling his little daughter the story of the little goblin which came out of the woods on St. John's Day (24th June) to reward good children. Presently he drew a picture of the goblin on a piece of paper, a tiny dwarf with a long flowing beard, and a lovely golden crown of corn ears, a gnarled stick in his hand, and a big sack on his back.

He did no more work on the fairy-tale book. He was engaged in important business. One day a crusade began for the celebration of

St. John's Day, the Children's Feast (24th June). 'Make the children happy,' wrote the newspapers, and in the feuilletons there were nice articles about the old German custom which had taken on a new significance. In the trade supplements Councillor X spread himself on the economic and social effects of the toy industry of Central Germany. In the Children's Hour Aunt Molly told charming stories about St. John's Day. In the stores and toyshops hung placards emblazoned with the words, 'Make the children happy,' around a picture of the St. John's goblin, a tiny dwarf with a long flowing beard, and a lovely golden crown of corn ears, a gnarled stick in his hand and a big sack on his back.

But Dr. Schaffer sat quietly in his office, the headquarters of the Syndicate of German Toy Manufacturers, which was amalgamated with the Co-operative Society of the Chocolate, Sweetmeat and Gift Industries of Germany and the National Federation of United German Gift-Card Designers to form the central organisation of the National Federation of German Toy, Chocolate and Card Manufacturers, known as the N.F.T.C.C.

Dr. Schaffer sat quietly in his office—his little daughter was not allowed to talk about the St. John's goblin any more—and worked seriously, conscientiously and industriously at extensive and far-reaching plans, a personage so highly esteemed that no voice could be raised against his being elected to the National Economic Council.

But one evening in the week a group of men met together, whose only common interest was their desire to expound and exchange their opinions, views and experiences in open discussions which, under the direction and control of Dr. Schaffer's incomparable controversial gifts, touched on practically every subject worth mentioning. Ive had first come across Dr. Schaffer again at a lecture ('Give us back our Colonies,' delivered by a Social-Democratic member of the Reichstag. What next! thought Ive), and had gladly accepted his invitation to spend an evening with the Circle, of which he had already heard.

On the fourth floor of a new block on the West side of the town he found about fifteen gentlemen sitting round an oval table in a sparsely and simply furnished little room, low-ceilinged, with pale blue walls, and lamps with yellow silk shades. When he entered no one took any notice of him. His host merely beckoned him to his side and, without pausing, finished his sentence, which consisted of a considerable number of intricate and involved periods.

As far as Ive could gather the subject under discussion was the latest increase of the goods tariffs on the National Railways and the effect of this on German home trade, with particular reference to traffic conditions in the Rhineland-Westphalian industrial district where, on this account, a project had been formulated for the establishment of a canal system, whose course could not be finally settled owing to the competitive feud between the crude steel combine and the iron-working industry on the one hand and the Hamburg-Amerika and North-German-Lloyd lines on the other. These interests had embarked on a fierce battle arising out of the necessity for opening new markets, which, owing mainly to the unrest in China and India, involved the Far East, where, on account of the continual curtailment of German capital support, no business could be put on a sound financial basis without the help of the leading English banks. But these banks, owing probably to the disturbing influence of the Russian Five Year Plan, were forced to concentrate their interests on the aforementioned markets. Thus at last the intervention and assistance of State Commissions and of the Reich were found to be indispensable. This, of course, represented a decisive step in economic planning, which gave rise to by no means unimportant differences of opinion between the parties concerned as to its socialistic or state-capitalistic significance, and every effort had to be directed towards preventing the ground gained from being critically assailed by private-capitalistic influences, involving a danger for the whole future. This proved that the increase on tariffs on the National Railways could not be the right measure, if only in consideration of the probable extension of motor goods-traffic, which, owing to the monopoly dispute between the National Postal Service and the National (though under foreign control) Railways, was becoming more and more dependent for its economic existence upon the initiative of private enterprise.

Ive felt very small and unimportant. He leaned back in his chair and watched the men who were debating with such liveliness and intense earnestness these problems, of whose importance and difficulty he had some faint inkling—he had too, a faint inkling of the trend of the discussion—without in the least understanding the underlying facts.

Nobody there was probably over forty years of age, and, although Ive knew that they belonged to the most varied and opposed political parties and social circles, it was impossible to observe anything but a most extraordinary unanimity as to the essential point, the final inference from which might be summed up in the sentence: Everything must be changed. This delighted Ive.

The only unknown quantity in this group was a young fellow, probably the youngest present, who perpetually interrupted the pleasantly rolling flow of the discussion, unmercifully seized on every statement, insisted on its being further examined, and with his almost academic pedantry acted as the disturbing and at the same time enlivening factor of the argument. Ive, who was obliged to limit himself to studying the manner in which the opinions were set forth rather than their actual validity, and to tracing the points of contact which they indicated, was deeply interested in this young man. He had plenty of leisure to observe him. The young man was sitting in a corner, formed by two couches which had been pushed together at right angles to one another, the most uncomfortable spot in the whole room. He sat in a humped-up position, his legs crossed so that Ive could see his thick worn-down shoes, with a large hole in one of the soles, and his grey washed-out socks hanging in untidy wrinkles round his ankles. One hand lay on his knee, a broad, rough hand, with square-cut, not over-clean fingernails—a scarred horny hand which doubtless was capable of hard work; when he raised it once to crack a nut between his fingers, Ive saw that he had only placed it on his knee to hide a hole in his trousers which had been clumsily darned with wool of a different colour. When he spoke the impression of tremendous strength was increased. He spoke slowly and very softly, the words forming themselves with difficulty between his thick lips which covered a mouthful of sound teeth. His whole firm-chinned face seemed to work when he spoke, particularly the low bumpy forehead, and under his heavy brows his small deep-set grey eyes were placed very closely together. He was not pleasant to look at, with his greyish pale skin, beneath which the movements of his jaw muscles could be seen; his thick, unkempt, light-brown, rather greasy hair, the ends of which hung over his dusty coat collar; his ill-fitting suit, shabby shirt and dirty, frayed collar. But the directness of his personality immediately appealed to Ive, showing him to have the only type of mind worth tackling. The only thing Ive wished was that he would free himself from his one remaining atavism, and remove his hand from his knee. Ive had formed the habit, whenever he made a new acquaintance, of asking himself whether he would wish to have such a man as a battle-comrade. In this case he thought at once: Most certainly. It was not only that everything he had to say had a sting in it, his manner of speaking, too, was remarkable. It was noticeable that as soon as he began to speak, he always received the closest attention even from men who had just holding forth with astonishing objectivity and with a wealth of impressive statistics and technical knowledge concerning interesting economic facts. For it was evident that, however far from the point and contradictory his casual interruptions might seem, sooner or later what he had to say proved to have a direct connection with the argument on foot, illuminating it, as it were, from a completely new angle. Ive who, with the rapid growth of his sympathy, had feared that the young man might not be at home in the realm of complicated economic problems, soon had an opportunity of realising that he was nonplussing those present by his exact knowledge, for example, of certain financial transactions of the Canadian Electrical

Industry. That was it: from his whole attitude towards these things it was obvious that for him, the actual facts which he mentioned were not so important as something quite different, quite impalpable, and in relation to this the irreproachable statistics which he could produce had significance for himself alone. Ive realised at once that his theories were based on a phenomenon which had its roots in a quite different soil from that in which the normal deliberations of the economic intellect usually flourish. What this was Ive was no more able than the others to discover from the abrupt, obscure hints given by the young man, yet even these disclosed dazzling prospects which could be extended and developed according to individual fancy or temperament. At all events the actual significance of these transactions which were being exposed with such indisputable clarity, lay in the fact that, now that they were no longer seen from the customary point of view and justified by the usual explanations, they seemed to be no longer entirely subject to the laws of causality. They displayed themselves in all their nakedness; and viewed thus they might have been described as the mad or self-destroying caperings of an overstimulated imperialistic will, but most certainly not—and that was the obvious point—as the result of calculations, however mistaken or farfetched, based on any prosperity-theorem. If one tried, despite all, to get at their meaning, they revealed themselves as a terrifying example of complete barbarity, with the emphasis on 'complete' rather than on 'barbarity,' unconsciously making use of the subtlest resources which a highly developed order could afford it in order to call into question the basis of this very order. The young man saw very turbulent forces at work here, even in this dry and unimaginative setting, and it was apparent that he viewed these forces with a definite and friendly interest. Naturally this attitude was extremely disquieting. True a few voices were raised immediately to call attention to the inevitable results of the Canadian event—a violent upheaval of the market—but the whole basis of the discussion had suddenly been shifted. For, from the moment that the question of meaning appeared on the horizon of the discussion, it seemed as though almost every member of this heterogeneous circle suddenly felt prompted to descend into deeper mines of knowledge, and from thence once more to explain his point of view, which after all was quite clear, a proceeding which had an unpleasant savour of justification. Each one of these men, who but a moment ago had been so sure of themselves, and for whose experience and knowledge Ive could not help having the strongest respect, could not but realise that it was not sufficient to establish facts, but that it was equally important to examine and understand their causes and their origins, and, using the greater power of discrimination thus obtained, to incorporate them in the present-day conception of the world. But as more and more individuals thrust themselves into the embittered argument, stranger and stranger groups were formed, only to fall asunder again as the next controversial point arose and to re-group themselves in surprising new formations. In the hot, acrid atmosphere of the little room the faces seemed suddenly to cast off their dull pallid masks, to thrust themselves through the blue smoke and stare into each other's eyes as though driven by a secret fear, which said plainly enough that now things were being discussed which must be taken seriously.

Men who a minute since had been riding the hobby-horses of their economic convictions in harmonious companionship were now crossing swords in enmity. Worthy business men, with bitter experience behind them, were wrestling on the quaking ground of metaphysics, were steering themselves despairingly through clouds of mysticism, mounting with every statement to more and more dangerous heights, until one of them, a temperamental gentleman in the motor trade, craftily lured on by the young man, reached the climax and shot out suddenly, 'In the beginning there was Chaos.'

VII

IT was late when they broke up. As soon as they stepped out of the house into the dark street, the cold night air struck their faces sharply. The picture of the room they had just left faded—the little pale blue room where the clouds of smoke had given a ghostly unreality to faces and thoughts. All the excitement released in the debate was now concentrated in the single desire to find their way out of the labyrinthine passages of discussion on the safe leading-string of natural speech.

Ive loved this hour of the night, when footsteps resound on the deserted pavements, making a perfect accompaniment to thought, giving it a temerity rising to the point of inspiration. The light sweat which breaks out over the skin lubricates as it were every fibre of the brain, so that the most irreconcilable ideas unite in a perfect pattern. In such hours quick friendships are made which as quickly fade in the crude light of the morrow when nothing remains but an insignificant residuum of embarrassment. Ive looked at the young man at his side. He had asked Dr. Schaffer who he was. But Dr. Schaffer knew no more than that he had turned up one day and had at once quite unaffectedly joined in the discussion, and, since what he had to say was at least the product of original thought, he had always been welcome, and nobody had found it necessary to ask him for further information.

Walking side by side they realised that it was no longer possible to avoid the rather ridiculous and disconcerting comedy of a belated self-introduction. Pareigat was the son of an elementary school teacher who had been exiled by the shifting of the frontier. At the university he began by studying economics, but passed on, first to philosophy, then to mathematics and physics. He had never taken his final examination in any subject for the simple reason that he could not raise the money for the fees and, even if he could have raised the money, he would not have wished to enter. In any case, the prospects of obtaining a post on academic qualifications were nil. So he stayed on at the University, making the utmost use of its educational facilities, until he was sent down for Communist activities. He was a Communist as a protest, out of defiance, out of sympathy for the Russian experiment, for hundreds of reasons, but not because he shared in the least its materialistic conception of history or accepted its economic doctrine. During his student year he kept his head above water by doing night-duty as a taxi-driver and later, when he needed the night for work, he drove a bookseller's van through the town. He had no independent means, and he had never had a regular job. His article on the Canadian Electrical Industry, which was published in an economic journal and reprinted in American and English trade-papers, had brought him in altogether eighty marks. This sum enabled him to begin a book on 'Long-distance Gas Supply,' and he had been working on this for the last six months. Ive gleaned no idea as to how Pareigat actually lived, and everything pointed to the fact that he himself could not have said how. However, it was obviously not a matter of fundamental importance to him. All that he said about himself seemed to be simple, straightforward and free from any trace of social resentment. He walked beside Ive, his head slightly bent, his face shaded by a wide-brimmed black hat, and his coat, worn through at the elbows and at the sides, was fastened by a single button swinging from a long thread. Ive spoke of Claus Heim, and, without quite knowing why, he laid emphasis on the contrast, which spoke for itself, between the picture of Claus Heim, silent in the midst of violent attacks, and the picture of the nocturnal controversialists whose company they had just left. He went over the evening's discussion, saying almost angrily that it amazed him that these gentlemen could reconcile what they said with what they were. It did not amaze Pareigat. He said that nowadays everything was reconciled with everything else and spoke of the phenomenon of transference of consciousness.

Ive found it difficult to follow Pareigat's train of thought. If he had himself developed any theory from the farmers' battle and particularly from his own demagogic activities— and it really did seem to him that demagogy was the only means of making a direct attack on democracy in its everyday manifestations—it was the theory that it was dangerous to succumb to the magic of one's own words. There was no doubt that in this struggle the best and most effective method was the simplest. The opponent and every phenomenon which arose in the course of the day should be labelled, the idea transformed as it were into an image; instead of juggling with abstractions one should bring concrete figures into action. But this could only be accomplished if he himself did not confuse life with one of its manifestations. This fellow Pareigat did not fit into any category. Not that Ive wanted this exactly, but, again and again, at almost every one of the Pareigatian expressions or statements, he caught himself hastily assigning him a suitable place, only to recognise his mistake at the very next sentence.

This made him fear that his arguments were bussing fire, although Pareigat always took them up immediately, turning them playfully this way and that and then calmly establishing them on a new basis. It seemed to Ive as though this fellow carelessly made use of the terminology of every movement, yet he got no result by parrying with his own; Pareigat skilfully twisted its meaning and, when Ive defended himself, swooped down on him like a hawk on its prey, and forced him to examine the debated expression for its actual significance. Ive stumbled from one pitfall to another. Nevertheless he enjoyed the discussion. Conversing heatedly they strode through the empty, dim streets, where the facades of the houses rose steep and silent to the narrow strip of sky; they leant over the bare iron railings of bridges, looking down into the black depths intersected by a mesh of shining railway lines; they penetrated the sudden floods of light from isolated street lamps; glided past the immovable figures of policemen in shining helmets, of tired girls emerging ghost-like from dark corners, towards the sooty-red halo surrounding the massive silhouette of the church which stood at the end of the broad street, dark and menacing with upstretched, accusing finger.

After every digression, after every deviation into the tangled thicket of elastic definition, they returned to the narrow path of the discussion, just as they had returned to the street, as though their progress had been uninterrupted, from the beer-house where Pareigat, leaning against the counter, had ravenously devoured a pickled herring.

Returning to the phenomenon of transference of consciousness, Pareigat said he regarded it as a result of the pretentious attempt, conditioned by the passing generation, of the individual to free himself from the dynamic unity of life, an attempt which had succeeded constructively through the disruption of this unity. Thus all intellectual battles must of necessity take place on some other plane than that of 'being.' The character of these battles was indicated mainly by the fact that the problem of 'meaning' was removed from the intellectual plane, but not from the spiritual plane, where alone it could be united with the problem of 'being.' Consciousness, said Pareigat, had been transferred from the plane of 'being,' so that now all orientation must be from a hypothetical line, on which the moving points of interest served to guide the few. Thus the strange phenomenon that capitalists and socialists found themselves in agreement in so many fields and, indeed, united in one front, though at times it might be a somewhat thorny contact, against all assaults of a spiritual nature, only retained importance as a phenomenon.

'All the same,' interrupted Ive, 'in all these intellectual battles, leaving out of account, though I admit its truth, the example you cited of capitalists and socialists, the attempt is to transform a conception of life into a reality, or vice versa.'

'That is the very thing,' said Pareigat, 'that must of necessity end in disaster.'

For actually this attempt was not obeying the direct appeal of the personality, but, as it were, that of its reverse side—the fear which expresses itself as a wish for new orientation, a change of position. This wish really belonged to the unconscious rather than to the conscious, and its destructive tendency was obvious and could be demonstrated by the fact that, while it claimed to express the communal spirit, it was splitting it up into innumerable sects and conventicles, political and religious.

Ive said that he himself, in criticising an attitude, had always considered the decisive criterion to be whether its aim was success or fulfilment, and, from this point of view he did not like the idea of calmly dismissing the tendency they were talking of as unfruitful.

But Pareigat would not agree to this. Fulfilment, he said; was only one of the sources of success, and the thing to discover was in how far success was at all possible nowadays. Greatness, in no matter what sphere, was only tolerable today in the form of eminence, and wherein lay the essence of eminence? Certainly not in the development of one's own personality, but, on the contrary, in emptying it, making it serve as the container for the greatest possible number of wish-fantasies. Eminence was not self-sufficient, it relied on its reflection; what it accomplished was the means to an end, which has no relation to its own responsibility; it was pure instrumentality, whether it were a question of eminence as boxer, singer, film-star, artist, preacher, administrator, or politician. But even in such cases, the higher degree of the eminent significance had been transferred more and more from the actual doer or leader to the instrument, from the actor to the producer, from the industrialist to the banker, from the statesman to the demagogue, from the man of learning to the writer, an astounding principle of depreciating counter-selection, a principle which was more or less illustrated by the position of a Russian People's Commissary at its most typical, a position, the essence of which was that its holder could be no more than the bare instrument of a mass will.

'The fact remains,' said Ive, 'that in principle this attitude satisfies an imperative claim.'

'The fact remains,' said Pareigat, 'that the imperative nature of this claim is open to question, so long as the claim itself is not justifiable. How can the claim be justified? By the mass-will, the justification of which can be called into question at any moment; and how is the mass-will to be justified? By its existence; and how is existence to be justified? By the declaration of the claim. A delightful game, an intellectual *perpetuum mobile*, which must be continually rediscovered, because without the question of justification no order is conceivable. But the question of justification is the question of existence, the question of existence is a spiritual question, and every justifiable plan must be a spiritual, that is, a hierarchical plan.'

'That is reactionary,' said Ive quickly, and regretted it immediately.

'It certainly is reactionary,' said Pareigat, and gave the illustration of the wheels of history, which cannot be turned backwards. And it was futile to want to turn them backwards, for they did it themselves without any help.

'History,' he said, 'is the expression of living development, and its periods run the same course of growth, maturity, and age as the span between birth and death. Those who deny this, deny life itself.'

'And indeed they are trying to,' he said, and Ive was astonished at the wild hatred which he could hear vibrating in his companion's voice—'they are trying to argue death away; simply because they cannot deny it as a phenomenon, to deny its importance as the boundary-line and keystone. Does not life reach its highest potentialities in the shadow of death; is not its whole course ennobled by the pain and horror which are sanctified by death?'

'That is the great illusion,' said Pareigat, coming to a standstill in the circle of light from an arc-lamp and pushing his hat back from his forehead and seizing Ive by the coat—'to want to explain death, to explain it as a simple transmutation of matter, as a material act, to postpone it with their miserable hygiene, to destroy its force as an expiatory fulfilment, to banish it as the seal of a heroic stake, to debase the sacred significance of the plan to sordid security in the name of their cowardice—an optimistic cowardice, and therefore the vilest and most contemptible, which they find it necessary to exalt to the status of a law, because they know that the man who demands dignity in his life will never submit to it.'

He released his hold of Ive and said in a quiet voice: 'They exist in a state of "being" which is a denial of "being." They do not live, they explain until nothing is left but a vacuum containing the slimy web spun by their own brains.'

'But,' asked Ive, 'does it not follow from their very insistence on an unconditional life based on their own personality that no imperative association and, therefore, no plan of any kind is possible?'

Pareigat would not admit this. 'No,' he said, 'since life encloses them within its boundaries, it encloses them completely. Conscious "being" embraces the whole plan, and thus is its most important element. In it and in it alone can the individual be identified with society, with the nation, with thought, for, of necessity, he strives in every direction, he is subject to an immediate urge to complete the synthesis, and thus he is one pole of the plan and between this pole and its opposite alone can develop the only possible, the only noble, the only justifiable organisation.'

'Which?' asked Ive.

'The Church,' said Pareigat.

Ive was silent. He wanted to question further, but he was silent. He felt as though he must throw himself down from a great height to break with the weight of his body the whole confused web of the embarrassing discussion.

The keen wind whipped their coats about their bodies as they walked on across the square. On the roof of one of the houses they were approaching the blue-white incandescence of an illuminated sign shot up like a stream of oil and flowed with silent mechanical speed along the line of invisible letters and then was extinguished. A car, a black, gliding shadow with dazzling, rapacious eyes, swept round the corner and disappeared.

Presently Ive asked abruptly: 'How do you pray?' Pareigat stood still with one foot in the gutter and one on the pavement. The headlights of a second car shed a flickering light on his face. It was grey, and round the eyes lay deep shadows.

'Must I tell you?' he asked softly.

'You need not,' said Ive.

Pareigat whispered: 'Then I would rather not.'

They walked slowly on. They turned into a side street, an alley which branched off obliquely, with a few straggling lamps, whose pale green light encircled and united the disconnected outlines of pavement, houses, and gutter. The people they encountered had different faces from those they had met previously. As before, they were masks, standardised to the same expression of strained, cold absorption, with dead, glittering eyes, but, whereas the features of the others had set after intelligent animation, these were rigid as though in preparation for a gloomy, pointless vigil without intermission or end. They were underground-railway faces, as Ive described them, the others taxi-faces—in both cases alien, another race, the race of the town.

Ive was seized with a mad longing for the Marsh, blue caps pulled over ruddy, healthy faces, the soft crunching of the earth beneath an easy tread, the warm pungent smell of placid, cud-chewing cattle. Suddenly, empty and exhausted, he put one foot before the other mechanically, then pulled himself together as the thought struck him that his face must have the same expression of deadly boredom to be seen on the wax models in the brightly illuminated windows of the fashionable shops. It was just past midnight. Ive looked apathetically at the long rows of waiting taxis which the darkness enveloped, listened to the distant roar of the town, borne by the wind over the blocks of sleeping houses, to the intermittent wail of saxophones, which issued from the doors and windows of small night clubs, where in front of the shining portals, ornamented with strange emblems in metal, gigantic commissionaires stood in brown, gold-braided uniforms, beside placards on which were depicted in broad, sloppy lines scantily clad ladies in ridiculous dance postures and clownish musicians in dinner-jackets. The distant roar seemed to be increasing, more and more people crossed their path, until they filled the pavement and the road. They dispersed at the shrill hoot of a fire-brigade car which every two seconds unmercifully sounded its signal of grave danger, the sound filling the street to the farthest corner, while the car, a bright red, bloodthirsty eye on its bonnet, rushed by at full speed, leaving the crowd in a vast eddy behind it. All at once the police were there; in a side street, where Ive and Pareigat had been pushed by the on-rushing flood of people, stood the constables, some in close formation round a car from which firemen were still leaping down, some ranged up in front of the houses, and a few posted at the corners of the streets, a surging confusion of shakos, heavy coats, and carbine-barrels. Ive pushed forward. The whole main street was a whirl of movement, a silent confusion of aimlessly marching crowds, who from time to time strove to disentangle themselves. There were far more men than women; a lot of young fellows without hats or coats, looking about them defiantly, came up in small groups, chatting gaily together; as they came to the corner where the police were stationed, they ceased talking and formed a small semi-circle to make room. From the wide-open doors of a dark building with shuttered windows the black crowd streamed, in the mass resembling a swarm of almost identical figures; as they emerged onto the street they formed into a procession, which proceeded slowly in Ive's direction. Ive could not make out whether they were Communists or National Socialists; in all the numerous demonstrations he saw, there always seemed to be the same young, eager faces, the same thin, under-sized bodies of the generation that had grown up in the starvation period of the war, the same stiff standardised clothes made out of cheap material.

'Germany,' cried a clear falsetto voice, and the chorus answered with a reverberating shout:

'Awake!'

Ive stood still, looking for Pareigat, whom he had lost in the crowd. As he looked all round, peering into the faces as they pushed by him, a hand came down with a resounding friendly slap on his shoulder.

He turned.

'Hinnerk!' he cried.

'My name is Emil,' said Hinnerk.

'When did you join the Nazis?' asked Ive.

Hinnerk laughed.

'Why, a long time ago, actually when the Party was first founded, didn't you know?'

Ive had not known.

'You can put me in touch with the Party office then,' he said, 'I want to see them about the Farmers' Movement.'

'Righto,' said Hinnerk.

He waved a friendly hand and took his place in the procession which was now hurrying down the street with a rumbling roar.

'Look out, the police!' Ive called out after Hinnerk, pointing to the corner where he had seen the posse standing. The chain of police was already forming an oblique line across the street. At the sight of them, the straggling crowd split up, pressed themselves against the walls of the houses, so that a space was cleared between the approaching procession and the chain of police, a little way behind which another line formed, this time armed with carbines, and followed slowly. The free space quickly grew smaller. Suddenly the police increased their pace; the constables, tall, lithe, strong men with chin-straps beneath their clean-shaven jaws, manipulated their belts with practical skill to unloose their rubber truncheons. As though at the word of command, they began to run silently; they raised their truncheons; they ran faster; now they had arrived; there were a few seconds of confusion at the head of the procession; Ive stood and watched. The constables raised their arms, they drove like battering-rams against the massed crowds, like giants amongst the slender young men with pale faces, human mountains letting fly their blows, with practised technique and the utmost precision, on the swarming throng, like rocky boulders whirling down into the valley. Nimbly the young men in their threadbare suits, their arms thrust up over their heads in defence against the hail of blows, pushed themselves between the gaitered legs of the uniformed athletes, intending to rush the chain and break it. But the chain was solid. Already the front of the procession was broken up—Hinnerk alone remained, wedged in among the bluecoats, pushing with his clenched fists among the helmeted heads. Ive, seeing this, sprang forward to help him. A blow crashed on his shoulder; he turned, staggered, fell, and pulled himself up again. He saw the swarms, the confusion of moving, black, fighting shadows; Hinnerk had disappeared; a broad wall of strong backs, with shining belts, marching in step, pressed back the seething flood, the confused tangle of raised arms, the raucous medley of cries. Out of the door of a house came a young girl, very slender, in a close-fitting coat, carefully holding a number of parcels in her arms. She looked to the right and to the left, stood hesitating, stepped into the street, made a half-turn in order to cross the road. The second chain of police had arrived at this point. 'Move on,' roared a voice; the girl halted and looked round. Ive was standing stupefied in the middle of the road, rubbing his shoulder. The girl, police in front of her and police behind her, hesitated in alarm; then a blow crashed down on her head, she swayed and fell; her parcels were scattered in every direction, a bottle broke with a resounding crash. Ive rushed forward to the prostrate figure, lying in a queer crumpled heap in the dirt of the street. All at once Pareigat was there; he bent down with Ive over the girl.

'Move on,' snarled a hoarse voice.

Ive could feel the breath on the nape of his neck. In uncontrollable rage, he flung round and stared up. A police officer stood before him, his shako pulled down over his eyes. Ive saw distinctly the broad, flat face with cold eyes, now blinking in excitement, whitish flesh bulging over the silver-braided collar.

'Brodermann!' cried Ive suddenly. The officer started, pulled himself together and looked at Ive in confusion.

'Move on,' he said quietly, turned and followed, almost laggingly, after the advancing body of constables. The girl raised her head and shoulders, supported herself on her bent knee, pulled herself up, and without a word took the parcels which Pareigat had collected. Then with her free hand she awkwardly brushed the dirt from her coat.

'Leave me alone,' she said sharply, when Ive began to speak.

She then took a few steps, turned again, and said in a low voice: 'Thank you,' and walked unsteadily away.

'You know that police officer?' asked Pareigat.

'An army comrade,' said Ive, looking after the girl.

VIII

THE defendants in the big bomb-case in Altona had decided to follow the example of Claus Heim, and to refuse to make any statement in their examination. So the proceedings dragged on, day after day, with nothing but the monotonous reading of thousands of affidavits. Police-Commissioner Müllschippe rattled out his answers when questioned on oath; County Court Judge Fuchs was promoted to an Administrative Court, which not only meant an increase of salary, but the pleasant prospect of not having to take any further part in political cases; Hinnerk sat in the body of the Court and was surprised to notice how often 'a certain unknown person' cropped up in the affidavits. But Claus Heim was sentenced to seven years' imprisonment. This sentence, if it did not do much to further the Movement, gave it great moral support. In silence Claus Heim had taken his place in the dock, and silent, morose, without turning his head, he returned to his cell.

Ive, who had been acquitted, was allowed to speak to him again. The farmer of St. Annen Klosterfeld realised what he had brought upon himself. Ive told him of his attempts to stir up the nationalists to take action on his behalf; and of the somewhat discouraging results of his efforts. Heim asked Ive not to deviate a hair's breadth from the demands of the Movement on his account, and to keep any action on his behalf free from the interference of sentimental fools. On no account, he declared, did he wish to be released even a day sooner than any of the other farmers who had been sentenced. Ive decided that he had better not even mention the question of an appeal.

He was very depressed when he left the lonely man; he had not been able to hide from him that on his journey through the province before the trial he had found many weak spots in the Movement. The main body of the farmers was standing its ground uncompromisingly. The Land League and the other associations of the Green Front, which was only superficially a united front, at the conference tables in the town and in the official press, and not always there, responded to the impetus of the Movement, by adopting the watchwords of the militant farmers, and attempted to bring their local organisations into line with the emergency committees and sometimes even excelled them in the severity of their demands and in their bombastic announcements of tactics. But their actual functions were carried out not by the tenant farmers, not even by working farmers, but by industrious quick-witted business men and syndicates, by gentlemen in offices who did not possess a yard of land or a blade of grass, by pensioned officers and officials, and they were quite content to remain, as old Reimann expressed it, with their fingers in the Movement and their arses in the System.

That was just it: where did the System begin and where did the Movement end? There were all sorts of temptations; the Government tried once more to set the Beelzebub of credit to drive out the devil of debt. Every farmer realised that that would do no good in the long run, but it was difficult to resist, since it helped them to get over the hardships of the present moment. For misery was increasing in the country; prices of farm produce were steadily declining; one minute it was produce as much as possible, another, produce as cheaply as possible, one moment a wheat tax and the next a reduction in forage prices, still prices declined and a decrease of trade returns led to an increase in trade costs, and if business increased and with it taxes, then prices fell and with them purchasing power.

It was not much comfort to the farmers to know that they were not the only ones in this plight, that industry was in the same plight, and industry in other countries also, and the farmers of the whole world. There were clever people who set about to prove to the farmers in their newspapers that from the economic point of view their existence was no longer justified, which did not increase the farmers' love of the newspapers nor of economics (they had never had much opinion of the clever people). But every calculation, on whatever it was based, only went to prove what they had known from the outset, that their battle was a life-and-death struggle. There might be a crisis, but they wanted to live, to live fully, and any one who put obstacles in the way of this desire was an enemy. The System was the enemy, and within it the Government, which, involved in the same network, tossed to and fro by the same whirlpool, did the only thing it could do, and for this very reason was intolerable; that is to say, it used the formalities of the law and a perfectly disciplined police force to preserve the status quo and left no way open—open for what?—For chaos? But it was the farmers alone who could find the way out of chaos, and it was from them therefore that the new order must originate. The new order? But it was not a question of new order or old order, but of any order at all. So the farmers were striving for an economic autocracy; not because they considered this to be the only panacea, but because they saw that it was inevitably approaching in every country, and they regarded this development as good, because this retrogression was a progression towards the natural basis of production—the farmers had already begun this retrogressive progress, it was the farming-community not the System, which was in sympathy with the tendencies of the times. There might be a crisis, they had to go through a zero-hour in order to grasp the meaning of the order. They had to be prepared for this moment, and they had to have a longsighted policy to carry them still further. It was useless to encounter the forces which were leading to it with ridiculous specifics, as the System was doing.

The Government was ready to step in with subsidies, whether it be in the form of a moratorium, credit facilities or reduction of taxes. This began in East Prussia and the other Eastern frontier districts, and actually it was there that the System itself was exposed to the most direct danger. The importation of foreign capital into industry, into municipal affairs, seemed bearable, almost to be welcomed, for the thirty milliard marks of foreign capital, which was the amount the Reichsbank estimated to have been invested in Germany, came in in a quiet and friendly way and silently mounted up. The transaction was welcomed as a benefit, indeed had been called in as a remedy. If the political reparation debts were fraught with a feeling of humiliation and degradation, a feeling that they had been incurred under duress, in short were tribute, the private debts, to which the political debts had given rise, were a voluntary responsibility. Moreover, with so many foreign interests at stake, guarantees must have been given, and in guaranteeing the security of foreign capital the System guaranteed itself.

But in the East it was a different matter; agriculture was in a different position.

'What is the position in the East?' wrote Ive. 'To all the other menaces has been added that of an arbitrarily drawn boundary line. The farmers of Northern Schleswig know what it is to lose the inland provinces, to have to seek new markets for their farm-produce, and the Danes may well gaze with sorrow at the grass which is sprouting up so gaily between the stones of the market-place in Tondern. But East Prussia is alienated from the Reich; Upper Silesia, the Grenzmark and the agricultural district of Further Pomerania are even more thoroughly divided up than the Nordmark. Statistics prove that East Prussia, the whole of East Germany, is denuded, that our provinces in that district are on the way to becoming an area without population. How is this happening? There are landowners who can no longer keep their farms, there are landed proprietors who can no longer keep their property, who own, perhaps, two properties and are obliged to sell one in order to keep the other, and naturally they try to get rid of the property which is most endangered, which is near the frontier. Where are the purchasers? Where are even tenants to be found? Who wants to buy or to rent an undertaking that he knows to be unprofitable? The Government refuses to buy; it is already overburdened with estates. To parcel out the land in small holdings is impossible, for small holdings involve buildings, and buildings require the investment of capital, and there is no capital. Then a German Land Acquisition Society is advertised in Kattowitz, and an Association of Estate Purchasers in Danzig with attractive offers. The landowner makes inquiries; the results of his inquiries sound satisfactory; the societies seem to be well established and have extensive connections; nothing is discovered against them, in Kattowitz, Danzig or Berlin. Soon there are new masters on the estates. But the estate is always changing hands, and sooner or later there appears in the Estate Register a name full of consonants ending in *sky*. The new owner avoids any neighbourly intercourse; he seems to be a quiet, thoughtful, active man; there is a new impetus to business, expensive innovations are introduced. No one knows where the man gets his capital, but he has it. For capital is necessary for the ambitious afforestation schemes, the installation of a saw-mill, a cement works, saw-mill. And workmen are required, and the workmen who come are Polish workmen, with large families of children, who need a Polish school and a Polish schoolmaster; and one after another they come, and a Polish baker turns up in the village—the German baker cannot stand out against the competition and disappears—and a Polish butcher. The majority of the members of the District Council are Polish, and the Polish landowner is a patron of the German Church.

This is not an isolated case. It is like this all over the East. German opposition is strong, but Polish capital, very carefully laid out, is stronger. What is the Government doing about it? Is it turning a blind eye? Most certainly not. It is turning a particularly keen-sighted eye. For there is one thing that they must not allow to become an accomplished fact: loss of German land while they are in power. For that would mean the secret would be out, the bitter truth that had long been hidden would be proclaimed to the whole world, that the terrible fiction that there still is anything in Germany that belongs to the Germans is, indeed, no more than a fiction!'

Ive was amazed at the energy with which the Government by virtue of its East Prussia Relief Act sprang to the help of the threatened provinces. For years past millions had been pumped into the Danaïdean sieve. Now the law was to be developed into a general Eastern Province Relief Act, and, although Ive was aware of the danger, it could not be averted by the Movement. For every individual farmer in turn was faced with the question, which was dangerous because it was tempting. Schleswig-Holstein was a distressed area and the System offered relief, but did it not offer this relief in order to save itself?

Ive wanted to say: 'Don't accept,' and so did old Reimann, and Hamkens, and all the old brigade. But ought they to say that? The Unions urged acceptance and made preparations, for eventually the administration of the subsidies was delegated to them and the Board of Agriculture. But the decision for the individual farmer boiled itself down to this: If I do not accept, another will, we all have need of it and are we to go bankrupt before the zero-hour has arrived?

'The East must not go bankrupt,' said Ive, 'System or no System, but do you want to accept with one hand and attack with the other? Think of Claus Heim!'

'Claus Heim would say: "Take what you can get,"' said the farmers. (But Claus Heim had said to Ive, 'I cannot decide from here, but I should probably not accept myself.')

'Everyone must decide for himself,' said old Reimann finally, and the farmers, not all, but many of them, and particularly those, of course, who were in need of the subsidy said: 'For many a long day the System has got nothing out of us, but we have to pay our private debts with our very blood. The System must help us to get out of the debts to which it has driven us, or are we, too, to refuse to recognise private debts? We might as well become Bolsheviks at once — we should be rid of our debts, but of our farms as well.'

And Ive returned to the town, in a state of despair and agitation. Every question and every consideration struck him painfully, like the lash of a whip. He felt the whole question so intensely that he seemed to be on fire. Every force within him seemed to have condensed and become fused into his being, giving him a feeling of deep depression.

IX

IVE's interview with the Secretary of the National Socialist Party led to nothing. The Secretary, a youngish ex-officer, said to him immediately:
'Why are you not a member of the Party?'
'I will tell you frankly,' said Ive, 'what is the main thing that keeps me out of your Party; it is the officialdom of the Party.'
The Secretary made a gesture with his hand, and Ive waited expectantly for what he had to say, but he said nothing.
'It was this officialdom,' continued Ive after a moment's silence, 'that made your leader offer a reward in connection with the bomb outrages to any of your adherents who could produce evidence to prove that the outrages did not originate in your Party. This action of your leader has not unappreciably assisted in the discovery of the plot and the arrest of our leader. I have come to you to ask you if the Party is prepared to co-operate in our propaganda-crusade for the liberation of Claus Heim and the other sentenced farmers,'
'What do you suggest?' asked the gentleman in a curt tone, which he considered extremely military.
Ive explained that the Farmers' Movement had never opposed the National Socialist propaganda work in the province, and that there was no intention of changing this attitude in the future, but that this undoubtedly depended on the attitude adopted by the Party in the vital questions of the Movement. He could very well imagine that there might be extensive co-operation.
'And since it has a programme,' said Ive after a short pause, 'it naturally expects adherence to its programme.'
'The programme of the Party,' said the gentleman, 'undoubtedly aims at class organisation.'
'The programme of the Party,' said Ive, 'can only in the event of victory...'
'We shall be victorious,' interrupted the secretary, and Ive assured him politely that he had no doubt of this. But he had doubts as to whether, after their victory, class organisation could, as it were, be constitutionally effected in, say, the form of § (1) The Third Reich is a class organisation; § (2) This regulation comes into force immediately.

It was much more important to get a foothold where the germs of this organisation already existed and were developing, and to carry out the attack from that point.

'That would disintegrate the attack,' said the secretary. 'That would provide the reserves without which the attack would be disintegrated,' said Ive.

'What do you demand, of us?' asked the gentleman.

'We demand of you an attitude consistent with your official aim; that is, we demand that in the affairs of the farmers you recognise the objectives proclaimed by the most militant section of their community.'

'And,' asked the gentleman, 'if we do not, if we cannot comply with this demand?'

'Then,' said Ive, 'doubts must arise as to your integrity of purpose-doubts which will not allow us to regard you as any better than those whom you profess to be combating.'

The secretary shot his head forward: 'Anybody who opposes us...'

'Will be shot, I know,' said Ive in a bored tone, 'and we are back in the fields of Philippi... Don't talk rubbish, sir, you are addressing Dithmarsch farmers, not Ullstein editors.'

'Moreover,' said the secretary, 'binding agreements can only be made by the National Headquarters, Department of Agriculture.'

'I think that settles the matter,' said Ive, and departed.

'If you want to be treated properly don't go to bureaucrats,' said Hinnerk, when Ive told him of the failure of the interview.

'Why don't you let your bureaucrats go to the devil?' asked Ive.

'Because we are a party,' replied Hinnerk.

'And why are you a party?'

'Because we have bureaucrats, but, seriously, bureaucrats are always there, and the middle class is always there; so long as they are on top, let them have their form, the Party. But we are the Movement.'

'Who is "we"?' asked Ive.

'The young men,' replied Hinnerk. 'Come with me to my storm-troop; tough nuts, I can tell you; there are fellows there combed out from every pot-house in the town, sixty percent ex-Communists, expelled grammar-school boys, rusticated students, old ex-service rascals and young Indian princelings; nobody who isn't down and out counts.'

'A pleasing prospect,' said Ive, 'are you official?'

Hinnerk grinned: 'To the official all things are official!'

'And what is the Movement doing? It is marching on, I know that,' said Ive bitterly, 'and it is all the same to it where its marches lead it, but the bureaucrats know where it is marching, and it isn't all the same to them; we've been through that already.'

'And wasn't it all right when we went through it before?' asked Hinnerk. 'What happens is not just by chance, after all, and the simple fact that people are marching on has always brought things to a climax. Who is to know whether a cause is good or bad? If it is good, it must prove it, and if it is bad, then its odour must be palpably foul. We march for a cause as long as it is good, and if it goes bad, then we don't march for it any more; do you think we are so entirely without perceptions as to march without any reason?'

'The upshot of all that,' said Ive, 'is that a cause is good as long as it can carry you with it. Are you content to be merely baggage?'

'It means that a cause is good so long as we can bear it, and if the baggage hinders over much, we throw it away.'

'But the meaning, the meaning?' asked Ive.

Hinnerk replied: 'The meaning is that we are indispensable. For what Movement can do without its military organisation? Those who thought they had buried us once and for all, are scratching up the earth with bleeding fingers now to get us back again. The young men are needed in every camp and in every camp they are in uniform.'

'And from all the camps they are setting out to give each other bloody heads, so that the bureaucrats can settle their fat backsides more comfortably into their arm-chairs.'

'And if so, why grudge it them? And why shouldn't we fight each other? It keeps us up to the mark; practice is practice.'

Hinnerk laughed. 'Come to my storm-troop,' he said, pushing Ive forward.

'Why do people hate each other?' asked Hinnerk, with a troubled expression, 'because everyone is a renegade to his neighbour. We are all descended from the same Mother Eve, but opinions are opinions, and it doesn't matter what opinions one holds, so long as one takes the opinions one has seriously and sticks up for them. If I land a Red Front man a blow on the jaw, I don't do it because he is a Communist, but because he is not one of us, and he probably feels exactly the same as I do.'

The meeting-place of Hinnerk's storm-troop, on the north side of the town, was a beerhouse, the entrance to which was at the foot of narrow stone steps without any railings, and whose signboard showed traces of having had stones thrown at it. In front of the door two young fellows were patrolling up and down, and Hinnerk greeted them with raised arm. The beerhouse itself consisted of a vault divided into several rooms, of which only those on the street side got any daylight. It was filled with tables and benches, piled one on top of another as though they were meant to serve as barricades. The counter, a block of solid wood, had a railing round it to protect the glasses. At almost every table young men were writing, smoking, playing cards, or talking, and looking at newspapers. Their faces wore that expression of unconcerned imperturbability which the faces of soldiers might wear in the lull between two battles. The air, the whole tone of the room, with its clouds of smoke, its figures, its atmosphere of pointless activity, at once brought to Ive's mind the picture of a billet in the Great War, and he was not surprised to hear that many of the young men who had no homes were in the habit of spending the night on the narrow benches of the beerhouse. Every hour the sentries were relieved according to regulations, and the desultory conversation was mostly about duties. Duties were more important than politics, in any case they lay nearer home, for immediate danger was always threatening, whether from the bourgeoisie and their guardians, the police, or from the militant organisations of other factions.

Outside in the street pedestrians hurried along, tram bells clanged, cars rolled by, but all over the town were scattered the hiding-places, the underground meeting-places of the active section of young people, who were ready, when the time was ripe, to throng the streets of the town, to hoist their banners on public buildings, or to engage in murderous battle in the dark corners and doorways of the town and die like beaten dogs.

Ive realised that in such a place it would be senseless to ask about the why and wherefore, and if he immediately felt a strong attraction towards the men in this room it was nothing more than the attraction he felt towards the homeless sons of all periods of upheaval.

Exactly opposite, on the corner of the street, Hinnerk informed him, was the meeting-place of the Communists, which, since the entrance-door was at the top of some steps, was very difficult to attack, but it was easier to clear off after the attack, whereas here the position was reversed; and, pushing chairs and tables into position, Hinnerk demonstrated the last battle, in the course of which the Communists had succeeded in getting into the rooms, but had only been able to escape with heavy losses.

Day and night the enemy armies were on the watch, ready to fall in furious onslaught upon their opponents, though they were all friends, to seize them by the throat, to hurl them to the ground in the wild battles of the night which were only broken up when the cars of the flying-squad came rushing up. From time to time one or other would change sides, knowing full well that this meant that he could expect no mercy from the faction he had deserted. Hinnerk's storm-troops had had four deaths within a few months, and very few of the men remained long without a wound. Hinnerk had added several scars to the injured hand he had got in Neumünster, and the student who was sitting at the same table with him and Ive, a broad-shouldered young man with fair hair and blue eyes, did not owe the deep cut on his cheek to a duel.

'What are you studying?' Ive asked the student, who answered: 'F.I., Faculty of Idiots, Economics, Social Science.'

On being asked why, he replied because of the ninety-nine percent, certainty of scientific error; because of the possibility of immediately recognising as nonsense everything that he had laboriously crammed, even when it presented itself to him in the proud cloak of abstruse learning. What had not only made him wish to be, but had forced him to become a National Socialist was the fact that the Movement was not based on a hard-baked economic doctrine, that the leader had given a meaning to learning in that he had emancipated it merely by providing, through the simple combination of the words National Socialism, the common denominator from which all learning derived.

But surely the ideas of a nation and socialism had existed for a long time?

But it was not until the pronouncement of their combination that the conceptions of nation and socialism had opened up such breathless vistas; just as the watchwords of the French Revolution, though they had existed as conceptions and ideals for centuries, had only become effective on their pronouncement, and then had changed the face of the world. What prospects had learning to offer the individual since the war? The meagre prospect of picking up some wretched job.

'But we are not studying in order to pick up a job, in any case' — the student made a movement which accentuated the scar on his cheek— 'and perhaps we shan't be asked in future: "Which Students' Corps did you belong to?" but: "With which S.A.* troop did you serve?" I am an S.A. man,' he said, 'because I belong to the Movement, and I belong to the Movement because I am a student.'

'How does the Movement,' asked Ive, 'justify its claim to power?'

'Through the fact of its existence as a movement,' said the student, 'for the effective principle of every movement lies in its continually renewed act of self-creation. We make no claims on the nation or on socialism, but we are nationalists and socialists, and the fact of having the power in our hands is a guarantee for socialism and for the nation.'

'You do not, then,' said Ive, bending forward, 'conceive of the nation as a statistical constant, as it were, and you do not conceive of socialism as a plan?'

'I conceive of the nation as a perpetual act of volition of the people,' said the student, 'and I conceive of socialism as the economic form which, being in any case most strongly bound up with the State, endows this act of volition with the greatest possible

---

* The *Sturmabteilung*, or storm-troopers, were the street fighters of the early days of the Nazi Party.

motive-force—that is, it is based on a plan, but a plan elastic enough always to adapt itself to the changing requirements of the nation. Private property...'

'...must be abolished,' cried an S.A. man from three tables away, and every one laughed...

'...exists even now merely as a juristic idea,' said the student, 'whose usufruct is exercised in a sense contrary to the service of the nation; we shall not abolish private property, but we shall control its usufruct.'

His whole face lit up with pleasure.

'I don't know,' said Ive, hesitatingly, 'in how far what you say expresses the aims of your Party, and I don't know whether it will not come to the same thing in the end as Communism is forced to do, and indeed every form of State power will be forced to do, if it is not willing to abnegate itself; but, at any rate, you must be aware that your language will be open to misconception, if, for example, in your propaganda, which strangely enough, though it is one of the political tools of democracy, you cannot do without, you use terms like socialism, which, in the minds of the public to which you are appealing, already have a set meaning, and that in the sense in which it is used in the programme of your opponents. I could accept the possibility of using misconceptions as instruments to confuse the issue, but can you venture to do this without this instrument turning against yourselves?'

'We can,' said the student, 'we can, if that were our intention, which is not the case. We are in a more fortunate position than that. The ideas of a complete age have had all the meaning wrung out of them and are now open to any interpretation. We have been lucky enough,' he said, 'to discover that, as soon as the peak of an epoch has been passed, every idea, even if it has been conceived in the spirit of the epoch, turns against it. For the past thirty years every dogma has contributed to the decay of the epoch, undermining its characteristic structure; and the critical break in the rhythm has now been reached, for today for the first time it is possible to think without prejudice, take ideas dispassionately, just as they present themselves, and exploit them. We have already left the last period behind us, the period of senile reflection, and it is no longer the dogma which concerns us but the facts on which it is based, and facts are no longer important as the result of scientific research but as a weapon to be used against it.

Practically speaking, today every really national act is a socialistic act and every really socialistic act is a national act; and the thing that differentiates us from our opponents, who are also socialists and also nationalists, is our knowledge of the relations of ideas and the expression of this knowledge in a clear, reasonable, simple sequence unclouded by dusty theories; we are fighting as members of the proletariat—for the German people has become a proletariat—against exploitation by capital, for capital has become foreign capital; and anyone who doesn't fight with us can no longer be considered a member of the proletariat, can no longer be considered a German.'

'Heil!' cried an S.A. man from three tables away, and every one laughed. Even the student laughed. But Ive did not laugh.

'In the end then,' said Ive, 'you ask of the individual nothing more than a single intellectual decision—with all the consequences, of course. Intellect,' he said unhappily...

'Intellect is a disease,' said Hinnerk suddenly, getting up and walking round the table to where Ive was sitting. 'Have you joined the mental acrobats?' he asked softly. 'My dear fellow,' he added, 'don't crack your skull. Intellect is a disease, a useless mucous secretion; no matter how much you may try to tone up the membrane, the sequel is general debility. Do you imagine that I have never been to bed with the harlot? Everybody steps in muck some time or another, but a decent man draws his foot away. The clever fellows with their intellects have had the whole apparatus in their own hands for twelve years. They have talked and written and split hairs and cried woe to us silly idiots, and where have they landed themselves with all their intellect? In the gutter. They are still slaving away and the whole cartload has gone astray and they won't be able to save ten thousand clever books out of the morass. It makes me want to vomit even to hear the word. With all their intellect they haven't produced a single decent man, but they have driven many a decent man mad with their intellect. Intellect is the beginning of betrayal. Look out for yourself, Ive. Have a drink.'

'Here's to you,' said Ive, lifting his glass. 'Comrades shot by the red front and the reaction, march in spirit within our ranks,'* he said, lifting his glass again. 'Here's to you, Hinnerk, sit down here.'

Hinnerk sat down. 'Well, well,' he said, and took his notebook out of his pocket.

'Sunday morning at seven o'clock,' he announced, 'we assemble for the propaganda tour. Meeting place Pankow, at the committee-room. Come here, Schneider, you have to collect the pamphlets at the district office. Schanzek, you've to bring the flag. In your working clothes. And leave your guns at home. Hermann—you're in arrears with your S.A. insurance; 1 mark 54, on Sunday! Ive, you must come with us,' he said, and Ive promised he would be there.

---

* Iversen is quoting from the 'Horst Wessel Lied' — the official song of the S.A. and the N.S.D.A.P.

They sat on together till morning, drinking and throwing their cigarette ends on the floor, and Ive felt he would very much like to join the S.A. But Hinnerk did not press him, and Ive did not suggest it. But he turned up punctually at the rendezvous to take part in the propaganda tour with Hinnerk's storm-troop. This was a week before the election which created such a sensation, and which produced such an astounding increase of National Socialist votes. The swastika flag was hoisted on the lorry into which the forty S.A. men were tightly packed. Hinnerk gave the last directions; Ive climbed up in front beside the driver with the student, who spread a map out on his knees. The lorry set off with a clatter, and the men began to sing their campaign songs. The streets were still empty, but windows were opened, and customers came out of the barbers' shops to look after the lorry. Just as the 'Deutschlandlied' was pealing out in quick time, the lorry passed a group of constables, who had collected at a corner of the street. The singing ceased, but at the word of command they shouted in chorus:

'Police! Join in!'

The constables stood unmoved, looking straight in front of them.

'Germany!' cried Hinnerk.

'Awake!' answered the chorus.

But the police apparently did not wish to represent Germany; not a feature moved in their set faces. Gradually the road widened as they neared the open country; the houses were low, with little gardens between them. In the bright, clear light of the September morning the lorry rolled into the forest. Ive looked at the low brushwood at the side of the road, at the tall, straight-trunked trees with their reddish bark, surmounted by a tuft of foliage, at the patches of fine yellow sand between the greyish-green and brown of the scattered pine needles. At a bend of the road the lorry halted; the men jumped down; they flung their civilian clothes into the ditch, while out of rustling paper parcels tumbled brown shirts; straight, naked legs were pushed into the uniform trousers; ties were pulled on and belts clasped round the suddenly attenuated figures; red armlets with the black swastika on a white ground emblazoned their sleeves.

'The police,' said Hinnerk, 'are strange creatures; they only appear singly, and the arm of the law is paralysed in the open country; in the Third Reich that will have to be changed.'

They drove on. Whenever a house appeared on the roadside, whenever they encountered a vehicle, the leaflets fluttered down; not a soul passed without receiving his sheet of paper. A village emerged, spreading out peacefully between the wide fields, which, fringed by the dark outlines of the trees, caught the light of the sun in green and gold patches. Smoke rose in thin spirals above the gleaming white walls of the houses and the red roofs. The picture of this landscape and this village roused in Ive the same feeling of ashamed irritation with which the sight of certain kinds of trashy art affected him. Am I so urbanised already?, he thought, sniffing up the hot fumes of petrol, while the driver cursed the roughness of the village street. In the lorry they were singing the S.A. March; hens fluttered cackling across the road; curious faces peeped through the clear glass of the low, flower-fringed windows. The lorry drove slowly along the main street, and stopped in the square between the church and the War Memorial. The S.A. men lined up. From the church came the sound of the organ and the choir. Ive walked slowly round the War Memorial. It was a large, square sandstone pillar surmounted by an eagle with half-spread wings; on three sides of the pillar were the names of the fallen. Ive counted the names, then turned to look at the village. Not a house could have been spared. Yet in the frame on the door of the parish clerk's house were posted four conscription notices. The church doors opened and the villagers poured out in a black swarm. They started at first at the sight of the brown-shirted men; then slowly passed on. Hinnerk waited a little longer; then the group formed up in threes and, at the word of command, marched back along the main street, singing, the flag at their head. In even ranks, their hands on their holsters, the men marched, Hinnerk at their side. If he held back a bit to inspect the line and the leader, he kept in step, marking time as prescribed in the Prussian Infantry Instructions for a sergeant. 'Emil is right,' said the van-driver to Ive, 'he is certainly not a good Nazi, but he is a good leader.'

Ive followed the procession. When they came to the last house in the village, the column, surrounded by a crowd of children, came to a halt; the men broke the line and retraced their steps, distributing leaflets from house to house and selling 'bricks,' little square tickets printed with the words: 'A brick for the S.A.' at 30 pfennigs each.'

All the villagers were at their cottage doors; looking silently and distrustfully past the brown troop, but they took the leaflets, reading them carefully and then folding them up. Once more the lorry with its singing load rattled down the street, saluting every group of villagers with a resounding 'Heil,' and here and there they even received a salute in return, They drove about the countryside, between woods and fields, methodically visiting and working each village. Out of five cars they met on the way, the occupants of three responded to their 'Heil.' Whereupon up flew the arms of the S.A. men in salute, and for a few seconds the soldiers became party-men, and again Ive experienced, as before at the sight of the peaceful landscape, the faint feeling of uncomfortable shame. The men sang themselves hoarse; they repeated the same songs again and again, striking up as soon as they sighted the first houses of a village. They were the old melodies, but the words were new. They had been for Kaiser Wilhelm in the war; what matter now if they were for Karl Liebknecht or for Adolf Hitler— the words rolled out just as well. At midday the column stopped at a large agricultural village. The inn was filled with the brown uniforms. In one corner the farmers sat crowded together over their glasses, a silent fortress in the midst of the hubbub that suddenly filled the bar. The student took the opportunity of explaining the aims of the Movement to the farmers. They listened to him quietly, but it was impossible to guess their reactions from their faces. Ive was rather pleased. Farmers, he thought to himself, farmers.

Ive sat down in the sun outside the inn. The square stretched before him, wide and empty. From the open windows he could hear the hum of voices. He lifted his nose to snuff up the warm smell of a dung-heap, he looked with concentration at a pig wallowing in a dark iridescent puddle. Fourteen stones live weight, he calculated, seventy marks, delivered free from the farm after seven months, fattening. In the shop, he thought, a pound of pork costs ninety pfennigs. The difference is swallowed up by the middlemen.

The student was standing at the window with a hunk of black bread in his hand.

'Subject, "Middlemen"!' Ive called out to him. The student laughed and began straightaway:

'The Jewish middlemen.' Ive heard and smiled. He too had written about the Jewish middlemen in *The Peasant*. He had got the expression from the farmers and the farmers took it up from him. Until he discovered one day that in the Nordmark there were no Jewish middlemen. Ive would have liked to see the Jewish cattle merchant who could have got the better of old Reimann.

'International financiers...' the penetrating voice of the student, trained in turbulent meetings, reached his ear. He's lost no time in collecting an audience, thought Ive, and continued his desultory meditations in the hot midday sun.

Later on, when the lorry was rattling along a country road, the student said there would probably be a row in the evening. Their goal was now a labour colony, close to the outskirts of the town, and they expected to reach it at sunset after an extensive tour of the villages. Ive had heard them talking of the colony that morning, it had never had a National Socialist meeting before. The whole day seemed to be an unexpressed preparation for the evening. The lorry roused village after village with its propaganda; duty is duty; but, although no one mentioned it, the colony was the main objective of the day. It cast its shadow before it, and Ive observed that it was a powerful shadow. They clattered through the last village; Hinnerk looked at the time.

The lorry continued its journey slowly. It left the wooded country, its wheels crunching the newly laid road, edged with thin, wretched little trees without foliage, driving between fields covered with garbage, through a grey, patchy landscape. In the distance the Colony could be seen, irregular rows of monotonous red huts against the bare horizon! Every voice in the lorry was silent. The student adjusted his belt and looked fixedly in front of him.

'Halt!' commanded Hinnerk.

The lorry came to a grinding halt before the doors of an inn. Several men hurried out of the bar, raised their arms in response to a resounding salute, and turned eagerly to Hinnerk. They were the local Party members. They had rented the largest hall in the neighbourhood for a meeting, but the Communists had arranged to hold a meeting in the same hall exactly an hour beforehand. They were already beginning to assemble. They had stationed their young men in the most favourable positions for defence and had organised a look-out in relays to give immediate information of the arrival of the enemy. Hinnerk studied the map, running his finger along the intersecting lines, asking questions meditatively. One of the men drew a plan of the hall and the surrounding neighbourhood, and showed the position of their opponents' committee-room.

The National Socialists had already established their quarters outside the colony; today they were going inside it for the first time. The S.A. men proceeded in close ranks; the flag flew high, guarded by four men. In front was an advance guard of three men. On the pavement, on either side of the solid nucleus of the troop, marched the flank guards (with them Ive). The men, their caps strapped under their chins, their left hands on their holsters, knees bent high at every step, eyes fixed straight in front, their mouths opened wide as they sang, pushed on into the road which stretched ominously before them, with as yet only a few straggling huts on either side. Behind the wooden palings of wretched little gardens, behind the cement posts of narrow doorways, isolated figures appeared, looked the troop rapidly up and down and disappeared again. Cyclists shot out of side streets, turned at the sight of the marching contingent, and pedalled off in the opposite direction. Windows opened. A woman in a grey blouse, with a broad red face, her immense bosom spreading over the sill, leant out grinning into the street; she began to laugh, a shrill, fat laugh which turned into a screech, spitting out scorn, malice and bitter hostility, like a poisonous reptile, at the men and their flag. The street filled up; children and youths, men in blue jerseys, accompanied the procession, mostly in silence, their eyes fixed on the marching men, pressing close upon the flank guards who strode on unflinchingly. People poured from every side street. Figures with pale expressionless faces and impenetrable eyes, with high shoulders, their arms hanging stiffly with clenched fists, came rushing up and thronged in front, behind, and at the side of the procession. The accompanying crowd grew thicker and thicker, a solid mass, an undulating sea of people on which the troops, heads in air, rode like a ship dividing the waves with its bows. Ive forced himself to take no heed of the crowd. He looked at the houses, the shops; he tried, for old times' sake, to find, among the advertisement-placards of various oils on a petrol station, the black-and-red placard of Veedol, and was annoyed because it wasn't there. Someone pushed him roughly so that he nearly fell into the road. He looked round. A young fellow, with his cap on the back of his head, was walking at his side and looking unconcernedly in front of him. There were dark smears of oil about his ears; his face was gradually turning red. The S.A. sang. One song followed another. The closer the crowd thronged round the troop, the more loudly the men roared out their songs. Between each verse Hinnerk boomed out over their heads, 'Germany,' and the S.A. replied, 'Awake.' It resounded like a thunderclap against the houses.

They arrived at a square. In front of an inn with a white facade a silent crowd was waiting, clustering in dark masses. They were congregated most densely in front of the door of the adjoining building. The S.A. wheeled round, the advance guard stopped short, Hinnerk ran forward. The flag was lowered, the point with the swastika was thrust straight forward, threateningly, over the heads of the obstructing crowd. Ive suddenly felt himself shoved and pushed against the troop, which was thrusting its way through like a wedge towards the entrance. Their speed increased. Hinnerk raised his arm; there was a short sudden rush; the flag waved aloft; the S.A. had arrived; figures rushed to one side; a table was knocked over; the doors were flung wide; the dark passage, swept clear, swallowed up the brown troop. Ive stood in the hall. The hall was large and light with yellow walls, high up in which were narrow windows. Opposite the entrance was a platform with tables, chain and a desk. It was crowded. Row after row of chairs was filled with black figures; as though with one movement all the faces turned towards the door, pale discs in the dark confusion. The gigantic red flag which hung down straight over their heads, a flaming beacon, was blown out in billows.

'Germany!' cried Hinnerk into the hall.

'Awake!' resounded the answer.

Hinnerk, followed by the S.A. men, leapt over the chairs on the right, and seemed to whiz like an arrow through the tumult towards the front of the hall, scaling the rows of seats with the agility of an acrobat—the head of a writhing serpent before whose rapid movement the heavy body of the crowd bent back in trepidation and swayed to make way. When he was near the platform, he turned, and, using the table as a jumping-off ground, landed with legs and arms widespread on the space cleared for him by the dumbfounded S.A. men to whom he had indicated the direction and goal of his leap. He waited for a moment for his soldiers to take up their positions. Then he bowed smilingly to the crowd, which had sprung to its feet, shrugged his shoulders apologetically, pointed politely to the platform to remind the men there of their duty and their purpose. Gradually the tumult subsided, leaving only a tremulous excitement, a dangerous tension, filling every corner of the hall with expectation. The lamps shed a lurid light over the crowd, colouring their faces yellow and green. Ive looked them up and down appraisingly and seemed satisfied. On the platform a man left one of the tables and, standing behind the desk, rang the bell. He began to speak slowly in a clear, calm voice. He opened the meeting, greeting all those present, emphasising the word 'all,' and said that he relied on their enlightened proletarian intelligence and their ability to distinguish between true and false, between the will of the proletariat and capitalist corruption. Comrade Melzer would now address them.

Comrade Melzer was a robust young man with a low furrowed brow, behind which one could fancy one saw his thoughts taking form and point. He was in his shirt-sleeves. He took his position beside the desk, near the edge of the platform, directly over the heads of the S.A.

'Comrades,' he said, waited for silence, scrutinised the corners of the room from which a group of young workers were imperceptibly pushing forward, made a wide, all-embracing gesture towards the body of the hall, as though he were concentrating all the forces on himself, smiled, and bowed. He began to speak of the decisive struggle of the proletariat which had now reached its last stage, a truth which was demonstrated by the fact that the bourgeoisie of the whole world were manning their armies with any one they could find. The S.A. men looked attentively at the speaker. The latter only occasionally raised his voice slightly. What he said was simple and revolved round one clear point, from which he never deviated. At the present moment, continued Comrade Melzer, all the efforts of the capitalistic world were concentrated on producing confusion in the ranks of the proletariat, in dividing them in order to be able to continue their rule, with the short-period end in view, as soon as the achievements of organised labour had, through the treachery of its leaders, proved themselves to be achievements against the interests of labour, of establishing class rule once more and this time for ever—and, on the pretext of dealing with a crisis, to reduce wages to a brutally low level and artificially to increase the industrial reserve and, with its hand at their throats, to keep the Proletariat in such a state of misery that the revolutionary masses would become an army of half-starved slaves who, unable to make a stand against class-supremacy, would simply vegetate like a docile herd of cattle, perpetually creating the means for others to live. In this effort, went on Comrade Melzer, capitalism had been able to find hirelings in the ranks of the proletariat itself. The S.A. men stood behind Hinnerk in dumb expectation. The eyes of the whole room were drawn, as though by an invisible magnet, to the brown shirts, every breath that was drawn in the death-like silence between the sentences seemed to be fraught with cold, implacable hatred against the group. Comrade Melzer spoke of the Russian example, the example of a people, of a nation, which under the red flag of world-revolution had, by the emancipation of the proletariat, accomplished its own emancipation. Only through the Social Revolution, Comrade Melzer suddenly shouted into the hall, is national emancipation possible. 'Bravo!' burst out Hinnerk right in his face. With one accord the crowd rose to its feet. From all corners of the hall it pressed forward.

'Only the international solidarity of the working-class, whose head and heart is Moscow,' said Comrade Melzer, smiling, almost in a whisper, but accentuating every word, 'can guarantee the Social Revolution.'

Relieved, the crowd laughed, burst into shouts, which rose to resounding applause, stamping of feet, and shrill cat-calls. The S.A. men closed up, their hands dropped from their holsters. Ive looked intently at Hinnerk, who nodded laughingly to Comrade Melzer.

'The revolution will be a Marxist revolution,' said Comrade Melzer, 'or there will be no revolution at all. Marx said—' he shouted into the hall.

'Have you ever read Marx?' roared Hinnerk's voice up at him.

Comrade Melzer gave a start. 'Certainly!' he shouted in Hinnerk's face.

'Have you read all four volumes of *Das Kapital*, asked Hinnerk incredulously.

'Certainly,' hissed Comrade Melzer, bending down to him.

'He only wrote three volumes,' declared Hinnerk.

The S.A. burst into a roar of laughter. With wide-open mouths, the men slapped their legs, laughed for all they were worth into the hall, they laughed up at the silent, dark walls, they laughed down into the menacing, dismayed faces. By this time the group of young workers had pushed their way forward to the front rows.

'With the volume on the Criticism of Political Economy there are four,' said Comrade Melzer, shrugging his shoulders. The bell rang, Hinnerk motioned to his men—they were silent.

Comrade Melzer continued his speech calmly; he spoke more rapidly; from time to time his eyes wandered to the front rows, between which the young workers were standing with non-committal faces. Hinnerk looked at the time.

'Comrades,' said Comrade Melzer, raising his voice, 'capitalism is digging its own grave. By immutable and iron laws it is running full steam ahead to its own destruction. But the vultures and hyenas are getting ready to devour its corpse, to rob you, comrades, of the goal of your desire, of your desperate struggle, of your heroic sacrifice! Do not trust them, the wolves in—brown—sheep's clothing.'

A ripple passed through the rows, eyes met in consternation.

'Do not trust those who cry to the four winds that they are the saviours: they are the traitors...'

A groan reverberated through the icy cold, keen atmosphere.

'...And let your watchword be now and forever: "Shoot the Fascists, wherever you meet them!"'

'Up!' roared Hinnerk. In one bound he rushed forward, his arms flew up, the leg of a chair whirled through the air, a table fell with a crash; cries shrieked from every throat, and they were at each other. Ive ran forward, his head lowered between his shoulders, one arm bent above his head; a blow crashed on his arm, his fist shot out and encountered a soft belly, a cracking thump landed on his chin from below, a chair rolled between his legs, he caught hold of it and held it high in the air, the student clutched the back of it, they tugged, the wood cracked and broke. Ive brandished the jagged cudgel, swung it round his head and brought it down with a crash on a cap. The platform seemed to be cleared. S.A. men sprang up from the boards. The men worked their way forward in two rows, forming a partition right across the hall, the first row with narrow spaces into which the men of the second line sprang. Outside, stones whirled against the windowpanes, the glass fell in shivers to the floor, Hinnerk jumped back, he bent his trunk backwards, he hurled a chair, which turned right over in the air and hit the big lamp in the middle of the hall. It broke with a deafening crash; the light went out, chips of glass rained down on the fighting turmoil. New contingents came surging into the attack from the entrance—Ive hit about him blindly, cries were silenced, gasping figures clutched each other round the neck, wrestled, raged, staggered, rolled, tossed hither and thither by enraged kicks. A shot whistled through the air, and then another. For a moment the black figures loosened their hold of each other, a long-drawn groan echoed through the darkness, then they set about each other again, tumbling over broken furniture, over prostrate bodies, with one mad purpose, to drive back the barely visible opponent. Behind the S.A. ranks a black empty space yawned, gradually extending, hot dust falling heavily on the floor. Suddenly the struggling crowd fell asunder—the trample of hurrying footsteps was heard, the door banged to. Breathing heavily, the men stood and listened.

'What's up?' cried Hinnerk—and, 'Light!'

Pocket torches flashed, and the rays searched. There was a movement beneath the overturned tables.

'The student!' cried someone. There lay the student; blood streamed round him.

'Bring bandages!'

'What's the matter?'

'A shot in the chest,' said someone, wiping the blood from his face. The student moved his hand feebly, groaned and twisted under the quick hands which were trying to bind strips of white material round his chest. A noise at the door. It was opened. All the torches flashed towards it. A military policeman stood at the door, his sword pressed against his body. He lifted his hand. He said in a shaky voice:

'The meeting is dissolved!'

The pocket torches were turned. They shone on to the platform, illuminating the immense red flag which hung across it with a black swastika on a white field.

X

ON the evening of the elections Ive rang up Dr. Schaffer and told him with amusement that he had just met Herr Salamander.

Herr Salamander, one of the gentlemen who frequented Schaffer's circle, had seemed to be in a great bustle, as though he were in a terrible hurry to get away. He said he was going to pack his trunk and take the train to Paris. He realised, after the results of the elections, that every sixth person he met in the street, on seeing his pronounced Jewish appearance, would be possessed of one wish only, the wish to kill him, and therefore there was nothing left for him to do but to flee from these insupportable conditions, and to put a frontier between himself and the country in which such things were possible. Ive asked Dr. Schaffer whether he too was packing his trunk.

Schaffer laughed. He was not packing, he said, and had no intention of doing so.

'So our friend Salamander has suddenly realised the value of frontiers. I tell you what, he continued, 'why not come round and see me and finish off this exciting day by an evening of talk?'

Ive agreed. A relationship had grown up between him and Schaffer, which might have been described as a cautious friendship. In spite of complete sincerity on both sides, there was still a trace of shyness, a barrier of reserve, which needed the expansive relief of complete loss of self-control to break it down, and this had a stimulating effect on their association. Ive, who had an idea that his own character was not sympathetic, was inclined to be very reticent about personal matters. The only binding absolute relationship he recognised between himself and others was that of comradeship, and, even in the case of Claus Heim, this was based not so much on affection as on their common cause. Comradeship, however, seemed to be the one thing that was impossible between himself and Schaffer, and Ive knew that this was almost entirely his fault. Just when the discovery of their similarity of opinion on essentials seemed to be bringing them together, Ive would lay stress on their differences and refuse to do anything to reconcile them. Schaffer's point of view alone was enough to drive him into defending positions which were really not his at all; he had a way of disputing the authority of Schaffer's views even when he shared them. Thus, on one occasion, when Schaffer said something insulting, though actually true, about the Kaiser, Ive put up a ridiculous defence, although he did not in the least disagree with him. Similarly he regarded it as almost presumptuous in Schaffer to have such a deep and sincere admiration for German art, although he could not but admit that this admiration arose from a much sounder knowledge and a profounder study of the subject than in his own case. Schaffer was very patient, and Ive often left him admitting to himself that he had behaved badly but was undoubtedly in the right, whereas Schaffer obviously thought him a nice fellow but wrong-headed. This did not prevent him from seeking Schaffer's company, attracted chiefly by his absolute sincerity and the fact that every one of his actions, however odd it might seem, had convincing reasons behind it. In fact, as Ive discovered later, even the St. John's goblin was the outcome of an extremely thorough and complicated intellectual process, in which solid research into folk-lore, child psychology, and the laws of creative art formed important stages, without however adding to the homunculus's diminutive stature.

Ive found Dr. Schaffer at his desk looking at a collection of old prints.

'We must not succumb to the general hysteria,' he said, putting the prints carefully away into their portfolio. 'If this election should really prove to be a historical event it will certainly be an event of very doubtful value.'

'Make no mistake,' said Ive, 'even supposing the Movement should fall to pieces under the weight of our disappointed hopes, one thing is certain, whatever rises from its ruins, it won't be anything that has ever existed before.'

'Why,' asked Schaffer, 'do you even mention the possibility of this Movement falling to pieces?'

Ive thought a moment. Then he said: 'It is understandable that you—as a Jew—are obliged to oppose the Movement; but what is to prevent my joining it unconditionally? You may well be anxious, even though you won't admit it, but how much more reason have I to be anxious, when I see the Movement blasting with its rapid explosions everything that I consider right and necessary and true, everything for which I have been fighting; and the goal which has been my ardent dream, not transformed into reality, but reduced to a hollow, vulgar formula? When I see that, even though its possibilities may be infinite, it is pursuing a path whose landmarks I should on no account wish to see taken as indications of the future? When I see that all the values which I acknowledge are having their deep and binding significance destroyed by the Movement, or by those who have made it their public duty to represent it; that the only values which make life worth while are being corrupted and stultified—for instance, the nation?'

'I admit that I am anxious, but why should you think it is because I am a Jew?' said Dr. Schaffer. 'Why shouldn't it be for the sake of the only values that make life worth while; for instance, the nation? Do not misunderstand me,' he added quickly, 'I have been a Jew, today I am a German, but certainly not in the dull manner of Liberalism, which changes its nationality in order to make existence easier, making this expedient change the basis of a comfortable principle, a principle which represents all nations, if not as similar, yet as equal, and therefore interchangeable, and by this false interpretation destroys the principle of nationality. If I have been a Jew, and am today a German, it is because I recognise the principle of nationality, that is, because I can only live as a responsible member of a nation.'

'What do you understand by the term nation?' asked Ive.

Dr. Schaffer looked round at him, and said slowly: 'I can only interpret the term nation as the sovereign will of the people endowed with power and form.'

'I,' said Ive, 'cannot understand the conception nation at all. It is simply something that is there making a demand, a compelling cry of the blood.'

'Of the mind,' said Schaffer. 'If it were merely a question of race, the choice would be easy. I am not so foolish as to deny the significance of race. For the very reason, that my origins are Jewish I could not do that without betraying my principles. But in the question of nationality race is only a supplementary factor.'

'If,' said Ive, 'class-consciousness is creating the social revolution, with the object of bringing class into power, will it not be race-consciousness that will create the national revolution?'

'With the object of bringing race into power? But the social revolution does away with classes through the supremacy of one. That is its object. Is the national revolution to do away with other races?' asked Schaffer, and went on: 'That would be only in the last resort. I by no means minimise the importance of last resorts, but I cannot wait for a German Genghis Khan. You and I are responsible for what has to happen. And it is ideas alone which can create a revolution.'

'It is revolutions that create ideas,' said Ive. 'War is the father of all things, and civil war is the mother. I cannot wait for ideas. Thoughts may be winged, but you must destroy the cage if they are to fly.'

Schaffer gave Ive a cautious look. 'Destruction,' he said, 'is an evasion and an easy one, for it brings pleasure with it. I am thus far no longer a Jew, that I might describe this painful pleasure simply as a *goyim* pleasure. I recognise the significance of destruction, but I do not at the present moment see its practical necessity.'

'Are you one of those,' asked Ive, 'who demand a fifty-one percent of certainty of success?'

'A hundred percent certainty,' said Schaffer, 'for it is the risks of revolution that destroy its value as an act of violence. Don't imagine that I wish entirely to repudiate the Terror as a means. It lightens the task, and I cannot conceive how my own personal revolutionary motto could be more easily, more quickly, and more certainly fulfilled than by the Terror: "Down with arteriosclerosis as the sole criterion of capacity." But the means is not the end, the Terror is not the revolution, the conclusion is not the premise. Above all, revolution is an intellectual change. Without the ideas which were discussed in the salons of the French aristocracy before 1789 there would have been no attack on the Bastille, without Mirabeau no Robespierre, without Marx no Lenin. The revolution is there with its intellectual nucleus, the crystallisation of the change which is justified by the promulgation of ideas, by the new outlook. This nucleus alone is capable of deciding the degree of destruction necessary to attain the goal.'

'The question is,' said Ive, 'whether it is to be our ambition to produce the only hygienically justifiable revolution in history. The question is whether, deprived of its elemental quality, it will not be defrauded of its actual significance. You can demonstrate to a prisoner the practical impossibility of escaping from prison. But that will not prevent him from rattling at his bars. I know that it is impossible to attack tanks with walking-sticks. But if we have not the courage to attack tanks with walking-sticks, are not prepared to do it at any moment, we have no right to talk of revolution.'

'We have no right to talk of revolution,' said Schaffer, 'so don't— let's do it. Everybody calls himself a revolutionary. Since I discovered that there was even a League of Revolutionary Pacifists, I have given up calling myself a revolutionary; otherwise I should find myself in too embarrassing company.'

'You might call that hiding your head in the sand on aesthetic grounds,' said Ive, laughing. 'In the Third Reich...'

'In the Third Reich we two will probably meet again on the same sand heap,' said Schaffer.

Ive shrugged his shoulders. 'Possibly,' he said. 'But that does not seem to me to be a reason for escaping from the prisons of the bourgeoisie in order to settle down comfortably in their dungeons. You and I are responsible for what has to happen. How do you justify your responsibility?'

'I am a German for the sake of the principle of nationality,' said Schaffer slowly. 'This faces me with responsibility; I justify it by striving to carry out the only task, the only revolutionary task if you will, which can exist today: to co-operate in the formation of an intellectual aristocracy which will find a way out of the complete planlessness of the German position.'

'The nation as the sovereign will of the people, that was it, wasn't it?' said Ive. 'Then we might as well rest content with parliamentary democracy. Why don't you stand for the Reichstag, sir?'

Schaffer leaned back. He closed his eyes.

Ive gazed at his pale, yellowish face, the bumpy forehead, with its fringe of thick, wiry black hair, the pointed nose, the full-lipped mouth, the slightly receding chin, blueshadowed. He looks very Jewish, he thought to himself, and was suddenly overcome with an uneasy feeling of compassion that he would not for the world have owned to anyone.

Schaffer said quietly: 'We shall never get any further like this. In the end, the only common ground between people is faith. And even there, every individual has his own kind of faith. Every one finds his own way to objective conception, to absolute truth. Your faith is the result of strong feeling. But do not imagine that mine, which is the result of intellectual unrest, of sincere questioning, is any the less ardent, any the less violent, subject to claims any less urgent, or to less exigent responsibilities.'

'Put it to yourself,' said Ive, 'do not you love the principle of nationality more than you love the nation?'

Schaffer replied, 'I believe in the principle of nationality, therefore I must love the nation—the nation which does not yet exist, which we still have to create. I find myself in the strange situation in relation to you,' he said, 'of having to defend National Socialism. By its mere existence, it has forced people to recognise the nation, if not in principle, at any rate as an actuality. The mistake lies in the overemphasis of the fact that it is an actuality which has yet to be created. It is this that makes me anxious: the failure to realise that a beginning has been made, preposterous, but at the same time a beginning that must be universally recognised, National Socialists dream of a Third Reich, and so they are at liberty, as in the case of the various Internationals, to label every intermediate step Reich 4A or 5B, as the case may be.'

He raised his hand.

'Let me go on,' he said. 'You know that the convert is always stricter about questions of religion than the man brought up in the faith. I am a convert to nationalism. I have tried, as a Jew, to have faith. I have ventured, and I have to venture, on to the thorny path through the thicket. Men who live on a frontier do not see half, they see double—as it were stereoscopically. They can never shirk decision without surrendering themselves from the national point of view. It is an intellectual decision. I have decided. I am more insistent about the question, because I see it as a more urgent issue. The road I am travelling is a private one, I know, but the prospect is not private. I have decided to be German. Why? I love French literature, English will-to-power, Russian breadth, Chinese ethics, German depth; you might, therefore, say that I love all these things as visions, but I see the fulfilment in German nationalism. I see the meaning of the world here'—a note of distress came into his voice—'after failing to find it in Judaism.'

'If National Socialism were consistent,' he continued, 'it would realise that nationalism is a Jewish discovery. Moses was the first nationalist, and the ten commandments are repeated in the German criminal code. It is in no sense of cheap triumph that I make this apt comparison. The fact remains that the first manifestation of Judaism, that of the tribe of Israel from Mount Sinai, contains in it all the elements of nationalism, expresses the sum of the experiences of a nation in race and history, embraces its whole desire for self-expression, its culture, and, over and above all these, the element which is most important in developing national feeling, the will-to-power, which, in the knowledge of its unique individuality, reaches out towards a God, an only God, the God that has made this nation his chosen people, to rule so that in his name it may redeem. It is the covenant between a people and God that makes it a nation.'

The Covenant and its law:

'Now therefore, if ye will obey my voice indeed,
and keep my covenant,
then ye shall be a peculiar treasure unto me
above all people:
for all the earth is mine:
And ye shall be unto me
a kingdom of priests
and a holy nation.'

Schaffer rose and walked up and down.

'Two thousand, and again two thousand years!' he said. 'The blockheads should have the word nation torn out of their impudent mouths.'

'They should!' said Ive. 'Who has given you the right to this formula, what siren's voice has lured you from the covenant?'

'Anti-Semite?' asked Schaffer.

Ive replied: 'The Jew today is the most visible defender of the Liberal stronghold. I attack him because I want to see the stronghold stormed.'

'Exactly,' said Schaffer. 'The Liberal Jew is the most dangerous enemy of Judaism itself. You as well as I have the right to attack him so long as Judaism is not prepared to whistle him back to his responsibilities. And it is this that has made me despair of Judaism: that it has failed in its will to power; that it has complacently given way where, in all the circumstances, it should have resisted—in the intellectual field; that it does not recognise its hour, does not stand up to bear witness once more, once again to cast down the tables of the law; that it is allowing its power to be broken, after allowing its form to be broken. This and much more. I have not lightly cut myself off; I know what is going on in Judaism today, and particularly in Germany, where the atmosphere has not been propitious to narrow adherence to the law as in the East, nor to an expansion of the law as in the West. I know all about the signs and wonders, about Herzl and Buber; I know that today Judaism also has been caught by the tumultuous waves of the constructive ideal. I know, too, that the vessel is broken, the spiritual form, the theocracy; I know, too, that the foundations are not there for a new development—have not yet been renewed—a calm, deep faith springing up from the depths of the soil; I know, too, that all that Judaism has to win nationally will, at the best, be a matter of pleading, of begging, but not of conquest. I have cut myself off because I have lost my faith; because I can no longer find the organised community. The prophets are silent for me now, when Goethe speaks. I cannot rejoice over it, nor can I bemoan it; it is so. Four thousand years! In yet another thousand years, perhaps! Let him who can believe, have patience and experience in himself the Renaissance of which he dreams. This is the hour of the German nation. The intellectual riches which I sought in Judaism, in the tradition of my people, I have discovered fuller and more alive— and younger—in the German nation.'

He continued: 'Of course, it was not in the columns of the daily press that I made this discovery, but in obedience to the call of a future, which, while marking off an epoch, reveals the germ of historical development. The very first movements of a nation indicate its destiny; whether it recognise or reject it, it will have a history, or changing conditions of existence. Let us do away at last with the stale ideas which have been confusing people's minds since the French Revolution, and allowing every village community of Europe to set up "national claims," without ever having given the world a single constructive idea. A people justifies its claims as a nation when it proclaims its universal obligations—obligations which are fulfilled in the heroic figures of history. War and murder, and pestilence and insurrection have existed at all times and among all peoples; but the criterion of a hero lies in his ability to fulfil a task which, though the people know nothing of it, is the very essence of the nation. Jeanne d'Arc is the French national saint and heroine; for, long before the events of the French Revolution which made of her people a nation, she was striving to fulfil its mission. Hers was a divine mission, of course; she fulfilled the vows of the most Christian daughter of the

Church, and the Church could not do otherwise than proclaim her a saint, thereby acknowledging the national claims of her most Christian daughter. Just as she can and will acknowledge every national claim if it is expressed in terms of Christianity. Just as she recognised the German claim in the Holy Roman Empire of the German nation. But that is just it: the universal responsibility was not laid down by the German People, but by the Church; the nation as mediator, not as prime-mover. When it wanted to be prime-mover, it was in a position of protest, and in its most violent protest, in the Reformation, so far the most national manifestation in German history, it attacked the foundations of the Church, the foundations of the Holy Roman Empire, for the sake of the German nation. And I regard it as a sign that at that moment the closest bond was formed with those people who alone by their inexorable exclusiveness preserved their national claim in its purity: with the Jewish people. I refer to the translation of the Bible. By deliberately incorporating in its own culture the one universal document of the world it established its own universal responsibility against the claims of the Church. Nothing is more natural than that it should be for German culture only that this event preserved its deeper religious significance; that for all the peoples who were caught up in the whirlpool of this event the consequences were mainly other than religious; that Gustavus Adolphus fought and fell in Germany; that Cromwell, in obedience to the Puritan command to propagate the Gospel, was obliged to turn immediately to the imperialistic ambitions which found a barrier everywhere where the Church had already established her political sway; that the Gospel of the Rights of Man, the last powerful missionary idea of a nation, directed the whole impetus of the French people against the Roman Empire of the German nation, and reduced it to ruins; but never ceased and never dared cease to direct it against the German nation, and in all the churches of France the tricolour hangs with a golden cross on its white ground. Every nation extends as far as its power extends. Does not Fascist Italy claim to be the heir to the Roman Empire and, therefore, today the head of the Latin peoples, and tomorrow the proudest son of the Church? And is not the missionary idea of the Russian people world revolution, and has it not its irredentist armies in every country of the world? The principle of nationality is always the same; only the nations vary; part of a whole, they suffer all the processes dictated by life, they come into being and grow, subject to eternal world-laws; they gather in and dispense and hand down, they change and fulfil themselves and pass away, and the traces of their spirit are indelible. When a period is pregnant the world awaits the birth of a new idea. The present time is pregnant; and the world is waiting. There is only one idea that can be brought forth, destined to bring a new order, to give its character to the coming centuries, possibly to the next thousand years. And it will be a German idea.'

Schaffer continued: 'I regard it as a sign that in every province of German life there are signs of a change of heart, but only in German life. India and China are fighting—for their national freedom. And what do they announce as their aim? What do the theses of Sun Yat Sen and the Indian Congress mean? What does Gandhi dream of and what does the Chinese student talk about? The self-determination of the nations, a new order on the lines of Western democracy. The Russians speak of a new sense of life and point to the powerful, dazzling, economic plan which is changing the face of a portion of the world. The complete shifting of values, stressing the economic basis of life, may signify to the Russians the dawn of a new era. But America achieved the shift long ago, and is writhing in the wheels of its mechanism, whilst the same ambition which created this mechanism is changing the country of the Soviets into a paradise of iron and concrete, of tractors and boring machines and Americanising its people. I regard it as a sign that today, for the first time, we Germans are no longer contesting the claim of France to be marching at the head of civilised nations, but we are contesting the claims of civilisation to be a redeeming force! That we, the most highly developed industrial nation of the world, the possessors of the greatest number of technical inventions, have begun to attack the foundations of this development, to turn mind against one of its forms. I regard it as a sign that we are daring to think in other than utilitarian terms, to seek for other standards, to replace technical conceptions with metaphysical conceptions, to direct intellectual forces to the sphere of the spirit. All over the world men are racking their brains for a solution. But if there is a solution at all, one thing is certain, no solution can suffice unless it come from the spiritual sphere. If it is possible at all, then it is possible to us to wage the world's wars, to taste the blood of battle, to pass through that purification which alone gives the right to speak for the whole world. It is not by chance that the capitalist era was made éclatant by German prestige; that it is only in the German sociological structure that you find an era spreading over four centuries, that it is only in German consciousness that Western history is conceived merely as an act of preparation. It is not by chance that not one of us, if he wishes to act responsibly towards himself, can resist the necessity of acting with universal responsibility, that freedom of action has been taken from us; vocation is not a matter of chance, but a command. The world is in a state of unrest and expectation. The world is thrown open before us; let us throw ourselves open to the world.'

Schaffer was silent. He did not look at Ive. And Ive did not look at him. Ive could not doubt the sincerity of this confession, but this very sincerity led him to assume that Schaffer's credo was without any actual centre of gravity, or at least without any consciousness of a centre of gravity. He said: '"Let us throw ourselves open to the world." What does that mean but "let us leave the German question open?"'

He hesitated, then continued: 'Whatever our task may be, it is essential that first of all we should fight for our existence.'

Schaffer said: 'It is essential that first of all we should arrive at a conviction through which our existence is justified. To throw ourselves open to the world means that we must solve the German problem for the sake of the world. I could not call myself a German if I regarded the matter in any other light. And this is the way in which we must solve the German problem, everything points to it—don't interrupt me—by German socialism. That is by a metaphysical socialism, not like Russian socialism which only embraces a part of reality, and forces men within the bounds of the part—but the whole of reality, with God as the highest reality within it. And this highest reality expresses itself through a law which, in the first place, demands of man an unequivocal attitude towards his fellows, that is, through an ethical injunction, the one which has always raised Judaism above its environment, the one which can raise the German nation to stand alone above its fellows.'

Ive said: 'I knew it. And here is the mistake. I am in the extraordinary position in regard to you of having to defend National Socialism. Merely by its existence it has forced people to recognise a German socialism, if not in principle, at any rate as a possibility. The error lies alone in the overemphasis of the fact that this is not socialism. That is what makes me anxious: the concealment of the knowledge that every form of equalisation—and every socialistic theory, however it may be constructed, must, when applied to mankind, be based on some such principle—is contrary to the intrinsic German character. The propaganda of the Movement with its slogan of National Socialism, whether it be meant seriously or not, or whether it change according to circumstances or not, could actually be effective anywhere. Even where property is in question, and particularly there, the slogan penetrates without fear, to the upper and lower, middle classes, to the entrepreneur class, even to the manufacturing class. For even in the case of the most radical realisation of the slogan, as things stand today and as they will even more unequivocally stand tomorrow, all that will happen is that a de facto state of affairs will be turned into a de jure state of affairs. For every form of property has long since been bankrupt. But what is the reason that the Movement is forced, forced in order to have success, to avoid even the suggestion of socialism in that class where, although the actual conditions of property are exactly the same and where, if not the most violent and most ardent, certainly the most spontaneous national feelings are to be found—in the country, among the farmers? Because the most spontaneous feeling is not based on intellectual conceptions. Because it requires no ethical injunction to make it what it is. War, murder and insurrection have existed in all times among all peoples; but eventually it was always a question of land. It is at frontiers that the feelings are inflamed which cause a nation to make its stake, and in changes of frontier the course of history can be read. Why is it that since the Destruction of Jerusalem Judaism has been nothing but a theme of history? And why is it that Zionism, the beginning of the Jewish Renaissance, turns to Palestine, the country that is the holy land of Judaism, that since the days of Moses, the first nationalist, has been the promised land, Canaan? The history of Judaism since the Destruction is an intellectual history, it is true, and it is only an intellectual history, and it is fundamentally always the same intellectual history, the history of the preservation of its intellectual content. Actually Judaism has developed in itself all the elements of a nation except one. Judaism has at its service the complete sum of experience in its positive national sense, faith, race, history and culture, from the revelation of its destiny as the chosen people to the missionary idea of the redemption of the world through an ethical injunction; from the struggle for an order to the justification of this order by the transmuting, but in itself immutable, law. So strong is the Jewish conception of nationality that until it was faced with its greatest danger—Liberalism, it was able to do without any State organisation. And it has had to do without any State organisation because the Jewish nation has no country. But one fact is certain. What happened to the Jewish people as such was not merely by chance, and the sources of it were beyond their reach. If there is an ethical injunction which is capable of elevating Judaism in the eyes of the world, it is the law of justice. I know it is an Old Testament law set up at a time when Judaism could not only make demands, but could give guarantees. God, the highest reality, set up this claim for this people and no other. And it was this people and no other which was chosen to fulfil it. I don't know how the Jews interpret their dispersal—as a punishment or as a trial. But I do know that it is only through the dispersal that the Jewish missionary idea has gained its terrible weight. And this is the mad temptation to which the German nation threatens to succumb today: in its state of despair, deprived of country, its existence imperilled, and conquered at every point except in its essence, to set up a claim for justice! A temptation, because this claim is not urgent in our case. For us justice has never been of the kind that demands from mankind an unconditional attitude towards his fellow-men. If Judaism can excuse itself for having listened to the siren-voice of Liberalism, proclaiming the rights of man, because the voice was so like that of its own prophets, what excuse is there for us? If Judaism succumbed to the dangerous illusion of setting up the law of man instead of the law of God for which it was seeking, how much greater is the danger for us, since it is not our forms which are being attacked, but our very essence. If we are venturing to search not for ideas, but for events, not for ends but for means, in short, not for abstractions, but for the original and essential factors, it is clear that it has never been with a view to equalisation, but to organisation. This power is so strong that even Protestantism, a religious form of democracy, set itself up in the form of an evangelical theocracy. We may take it as a sign that even in the widest public consciousness our whole history has only been considered as a preparation; in the long run none of our desires has had a lasting fulfilment. Perpetual hope goes hand-in-hand with perpetual danger, and the stronger a faith the greater its temptations. Whatever we have accepted, we have always accepted it in our own sense. It is when we speak in strange tongues, expressing accepted ideas, that we are incomprehensible. It is not that we are different, but that we are different and yet want to be as others, which makes us, so it seems to me, incomprehensible, and worse still, gives us the appearance of insincerity. We are struggling for a socialism that in effect is no longer anywhere accepted as socialism. We call ourselves a nation and do not recognise a nation's perpetual responsibility, since we have no regard for treaties, which though they may have been signed in different circumstances and by governments, which have disappeared, none the less were signed in the name of the nation. We boast of living in the age of Liberalism; we accept its forms, are ready to adopt its institutions, and can anyone deny that we are incapable, under this banner, of attaining that state of equality, at a happy average cultural level, for which the French nation strove, and achieved with complete naturalness. Viewed from this level and taken all in all, our whole standard of life is, indeed, one of barbarism; our literature is a cacography; our discipline, based on the idea of a recruit clicking his heels before his superior officer, is a horror. The discussion that we two are carrying on at this moment is the height of folly, and all we hear on every side, be it shouted or whispered, points to chaos, to the decay of Western civilisation. I think that this should be enough for us, if we only have the courage to draw the conclusions. We declaim against the corruption from the West, from Rome, from the East, but it must surely be deeply rooted in ourselves, since everything we are capable of saying is no more than argumentation, and in any case our polemics are directed against ourselves. We set ourselves against the economic entanglement, which has made us bankrupt, and are not prepared to set ourselves against the intellectual entanglement, which has made us intellectually bankrupt, in spite of the fact that on every side the thin flow of universal literary diarrhoea is proclaimed as the product of the highest culture? We cannot go in for politics because we are not a nation, and we are not a nation because we do not possess the attributes of a nation; one of these attributes, and at this juncture the most important, is the integrity of the land. Of the land, the tangible, solid earth, Dr. Schaffer, with which you as well as I have lost all direct relationship, a relationship which the whole world is trying, not without success, to commercialise out of existence for those who still possess it, a relationship which, in truth, carries with it consequences of greater material, metaphysical and ethical significance than we are capable of imagining. For we live on the pavements and our love of nature, considered practically, can never develop beyond the futile endeavour to milk an ox. Until the integrity of the land has been attained, secured for all time, by whatever means you like, any attempt to proclaim universal responsibility can only be designated as transcendental prostitution! What German history will look like in the future I don't know; but this I do know, that we must not rest a second, that we must make every effort to be able once more to take our place in history as a nation. It is the land which is issuing this command, the land weighed down with unfulfilled history, it is the latent, unexhausted strength of the land which is driving us on. We Germans cannot live in disintegration, and wherever Germans live in disintegration, any attempt to obtain arbitrary power by the preservation of individuality has always been doomed to failure. A spiritual Jerusalem might be enough for the Jews, but a spiritual Germany is not enough for the Germans. The strongest German tribe, beyond the frontiers of Germany, the Baltic tribe, lost its power after seven hundred years, when the German Reich lost its power. And the power of the Baltic people was based on the possession of land. Wherever Germans settle in foreign countries they are drawn to the land; and where they have settled in towns they have lost their power more quickly, more absolutely, and have given themselves more quickly and more absolutely to the service of the foreign nation. Bismarck knew what he was about when he demanded the ear and the blade as a symbol of his chancellorship. And we, who possess neither ear nor blade, and never shall, we who live in the disintegration of the towns—shall we not, in God's name or the devil's, develop an even stronger sense of the land? Does not the Jew in foreign countries, the Catholic of the Diaspora, feel the more strongly the need of intellectual anchorage? And we in the towns feel the need of anchorage, intellectual, if you like, or spiritual, or moral, in the land. It is not the relationship of man to man which is important for us, but the relationship which he sets up for himself to the land, to the community, which is united to and through the land, no matter in what way. That is the only claim which holds good for us in all circumstances when we speak of the nation. It is a German, not a Jewish claim.'

Ive raised his hand. 'Don't interrupt me,' he said. 'Whether I am an anti-Semite or not is beside the point. In fact, anti-Semitism is never more than a manifestation of secondary importance, and the fact that it is always regarded by each of the parties involved as the problem of the other, and is attributed to the responsibility of the other, leads to the conclusion that it is not a problem at all, but a not always unequivocal phenomenon which must be left to the wisdom of the State authorities to deal with. It seems to me rather useless, after a long period of suspecting one another for being Jews, now to be railing at each other for being avowed Nazis. It is only confusing the issue. And in the end it is an idle speculation as to whether, biologically considered or otherwise, the freckled son of a Pomeranian inspector is of greater value to the nation than a German Jew of high intellectual capacity. The nation establishes standards, it is true, but how can functions be compared? Whether a man fulfils his function well or ill decides his value. When I said "a Jewish claim," that was of course a criticism of standard. That was how you understood it and how I meant it. The important thing is that functions should be fulfilled according to the standards set by the nation. What the Jewish claim asserts is that the nation can never be the primary authority; it can never determine our rule of life and its structure, the State: it cannot determine the intellectual content of the State, the law. Judaism has taken advantage of the fact that it possesses no territory; it was able to do without the State and it was obliged to make a stand against authority. But we do possess territory and cannot do without the State nor the authority of the State, and, in no circumstances, is the German will-to-rule, in whatever degree, in whatever form, or in whatever direction it may manifest itself, restricted to the intellectual sphere. It is so, and we do not wish to change it. If there is such a thing for us as universal responsibility we must not repudiate it, because the first thing it demands of us is the sacrifice of our individual power. This responsibility must be with ourselves, based on our abundance, not on some more or less voluntary deficiency. For that would be making a bad virtue of a good necessity. If we examine ourselves as to our possession of extreme possibilities, the momentum is always at both poles.'

'The basis of our life is the land, so that our universality can only be realised imperialistically. Why should we hesitate to express what every one is accusing us of? Nations have their beginnings in the heroic period, the highest they can attain. They come to an end with the abstraction of a world philosophy. If at this moment we believe in a German beginning, we shall act without scruple. We will leave the justification of our actions to life, not to theories about life.'

Ive ceased speaking. Schaffer in his corner of the room did not move. They did not look at each other. Schaffer got up and broke the spell by pouring out a cup of tea for Ive with the utmost cordiality.

When Ive left the house in the early hours of the morning, Schaffer accompanied him down the stairs and, laying his hand on his shoulder, asked:

'What is "German"?'

As he shook hands at parting he asked once more:

'What is "German"?'

XI

THE battle of Neumünster ended with almost complete victory for the farmers. The town, mainly under pressure from the restaurant proprietors and tradespeople, accepted the farmers' conditions, the flag was returned—with ceremony—the police-superintendent was pensioned off, and negotiations were set on foot for paying compensation to the injured farmers. The burgomaster, left in the lurch by his town and no less by his party, owing to the commotion caused by his strictly upright conduct, out of favour with his superiors and his inferiors, faced the consequences and resigned his position. The victory produced no unseemly rejoicing among the farmers. Not that they thought it had been too dearly bought, on the contrary. But, with the capitulation of the town, the farmers had lost a symbolic goal.

It was inevitable that the province in spite of its inherent doggedness, should succumb to the suggestive appeal of the fierce National Socialist propaganda, with its flags, uniforms and route marches, its rough plain-spokenness, and its exaction from every individual of a high degree of personal sacrifice and personal work in the service of the Party. Ive felt that it was necessary to resist this influence. The farmers had the same interest as the National Socialists in destroying the System, but Ive did not want to be subverted into changing his view that, in the long run, it was absolutely necessary for the farmers to make a stand against National Socialism; and he could not see what the farmers would gain by having to fight against what would probably be a very hard system instead of against a soft one. True, he anticipated that the stronger opposition would act as a stronger incentive, but in the end the whole thing was a question of time, and the Movement could not afford to lose time. So he faced the bitter truth that some means had to be found to oppose not only the System but the Movement which was showing itself to be the System's strongest opponent. Unwillingly Ive sought for a compromise; he realised that when it was no longer merely a question of the strength of the Farmers' Movement—and, as things now were, it was impossible to rely on that—it would almost certainly be a losing game. He was accustomed to see things as clear-cut issues, and the thought that victory was not certain had an oppressing and paralysing effect on him. This reduced his zeal for his negotiations in the town, especially as he was in the position of having nothing to offer but everything to ask. He met with a disappointing reception everywhere, and it was no comfort to him that the farmers' leaders who had been sent to South, West, and Central Germany were in the same plight. There were ready listeners enough, but their ears had been attuned again and again to other voices, amongst which the voice of reason, that is of complete perplexity, had a prominent place. Ive felt as though he were slithering through soap suds. The ground he trod, the hands he shook, the words he heard were slippery and unfriendly. When he was not dashing his head against trees overgrown with the ivy of smooth phrases in the forest of self-interest, he was getting entangled in thickets of wordy, ineffectual discussion in the intellectual undergrowth of the town. Even in the most barren soil ideas grew in rank profusion, throwing out strange, alluring blossoms, which filled the paths with their overpowering scents, and twisted themselves into a variegated wreath that could serve no better purpose in the end than to be laid in the grave of a dead hope. The climate of the town seemed to encourage a wild and terrific fertility; unsuspected thoughts took form, displaying at first a strength which seemed capable of lifting the whole world off its hinges, only to quail before the task of drawing a cork from a bottle. The simple recognition of the fact that the world was not sick but drunk gave rise to the highest hopes, flung out a vast abundance of deductions, each one of which, when carried to its logical conclusion, led to the indisputable fact that the world was not sick but drunk.

Ive was lost in this enchanted garden which, after all, he had only entered reluctantly; it was his reluctance which led him astray. He saw so much serious endeavour, so much devout confidence, that he did not dare think that the whole struggling effort was for nothing; he gave heed to wrinkled brows and assurances, which might be true or false, that events were uncontrollable; that, so far as the ultimate success of their cause was concerned, this hardly mattered so long as they had courage—and they had courage. But the fact that they imposed no obligations, that they inspired no virtues, that they laid down no specific laws enjoining a definite and immutable attitude, made them ineffectual. Many of the ideas were in themselves rigid, but they displayed tolerance towards those who asserted that it was possible to be a Communist and have a banking account, or to be a Jew or a police-sergeant and at the same time an adherent of National Socialism. Since the ideas appeared to be self-sufficient, the position one took up hardly mattered. Nothing much really seemed to matter. Ive realised this in regard to himself. Like nearly all those with whom he was living now, he was striving for a rigid scheme, for a more and more exclusive organisation, which would keep every individual at his post, but he was also in favour of the utmost personal freedom. Since he could only think in alternatives, he professed himself on the opposite side of what he was really aiming at, simply because his aim had not yet presented itself in an acceptable form. He could not make up his mind to look for some useful and remunerative occupation. Schaffer had offered to give him introductions— because he was certain that he would only be able to work half-heartedly. He did not join Hinnerk's troop, because he felt himself too much of a soldier to be that kind of a soldier. He joined no party, because even where there were prospects of being more useful to his farmers, he would not be working for his farmers alone. A discontented creature, born of discontented times, he rushed from one problematic theory to another, and here too he had to be on his guard against letting his problematic theory assume the nature of a problem. The complete shattering of the general line of thought, the disintegration of the daily growing army of people, who, flung down from their positions of security, huddled together in masses, whose similarity of party-label could deceive no one as to their lack of cohesion—the colour of this picture, a deadly grey generated from the vibrating whirlpool of black and white; all this led Ive to place the final *denouement* in a remoter and remoter future, while the moment of disruption seemed to approach nearer and nearer.

The more Ive lost touch with the farmers the more difficult he found it to orientate himself in any particular direction. His life and his actions were all makeshifts. On all sides people talked of values—never more—and yet no values were respected. Everything he encountered lent itself to hundreds of interpretations, with the result that it had no meaning at all. He realised to the full how justified was the condescending reproach made against him and his like by wise and sober people with enlightened ideas: that it was a sign of immaturity to construct a valid and durable vision of the world out of the imponderabilities and intangibilities for which he was searching, and which he was turning to account while still barely convinced that he had found them —a sign, so to speak, of a fixation in puberty. Ive was even more severe with himself, repeatedly anathematising all his furious, and occasionally futile, attempts to arrive at a clear and well-founded point of view; at the same time contesting with the wise and sober people the possibility, on their side, of constructing round the dried-up axle-tree of their statistics the glorious structure within whose walls it would alone be possible to live to any purpose. It is true no one denied the great, the infinite synthesis, and it must, therefore, be possible from every point of view to reach it, to arrive at the laws of totality. It was only a question of the way, as people were always fraternally assuring each other, with the result that, in the privacy of his chamber, each one felt that he was the saviour, only to be laughed to scorn when he announced his claim. The fact was that great figures were no longer tolerated. Even the most despised epochs of history were richer than this period in great figures, men around whom the battle raged, who personified a world, for good or ill, lighthouses of the intellectual voyage, ironclad breasts, in whom the blood of their era seethed and boiled, stern minds who, whether in cruel scorn or in deadly earnest acted, even in their decline, as the motive-forces of reality—figures who could be likened to machines roaring at full capacity: but in these days machines could be likened to nothing but themselves. Yet in the world-war, so it was said, flung together by machines and material, men experienced once again the dawn of an era, the passionate certainty of a new destiny. And twelve years after its end the world-war survived in thousands of tons of printed papers, in monuments erected to the memory of millions of unknown soldiers, in the solemn declarations of a hundred and twenty-five black-coated prime ministers, whom nobody took seriously; whilst in the streets of the town brutal guerilla warfare raged, warfare between those who, though fundamentally in agreement, were engaged in a mutual massacre. No great world figure was taken to the scaffold or led out to be shot: because there were no great figures worth martyrdom—who could deny it? Great figures might have ignited the pulverised mass of the world, might have set the gaseous vapours, which hung heavily over the countries, ablaze, to burst in tearing explosions—figures, yes, but not the ghosts and masks which glided unobtrusively through the streets, heroes of the Ufa news-reel, or to be heard from 3.30 to 4.15 on wave-length 1634.9.

To Ive his environment seemed so unreal, he himself seemed so unreal, that often he found himself standing in front of his mirror at midnight in astonishment, feeling his face and his limbs, terrified by the certainty that he really was still there, flesh and muscles, bones and sinews, blood and brain, and not a shadow, although he looked rather blue, not a ghost that would fade away, although he felt like one. In his mind rose memories of moments at the front when, after days and weeks of painful preparation, suddenly the enemy sprang up from the deserted battlefield, men came into view out of the clouds of gas, out of the shadows of the convulsed earth—terrible moments in which all consciousness of time was destroyed, when shattering currents surged through the tensed body, shaking it from head to foot with powerful excitement, when the heart thundered against its walls, until burning expectation was quelled into petrifying reality. He sought for a reflection of that experience in the streets of the town. He sought friend or foe—no matter which—so long as it was a piece of living reality on which his fluttering passion could break and take form, a personality in the midst of the carnival procession of busy, noisy modern men and women, pale underground-railway faces, repressed emotions and fleshless thoughts—an image, arresting, rising up out of the grey town, a guide, silent and challenging, heroic, reassuring by its presence—a human being. He felt, indeed, that this desire was too personal; he asked himself whether he was not trying to escape, whether this was not a sign of treachery, of failure at the test, but he was at such a pitch that he could not face the answer.

When he carried his mind back to the time of his arrest, nothing stood out clearly except the picture of Claus Heim, unbending, in the dim light of his bare cell, and that of a slender figure lying on the ground in the dirty dark street, with a rubber truncheon whirling threateningly over it. Ive did not know who the girl was, but Pareigat had made enquiries and had found her. He came to Ive and told him that she would like him to go and see her. The girl—Ive called her Helene because, as Pareigat said, he saw her in every woman he met—lived in an attic studio with a painter. Helene, who was nearly thirty, came of a well-to-do family. Her father, a distinguished scholar, a pupil of Haeckel and a friend of Ostwald, had died young. Her mother, unequal to managing the family estate, had lost everything except a little house in the country. At sixteen Helene ran away. She eloped with a young man two years older than herself, whom she married. Later on Ive saw a photograph of Helene in her infancy which moved him greatly. She was two years old and was squatting on a chamber-pot—a favourite photographic pose for children in those days, and not only in those days—but she was not squatting as children of that age usually do on such occasions, smiling contentedly in anticipation of fulfilling the salutary function. She was eager, bending forward, her baby forehead puckered, with a dangerous, alert seriousness, obviously determined not to be content with the pose, but actually to do what the photographer certainly was not expecting her to do. This was a child who tolerated no kind of deception, and one could picture her tearing about the garden, long-legged and nimble, filling the house with rapid movement and impatient cries; when she loved, really loving, and when she hated, hating with a wild finality of hatred. The narrow span between hope and danger in which every really young life struggles along, threatened in her case to be snapped at the slightest test. If it be true that all the possibilities of life lie between the two extremes of crime and sanctity, in her case they were only at the poles. She had none of the small secret pleasure in innocent games, in half-dreams, half-experiments. For her a dream was a complete reality, or reality a complete dream, and only in full development could she find security and sanctuary.

Undoubtedly it was Helene who drove her playmate to leave the narrow confines of a garden with her, tore the laggard from his home with stinging words, demanding absolute courage when his half-bold boyish passion kept him hesitant; just as it was she who ended the relationship as soon as she realised it had become untenable.

She was expecting a child by the man whom she could no longer love, whom she could no longer respect, from whom she felt estranged; bound to him only by a memory, which she accepted and acknowledged, but no longer bound by the ardent force which had created the child that was growing within her. So she got rid of it. She did not put herself into the hands of a doctor. In black despair, though fully aware of what she was doing, she went to a woman, whose action, denuded of the hygienic magic of a professional operation, could in no way gloss over the enormity of the crime. She willingly exposed herself to the danger of death, with the desire to destroy in herself something more than the child. In token of this destruction, yielding to a pitiless anarchy, she drove herself on; an insatiable empiricist, content in the strong conviction that she could not fall, but always submitting this conviction to fresh tests of strength; sullied, but purified by excess of pain; she never gave way and could not tolerate the thought of giving way; armed with an unquenchable pride, she set about living where she could live independently. Thus she was never corruptible, embarrassingly exacting, searching beyond and through every circumstance, never forgetting for a moment, in misery or in triumph, that somewhere at her command the complete, the only and the real task was waiting for her. After a wild period of unrest, she found it; she met the painter.

He was sitting in one of those beer-houses where artists and writers meet together, to enjoy from their high altitudes a little colleaguely sociability without too far demeaning themselves. He sat neglected in the midst of the smooth-tongued, quick-witted, elegant crowd, a broad-shouldered, countrified figure, his greying hair straggling untidily over his brow, his dark eyes gleaming through his glasses, a figure of fun, elbowed to one side with light jests, like a dishevelled old owl sitting on a branch, belonging more to the night than to the day. Helene saw him and compared. With timid glances, hunched shoulders, his hands clasped together, resenting yet attracted by her overwhelming presence, he broke through his crust of reserve. He plunged into the conversation, with wild, coarse anecdotes, the impact of his words resounding hollowly; his awkward gaiety rebounded on the chain of quick sentences, a metallic prefiguration of some future subject of his brush. The stories he told in his strong, rolling dialect, seemed to have no point or interest. His listeners were probably laughing more at him than at his words, in their embarrassment encouraging him with a semblance of amusement. Helene listened and compared. The painter, naively delighted, more concerned with his own outbreak than with its effect, went on declaiming in the unfriendly atmosphere, telling his simple stories, revealing a background of wild landscape, interlarded with queer, crude jokes and coarse situations. With rising enjoyment he kept up the flow of macabre anecdotes, the very tone of which was making an abrupt rift in the brilliant net of light conversation. Helene recognised a kinship of blood; recognised, too, the poison in the blood; it drove her to fury against the babbling insolence and the bursts of laughter of these people. She attacked their scorn with a sharp sword, took sides with a violent partisanship that allowed of no more mockery. Incredulous, the painter shrank back into himself. Afterwards Helene found it difficult to get at him, to tear him out of the shell in which he tried to take refuge for fear of exposing himself to her. She forced him to meet her on several occasions and each time he turned up like a timid schoolboy. Eventually she went to live with him in his studio.

The painter came from a little valley in the Black Forest; one of those valleys not yet overshadowed by majestic heights, nestling beneath the spreading highland with its steep gorges and wild, rugged declivities, where the mountains are, as it were, taking breath for their final towering ascent. The little house beside a rushing river, half-way up the mountain-side, where he was born, was the last house of the small town, in whose narrow alleys were collected the outcasts of the forest who had fled from the desperate poverty of the land which had no nutriment to offer them. Grouped round one industry, the handicraft for which the whole district was known, the population kept itself proudly aloof. Though of pure peasant stock it was already completely urban in character. This character, matured and crystallised, scornful of any change, bent to its will those who, strong in the memory of their not-so-distant heritage, found its walls too narrow for their growth and sought perversely to burst their bonds. The seclusion of the valley had nothing to offer to men who, in wanton pride, were discontented with its wealth of natural advantages. Thus the little town acted as an excellent sieve. Only the strongest could force their way through its meshes, and gave it a name for puritanical hardness, while the weaker remnant stayed rooted to the valley like rugged trees spreading out luxuriant branches. Every thought or desire that found its way into the valley from the world behind the mountains, bent in cowardice before the unyielding obstinacy of the townsmen; every power that encroached on the highlands, had to submit to the tyranny of the forest-sweepings. This soil was no doubt favourable to art, but certainly not to an artist, if he imagined that by staying there he would ever be able to pluck laurels from the dark pine branches.

The boy, brought up in direst poverty, travelled in his dreams far beyond the black, wooded mountain walls. It was not the slopes and meadows, not the wild thickets, not river and mountain that led him away from childish games of adventure and conspiracy, in which boldness alternates with timidity, and which, indeed, like the landscape in which they were set, already contained the germs of what later, purified by the incorruptible will of an artist, was to develop into a new reality. Stories of distant wars, bloody battles, heroic risings and massacres, the terrible sufferings of saints in bright robes, the proud majesty of royal courts, the blood-curdling adventures of lonely and noble brigands and highwaymen, and finally the picturesque figures of folklore took form on every sheet of old paper he could find. They were drawn with clear, firm lines, which might later perhaps gain in sureness, but certainly not in liveliness. He did not shine at school, and, entangled as he was in a mesh of passionate fantasies, it was only natural that he should be misunderstood by those around him. The rare occasions on which the safety-valves at the disposal of every child relieved him from the tense oppression of his inner world, only served to teach him to retire more closely into himself. So the seething torrents of his imagination turned against him, torturing his body, mind, and spirit to the point of exhaustion with their wild extravagances. He was sent to the factory as an apprentice and here his obvious talent was given a chance to develop, over a period of nearly four years, in the depiction of artistic designs of delicate flowers and angels' heads on enamel. He attended the polytechnic and copied plaster-casts and stuffed cockatoos from thirty-four angles, and was the butt and scorn of his fellow-students. Finally he went to the School of Art, where his individual gift was cruelly cramped but where he was at least given a start. In the war he was a most inefficient convoy soldier, perpetually in trouble with his N.C.O.s. He went through his training in a state on the precarious borderline between dream and reality. All this gave to his line the acrid bitterness of a pamphleteer indicting God and the world; gave to his palette, in which a glowing metallic red was the dominating colour, its merciless realism; gave to his own world, every disturbance in which beat against the thin glass wall of his consciousness with indescribable violence, the perpetual explosive force, which expressed itself outwardly in frenzied outbursts against all restraint, against all social authority, but inwardly tore up the living soil which fed a rank eroticism—manifesting itself in every kind of abnormality apart from actual perversion—and rent the tissue of living fibres, transforming them into a wild confusion—of morbid phantasmagoria, whose content no theory of psychology could have analysed, for it manifested itself already purified by the medium of the spirit—art.

Nothing was more natural than the protracted outbreak of this force when the shackles inspired by his environment became weaker. The painter was whirled into the midst of the town shaken by revolutionary eruptions, and he rushed into the conflagration where the flames were fiercest. But no aristocrats' heads were borne on pikes through the town, no capitalists' bellies were impaled on lamp-posts bending under their weight; the blood that flowed in the gutters was the blood of soldiers and proletarians. There was no mighty gust of freedom announcing the dawn of a new era, but the stench of the putrefying corpse of an epoch that brought with it destruction even in the process of decomposition. Gradually driven from the storm-centre of the movement, the terror, to its periphery, into the dull domain of braggart bumbledom, of literary sparring on the barricades, his insatiable craving drove him to more and more ardent expressions of his revolutionary will. But the staggering procession of the oppressed and wronged was no more than companionship in misery, unutterably alone in their wretchedness, defrauding him of the sacred import of the solidarity which he served.

In Dadaism, the great farce of artistic exaltation, he was once more exposed to the collective scorn of an unruly coterie. These artists soon tamed themselves to servile entertainment of a public made up of comfortably horrified bourgeois, who, in their amiable attempt to understand, were ready to tolerate the ridiculing of the army and a number of other sacred institutions, or the disgraceful proclamation of the age of machinery in art through the medium of pieces of rag, toothbrushes and horseshoes stuck on to canvases smeared with blobs of paint, but, when confronted with an impudent pictorial criticism by the painter, symbolised by a blaring toy trumpet, of Germany's noblest figure, they rose as one man and left the gallery in a fury, crying: 'Goethe!'

The studio became a den of thieves, a meeting-place for harlots and pimps, criminals and madmen, a night-refuge for persecuted artisans and terrorists, an inferno under the gigantic dusty glass roof, above the grey stone block, crowded with musty, bourgeois activities; and in the midst of the inferno stood the painter working industriously and with painful accuracy at his easel—he was at the next stage by now, Verism, neo-realism—placing his colour with meticulous exactitude, amid a buzz of obscenities and dialectical vapourings, of stormy declamations and arrogant threats, in the stifling exhalations of dust, sweat and filth, himself starving, ragged and devoured by an eternal fire.

Helene came, she saw, and set to work. She set to work, a beacon of passionate protest. She planted the high heels of her dainty shoes firmly on the rotten floor, and, in one whirl, the whole fine company had flown from the temple. She swept, a raging fury, through the wide room suddenly charged with electric currents; screaming women, with dishevelled hair, filled the staircase with their yells; revolver shots resounded; broken china was sent flying; the air was rigid with hissing, biting insults, with rumbles of discontent; in icy, silent fury the men departed from the inhospitable spot. Helene stayed, and brought up all her reserves to establish the victory. She set about it with innumerable pails of clean water which she poured in streams through the room; with scrubbing and sweeping to efface the last traces of the filth; with needle and thread, for missing buttons and torn trousers were not to be tolerated; with paint-pot and brush; with hammer and nails; with epistolary compositions and telephone conversations, addressed to all the relevant authorities, demanding the installation of a lavatory. There was not a moment's respite.

The painter lost the connection which after all had brought him bread and butter, so Helene made his existence secure by her own work. She wrote, translated, acted in films, seized every opportunity with the tenacious grip of her slender hand. She sat upright and taciturn in editorial waiting-rooms; she pushed her way into the narrow corridors of film studios, exposed to the fire of impudent glances, unmoved by the friendly pawing of popular favourites, the sloppy innuendoes of trash-producers. The centre of her thoughts, of her actions, of her burning anxiety, her radiant pride was always the strange man in the studio.

The painter had done his best to resist. In nights of raging anguish, in hours of bitter despair, he rose up again and again in uncontrolled outbursts against the restraint, trembling for the fruitful abundance of his art. Then, overcome by Helene's strong, cruel will, in terrifying eagerness for the amazing gift she had brought him, he would collapse, writhing at her pain, clinging to her steel-strong, wiry body, in frenzied fear lest he should lose for ever this piece of reality which had fallen from heaven, and with it lose himself. Helene did not spare him. Everything that he had painted so far, she declared, was rubbish. She led him round the pictures, pointing out where his work had been corrupted by fashion, or distorted by doctrine, unmercifully tore to shreds, wounding him mortally, with her quick words, anything that did not pass muster in her eyes. But when in abject despair, he already felt the very breath of annihilation about his trembling limbs, it was she who, by a gesture, by a tear, by impetuous surrender, by a startling fulfilment of his wildest dream, gave him such wonderful courage that his inhibitions were swept away, his perplexities solved as if by magic, and all his torments and black doubts stilled and transformed into delight. She did not relax her care for a moment; the struggle continued for three years. Helene, with her finger, as it were, on every sensitive nerve, gave way where she felt a real urge for fulfilment, but dammed with a stranglehold the stream that sought an unworthy outlet; she remained always the one critic who was entirely for or entirely against him.

Time showed that dirt and degradation, confusion and corruption had never fundamentally destroyed the painter. It seemed as though the town had enveloped him like a glass case, under which he had lived alone in his own domain, and that, as soon as the glass case was lifted or broken, the boy from the Black Forest sprang out, stretched his arms and began again from the beginning to live his own life. It was not actually a cure which Helene effected in him, for he was not ill in any respect; it was not a transformation, for the essential in him remained immutable. Helene had known this, and it was this knowledge that had given her the courage, and still gave her the courage, to stake all and, by an indissoluble union, to lead the indomitable spirit, to direct the ebullient force, to impose order upon the elemental urge. If he as an artist was incorruptible, she was equally so as a human being. But now that his liberated creative power was working its way up in bold spirals from its mysterious first principles, the final fusion was consummated. Helene, in order to encourage by example, inspired by her positive will, began to paint herself; and herein lay the test, that she did not paint as he did, nor he as she did, that their very method of attack differed. He visualised things plastically, in speech could only express himself plastically, and the composition of his pictures was graphic; he experimented and sketched in water-colours, but he gave the permanent form of delicate oil-colours to his powerful visions only after a final sublimation. Helene, on the other hand, laid her colours on the canvas broadly with a sure brush, with a faultless sense of composition, and, since she never needed to erase, could do without the skeleton outline of a drawing. Thus this woman was for this man everything at once that a woman can be for a man, and she was inexhaustible.

The painter, who was nearly forty, experienced his renaissance— a renaissance which did not release him from restraints, but only attained its successful development by moderation and direction, so that, exalted, though not diverted from his path, he was enabled unfalteringly to break through the encompassing limitations which had imposed themselves upon him like a layer of skins, the distant goal before his eyes, the goal that was his and Helene's, and which drew ever nearer and shed a clearer and clearer light on the gloomy foreground, nor could he appreciate to the full each stage of this development, with its torturing doubts as with its promise, without the ever-ready second presence.

The first time that Ive visited the studio he found Helene, her face smeared with paint, sitting motionless in a state of rigid, strained absorption at her easel in the middle of the room, with two large cats beside her, while the painter, quill in hand, was standing wrapped in his white coat, bent over a large sheet of paper. The only audible sound was the scratch of his pen.

When Ive came again, and he came often, so often that it became evident how much he was in need of an environment that brought peace with it, the same sight met his eyes.

For the first time since he had been in the town he had found people whose whole life, in form and direction, developed from an invisible central point, enclosing every temporal event within a circle, where alone it could be subdued and all true strength allowed full sway. It was Helene who insisted on a dramatic seclusion which was always shattering the abundantly productive temperament of the painter and calling it into question, so that the internal conflict perpetually enlarged the circle. Eloquent testimony of this struggle was given by the pictures on the walls of the studio and in the portfolios on the table.

Ive's life had been completely uninfluenced by any form of art—his musical education had been very casual and entirely restricted to the mechanical side—in literature he had had to be content to pick up, eagerly but without any plan, whatever chance brought his way; in the years of development, the most favourable time for enriching the mind with knowledge, like many of his kind, he had been knocking about in the mud of the trenches and had never been able to seek his pleasure in books, theatres, or concerts. And it was with full consciousness of his limitations that he stood in front of the pictures. Yet he could not regard them in silence. Often enough, under stress of emotion, he had quite naturally allowed himself to be led into the mild deceit of speaking in *terminis technicis*. Yet it only made him feel an impulse to sincerity when he saw the painful twitching of the painter's mouth, such as a hunter might be unable to control, if a harmless pedestrian told him that he had seen an antlered stag grazing on the edge of the wood, and that it had fled at the sight of him. In fact Ive, whose first intimate contact with the sacred art had come so late, could not give himself up to a pure visual enjoyment, looking rather for the strange, involved paths, the spiritual undercurrents. After all, he was himself finding his way, and had laboriously to work towards everything that seemed to him to be attainable, encouraged merely by the pleasure of observing the governing laws more closely as they joined issue with his will.

At first Ive's untrained eye could see no chronological stages of evolution in the pictures, nor any path of development. Overwhelmed by the flood of impressions, he registered his reactions by a naive reference to his own experience, thinking back and forward, and realising the parallelism of fate, by which he saw here in pictorial representation what he himself only ventured to think. Before these pictures his shyness of everything personal evaporated, from them he derived for himself the succinct dictum that every human being should be an artist, since everything could become a fine art, if one could only isolate oneself from the vulgarity for which 'mediocrity had become complete nature.' The importance of politics as a statecraft was confirmed for him, with its immense vistas of responsibility, all-embracing and by its multiplication of difficulties creating an infinite progression of power. He experienced once again, and this time in images perceptible to the senses, the satisfying certainty that the same laws applied everywhere, springing from the same invisible, fertile soil, animated by the same supernatural, creative force, for which even the highest form must remain a fragment, even classical perfection no more than a mountain boulder polished by storm and wind, a monument of transfiguring nature, beneath whose icy shadow man's restless spirit cannot bear to linger, although he must recoil from the sight of busy hands working persistently to injure the resplendent beauty. Thus the highest achievement can only be attained by him who has seen the shining goal rising high above it—by the violent dreamer. Ive had always felt the attraction of this type of genius. Confronted now by the work of his new friend, it is true, he at first recoiled in horror. But the insistent delight of being able to absorb, as it were, in a well-cooked morsel what in its raw state so much in his nature refused to swallow, drove him on with palpitating eagerness, and, if the desire to pass the test of Helene's exacting judgment was great, still greater was the urge to fortify his own attitudes of defiance; and his increasing enthusiasm was genuine.

Ive knew nothing about the painter except that he had been an active Communist, and his first impression of him had been of a good-natured, introspective Bohemian, with an awkward, disarming smile, whose feelings he would not have hurt for the world. He had feared when he visited the studio that he would encounter a modernised dusty museum atmosphere, but this was by no means the case. At once he realised how much the pictures on the walls appealed to his deepest feelings, and when the painter opened the portfolios for him and brought the canvases down from the gallery, and, as he himself by repeated effort—which soon lost the character of effort, developing rather into the finding of a haven—became more familiar with the strange, mysterious world full of stimulating demands, he found that his interest was completely absorbed. Actually it was amazing that the daemonic revolt, which actuated every one of the artist's strokes, should still have had a message for those who had long ago conquered and subdued the forces of heaven and hell, but who believed that the creations of the imagination had to be accepted because they fitted in with their social theories. Helene pointed out the unworthiness of this attitude, in order to free the painter from his ideological fetters, and she succeeded, not so much because his pride was offended, but because he realised that the roots of his art were already shrivelling in this soil; for to divorce life from the soul signified divorcing it also from the noblest instrument of the soul.

The painter had become known through his caricatures, through the shavings of his work as it were, which he only published against his will, through drawings which it was hard labour for him to produce, and which through their merciless realism renounced their claim to be caricatures. Ive's laughter was arrested when he saw those grotesque figures, grotesque figures which none the less were those he met at every turn, whom he knew to be the authorities and masters of the world, and who in these drawings, it seemed to him, were attacked not for their grotesqueness but for their virtues, in spite of the glamour they might think these lent them. These drawings were disconcerting because they did not signify so much an accusation as the objective acknowledgment of an actual state of affairs. And to Ive's searching questioning the answer came that the painter's daemonic power lay in the fact that he could still see apocalyptic visions in the clash of sheer greed with violent claims, and so did not express himself in a cheap anarchism but showed the possibility of a higher order, as much as to say, without this nothing would be left for a noble man but to shoot himself. Thus the theme and scene did not give to the drawings so much an arresting hardness and devastating effect, as the cold defeat of a life, which, in the brutal self-laceration of a soul which could never find satisfaction, had become the battle-field in which legions of spirits were let loose for a struggle to the death—spirits precipitated from the clouds and rising up from the mire, to drive the world to fear and horror, to impulse and counter-impulse, to growth and destruction; the laughter of hell and the trumpet blasts of heaven; a life, expressed in dramatic lyrics, which places defeat before victory and puts faith in no security which is not attuned in this way. The presentation, as though etched on ice, of the massacre of the Bethlehemite children by Herod's Roman soldiers obviously pointed to the conclusion that it was not wild bloodthirstiness, but pure professional zeal which led the Prussian police to shoot down men, women, and children like rabbits in the proletarian quarters of the town; thus in limitation was shown the wide range of human possibilities, the degree of insensibility which seems to be necessary in order to be able to function in the outworks of a rigid order when behind all the battlements the demons are lurking ready to hurl themselves through the gaping cracks into the ethereal spaces of defeated discipline, the first heralds proclaiming to terrified satiety the beginning of a new era. None of that suspect deceitfulness which gives to the poor man the halo of a new hero, which he is not able to bear; but the naked ugliness of crime with its annihilating demands, the pitiable desire to imitate glory, the barren hopelessness of a position in which courage has flagged, which brings disgrace to him who succumbs to it, and disgrace to him who tolerates its existence. What a fatal mistake, what madness, still to seek order in the inferno of times that are out of joint, of a world whose foul breath stinks, which makes a parade of its sores, proud of its misuse of the healthy blood-stream, allowing it to flow through the decaying tissues, until it emerges as putrefying matter from a scabrous skin; of a world of the pavements with its rustling harlots, who remain harlots, however much they may assume the pompous poses of the bourgeoisie, with their fancy-men from filmland, the Press and finance, with cheap politicians, knights of the bridge-tournament, heroes of the American bar, braggarts of public order, a world of slime, with its leading articles and short stories, its revues and sessions, its Riviera films and State ceremonies, its governmental decrees and its cooked balancesheets. But only a superficial world by the mercy of God. For where would be any hope, except in the certainty that even the crudest actors on the limelit stage, the nightfigures of the gutter, the exhausted bodies on the tops of omnibuses, the apoplectic masses of flesh outside the little hells, that the whole carnival procession spewed out on to the streets from every door and entrance, is the plaything of an untameable force, tossed hither and thither by dark menacing forces, exposed and surrendered, torn between the choice of being the salt of the earth, or dust and ashes, whipped on by the all-powerful will which knocks at every door, surrounded by breakers like an island in the midst of the sea? Where would there be any hope, if not in the torment of icy desolation, in the raging battle of the hosts of spirits in one's own breast, which come whirling up out of mythical abysses, where the noble spark of life has not yet been extinguished by petty, spurious activities? Where would there be any hope, if not in life itself, in whatever direction it may be driving, in busy market-places, in grey factories, in machine-rooms and offices, in palatial restaurants and in starving slums, in the confines of museums, or in scientific laboratories, in ornate churches or in the barren, neutral ground of dull sophistry? When men are silent, the stones speak, and not only they. Bush and field, forest and mountain and water bear witness; from rugged chasms it creeps unwaveringly up the steep precipices, in a wild, rank vegetation from dark damp grey to deepest green; the last rooty tentacles cling to the brown rock, which, worn smooth by the rushing water, and shattered by its hurtling fall, buries its jagged corners in the bosom of the earth, overgrown with a brilliant coat of moss, holding in its dainty network milliards of glittering dewdrops, bearing nourishment for the mighty upward striving stem, and a death potion for the putrefying wood. The tree trunks stand pale in the dark, towering forest, are flung down by the wind that sweeps round the summits of the mountains, falling at last into the valley washed by the loamy stream; the black, crumbling earth of the slope tears at their roots until they bend, their swaying, shivering branches entangled in the foliage of their neighbours falling with them, catching and thrusting, resisting and breaking away; the tenacious thin tendrils climb up with choking stranglehold, hosts of pallid fungi block up the pores and cracks of the bark, the scabrous skin falls off in shreds, the pale bones gleam nakedly, while thousands of seeds in their hard cases batter clamourously on the earth. It is not the Pan of the dark olivegroves fanned by soft warm breezes who is man's opponent here, but the great adversary himself. He lets the bleeding wounds of the trees heal up into lewd swellings, from which sap oozes through capillaries and crumbling bark; he tempts the simple mind with dreams of fantastic lust; with magic spells he transforms the swelling wood into voluptuous flesh, whose cries for love re-echo through the forest; he fills bush and thicket with ardent, grotesque gestures, and the light clearing with dancing shadows, the marsh with torchlights of nocturnal orgies. He chases through the narrow glades, which gleam in the dark shadows beneath the light of the blue sky, on scurrying, spindle legs, seizing the fugitive by the neck; his clammy breath is exhaled from rock and crevasse; in poisonous vapours he hovers over the sleeping chaos, cracking his joints in the terrifying silence. With his chuckles he scares the leaves out of their hiding-places, creeps through the ruins over the broad, crumbling ramparts and battlements, where vaults and pillars are slowly being smothered by the living dark green curtain; he pushes his way maliciously in among the decaying nests, casts a spell on the angry hum, the scurrying horror and fright of the insect world, he sates his devouring appetite on the mountain slopes until they are bare, until their plucked skin hangs in grey strands about their wrinkled heads; he raises his voice in the rumbling laughter of the storm, sends his bolts howling down upon the shrieking earth, batters the bushes, rends the trees, destroys the fields with hail, lashes fear into rage, until a last cry is forced from its strangled throat, beating rattlingly against the tightened skins of delirium.

From these forests the hordes rushed out, pouring through the valleys, filling the plains with their wild horn blasts, with their shrill battle cries; scaled the smooth sides of the mountains, carrying their spears into the distant, glittering towns, to burn and rob, to fight and fall, to set fire to the proud facades of royal palaces, of stately temples, to the abodes of sparkling, seductive wealth. In these valleys men strode in white cowls, staff in hand; they erected the bulwarks of the planning spirit, sacred galleries and spacious barns, gay paths and gardens; ploughed and dug and garnered their tithes; exorcised with the peal of happy bells, with tender music and rare scents; burned witches and sorcerers, to save their souls. In these mountains and hollows noble figures lived in solitude, sanctified by hard superhuman renunciation, completely absorbed in the service of the all-embracing spirit; writhed in shuddering agony before the visions impudently enticing them with loud lustful laughter from cleft and cave, with obscene bestial gestures—hairy, horned creatures, with swollen bellies, springing breasts, and lascivious lusts; and in their last trembling prayers they conquered them through self-renunciation.

The forest is still there, the smiling valleys, the towering mountains, the yawning, clammy caves; but on the dusty roads are heard the clattering explosions of benzene-oil driving the wheels with the whirring sound of good steel to rapider revolutions; the detonations of blasting operations resound in the mountains as great blocks of stone are torn out of their sides, split into slabs, broken up, ground down, to make building materials for houses and factories, rubble-stone, grey concrete; the tree-trunks roll down into the valley with a wide sweep, axes crash into the trembling wood, deft knives scale off the brown bark, saws grind, cutting the trunks into boards, planks, ship frames, mouldings, wood-blocks for pavements; machines grind and mash the wood into pulp, press and mill the seething mass into cheque-books and newspaper; rails are laid along the mountain-side, tall factories stand in the valley, the smoke of their chimneys rising straight into the air, and in the cool cloisters of the monasteries tourists wander armed with cameras; sharp-nosed spinsters stand, haughty and frigid, round the guide, looking with alien, inimical eyes at the stone vaults of proud abbots, at the gloomy cells, the dim refectory, all that is left of the strict order with its nightly prayers and daily penances, while outside the hotel the charabancs with their shiny leather seats wait in the grilling midday heat.

The same mysterious power which sent its zealous, fearless messengers to demolish the religious monuments in the pagan woods, and to fell the sacred trees, which destroyed the helpless superstition which endeavoured to form an alliance with the spirits instead of subjugating them to service and order; the same power which drove the monasteries, the abodes of militant peace, further and further forward into the threatening land, which in the towns enabled faith to establish itself in churches and cathedrals raising their spires to heaven to the glory of God and as a sanctuary from affliction, sheltering the habitations of men beneath their beneficent shadow, enabled a reign of glory to be established, enabled passionate lust to be quelled, united the conflicting forces by its guiding hand; this same power stood now in the centres of the hybrid world, and not only there, in bitter, rankling, almost hopeless, defence against the encroaching forces of an age which had withdrawn itself from her in wanton pride, its only security in the promise that the portals of hell would not overpower it. In those times when a gleam of happy certainty, of indestructible faith, was still to be seen on the most clerical face, no object left the workshop that a master had not carefully moulded to his ends, making the end itself subservient to the unity of a great purpose, had moulded artistically, in the endeavour to give the object the full dignity of worthy service, that is, had subdued through art, something that was spiritually striving beyond goal and service to fulfil itself, whether it were pot or pan, house or merchandise, implement or ornament. But with the emancipation of the temporal spirit from its ordering force—a process which began within the realm of this force—of necessity everything was emancipated; individuals as well as objects, together and apart, strove, with no limit save that set by the persistent struggle, to develop themselves to the utmost, regardless of the general balance, of that wise selectiveness, which for the truly religious soul must signify earthly redemption. The creature that nature has liberated, in his freedom scorns the hand that fashioned him and would guide him. He subjugates with a stronger and more bitter tyranny than the brain of man could ever conceive the life in the midst of which he is raised to the absolute. Ignorant of worth, the first principle of order, he lives eagerly absorbed in his own needs, the quantitative needs of a mechanical being; ignorant of the royal pride of power in the exercise of his blind strength. Like the adversary, the great ape of God, who secretly takes on every form, in order to establish his kingdom in every sphere, to make man the ape of man, and his work an apish imitation, the mechanical being approaches with the old clumsy trick, offering himself as a complaisant ally in spheres where he intends to have complete sway, until, with all the trump cards in his hands, he can place himself in the position of full power and exercise full power over men. Thus, in the light of an order that accepts quantity rather than quality as its principle, in the light of a law that reduces the diversity of creation to the dull formula of cause and effect, he was, indeed, able by his pretence of independence to change the face of this earth, to the very last wrinkle, into a mask that barely hides the devouring monster behind it. In this world every opposition is bound to develop into a struggle between daemonic unities, into a hopeless struggle for man, so long as he fails to make use of the special intelligence which distinguishes him among all other creatures; for until this moment of reflection, the only decisive factor can be, which unity has the greatest reserves to call upon, and there can scarcely be a doubt as to the answer: not man. In fact, he surrendered long ago, delivered himself up with the leverage which he celebrated as the act of his regeneration, and which indeed freed him from all bonds, and not only himself, but that which he thought to be a means, since he himself was a means, and had become an end in itself, because he had set himself as a goal. Now having become absolute again he was confronted by that which had become absolute again, and though there may be a biological limit to his development, what limit can be set to mechanical forces?

They overpower him with their will to augment, which exacts of capital that it shall yield interest and compound interest, of labour a multiplication of labour, which does not allow an invention which increases capacity threefold to mean a threefold lightening of labour, but a threefold increase of tempo, and the threefold increase of tempo again a threefold capacity, sucking every living thing into the maelstrom of production, only to spew it out again as a makeshift, subject to no force, so long as there are voices to murmur that economy is fate. Thus the time is at hand for a new order to be built up, which, possessed of the hierarchical secret, shall renew the struggle and claim the cooperation of every kindred spirit. The time is ripe and why should it not be the artist who is the first to realise its ripeness?

From the dregs of the gutter whose faces, distorted with the crazy fear of brutality, bore witness and gave warning, the eye turned to the bleeding, martyred Christ upon the Cross. But this was not the figure of a patient sufferer, the only one that the faithful seemed able to tolerate now, not the gentle, pale countenance that hangs over the poor-boxes in the church, or gazes in mild protest from the embroidered hangings of the altars, not that anaemic Saviour who, if he were to come to earth again now, would not be led before any high tribunal, before a Pontius Pilate, but before Dr. Sauerbogen, Officer of Health; would not be condemned to death on the cross, but would be housed for life in the Buch Sanatorium. This was the terrible face of one in the last torturing agony, who, with full understanding of the world, and full knowledge of the will of God, realises that more is being rent in him than muscles and sinews, full of an even deeper pain than that which is forcing open his dying eyes, and drawing blood and sweat in viscous drops from his greenish, sagging skin.

Ive stood in front of this picture, struck dumb as in the breathless interval between lightning flash and thunderclap. Once again it was not so much the power of the picture which put him on the defensive, but the seemingly irresistible urge which had led to just this final sublimation. To Pareigat it seemed quite natural. To him it was a confirmation of his own intellectual processes and, whether it was the experience of objective 'being' which led through ontology to this result, or whether it was the experience of the devil through the unruly flesh—it was only a difference of medium; but Ive felt that he did not possess a single theory which seemed to fit in with this. Therefore he shrank from the sudden solution, which denoted a retrogression for him and, even if this retrogression was a new beginning, it was one which demanded a new situation. This situation had yet to be created, and it was only possible to create it against the opposition not only of the historically founded world, but also against the opposition of the Church, itself historically founded in this world. Not that the task—and that was his first consideration—would have taxed him too greatly, but it extended over too great an expanse of time for him and he had not a moment to spare. He realised vaguely that this was no valid reason for shirking; he knew that this solution, even though it had presented itself as the only answer to the most powerful spiritual demand, could at this moment be no more than a personal solution and that his shrinking from a personal solution, for the very reason that it was so firmly rooted in his character, was eventually of a strongly egotistical nature, and arose from an arrogance which would break down under this solution—but this arrogance was his most characteristic strength. He knew, too, that, even though his ears might be open to every appeal, they could not listen to this appeal, which was resounding so loudly through his being, because its voice was already cracked; he knew that he could not follow this challenge, because he bore within him the heritage of a perpetual protest, which, even when subjugated to the laws of the ordering power, had never forgotten its own unfulfilled, all-embracing claim to recognition, and was now, after all the assaults, preparing itself for the last assault, he knew that the one thing that would be shirking would be to repudiate his obligations towards this heritage. He realised this vaguely, and he was filled with a fantastic fear that, since the violence of the artistic creed demanded of him a clear 'Yes' or 'No,' his 'No' would make a deep gulf between him and the noble, vitalising delight in a newly-born emotion which was fuller and purer than any he had ever experienced. So, spurred on by dreams of an intimate union, he tried to make a sacrifice of his 'No' and to avoid the shame of only being able to offer a vague, stammering justification of it; tried to enter the world of his friends, to enrich himself and them and at last to find the bridge which meant not only a personal union but also—far beneath the surface of visible endeavour, though on this plane indeed the results were clear and beneficent—a *rapprochement* between the opposing kingdoms. This was all the easier for him since Helene and the painter, themselves dynamic characters like Ive, like him too were standing in the light of a new adventure, so that the field which but now they had seen swathed in darkness was illumined by the dazzling beacons of an almost inexhaustible number of possibilities, every one of which had to be explored because every one promised to provide an essential part of fulfilment. Thus it seemed to Ive that it could not matter from what base the attack was launched, provided he was able to enter upon it armed with the weapons of his own reservations. In actual fact, they had very much in common. When their paths seemed about to diverge they forced themselves, in bitter discussions lasting all through the night, to formulate their aims precisely, weighing every admission and rejection and, if Ive followed his friends, it was not that their influence was so strong that he was obliged to follow them, but because he felt he could no longer do without the benison of their austere strength. Daily he was forced to find himself anew; he was so much enriched that he sometimes discovered himself indulging in the cold, malignant delight of the growing certainty that at last he would be able to measure swords with them, and he was horrified at the treachery that lurks, like an animal ready to spring, in every surrender that is not spontaneous. But to scare away this enemy he needed the presence of Helene more and more, and he gradually found himself in an entanglement which he could not bring himself to give up for fear of what he might lose besides. For the one means of relieving oneself of a burden, the confessional, which was open to the artist, was not open to him. Nor was it open to Helene.

On the day that Ive had seen Helene sitting so depressed in front of her easel, the Church had refused to receive her and to allow her to make her first Communion. It was she who had removed the sheltering glass case from the artist, and had thus prepared him for his abundant and fruitful development; with the flame of her pure will she had melted down their common stock of opinions and conceptions to the indestructible core of a faith which had suddenly revealed itself to their delighted perceptions as the one all-embracing faith—Catholicism. Yet on her the door was to be closed, the door to which she had found the way for herself and the painter. For him, a baptized Catholic, the painful period of preparation, into which she had thrown herself with wholehearted devotion, could be crowned by the simple act of confession; the simple act asked of her was to renounce the reward of the task in the fulfilment of which she had seen the whole meaning of her life.

At the last moment the barrier had been raised; half an hour before her reception, the fact that she had almost forgotten, and from which she had mercilessly tried to purge herself—her previous marriage and divorce—stood as an obstacle in her path. Her marriage to the painter was not valid according to the strict law of the Church. She respected the law of the Church, how could she have done otherwise?

Ive could not understand. He could not understand the strange submission with which she accepted that which, in one way or another, would destroy her.

She had found her way alone; no priest had guided her; no means of grace had given her strength; no word of intercession had been said for her. And the reply of the Church was: *non possumus*. The reply came through the lips of a young chaplain, a smiling boy, who confronted her and defended the glorious and powerful structure in which no rifts could be made; and Helene acknowledged this. Her first marriage was no longer valid to her, but in the eyes of the Church it was. She had never been married in a church, but once in its history the Church had given way and recognised marriage by the law of nature as marriage, and in the result this seeming inconsistency had tightened the bonds, enlarged its sphere, and lent a greater invisible strength to its enveloping power; and Helene acknowledged this. Her Catholicism was of an essentially different character from the musty, old women's consolation preached from the pulpits, of an entirely different character, too, from that of all the worldly-wise associations, congregations, guilds and parties, and of a different character again from that of enlightened youth who began by enthusiastic aspirations and demands for reform, then, mildly subjecting itself to discipline and guidance, settled down to the task of throwing new light upon the liturgy. Hers was a militant Catholicism, imposing rigid rules upon herself, and the world almost medieval in its uncompromising exactions, subjecting every smallest action to its binding laws, a lonely individual Catholicism, whose eager questioning the priests could only counter with dogma from which they derived authority for their prohibitions or reassurances; since they were rendered somewhat helpless by this onslaught of burning, stormy faith, before which Benedictine, Jesuit, and most certainly modern methods, arguments and definitions had to give way. Yet it was a faith which undoubtedly arose from a sincere need intolerant of any substitute. Indeed, so great was this need that Helene felt she could not bear to be excluded from participation in the sacraments. Once she had realised the significance of the Rule, which seemed to her to be the only one conceivable and indeed essential, she wanted to take a full share in it, to be, as it were, at the focal point of the rays, in the midst of the heavenly fire, in absolute enjoyment of the daily, eternal miracle of transubstantiation, which became possible and endurable only through this Rule. For her the Church was no longer a sanctuary but the holy land of her fathers, exclusion from which meant the Ahasuerian torment of banishment, which sees its love flung into the Void. Thus she could only regard as a horror every form of Christian culture, which out of the single phenomenon of the Reformation established a permanent act of apostasy, tearing the living flesh from the indivisible Church; by its attack on the whole sanctity of the altar menaced the very foundations of the Rule, and confined all the deeper emotions of faith within the frigid limitations of literal expositions, and so in its very cradle nourished the serpents which were later to poison the whole world with their venom. She could only regard as an abomination that cold, intellectual quibbling, which spreads itself in admiration of the wonderful power, organised to the very last pillar, without completely acknowledging it, but rather looking down with smiling condescension from the high watch-tower of modern objectivity, claiming to be more popish than the Pope. She regarded as an offence that stupid narrow-mindedness which has established itself within the Church itself, and has gradually filled the dome to its highest arches with its befogging vapours.

To Ive it seemed that the danger Helene was running was of becoming a horror, an abomination and an offence to herself. For, whatever she might do, the results counteracted each other; the mere possibility of being admitted to the sacraments not only separated her from her husband, but must of necessity destroy the sacred impulse which had driven her to knock at the door of the Church asking admittance for him as well as for herself, must, by its destruction of her work, at the same time destroy the Catholic spirit of her marriage. The priests whom she visited, who came smiling to the studio—and looked at the painter's pictures in silence—probably realised this with sympathetic regret, and anxious to console, directed Helene to the infinite mercy of Heaven, since the Church could not intercede for her, assigning to her the task, already self-appointed, of carrying the torch of her faith into the outer darkness and handing it on to those who sought the guidance of her light. The strength for this she was to find in prayer.

Helene, whose daily life was made up of the soul-destroying hack work, with which she had burdened herself in order to provide the bare necessities of life, managed to find time in a day in which every minute had its task, between art-dealers and film-studios, between cooking and washing and typing, to visit the bare parish church which stood in the ugly quarter of the town surrounded by grey houses with crumbling facades and poverty-stricken cellars and shops. Ive frequently went with her. There she prostrated herself, rather than knelt, on the cold and dirty stone floor, while Ive stood behind her. At first he was oppressed by the almost audible silence, and by shame at having only hypocritically dipped his fingers in the holy water. Then he was overcome by warm, sorrowful sympathy for the kneeling girl, and finally with eyes fixed in concentrated reasoning with himself he would fall into an empty trance.

He examined himself and found that nothing that had the remotest resemblance to devotion could move him. He forced himself to pray, and was alarmed at the meaningless repetition of a formula which, in spite of the sonorous cadence of the words, touched no chord in him. He tortured himself with contemplation of the Catholic Rule, which he could appreciate intellectually, and the objections to which could so easily be explained away, and which could remove the picture of the lacerated world to a dazzling perspective; and yet he felt that almost before he was aware of them, the refreshing waters had dispersed and anything that reached him only dropped into emptiness. No power seized him and forced him to his knees on the stone flags, no divine presence made him bow his head. The fear grew in him that he was an outcast, that the sense of holiness, all religious feelings were withered in him and that, therefore, his search for the meaning of things was merely a cowardly flight from reality, from the persistent demands of everyday; that, therefore he had no right to any other creed than that which the canaille daily spewed out in stinking spurts. But he was saved by the conviction that he was capable of fulfilling his pledge; that other bells rang in his ears with a message of certain hope; that there was in him the vision of another kingdom, pointing the way and importuning for fulfilment. And he told himself, so long as the vision continued to drive him forward to prostrate himself in the dust, as Helene did in the fervour of her faith, for him could only be the outward and visible sign that he was beginning to yield to a terrible mistake. He was almost pleased that the net of temptation was so widely meshed; that it lacked the final appeal that sets the heart aflame. He had heard this appeal in the past; it had burnt its way into his heart when he was on sentry-duty in the war; in the narrow streets of the Ruhr district it had sounded above the shrill note of the clarion; it had come to him from the farms of the Marsh and from the cellars of the town. But now he could hear nothing but the murmur of prayer, the sound of which filled him with shame, as though he had intruded into another's quiet and private sanctuary. But he said nothing of all this to Helene as yet, and when they stepped out of the dim nave of the church into the bright light of the square he did not dare to look at her.

XII

THE attitude of the public towards the painter showed plainly that Communism had become the fashion. The chief characteristic of the *élite* among the agitated elements in the town—referred to by the newspapers as the intelligentsia— was their capacity to accept any theory which had any bearing on their own particular activities, even if it was directed against themselves—which, of course, destroyed its original purpose. But they were incapable of accepting any point of view based on hypotheses alien to their own conceptions; indeed, they could hardly understand it so they ignored it. They ignored it even in the departments of life on which they depended for their existence: the powerful labour organisation of the town remained anonymous; the neighbouring country district, which catered for the town, remained anonymous, its principle of life an equation made up of unknown quantities. Indeed, it might often have been supposed that the town actually consisted of nothing but the Movement, that it had neither tradition nor any permanent cultural standard applicable to the present day. On the other hand, it seemed probable that it had a future of abundant promise, and that in its function, at any rate, it was completely independent of the aspirations of Klein-Dittersbach bei Bohlau. But when these aspirations began to be fomented, and their vile odours assailed the nostrils of the town, and were visibly smouldering within its borders, the town became transformed, as it were, into a great fortress of mourning against which the lamentations resounded hideously, whilst the only qualified spiritual guardians, as helpless as though confronted by a convulsion of nature, deserted their posts until the storm seemed to have abated, and then climbed up happily again to their old vantage points, and continued in the same old strain— a triumph of vitality, if nothing else.

The *élite* of the town was very modern, but the town itself was by no means modern, merely old and ugly and traditionally sound, like a mighty building of blackened grey stone, within which there was an activity as incessant as the electric current in the illuminated sign attached to its facade. Every one could see the illuminated sign; and the widespread sooty-red glow in the sky, shining over the centre of the town at night, might well make men's hearts swell with pride. But it required a very special incentive to make them penetrate into the hard and dusty activity within the building—for instance, to provide the symphony of self adulation with an industrious, rumbling bass. Indeed, it seemed as though some acquaintance with events beneath the surface was actually indispensable. It served, so to speak, as the fundamental and natural basis for their ideas, provided the material for dealing with social, economic and technical problems—indeed, by degrees the value of a thesis came to depend upon the quantity of material in it. A reporting style became the artistic ambition of every professional writer. Bare facts were as far as possible to speak for themselves. Thus the opinion of the man in the street was worth probing. The mere act of visiting a goods station, a market-place or a public-house provided their simple minds with a gratifying fund of new ideas. Reporters of every degree, up to members of the Academy of Poetry, found that they could learn about life, in its depths and heights, in a conveniently concentrated form by visiting the police courts, or by spending half an hour at a Labour Exchange, in an iron foundry or a doss-house; and they never forgot in the midst of their stylised prose from time to time to break into the idiom of the people, not so much with the idea of giving local colour, as in order to demonstrate that they actually had penetrated into the quarters of misery and grinding toil, excursions which undoubtedly bore the character of somewhat dangerous sallies. It was absolutely necessary to pay several visits to the district behind the police court in order to be able to talk about things at all, and the exultant satisfaction of having done their duty amply compensated for the painful shame they felt, after spending a gay evening in full regalia, at a chance encounter with the sinister tin-can battalions of labour. These useful exertions produced a comfortable atmosphere of tolerance towards every kind of social conviction. There was no circle in which Radicalism gave offence; it even guaranteed a modest livelihood; it had become a social quality, almost a necessity, and some well-known Communist or another was always to be met in the most exclusive salons, provided that his red was not too deep-dyed, and was displayed in conjunction with dirty fingernails. Nevertheless, there were many indications that the emblem of the hammer and sickle would soon be outshone by the newly rising Swastika. For, when all was said and done, the resonance of revolutionary declamations was due merely to the general readiness to be disconcerted by no form of truth, and this praiseworthy tendency in no wise meant that one need suppress a slight yawn when listening to the fearless exposition of stale facts or the determined demonstration of rather worn-out arguments; nor did it mean that the reaction to biting criticisms of social injustices in bourgeois society, or to gloomy prophecies delivered with noble earnestness need be anything more than a gentle and, on the whole, not unpleasant titillation. Thus even the unveiled threat of sometime or another abolishing private property no longer held any terror, for everyone knew that capitalism itself was slowly but surely accomplishing this task, and even the bold cry: 'First fill your bellies and then moralise,' did not so much arouse interest as the proclamation of an amazing new doctrine, but gained its sensational importance from the crude and brutal expression of what was common knowledge, and from the uncertainty as to who exactly it was who was going to be fleeced.

But the amazing progress of the National Socialists was attended with much greater excitement. In this there was nothing plain and straightforward, nothing that could be taken for granted; behind every word and every gesture lay a wide field for conjecture, and lurking behind its melodramatic presentation there might just as easily be the warm breath of a newly dawning world, as the cold calculations of beneficent iconoclasts; in any case, there was probably a new attraction in being able to introduce, instead of a youth in horn-rimmed spectacles from Hungary, Poland or Romania, a real live *Feme* murderer; and if previously ambitions had been centred in not being outdone by anyone in the subtleties of social conscience, the competition now was as to who could declare with justice that his was the truly nationalist point of view.

When the rumour spread that the painter had broken away from the Communists, the obvious assumption was, and why not, that he had become a nationalist, and nothing could have given more pain than the news that his defection was not of this order. There was nothing to do but to shrug their shoulders regretfully over the fall of this eccentric and drop the subject.

The painter had suddenly lost his market; not that there was any visible change in his pictures—he had never exhibited his religious subjects—but it was enough to have heard the rumour that the painter had given voice to opinions remote from every bourgeois standard, for him and his art to be considered completely outside the pale. For no matter what political colour the bourgeoisie might assume, they were still the bourgeoisie and remained susceptible to any intellectual arrogance which regarded them as a questionable phenomenon. Any attempt to establish a hierarchical rule of life was bound to rouse their bitterness, for, in that event, what would become, if you please, of Mr. Meyer, third attorney of the Central Assizes? But the Church had long since renounced her high position of task-mistress, and when she considered herself compelled to pay tribute to any form of modernity, it went very hard with her. The tame mechanical mind, the product of Benedictine teaching, seemed to be the utmost the Church could tolerate. Squeezed in between the forces of the secularised world, she had had to surrender her right to take the first step in any department, although she seldom failed to be second in the field.

Thus the painter found himself completely isolated in an almost hopeless struggle for existence. Ive observed this with a bitterness which sometimes made him regret that his friend had made such an abrupt and irreparable break with his former associates. Certainly, with the general and rapid deterioration of economic conditions, the prospects for art in any direction were meagre. It was this complete break-up of all professional organisation that made Ive feel that it would be a good thing to be at least in some active correlation to one of the rebel groups, whatever the future outcome might be. He had come more and more to despise political theories—and politics after all had become the articulate expression of life. He had no objection on principle, therefore, against an attempt—a temptation which often presented itself to him—to come to terms with Communism, or with any other form of revolt, if such a step had seemed to offer any immediate, or even more distant, prospect of good results. But his encounters with, the more or less approved representatives of the Communist camp were discouraging. He met with friendliness, and it would have been easy to be as thick as thieves. He would have been glad enough of this had it seemed worth while; but the one thing that would have served his purpose was absent: decisive action even in their own affairs, and in the end it made no difference whether he went to Hugenberg or Münzenberg; all they could tell him could have been found in a leading article, and was just about as effective.

'All is not gold that looks like shit,' said Hinnerk, to whom Ive confided his troubles. 'You're always putting the saddle on the wrong horse,' he said, 'why don't you join up with us?'

'With the Nazis?' asked Ive uncomfortably.

'With the proletariat,' said Hinnerk, 'the class-conscious proletariat.'

'Since when have you been a Communist, then?' asked Ive.

'For a long time,' said Hinnerk, 'actually since the Party was founded. Didn't you know?'

No. Ive hadn't known—he opened his eyes wide. 'Damn it all, on which side will you be, then, if it comes to fighting?' he asked.

'On the opposite side to the police,' said Hinnerk. 'But seriously, if anything is to be decided, it will not be in the Kurfürstendamm, and it doesn't matter which side you fight on so long as you are on the battlefield at all.'

'Oh, Hinnerk,' said Ive, 'is it really as simple as all that?'

'Join up with us,' said Hinnerk, pushing Ive in front of him. 'I knew at once that you'd come to no good when I saw you joining the fountain-pen brigade. You're so blinded with problems you can't see the simplest things. You've become too critical to be able to make a clear-cut decision. But, damn you, haven't you been playing the clown long enough? And now you're acting the tragedian as well, going around as crestfallen as a rabbit that can't find its hole. You must know whether you belong to the bourgeoisie or to the brigade of youth; all your scruples are stuff and nonsense.'

'You forget,' said Ive gently, 'that I have not lost my hole, that my brigade is an old and eternal brigade, that I have thrown in my lot with the farmers, that I have no tiling to lose, but everything to find.'

'Come,' said Hinnerk, 'all respect to your farmers, but you can't keep manoeuvring about in the no-man's-land between the lines, and not a soul knowing which side you belong to. I'll tell you what is the essential thing: to collect together all the brigades of youth from every camp—and, if there are a few broken heads from time to time, that's nothing among friends—and, with the united battalions, to drive the bankrupt cut-throats of big business and finance to the devil together with their hangers-on, the corrupt gang of profiteers and lickspittles, and then to set up the one decent law of comradeship. That's the essential thing; all the rest, my boy, will follow naturally. And you can call that socialism or nationalism, I don't care a damn which—'

'And win victories over France with the Red Army, and conquer Poland with the White Army. I know,' said Ive. 'And make a treaty with Russia and Italy. I know. Just see if that isn't what happens in a twinkling. Oh, Hinnerk, Napoleon wasn't such a bad fellow, was he, but stupid, stupid; can't we make a better job of it?'

'All right,' said Hinnerk. 'You talk as though you were already one of Ullstein's editors. You see if they don't give you a job on the Green Post. We can't all be as clever as you.'

'And we can't all begin kicking up hell and singing the International as though that were the only way to be a nationalist.'

'Rubbish,' said Hinnerk, standing still and seizing Ive by the shoulders. 'Heavens, man, I'd like to give you a good shaking...'

'The town is doing that for me all right,' said Ive despondently, 'and I only hope you are right. It really does look as though everything that I was doing here was sheer waste. When I weigh things up, the balance may be a little in my own favour, but that's all. It strikes me we are all marking time a bit—you as well, my dear fellow—and if that isn't enough to make one weep, it's enough to make one sick; and I have a great desire to land you one in the jaw, perhaps I should feel better then.'

'Always on the wrong horse,' said Hinnerk, distressed. 'Come with me, we've got a trial on today. Do you know Farmer Hellwig?' he asked. 'He's been kicking up hell, and enjoying it. He is working for the Communist Farmers' Union now, and perhaps he can tell you more than such a mental acrobat, or such a low-down idiot as I am.'

'What did you say—a trial?'

'Yes—a trial by the unemployed. Of the System. We often do it. There will be a few death sentences again,' said Hinnerk, delighted, paying no heed to Ive's objection that it seemed to him a bit premature.

Hinnerk strode along beside him laughing and talking, fair, tall and strong. He moved powerfully and easily in his green woollen pull-over, and Ive in his shoddy town clothes, all of them shabby by now, conscious of his own odour of dust, sweat and fatigue, was filled with envy. The town did not seem able to touch Hinnerk. Fundamentally he remained always the same. Only his voice had become rather hoarse from calling his fresh rolls or whatever he happened to be selling. Ive could well believe of this comrade, who was always true to himself and every one else, that he would always be able to hold his own with the forces of the age, simply by adapting himself to them without a trace of intellectual anaemia, and without for a moment forfeiting any essential part of his own personality; whereas Ive who, after all, had the same end in view, perpetually had the feeling that the pavement was slipping from under his feet.

'One wouldn't mind being a horse-thief with you,' Ive had said to Hinnerk once.

And he had replied: 'Not horses, motor cars.'

And Ive did not doubt that one day he would say: 'Not motor cars, aeroplanes!'

Since the times could do him no harm, he always moved with the times, and his strength lay in the fact that he was always unreservedly ready to do what the immediate moment demanded of him, and indeed it always turned out that the demand of the immediate moment remained the same, changing only in its outward form. Hinnerk's political opinions were of the most primitive order imaginable, but he had political opinions. Ive had none, but talked bosh, as Hinnerk said, and Ive wondered what possible justification there was for his own arrogance towards his friend. When Hinnerk said 'class-conscious,' he no doubt meant the pride of belonging somewhere, and he probably didn't care where he belonged; he might just as well have said 'race-conscious.' In any case, he believed undeviatingly in the great federation of good fellows and he could as easily have been the leader of a Russian workers' shock brigade as a member of the Fascist militia; he could as well have been the captain of an English Rugby team as an S.A. man in Wedding. There was a wide field for him and his like; he would have been at home anywhere except perhaps in the League for the Rights of Man. Ive did not know where he came from or what his circumstances had been. Hinnerk never mentioned the subject, certainly not because it embarrassed him, but because he attached no importance to it; he was here, and wherever he went he was sure to leave traces of his activities behind him. Further, there was no doubt that he was always ready to take action against all the legal forces of the world, but never against the laws of comradeship, so he could never go wrong, for Hinnerk was never guilty of treachery. If he was ready now to greet the troops of young unemployed men outside the hall in the centre of the town with a hearty 'Red Front!' or the Storm Troopers in the North with a 'Heil!' the thought was, and always would be, absurd that he could ever be acting as a spy. In fact, though the men came from different quarters they were all of the same brand, and the hatred between them was that of brothers at enmity whose actions, inspired by similar feelings, arc hot, unmerciful, and inevitable, but have none of the alien feelings that make hatred cold and unquenchable. Hinnerk moved among them with an unconcerned assuredness, and Ive's conscience pricked him sorely; he felt suspicious of himself, not just out of place. Actually I am a dirty dog, he thought, not to act as Hinnerk does. And when he had thus castigated himself he could reassure himself with the thought that all the possibilities of choice were still open to him, so long as no one thing had any impelling influence on him, and until then he must regard the disgraceful condition of freewill which he had naively substituted for time, as an annealing test.

Farmer Hellwig, to whom Hinnerk introduced him, came from the Hanover district. He was a youngish man of medium height with a thin, bronzed face and expectant, eager eyes. Ive remembered that he had met him before in connection with the formation of the Farmers' Party. At that time Hellwig had wanted the Party to be regarded as a counter-organisation to the Land League, had wanted above all that the political centre of gravity should be shifted to the farming community and was busy with plans aiming at a close affiliation between the agricultural producers' associations and the working-class consumers' associations. Ive had made no secret of his own doubts about these plans, less because he did not want to see the hegemony of the Land League interfered with than because it seemed to him that the Party form left no room for the development of the farmers' autonomy. The subsequent history of the Party had proved Ive to be right, and Hellwig smilingly admitted this as he pushed his way with Ive and Hinnerk between the rows of chairs and tables.

The hall, usually used for social festivities, was packed. About a thousand unemployed men and women were sitting and standing in crowded groups, but not in that state of gloomy expectation which is usually the atmosphere at a political meeting. They had the appearance of people defiantly prepared to fulfil a self-imposed duty. On the platform, on the narrow side of the hall opposite the entrance, beneath the red flag with the hammer and sickle, were three tables.

The middle one faced the hall, the other two were at right-angles to it on either side. As several persons began to take their places at these tables, the voices in the hall were silenced and every face was turned towards the platform. Four men and one woman seated themselves at one of the side-tables, and one man at each of the other tables. The man in the middle stood up and said: 'I declare the Court of the Proletarian Unemployed open. The prosecutor will open the proceedings.'

The prosecutor, his hands in his trouser-pockets, stepped forward to the edge of the platform. He said: 'One of the most monstrous crimes of the capitalist System against the working-class, and therefore against human development, is the completely successful attempt to put the instruments of power of the State into the hands of the possessing class. In the present state of proletarian enlightenment, anyone who takes part in this attempt cannot fail to realise the nature of his action. The working-class population confronts the weapon of class justice with the weapon of its own justice. It passes judgment on the misdemeanants and the sentences will be carried out by the executive bodies of Soviet-Germany. I call upon Witness No. 1 to give evidence.' The prosecutor sat down and a man from one of the side tables faced the audience.

'Comrades,' he said, 'I am a skilled iron-worker and have been out of work for two and a half years. I am thirty-nine years of age; I served in the War; I am a married man with three children.' He spoke like a man who is accustomed to legal proceedings, but his statement had a spontaneous ring about it. He said that he had a little home, but he added that he was not for that reason to be classified as a property-owner. A week previously, on the very day, as he had learned later, that some provision shops had been plundered—and then corrected himself: attacked—he had been waiting at his usual tramstop with his tools, which he could not leave at home or they would have been stolen. He had noticed that there was a commotion in the neighbouring streets, but he had paid no attention to it. Then some policemen had arrived, walking slowly as usual. There had been an officer with them whom he knew by sight, but the officer had stood a little apart. Two policemen had walked past him, and one of them had said to him:

'Move on.'

He had turned round and replied:

'I am waiting for the tram.'

At this moment the policeman had attacked him with his rubber truncheon, bringing it down with full force on his head—he pointed to the spot—and he had immediately fallen down, everything swimming before his eyes.

The prosecutor asked whether he had not perhaps said rather more than: 'I am waiting for the tram?'

No, he was sure he had said no more than that.

Had he perhaps made a gesture with his tools which the policeman might have misconstrued as a threat?

No, he was holding his pick and shovel over his shoulder, and on the end of the pick was hanging a bundle of seed potatoes.

'I did nothing more than turn round a bit and say: "I am waiting for the tram."'

However, he felt that he ought to add that probably he would not have fallen except that he had an old war wound. But in any case, apart from that, the blow had been no joke. While he was lying on the ground the officer had come up and had said to him in a loud voice: 'Get out of this unless you want to get some more stingers.'

'That is what he said; then he waited until I had scrambled up and collected my tools and had gone into the entrance of a house.'

The prosecutor asked whether he had not, in his dazed state after the blow, perhaps misunderstood the officer?

No, he said, he had understood him perfectly. He particularly recalled the expression 'stingers.'

'You told us, comrade,' said the prosecutor, 'that you knew the officer by sight. Who was he?'

'It was Lieutenant Schweinebacke,' said the witness.

The prosecutor told him to sit down, and called upon Witness No. 2 to come forward and give evidence.

Witness No. 2 was a pale, thin young man. He was a clerk by profession, had been without a job for three years, was married, had two children and was twenty-six years of age. He spoke in a low voice, hesitatingly.

'Ladies and gentlemen,' he said, not 'comrades.'

Yes, he had been evicted from his flat. He could not pay the rent out of the dole. He had hoped that the Friendly Society would pay the rent, because his wife was ill. But he had only had the same as the others. Yes, she was consumptive, and that was the reason he had not wanted to move. Yes, he had written to the estate agents.

'Who owns the house?' asked the prosecutor.

A foreign company who were the owners of several blocks of houses. The estate manager had said he could do nothing and had told him to clear out. He had not worried about this, however, as he had not believed that he could be turned out into the street like that, with his sick wife and the two children.

The prosecutor kept on questioning him.

The witness told him that he had said to the men who were removing his furniture:

'Why are you doing this, comrades?'

Then the policeman had told him to be good enough to keep his mouth shut.

'But where on earth am I to go with my sick wife and the two children?'

The policeman said that had nothing to do with him, and the removers carried his furniture out. Then he had gone to the restaurant to telephone to the police station. An officer had answered. He did not know who the officer was. It was not the district Superintendent. He knew him well because he had often had to go to the police station about signing documents.

He had said: 'Where on earth am I to go with my wife and the two children?'

He should have thought about that sooner, was the answer. The eviction order would be carried out; there was no appeal. And then the officer had rung off. Then he had just told the story to his friends in the restaurant, and they had all come with him to his flat. The furniture was already standing outside the door. Inside his wife was screaming terribly and the children as well. His wife was in bed. No, he had gone into the flat alone; his friends waited outside. Then the policeman had gone up to the bed and said he knew all about it, it was all put on. At this his wife had screamed still louder, and then the policeman had shouted, but more at him than at his wife. Then he had run out and called the people who were outside; there was quite a crowd by now, some of them people he did not know. And they carried the furniture in again, and even one of the removers had helped. They were not real removers, but unemployed men. Then the constable had become threatening and, when no one took any notice of him, had rushed off to the restaurant and telephoned for reinforcements. And the reinforcements had come in a car. Yes, the officer was with them. And they set about the people in the room and on the stairs with their rubber truncheons and dispersed the crowd. Then the policemen had completely cleared the flat, putting everything out into the street. The bed, too, with his wife in it. He had gone up to the officer and had wept, and the officer had said to him that the way he was going on he would have to be reported for obstruction and incitement. In the end a car had come from the Friendly Society and his wife had had to be taken to hospital at once.

The prosecutor asked if the voice on the telephone and that of the officer at the eviction had been the same.

Yes, it had been the same voice.

And had he still not known who the officer was?

Yes, one of his comrades had told him that it was Lieutenant Schweinebacke, said the witness.

The prosecutor told him to sit down, and called upon Witness No. 3 to come forward and give evidence.

Witness No. 3 was a young fellow, sturdy and bronzed, a handsome boy, as the woman next to Ive said. He greeted them not with the word 'comrades,' but with a hearty 'Red Front.' He was twenty-two years old and had never had regular work in his life. He gave the prosecutor no time to put questions, and told his story as though he had often told it before, in a lively manner and interspersed with obscene remarks. During the metal-workers' strike he had been at Siemenstadt, just by chance, of course, because picketing was forbidden, and he never did anything that was forbidden, on principle.

'When I got there I could hardly believe my eyes to see every one idle.'

'Is it a public holiday today?' he had asked one of the constables in quite a friendly way.

'Clear out of this.'

He said he hadn't known that taking a walk was forbidden; perhaps Mr. Constable could tell him of some better way of passing his time?

'If you don't clear out of this at once...'

Then he had gone into a pub to have a drink to get over the shock. The bar was full, but nobody wanted to stand a round. His pal Paul had been there, too, and had told him that there were some comrades there who thought things weren't so bad after all. So then he had stood up and asked if it was true that any of the worthy gentlemen present had joined the traitors to the working class? Heavens above, the fat was in the fire then. Yellows, every one of them!

'He's a Red,' someone in a brown shirt had yelled, and then everything was in a uproar. 'I ran behind the bar, Paul rushed to the empties and washing-up counter—five minutes later somebody went off to fetch the greencoats, and then we had all the colours of the rainbow.'

But honour to whom honour is due; the greencoats had been very kind. They had said to him at once:

'We've had our eyes on you for a long time.'

And then, like the grand fellows they were, they had invited him to take a seat in their car, but being a sociable fellow, he asked them to allow the young gentleman in the brown shirt to participate in the pleasure of a little drive. This, however, they refused to do. On the contrary, they pushed him and Paul into the van; then about twenty constables got in and an officer, 'all of them fine fellows, a couple of heads taller than me. Then we drove off with a regretful look at the pub where there wasn't a glass or a chair left intact. But Paul would not keep quiet. "Comrades," he said, "this is unjust..." "Shut your mouth," said the constable beside him, "we're not your comrades." I said: "Paul, be quiet, you don't know these gentlemen, you mustn't talk in that familiar way." "Shut your filthy mouths," said the constable beside me, and I made a sign to Paul to keep quiet, for I did know the gentlemen.'

At the station they were searched for a second time, and he had taken all his clothes off immediately and bent over to show that he hadn't a cannon concealed up his arse. For even though he was a natural child, he knew how to behave in polite society. But Paul, in spite of the signs he kept making to him, began getting argumentative again. Ten of them fell upon him. They came from the adjoining rooms and dragged Paul out of his corner. Then they set to work with their rubber truncheons and belt straps.

'Long live Liebknecht!' Paul had called out, and by that time he was down on the floor, and the fellows all round him, and they had pummelled until he spat blood. Naturally, the witness said, he had rushed forward to help Paul, but four men held him back, and turning on him with their rubber truncheons, had hit him over the mouth, knocking out three teeth. He opened his mouth wide and pointed to the black gaps in his jaw.

'Give it him hot, there's still some breath in his body,' one of the constables had cried out, when the others had wanted to leave off pummelling Paul. One of Paul's arms was broken, and his face looked like a piece of raw meat. So then they took Paul off to the police-infirmary and himself to the Alexander-prison, where he had found himself in decent company once more. At the end of three weeks they had had to release him, for he was a prudent man and had provided himself with a shooting licence four years previously. But Paul was still in the infirmary, and there were to be legal proceedings. And that's what came of making such queer friends; not a soul would admit to having had anything to do with it. Naturally Paul could do nothing, for one by one they would come forward and take their oath and give evidence that it was in Siemenstadt that Paul had been so badly treated, and that everything he said was a lie, and he himself could not be called as a witness in accordance with Section 51. So Paul would not be able to tell the true story and could sing in the delightful words of the poet:

'And if should break the ship's proud mast
The sails be torn to ribbons
Our bark we'll take and steer it fast
To Plötzensee and Tegel.'

The prosecutor asked:
'And the officer; what was the officer doing while they were beating him?'
Oh, the officer, he had been present the whole time and had turned his back and studied the guard-room inventory thoroughly.
Did he know who the officer was?

Most certainly, he had had the pleasure of meeting him several times. It was Lieutenant Schweinebacke, said the boy.

The prosecutor told him to sit down and called upon Witness No. 4 to come forward and give evidence.

Hinnerk made a note of the name of Witness No. 3, which he got from one of his neighbours.

'A grand lad,' he said. 'I must get to know him.'

The man whose turn it was to speak now was the typical hard worker, grown grey in honest, service; the treasurer of the Workers' Choral Society, an engine-driver, pensioned off a year ago; a widower, in a long black coat. He said that he could not agree with everything that the previous speaker had said, and he would like to point out that he was not a Communist; he did not belong to any party. When he had agreed to speak here it was merely as an act of friendship. For he could not allow that such circumstances should prevail with impunity in the world today, as those to which his friend had fallen a victim. For five years he and his stoker had driven the same engine every day, and he had found him a loyal, good, industrious, quiet man, of whom he could make a friend and upon whom he could always rely to do his duty. Even after he had been pensioned off, his stoker had often visited him. So that when one day the stoker was dismissed from the State Railways without notice on the grounds of undesirable propaganda, he had still had faith in him and had even given him a home. They had lived together exactly opposite the Employment Bureau. Every day the stoker had gone over to the Employment Bureau to ask if there was a job going, but he had always been disappointed. It is true that the stoker had often discussed things with the other men over there, but he had been a quiet man and had always made excuses for the officials, who after all could do no more than their duty, things being so uncertain in these terrible times, and so many necessary regulations having been made. Even on the day when the unemployed raided the office, the stoker had been against it, and had come back to him and said that it was very stupid destroying everything like that, and it would do no one any good. Often he used to bring a man in with him whom he had got to know over there.

'Heinrich,' he had said to him, 'don't make a friend of that man; I don't trust his face.'

But Heinrich thought he was a fine fellow with the right ideas, who had the workers' interests at heart, and that one could speak freely to him. But time had shown how much this friend was worth. It was this man who had finally incited the others to action.

'When Heinrich came in, he said: "This won't do, I must go over again, and speak to the man." And he went over again. But everything was in full swing by then. They were singing the International and breaking the windows; I could see it all quite clearly from my room. My stoker wasn't there. He was looking for the man, who had disappeared. When the police arrived the man was suddenly there again, and was speaking to the officer, and they arrested Heinrich. I hurried over at once to help Heinrich, but when I went up to the officer and began to explain everything to him, he simply turned round and went away. So they took Heinrich to the car. Just then the others came rushing out of the Employment Bureau, the police after them, and when they saw that they had got Heinrich in custody they picked up stones and threw them at the police and made a rush for the car. And Heinrich broke loose and tried to run away. Then the officer whistled and his men, who were still in the house, ran out with their carbines in their hands and fired on the workers. Heinrich had got a little distance away; they aimed at him. I called out: "Ah, no, no!" but they gave me a push, and then the shots sounded, and all at once Heinrich fell down. They wouldn't let me get to him where he lay and there was a terrible uproar. Then I heard that Heinrich was dead, and in the police report they said he was one of the chief ringleaders and had assaulted the police, and that in the confusion they had fired. But I know who was the ringleader, and how everything happened, and I went to the police, but they told me that I was suspected of being an agitator and I had better be thankful that they were not proceeding against me yet. And so I come to you and ask: "Is it just that a man's life should be of no account, and that the truth should be suppressed? And is it necessary to shoot right away, bang, like that, as though it was nothing? And is it right to believe a spy like that before an honest man?"'

The prosecutor asked him if he knew the officer. No, he didn't know him.

'Is that the officer,' asked the prosecutor, showing him a photograph.

'Yes, it is.'

'It is Lieutenant Schweinebacke,' said the prosecutor, and told the man to sit down, calling upon the woman to come forward and give evidence.

She spoke in a low voice and turned towards the prosecutor all the time, so that he often had to repeat what she had said and to keep asking her questions. She must have been sixty, and looked almost as though she were pregnant again, with her thin body and protruding belly.

Ive who had always regarded the posterlike drawings of Kate Kollwitz with some suspicion, realised how strong was the influence of satirical art, since the living model immediately transformed intended pity into indignation.

She said her boy had been seventeen years old and had not been able to find a job after finishing his apprenticeship. But he didn't like hanging about at home, so he had joined the young Communists and every Sunday he was off to the lakes with his tent, and she had always been afraid he would be getting into bad company, but he had always been so eager that she hadn't interfered with him. His father had been killed in the war, of course, and he was the youngest and hadn't had much fun in his childhood. She had enough to live on. It was difficult, but she had the pension, and if she was careful she could manage. But the boy had not been satisfied. He had made enquiries everywhere for a job, but there was nothing to be had. She had always been afraid he might be going to the public house, but no, he had never done that; he did all the housework and the shopping and the washing up, but that wasn't the sort of work for a boy. So he had gone out more and more with his friends, and once she had found a revolver in his drawer. She had been horrified and had asked him about it, and he said it was for the day of reckoning, and had looked very fierce. Then she had been frightened and had taken the revolver and given it to her brother-in-law. But he had laughed and said the boy couldn't even kill a sparrow with the thing, it was quite rusty and the spring was broken, and he gave it back to the boy and told him not to talk nonsense. She had often asked the boy whether he wasn't getting up to mischief with his friends, and he had looked at her frankly and said, 'No,' and she had believed him because he always spoke the truth. She had had four sons; one had been killed in an accident at his work, two were married and gone away, and then the youngest. She and the boy had lived alone. He had always been obedient, but restless. On the day of the shooting she had forbidden him to leave the house, and he had said: 'Mother, I must go to my friends, I cannot leave them in the lurch.'

But she had said that they were not good friends and had implored him, and told him that she didn't want to lose him on top of all her other troubles. For she had a presentiment of evil all the time and did not let the boy out of her sight the whole day. He was very restless and kept running to the window, and had wanted to hang a red flag out, but she had locked up all the red stuff. Then he had got into a temper and screamed, and she had said to him:

'That's right, turn against your own mother.'

Then he had burst into tears and gone into his room. She had not dared go to sleep that night; but the next day he was gone. Her neighbour told her that she had seen him going off very early and had told her of such terrible things going on that she had cried and had not known what to do and had only hoped that everything was over, and that he wouldn't find his friends. So she had run downstairs and out into the street, and it had all started again. The people were terribly excited and had said the police ought to be shot down like dogs. That was the way they were raging, and they told her she should shut all her windows because they would soon be shooting in at the open windows. At the corner of the street shots could be heard already. Then the people all ran on and some men had come up and told her that the police were firing at the Communist guard on the roof, and that her son was up there.

'I was in despair and began to run down the street. Then I saw the boy come running round the corner and I was so pleased, I called out to him and went quickly into the house, and turned round and saw him running towards me. Thank God, I thought, and was just going upstairs; then there were some shots and the boy ran into the house crying: "Quick, quick!" And I didn't know what I was doing. Then they were crying outside: "Here, here!" And then they shot into the house, again and again into the house. But the door had banged to, and I couldn't see anything, so I called: "Otto, Otto!" and I couldn't hear any answer because of the noise of shooting, which was terrible. Then they tore open the door, and there lay my boy. There lay my boy.'

The whole audience sat with bowed heads. The prosecutor went up to the woman. He asked her if she had found a revolver on the boy. The woman hesitated, and the prosecutor said that she must know that the party did not countenance individual violence. The woman said she knew nothing, except that her brother-in-law, who had arrived on the scene, had kept telling the police:

'No shot was fired from this weapon, the spring is broken.' And the officer had said he could not give an opinion as to that, and the weapon was confiscated.

Did she know who the officer was?

'Lieutenant Schweinebacke!' cried a voice from the hall, and a man stood up. 'I am her brother-in-law,' said the man, and the prosecutor told the woman to sit down.

The chairman stood up and asked if anyone in the hall could bring forward anything in defence of the accused, Lieutenant Schweinebacke, or in defence of the police superintendent. He announced that no one had offered any evidence in defence and called upon the prosecutor to speak.

The prosecutor came to the front of the platform, his hands in his trouser pockets. The aim of modern policy in the modern State, he said, was, in the words of the Right Honourable Minister of the Interior, to establish popular rule. What the unemployed court had just heard testified to the manner in which the police were setting about the fulfilment of this pleasant duty. Far be it from him to resort to the well-known emotional appeal of which professional suspicion-mongers made such ample and passionate use in the civil courts for the edification of their principals and of a hoodwinked public. Here the naked facts spoke for themselves. He might add that he had had the evidence of each of the witnesses taken down and investigated. He had not succeeded in finding a discrepancy, and he had had to restrict himself to selecting from a large number of similar statements five cases only to bring before the court. He had brought an indictment against Lieutenant Schweinebacke and against the Superintendent of Police, who was responsible, even in civil law, for all the actions of his subordinates. Once more he must emphasise that the class-conscious proletariat repudiated and must always repudiate all individual terrorism, but it could never abrogate its right to bring the enemies of the working-class to justice. He accused Lieutenant Schweinebacke and the Superintendent of Police of murder, and of counter-revolutionary activities. And he proposed that both the accused should be sentenced to death.

The chairman rose and said: 'I request those who are in favour of the prosecutor's proposal to raise their hands.'

The hands went up in rapid response—Hinnerk's arm shot up with a mechanical jerk, Farmer Hellwig raised his hand with a smile, and Ive, who felt himself turning red to the roots of his hair, hesitated, and then straightening his elbow stretched his hand high above his head.

'The accused are unanimously sentenced to death,' said the chairman. 'There is no appeal against the judgment of the unemployed. The sentence will be carried out on the anniversary of the Social Revolution by the functionaries of Soviet-Germany. The session is adjourned.'

With a loud scraping of chairs the crowd rose and immediately a hubbub of voices filled the room. The doors were opened. At the entrance there was confusion. The whir of motor cars could be heard. A sharp voice called into the hall:

'Look out, the shock brigade!' There was a roar of laughter. At the entrance appeared a policeman's shako. The meeting broke up. Slowly the crowd pushed its way out. Ive, Hinnerk, and Hellwig, jostled by the crowd, made their way forward step by step. Beside them and in front of them a murmur arose; one word was being repeated.

'Schweinebacke, Schweinebacke, Schweinebacke,' they all said, men and women.

'Schweinebacke,' murmured Hinnerk, and Ive pushed forward.

He looked through the entrance over the heads of the crowd. Outside was the brigade, the men lined up, straps under their chins, carbines in their hands. The officer stood apart near the entrance, a tall, rather stout man, with a gleaming silver collar and a broad face.

'Brodermann,' said Ive in an undertone.

'Schweinebacke,' said Hinnerk, as though to himself, and brushed past Brodermann.

'Schweinebacke,' said Hellwig, and passed on. Ive raised his head and looked into the face of Brodermann, who was gazing stonily in front of him. He did not move a muscle, but the contemptuous line round his nose became accentuated.

'Schweinebacke,' said Ive very loudly, and looked straight at Brodermann. Brodermann turned and looked at him. He shook his head gently, and turned away again, letting the stream of weak revenge wash by him, alone in the midst of the crowd, separated from his brigade.

XIII

Ive was not greatly surprised that they, Hinnerk, Hellwig, and himself, at once directed their steps towards one of the large restaurants of the town, to refresh themselves with a meal, a privilege not to be enjoyed by any of the thousand unemployed, whose legal proceedings they had just left, with the exception of the chairman and the prosecutor who had taken their seats in a corner not far from themselves. Ive had long since given up harbouring scruples which could only be labelled with the opprobrious term 'Liberal.' Moreover, there they were, and that was the end of it. At the same time his own and Hinnerk's financial position was such that they only ordered a small glass of beer each, half hoping that Hellwig would pay for it, and fell upon the rolls, while Hellwig pushed the menu-card on one side and ordered a steak.

'Blancmange,' he said, pointing to the menu, 'that means they put on the price shamelessly and serve you up a shapeless, flabby mass of pulp, that can only have been made to prevent the needy corn-flour industry from having to close its doors and deprive thousands of workers of their daily bread; there's no swallowing the muck!'

When the steak came, a piece of meat the size of a saucer, and three small potatoes, embarrassed by their loneliness, Hellwig began to make rapid calculations with his pencil on the back of the menu.

He cut himself off a piece of meat and said: 'Not much meat on this cow; according to the latest Berlin schedule, inclusive of freight and loss of weight, sixteen marks the hundredweight, so the farmer gets ex-farm about a hundred and ten marks—for a ten-hundredweight cow, which has taken three years to fatten for the market. There isn't even a quarter of a pound on my plate; price on the menu one mark sixty. In the shop steak costs one mark sixty a pound. On a high computation, very high, taking the most favourable circumstances, the farmers get sixteen pfennigs a pound. Deducting for the difference between live and dead weight, on a good average, say, fifty percent, then deducting another twenty percent, for bones and the inferior cuts, the retail price is still three times as high as the selling price ex-farm. Between selling price and shop price, per pound, mark you. This is not quite a quarter of a pound and is costing me one mark sixty, twelve hundred percent of what I get for it at home. What do they call that? They call it political economy. I call it a bloody swindle. Last time we met, Herr Iversen, you told me that an ambitious co-operative policy could not be carried through in association with a purely agrarian party, and today I admitted that you were right. And you were right in your prophecy that every agrarian organisation within the capitalist system, so long as it concerned itself merely with the conditions of agricultural production, must of necessity move on capitalistic lines, whether it be Land League, or Farmers' Party, or the most extensive agricultural association. What the farmer has to demand in the capitalist, as in every other system, is that his labour shall show a profit. But how is this profit to be guaranteed? Surely only through drawing a line midway between the claims of the producer and the claims of the consumer. I said guaranteed; that means that on either side of this line there must be only a minutely calculated space, just big enough for every natural advance to have an elastic rebound. Thus it is not the law of supply and demand, with speculation and market depressions, which must set the standard, but the exigencies of a common budget. Obviously this is not possible under the capitalist system. For it is not deficiency of consumption that is to blame for the prevailing overproduction, but deficiency in the organisation of distribution, and in the only possible future economic reform the two partners will no longer be called agriculture and industry.'

'But?' said Ive.

'But farmers and workers,' said Hellwig. 'For today industry is forced by the taxation policy of the agrarian organisations to lower its workers' wages, and thus to decrease the consumption of agrarian products, which in its turn leads to higher taxation on the part of agriculture. To escape from this vicious circle would really require a series of events based on a postulate of bloodshed beginning with the complete abolition of the private middleman, i.e. the elimination of the numerous money-making processes with their unnecessary raising of prices, and the restriction of the multitudinous transferences of goods to, at the most, two, from the grower to the co-operative pool and from the pool to the retail distributor, and ending with the monopoly of export trade.'

'The postulate,' said Ive, 'would be the victory of Communism.'

'Of course,' said Hellwig. 'Believe me,' he said, with sudden violence, 'my path to Communism was not paved with illusions, and I did not set out on it with an exaggerated envy of or hatred for the braggarts of the Land League. I am a small farmer, it is true, but I own my farm. I go in for retail produce and do very little wholesale business, it is true, but I own my farm. I have my farm down there, and my father had it before me, and my great-grandfather. My Lower Saxon blood dates back for centuries and, if I understand anything, I understand the doggedness with which the Herr von Itzenplitz auf Itzensitz defends his three thousand acres by every possible means, and his three hundred acres of forest-land and his herds of deer. I am not a firebrand, either professionally or emotionally, nor in the criminally frivolous spirit of the literary rodomontades of the coffee-houses—I am a tenant-farmer—a German, and always wish to be so, and I have a damned hard row to hoe, and I carry on my back a load of responsibilities which weighs me down at every step more heavily than a two-hundredweight sack of provender. And it is for that reason that I have to look about me and notice every stone beneath my feet; and if illusions come flying my way, be they but a featherweight, I cannot carry them, I have to examine everything and I have done so. I have looked about me and I know what the odds are, on our side and the other, and I know what my own stake is. Nobody is going to give me anything for the sake of my beautiful eyes, and as far as the National Association of German Industry is concerned I could rot on my dungheap if it were not that I had to buy machinery and potash; and if it weren't that the miner Kacszmareck makes his scrambled eggs with my eggs and eats my ham his fate wouldn't matter a toss to me, and that's as it should be. That's how things are today, and it's quite right, for it may force me to throw the whole ballast of false prejudices where it belongs, into the dung-pit, and, whenever I encounter a man or an opinion, to sift every theory and phrase to find the underlying motive of self-interest. I defend my farm, as my comrades in Holstein and Oldenburg defend theirs, but the farmer cannot and must not be content to protect what is endangered; capitalism too attempts that and loses through its short-sightedness. If we stay on our farms now, with our rifle-butts on the ground, we shall have to stay on the farm for ever with a pistol to our heads. If, now that the time is uniquely favourable, we do not march forward and take the position which is ours by right, then we shall never be able to take it. We have to seize the opportunities that offer and select the one most advantageous for the future. There is still time, and now is the moment to march forward, to secure the hinterland and reconnoitre the field in front of us; we know who is the opponent of today, and we know that the friend of today may be the opponent of tomorrow, so that with his help today we must make ourselves so strong that he won't want to attack us tomorrow. I have been through the whole *Kirchweih** on the quest, beating them all up, as you are still doing, Herr Iversen. I know

---

* *Kirchweih* is a German tradition celebrated locally, in connection with the name day of the patron saint of the community church. Here the term is obviously used metaphorically.

what is needful for us farmers and for the others, now more than ever, if our need is to be relieved, and, weighing all the pros and cons, I saw where our opportunities lie. I do not know whether Communism will be victorious in Germany, although many signs point to it, but I do know that it is only in Communism, as it would develop with us and through our work, that the possibilities of a radical salvation for the farmers are to be found.'

He ceased speaking and polished off the last potato. Hinnerk looked at Ive expectantly. The din of knives and forks rattling on the plates jarred on Ive's ears. He realised that he ought to say something, but suddenly his courage had forsaken him. How strange it is, he thought; here are we three, sitting in the middle of the town, talking, talking, talking about the farmers, who at this very moment, far away out there in their farms, are lying dog-tired in their huge feather-beds listening through the walls to the muffled clanking of the cattle pulling at their chains. Here are we three sitting, talking about the farmers, all three terribly alone in our sense of responsibility, a sense of responsibility with which no one credits us, seeing us sitting here, while the waiter in his white coat looks furious because we are taking up the room of more profitable guests. What the devil do the farmers matter to me? thought Ive. I've only one mark fifty left in my pocket. And what do they matter to Hinnerk, who is sitting there frowning and saying nothing, sipping his wretched glass of beer and in an hour's time will be going off to sell his rolls at the Kadewe? And what do they matter to Hellwig, to whom they have twice given a drubbing when he was speaking at the farmers' meetings? What does all this matter to us, slowly burning ourselves to ashes, while the cart goes rumbling on, regardless of us? Responsibility, thought Ive, responsibility, and not one of these dirty dogs questions us as to our responsibility. Where did I say that before? he asked himself. I should like to be questioned about what I am responsible for. Oh, I know, to Judge Fuchs, at the preliminary examination, when I was talking to him, and Claus Heim refused to speak. Claus Heim.

Ive recollected himself with a start and said: 'Perhaps you are right.'

Farmer Hellwig stretched out his hand slowly and laid it on the middle of the table.

'Why don't you join up with us?' he asked quietly.

Suddenly Ive was seized with a wild, frantic terror whose darting flames set his throat and eyes tingling with the envenomed torture of this ridiculous, stupendous, serious question. That's what will happen; we shall once more be cheated of ourselves—a hundred years lost through shamefully succumbing to the lure of the West, and now another hundred years in succumbing to the call of the East—will that happen? And if... Ive stared at the grimy tablecloth, and for a moment the absurdity of the situation struck him, but this sensation was immediately overpowered by the onslaught of terror—and if—what shall we have lost or gained? Lost, almost everything; gained, almost nothing. Gained the unity of little Germany and the certainty of a new beginning. Is that all? Gained everything that has been thought in condemnation of the age from Novalis and Holderlin, through Goethe to Nietzsche. That is all. Isn't that enough? It is not enough. Assuredly it is not enough, if we measure it by the hope that enables us to live, and by the power that we feel within us. And now that God's, mantle is hovering over us again once more, not to be able to catch it by the hem, out of stupidity, indolence, cowardice; our actions stultified, because we are vitiated and debauched, rotten to the core. Once more to have to renounce for a hundred years, because of a hundred mistakes, with the goal before our eyes and in our glowing hearts, the message that our clumsy tongues are striving to utter at our very lips, and to have to sink again and, who knows, if not for ever? And here we are snapping and snarling at the age, like a greedy dog after a bone that has been snatched from him? We must begin again, perpetually begin again; live— like Kleist, that's it, thought Ive, putting his hand to his throat—live like Kleist, and that will mean, must mean, to die like Kleist!

'Join up with us,' said Farmer Hellwig.

Ive sat upright. He stretched his hand out over the table, bent forward and said: 'I will tell you exactly what it is that above all estranges me from your Party. It is the Party's principle of internationalism.'

Ive waited expectantly for an answer, but Hellwig said nothing, he did not even move his hand. He turned a little paler and looked straight at Ive. After a short, expressive pause, Ive continued cautiously:

'This principle has prevented you—the Party— from giving to the different conditions of agricultural production in individual countries that degree of consideration which, for instance, gave such a virile mobility to Lenin's tactics. The Party is attempting, by its propaganda, to introduce into the Farmers' Movement elements which are alien to the character of the Movement, and is, in effect, working towards a rupture which is entirely opposed to the interests of the aim which we both have before us at the moment—the destruction of the System. Of course, no one can expect the Party to abandon a principle which it considers of vital importance, but it is to be expected that, in the exercise of this principle, it will use methods which will permit the farmers to co-operate with it provisionally, that is to say methods which do not endanger the vital issues of the Movement. And it is to be expected, because undoubtedly —to use the terminology of

Communism—the agricultural sector of the Party can only advance from the stage of theoretical resolutions to the stage of practical revolutionary action by close affiliation with the most militant sector of the German farmer-class. That is so and this fact is sufficient to put the Farmers' Movement in a position from which it can emphatically state its conditions.'

'Is not one of the vital issues of the Farmers' Movement,' asked Hellwig, 'that Communism should renounce the abolition of private ownership? From my close knowledge of the circumstances, and as a responsible official of the Party, I can tell you that this renunciation is possible on the assumption of a reorganisation of private ownership, which can only be carried out by the responsible body of the farmers.'

'But that is a fantastic idea,' said Ive.

'It is a Marxist idea,' said Farmer Hellwig, 'for the farmers' conditions of life make them into a class, because they separate them fundamentally from other classes. For this reason they must take a fundamental part in the class-war, but they have the advantage over the proletariat and the bourgeoisie of possessing the distinctive peculiarity of being able to make a change of front to preserve their existence as a class. With the same ease with which, without forfeiting any of their essential characteristics, they were able to take part in capitalist development, they will doubtless be able to adapt themselves to socialist forms of production; indeed, they will have to, for their own objects are driving them in that direction. Thus the reorganisation of private ownership among farmers will be conditioned by a change in their own position as a class but not in that of other classes. What the programme of the Communist Party of Germany does is simply to point out to the farmers who their consumers are.'

'The question is,' said Ive, 'in how far the control of agricultural production can remain in the hands of the farmer-class—on the assumption that Communism really will recognise such a class.'

'It will remain in their hands, under the control of the Communist Party,' said Hellwig, 'and the mere fact that I, Hellwig, a tenant-farmer, can be an official of the Party, ought to show you that it is not only Lenin's tactics that have a wide scope—'

Ive looked at him meditatively. 'I admire you,' he said, 'not only for the courage with which you read into the Marxist theories facts and views which do not directly and logically arise out of them, but also for the courage with which you imagine you can set about the practical organisation.'

Hinnerk said suddenly: 'D'you know, I liked you better when you were with the farmers.'

'So I did myself,' said Ive furiously.

Hellwig motioned to Hinnerk to keep quiet. He leant back in his chair and began to speak.

Ive looked at the farmer's hand as it lay on the table, a large, brown, firm hand, which did not once move during the whole discussion, and which caused Ive to exercise severe control over his own soft, white, nervous fingers. Ive listened to his companion's voice, in which there was no note of complaint or justification, no profession of belief, but simply the calm certainty of a man who has found his own path and certainly has no intention of letting himself be lured on to the ice of dialectic debate, on which arrogant asses like to disport themselves.

He said that he was just as far removed from the professional zeal of a beefsteak-theoretician as he was from the wild-eyed fanaticism of a long-haired revolutionary, who begins by repudiating every accepted idea and ends, if he's lucky, by preaching the regeneration of the world through some new erotic theory or through the moral influence of living on roots, or, if he's unlucky, as one of Mosse's young men, one day writing a pathetic article about starving children and another day a brilliant account of the latest fashionable ball. So much for the personal side; as for the cause itself, in all political convictions, in the long run, it could only be a question of calculating the parallelogram of forces in order to determine the magnitude of its diagonal.

'A simple calculation, Iversen, in which the component equations are sufficiently well known to reduce the possibility of error to a minimum. Well, then, the present crisis will be regarded by the interested parties—for obvious reasons—merely as a constructive reorganisation of capitalism, and not as a constructive reorganisation of the economic system as a whole.'

For the sake of argument he was assuming that Ive did not consider himself an interested party. Good. He admitted that it was not only economic considerations that made the farmers wish to change their conditions, but they were the only considerations which at the present moment compelled them to an immediate and unequivocal political decision. But the only movements which were in the end worthy of consideration as determinative representatives of the will to change were National Socialism and Communism. All the manifold activity beneath the surface, which he did not wish to and could not depreciate, must and would join forces with one of these movements, and only in this framework would it be able to take a constructive part in the shaping of the will. Moreover, it was an unquestionable fact that after, and in all probability before, the victory of one of these movements, important elements in the other would have much to say in determining the course of action. Eventually, therefore, it was a question —taking into account the retarding momentum of the influence of the bourgeoisie which could not be destroyed at one blow—not so much of taking up a position at one of the two extreme poles which were opposing each other today, but of shifting the centre of gravity, whose importance should never be underestimated, and which was the only thing worth investigating.

He continued: 'When we speak of Communism, we speak perforce of the Russian example, that is, of a national phenomenon of international import. When we speak of the Russian Revolution, we necessarily make a comparison with the French Revolution. This is inevitable the moment we endeavour to take an historical view. For the historical phenomenon is the same, and it is national. One might say that every nation has its day, and it is the day of Russia now. It is a bitter pill, of course, to think that Germany's future status will be decided in Moscow; her status but not her fate, that would be intolerable. Today her status and her fate are decided in Paris, London, and New York. And even the victory of National Socialism could not change that. We must not attach too much importance to professions of belief. The modern sport of guessing riddles— "Does National Socialism profess Socialism or private capitalism, monopolistic capitalism or State capitalism?"—takes place on a field, on which the only relevant question, namely, "What forms of production will Germany have in future?" can never be answered, and the only thing to do is to assume that, in its final result, National Socialism professes private socialism. For the question is whether, in the future, Germany will be able to decide for herself the nature of her forms of production. At first sight it would seem as though National Socialism has a greater number of possibilities at its disposal, because it leaves more open, but Communism has at its disposal more specific possibilities, and that is what matters. For the house is on fire, and it won't help matters to send for prospectuses of fire-extinguishing apparatus; and, since the worn-out hoses of our Western neighbour are useless, why not turn to the new buckets of our Eastern neighbour?'

'And in a hundred years' time we shall find ourselves in exactly the same position again,' said Ive.

'Sooner than that,' said Hellwig. 'But in that respect the League of Nations is about as much good to us as the Holy Alliance. If we were to listen to the upholders of the materialistic interpretation of history, the bourgeois revolution should not have occurred in France, but in the country where the economic and political conditions were more favourable to it, in this country, and the proletarian revolution, not in Russia, but again in this country. But fifty years later we had the miserable imitation of 1840, and the democrats of then are the Nazis of today, and the latter know just as much about the standards of Moscow as the former knew of the standards of Paris. Today we can and must avoid that detour. The more radical the decision the better, and the more primitive forces will be released. The whole coil of political questions which will envelop Germany immediately upon a National Socialist victory, bringing every subject up for discussion again, would disappear automatically with a victory for Communism. For Communism does not bring up subjects for discussion, it is forced to ensure its existence, to act at once and according to plan, and the simple fact of its existence, of the supremacy of Communism in Germany, establishes the German position unequivocally in the minds and feelings of the whole world. All the problems, which the era of National Socialism will have to attack at once, staking its all on their solution, will have been solved by the mere victory of Communism. It has been proved that for the Western world, that is the declining civilisation, resistance increases in inverse proportion to the degree of danger. Communistic Germany is the greatest danger in the world, National Socialist Germany is the most greatly endangered country of the world. That is just the difference. Maybe the Treaty of Versailles will be torn up under the Swastika; under the Soviet star it is already torn up, and all we have to ask ourselves is whether it is better to be a Russian battle-ground, or, if not a French, then an American colony. There is no third way, for that would presuppose an independent German economic field —and even more than that.'

'Well,' said Ive, 'we won't sit here in the Pschorr-Brauhaus dividing up the world; but the German economic field, let us say, the German economic battle-field of the future, would be Central Europe.'

'Of course,' said Hellwig, 'and Central Europe would be readier to join forces with a Soviet Germany than with a Swastika Germany, and, on the most favourable supposition of a purely German solution being attempted, then not only the whole of the Western world, but the Eastern world too, would be prepared, and would have to be prepared, to have a finger in the pie.'

Ive assented, and sat in deep meditation. He did not attempt to dispute what seemed to be flimsy arguments, because the objections that he could have brought forward had their origin in quite other spheres than those under discussion. Nevertheless he relied on the position he already held, without knowing exactly what its strength was, almost as though he were taking possession of a trench by night, studying its lay-out by the light of a candle-stump, while the threatening rumble of the battle-field mingled with the quiet breathing of the men, ready at any moment either to defend their post with technical skill or to make a sudden attack upon the enemy. Yet he wanted to join issue with Hellwig for he feared the farmer might think, although he showed no signs of it, that he, Ive, had only the same sort of stock objections which he was accustomed to hear. He only needed, for instance, to look around at the various people he came into contact with—officials, party-men, pressmen, the people he saw in the cinemas, in the streets, and in social life—to get a picture of the danger of mass terrorism which was well qualified to give him considerable pleasure; the memory, too, of his experiences in the Baltic provinces roused him to anger not so much because of what had happened as because of the method, which on the one hand had the regrettable result of usually missing its mark, and on the other hand, by its mass production of bleeding flesh through machine-gun fire from behind, even dishonoured death. Nevertheless he thought he might claim that he was able to refine the unexampled crudity of his feelings by his insistence on qualitative discrimination and, as regards the second great objection of the civilised world to Bolshevist barbarity, namely, that it suppressed intellectual freedom, he was making a serious but vain effort to discover anything in the German literature of the last thirty years, whose complete disappearance could have been deplored if it had permitted itself to be suppressed.

'It is a Liberal error,' he heard Hellwig saying, 'to believe that the institution of the International proves that Communism disowns the nation. What it does disown is the nation's permanent organ, the State.'

The national principle, in the significance which we attach to it today, was, in practice—as has been proved recently in China, for example—recognised positively by Communism. But even if this were not so, the most critical observer of the development of the Soviet Union could not dispute that all its measures, both political and economic, if they had from the outset been subordinated to national aims, could not have been better chosen or more effectively carried out. What applied to Soviet Russia under this heading must in all circumstances apply to Soviet Germany. In fact, Communism would be attacking itself if it departed from its fundamental principles, but it would equally be an act of self-aggression if, in the realisation of these principles, it disregarded the free will of its material. The completely different political and economic conditions in Germany were enough to guarantee at least the decentralisation of the administration from Moscow during the period of organised transition, just as the intrinsic strength of the people, translated into the forms of modernity, the existence of which was being put to the test, would guarantee the continuance of German history. This point of view might be objectionable to the economic pharisees, and the chorus of senile intellectuals might break into lamentations about reformist doctrines; but if this were reform, it was reform with a difference, not the reform of Kautsky, but of Stalin dissociated from Trotsky. From a certain point onwards after the zero hour of the revolution, revolutionary measures and opinions might, and must have, a counter-revolutionary character, and vice versa. The Russian example was certainly illuminating, but it would only bear fruit when it ceased to be regarded in the manner prevalent in the Western world, whereby everybody drew an abstract general line based on his own private conceptions, called 'socialism,' and greeted every deviation from that line either with completely unjustified spiteful pleasure and wild howls of triumph, or with bleeding hearts and more or less contorted lucubrations. There was, however, no such thing as an abstract line of socialism, but rather sturdy realities—exigencies, which must and would be reconciled with certain principles, derived from the general progress, for the advancement of a distant goal—a goal set by a point of view which had been developed and hardened by fiery trials and had therefore become organic.

'Now,' said Farmer Hellwig, 'if we turn away from the international accompaniment of the Russian "experiment," we have yet to prove that the Russian claim to be the representative of world revolution was not made at random and cannot be forfeited at random. The whole Russian position rests on it. If it had been a question in Russia of simply "introducing socialism," not, of course, as it is still conceived in the childish imagination of a number of bourgeois pedants, by merely abolishing differences of income and making a just distribution of existing products, but by introducing a really new machinery of production and raising the standard of life of the whole population to a higher level, in short by creating the "Communist paradise" of which the pioneers, and not only the pioneers, of the Labour movement dreamed—if this had been the only question, this could have been accomplished, in spite of the terrible upheaval of war and civil war, simply by the amazing possibilities of enhancing the productivity of the soil and increasing the extent of land under cultivation, which even today only amounts to about ten percent of Soviet soil, always linked of course with the adequate maintenance of the industrial apparatus in its development towards the necessary degree of efficiency, without uprooting the farmer-class from its more or less individualistic method of production in the violent way in which it has actually happened. And the Russian problem would not be a problem for the world if, today, ten years after the complete annihilation of the armies of intervention, the peaceful, disciplined and contented population of the Russian Empire, with their autocratic or non-autocratic economy, were meditatively contemplating the gentle gambolling of the lambs in the meadows of the Steppes. It is the world-revolutionary claim, which is conditioned not only by the position but by the opposition of the Russian phenomenon, which produces the danger of a new war of intervention, and, moreover, heightens the danger of all the interminable conflicts. To meet this danger the most extensive preparations are necessary, the "total mobilisation" of which Ernst Jünger speaks. And in fact this necessity is turning the whole of Russian life into a preparation for a war, which will not be carried out with weapons alone, and which is transforming the life of the nation itself into a heroic act, from the first spark of resolution in a man's brain to industrialise the land to the last stroke of the hammer; from the first deliberate sexual act of the enlightened young comrade to the executions of the Ogpu! It was the hectic *tempo* of industrialisation that first made necessary the increase of the means of subsistence by the revolutionising of agriculture.'

'The Kulak Hellwig,' said Ive.

'The diplomatist-landowner and tenant-farmer Hellwig,' said his companion, 'has at his disposal open ears and eyes, and has spent two years in Russia. I speak Russian, Iversen, and I was a prisoner of war in Russia. I know the conditions of the peasants over there, both before and after the Revolution, as far as it is possible for a prisoner of war, with his wits about him, to get to know them, and I know the conditions of the peasants there today as far as it is possible for a stranger to get to know them. What I know best of all is the position of the farmers in Germany. And that is the essential thing. In Russia the test is what is good for Russia, and here what is good for us. What then was the position of things "there? The revolution on the land was an agrarian revolution only because of the fat booty which tempted the poorer peasants. For the rest it was more or less a rebellion against despotism and incompetence, and it pursued its course by the same natural law that makes a stone roll down a mountain-side. The revolution gave the peasants land, more land than they could or wanted to swallow, and those who could and did want to swallow, afterwards the "kulaks," were hardly regarded by the peasants as "exploiters." The individualistic manner of production with its primitive labour methods, if the land was sufficiently redistributed, was enough to enable Russia to return slowly to its position as a great Power, but it was not enough to make Russia a World Power. For the process of industrialisation requires men, and the country districts provided them, and an indiscriminate colonisation of the country districts would have secured the means of subsistence, but it would not have set on foot industrialisation or achieved a surplus of exports. So that intensive, not extensive, agriculture is the watchword, modernisation, collectivism, corn factories. All that is clear and simple, and one is ashamed of having to explain it again and again.'

Ive blushed and said: 'The diplomatist-landowner Hellwig from the district of Hanover wants to remain a tenant-farmer and lays stress on the argument that the farmer must demand profit for his labour under the capitalist as well as under any other system.'

'He does and that is his demand,' said Hellwig, bending forward. 'I know, Iversen, that you are afraid you will have to put me down as a renegade, because up to now I have avoided speaking of the things which, in your opinion, must be of prime importance for every farmer—of the, shall we say, irrational values which alone give the farming community the right or the incentive to take its place as a vital unit with arbitrary power, as a class, or better still, as a profession; values whose obligation I will grant you as gladly as their bare material influence, and which the most inveterate materialist must take into account, if, at least, he does not wish to deny the whole irrational power of the proletarian consciousness of solidarity. Well, I avoided it, because, quite simply, these things do not come into the picture, or at least not in any decisive form, in considering the Russian example. If we compare merely the machines of production and the extent of trade, there is a damned deal of difference between Herr von Itzenplitz and me, and between me and small-holder Lohmann with his perpetually sick cow and his four dozen hens. But there is no difference in the bond we all acknowledge with the soil, whether it be three thousand or three hundred or only three acres in extent; no difference in the bond with our property, be it castle, farm, or cottage; no difference in our obligation to work, in our responsibility towards the whole country. I do not know and cannot know how these things are in Russia; but even if it does not seem as though collectivism, that is the radical abolition of private ownership, had come about particularly spontaneously, or had even originated with the peasants, certainly the so-called irrational values were not bound up with the things which with us are the individual essence, with blood and soil and heritage and the earth; or at least they had not the compelling force which demands death rather than renunciation. At any rate we heard nothing of the class-conscious opposition or professional pride that is always blazing up with us, on far less provocation, and only where religious standards still prevailed, among the Methodists, did we hear anything of the bitterness of the agrarian revolution. In this respect I think we could be depended on, if it were necessary. But it is not necessary. For with us there is not the incentive to that form of agrarian revolution; it would be a crime not only against the working-class, but against Soviet Germany itself, and against the holy spirit of socialism; it would be an attempt to build a power-station where there is no water, a saw-mill where there is no wood. For the process of industrialisation has long since been completed in Germany; the task of socialism is to take over the means of production and constitutionally to reorganise the industrial apparatus, but this simple fact reverses the whole scale of exactions. For now it is industry which has to aim at surplus of exports, to collect incredibly larger quantities of men, in all probability to restore even the forces liberated by the reorganised process of production, and, by guaranteeing the stability of the whole country, to guarantee also the stability of agriculture. The amount of land we have under cultivation cannot be increased to any extent worth mentioning, our labour methods cannot be further modernised to any appreciable degree, the productivity of the land cannot be noticeably enhanced. It is true there are still fallow lands to be opened up, large-scale holdings which can be subdivided; but there already you have the necessity of a new settlement, of a purely productive colony, coming into collision with the necessity for a more intensive economy based on collectivism. Collective work is only possible in agriculture, for it is only there that it can—possibly—be of economic utility, it is only there that it is possible to conceive of a limited number of machine- and tractor-stations for a largish number of collective undertakings. In Germany, however, pure agriculture only constitutes a quarter of the whole of agrarian production, and anyone who knows how closely the different kinds of production are united will have no illusions about the possibility of an agrarian revolution on the Russian pattern. What remains to be done is to produce one on a German pattern. This is dependent on the nature and result of the General Revolution. Therefore I am of the opinion that it is necessary for us farmers, on the one hand, to do battle with the existing System, not like the big landed proprietor whom I combat, not because he wants to live, but because he wants to live under the capitalist system and at the same time be the representative and director of the whole Farmers' Movement; and on the other hand to cling to it, not like the Nazi farmers, expecting wonders from tub-thumping megalomaniacs, and grumbling at the hard times; not even like your farmers, Iversen, standing in front of their farms in despair but in proud isolation, blindly attacking everything that approaches them, however distantly; but to join the only movement which can make the salvation of the farmers possible, even though it may not know, in any individual case, how; and, in order that it may know as soon as possible, to work with it. That is the essential thing and nothing else. In Russia the proletariat has liberated the peasants; the farmers in Germany can only be liberated by the proletariat.'

'He talks like a book,' said Hinnerk, grinning, and Ive motioned to him to keep quiet; the waiter came to ask if the gentlemen would like another beer, but the gentlemen declined, and Ive thought: how am I going to persuade Hellwig that it is necessary to intercede for Claus Heim? For, not for one moment did he doubt that it was more important to be completely at variance with Hellwig, here and now, over the question at issue than it was to gain some uncertain success in his continuous and painful importunings on behalf of Claus Heim.

Finally, he said that he might as well admit from the outset that any attempt on his part to give himself an air of high diplomacy could be nothing but a farce, for he was in a position which would not permit him to act from strength to strength. If he had succumbed to the psychological temptation produced by the nature of the discussion, even if he could succeed in hoodwinking his companion, this could be of no practical or positive importance. All he could do was to state that he himself believed in the necessity for a tactical association and he would undertake personally to see if arrangements could not be made for such an association.

'As a sign of a preliminary agreement which will immediately establish the necessary basis of confidence,' he said, 'you must be prepared to take a direct part in our propaganda crusade for the release of Claus Heim and the other condemned farmers. The Communist Party of Germany ought to realise what advantage it would reap from this.'

'This shall immediately be brought up for detailed discussion,' said Hellwig.

Ive took out his notebook and arranged a date for discussion. I must write to old Reimann at once, he thought, and said to Hellwig:

'You probably realise how difficult it will be, in view of the sinister effect which the word Communism still exercises, to induce the farming community and the whole militant peasantry of the northern provinces to come round to the ideas that you represent.' But on closer examination, it was actually only the word Communism which was a stumbling-block.

'I don't know,' he continued, 'if what you have been saying is in conformity with the ideas and attitude of your Party executive. I should be surprised if it were; for what the Party has up to now delivered in the way of slogans and manifestoes is not particularly calculated to arouse great respect for the world-shaking Communist intelligence. But that has no bearing on the question. I accept what you have been saying as an opinion which is possible within the meaning of Communism, and, if we choose to leave the field which you are considering, I am in a position to go very far in agreeing with you. No one can fail to regard Marxism at least as a very valuable tenet of belief, and so far the situation is favourable to Communism. The national aspect too is attractive, and I would even go a bit further than you and would assume that, even in the event of a Central Europe separated from the Western world, with a simultaneous tendency towards a world-revolutionary advance directed from Moscow, the sphere of German power and influence will of necessity detach itself from Russia, apart from the importance of German National claims, simply owing to the favourable position of the German industrial apparatus in regard to production technique. It is hardly conceivable that Communism, just because its task is to introduce a completely new machinery of production, is not also endeavouring to develop the apparatus to its full capacity and, therefore, to give it greater flexibility than is possible within the meshes of the capitalist system. At any rate it won't do merely to replace Western constraints and limitations by Eastern; that would simply mean driving out the German national devil with the Russian national Beelzebub. I beg of you not to take offence at what I am saying. It is because, with you, I do believe the indestructible power of the nation to be a reality, an element whose influence reacts perpetually on every theory and every constructive idea, that I am able to go so far in agreement with you, and the Russian example is of actual value to me—as a confirmation. I know that you and I are branded as traitors by the jacks-in-office of all parties and factions, but I know also that, at the present moment at least, it is more important to ignore all superficial clashes, in whatever form they manifest themselves, and to lay the foundations of a deeper union rather than to line the streets with avenues of flags and fill the marketplaces with the tumult of propaganda.

Ive continued: 'If then, I recognise the nation as an element of intrinsic importance, as the foremost historical force, our task is clearly set: it is our duty to force it to its full and unimpaired effectiveness, to allow it to attain, as it were, the unity of form and content to which it aspires. Do not misunderstand me! I, too, see no reason why sociological readjustments should not be made within the nation. If the proletariat is prepared to remove the corpse of the bourgeoisie, and, in spite of the protests of credulous physicians, bribed into asserting that they can still feel its pulsebeats, to bury it as quickly as possible, in order to escape from its pestilential contagions; if it can command the power, the unlimited control, to bring the class war to an end and abolish class, and if, at the same time, it has plans prepared which are in accord with the requirements of the nation, such action could only arouse universal approbation, and hardly a single reason exists for not supposing that the direct representatives of production, who as a natural consequence are those who must be most directly interested in production, are the best informed as to the requirements and necessary readjustments and are most fitted to do what is right. But if it is the will of the proletariat to submerge the individualistic economic islands, which wind, water and weather have so long been corroding, then the farming community must be at liberty to put its own house in order. That this order cannot be an individualistic one under the control of Communism you must admit, and when you have done that, I will admit that it cannot and must not be individualistic under any future control. If we assume the most primitive form of co-operation between industry and agriculture, or, if you prefer, between workers and farmers, that of simple barter, much as though the farmers said, "Give us machines and potash and we will give you scrambled eggs and ham," there must be some authority to establish the reciprocal values. But from what point of view? Surely from the point of view that will render the greatest good to the community as a whole. This authority, call itself what it may, will function like a department of state, perform a real public duty, only it will not guarantee complete freedom to the individual to strive for profit. This postulates, with the reorganisation of economics, a complete reorganisation of society, from which the farming community cannot be excluded. Through this twofold reorganisation the proletariat will be enabled to administer the means of production; but they will not, of course, be put into the hands of individuals of the proletariat, but eventually the machine will become the servant of those who serve it. I am rather hazy as to what the Communist remedies are, but I am prepared not to doubt their efficacy. But the farming community has from the very beginning had at its disposal the most important means of production, the soil, and is striving to make a livelihood from it. Under the auspices of the individualist method the farmer has become less and less able to do this, even when he has by partial renunciation of, but still in pursuance of, the method, sought to organise on a co-operative basis. In these circumstances, as a matter of fact, any alternative method would suit him, if only it would guarantee to him the essential result of his activity—production. Why should a collective organisation not be possible for agriculture? Why should it not be possible to erect corn mills in the East, and immense oxen farms in the Marsh, and an immense sheep farm on the heath, with managing directors, a technical staff, machine- and tractor-centres, potash stores and transport stations? Its advisability is questionable, but it is possible. Originally the farmer cultivated his plot and sold his products single-handed; later he cultivated his plot and sold his products cooperatively; why should he not in the future cultivate his land cooperatively and dispose of his products cooperatively? There is no reason why this should not be possible, but whether it is essential is a question. The pivot of the whole question is, and always will be, private ownership. And it does not need Communism to do away with it. Perhaps it is treachery to the revolution to say that private ownership no longer exists, because such a statement is calculated to confuse the issue. But that is the position for the farmer: he can no longer make a living out of his property, because the capitalist system has taxed him too heavily; he cannot sell his property, because there are no buyers. I do not know precisely what the position is in other economic spheres, but in any case there is food for thought in the remarkable phenomenon that, if private ownership is defended at all, it is only with an obviously bad conscience. There is probably a reason for this. And there is probably a reason for the fact that a farmer, if by chance he has the opportunity to sell his property and leave his farm, is regarded as contemptible, at least by his fellow-farmers. For private ownership is not only a conception of the economic law, it is also, I must say it, a conception of moral obligation. For, what else is the share of the individual proletarian in the means of production taken over by his class, that is by the whole collective proletariat, but a conception of moral obligation? For the farmer his farm is the embodiment of this idea, even when, under economic law, it no longer belongs to him. Originally, property in its most fully developed form, in the Middle Ages, probably possessed this corporate character, and this makes us think, doesn't it, of the phenomenon of the monastic orders of the Catholic Church? It was capitalism, and I trace its foundation to the Renaissance, that first destroyed the beneficent spiritual bond. The conception of property as a moral obligation was first lost sight of, certainly not with all individuals at the same time nor in the same degree, but it was lost sight of in the capitalistic tendency, and it is completely naive to try to differentiate between good and bad capitalism; good capitalism is always a bit late in appearing. Today capitalism is on the way to destroying the conception of the economic law, and private ownership is now no more than a fiction. The fact that the farming community never consistently took part in this development and, where it did spasmodically adapt itself to it, was obviously acting out of character; the fact that today, when the System has juggled away its power of disposal over property, it does not dream, nor can it ever dream, of giving up the spiritual bond of obligation, leads to the conclusion that there must be other ways of escape than the one, which has become untenable, of magically turning individualist methods of production and life into a collective method, by a simple addition sum of properties and owners of property. Just as it can never be forgotten that the farming community as a whole, whether as class or as profession, was never, and never could be, in a position to be exploited, it must also not be forgotten that, by its very nature, it cannot directly accept and take over the future forms of existence of those who have hitherto been exploited. The character of the farming community has always remained the same, and no agrarian revolution can be directed towards a fundamental reorganisation of its own forms of production and laws of property, but only against the more or less determining efforts which would like to impose alien forms of production and laws of property on the farming community, that is against the capitalist system today, and tomorrow—against the Communist system. I would not go so far as to assert that the unambiguous and natural acknowledgment in Russia of the particular conditions of production ruling in the agrarian sector as well as in every other sector leads directly to the conclusion that they were opposing the act of reorganisation and could only be brought into a more or less bearable agreement with the plan by the somewhat aggressive approximation of two scientific points of view; but it does lead to the conclusion that Russian agrarian production has not developed, or has not developed sufficiently, in accordance with its particular conditions: for obviously the costs of reorganisation are worth while. But they are not worth while in Germany. That is an assertion, but it is sufficiently illuminating if we consider the state of agrarian development. The only possibility of increasing profits is perfected mechanisation. This is, of course, not conceivable without a certain amount of reorganisation of the owner-farmers, of which the lesser farmers and small-holders particularly would have to be the victims; it is conceivable, however, if the farming community is able to take its stand, more than it has done hitherto, as a class or profession, or at any rate as a responsible unity, with full sway not only externally but also in its own domain, and this particularly, after the removal of alien disturbing influences, not so much owing to what one might call horizontal general limitations of ownership, such as inorganic large-scale production, but owing to vertical limitations, such as capital funds. If, therefore, Communism recognises the actual state of affairs, that is, if it realises that no advantage is to be gained by forcing itself with bloodshed upon the farming community, which is fully awake to its position and its needs; and further, if it realises that there is no advantage to be gained in urging those who are left, at most twenty percent, to the highest possible degree of agricultural profit by the crazily expensive attempt to bring about a radical reorganisation of agrarian production in a socialistic sense—abstract or not; that is, if it is ready to allow the farming community, as a class or a profession, sufficient scope to manage its own affairs reasonably, under the control of the State, then Communism might actually appear to the farming community to be not only acceptable, but even desirable.

'In other words,' said Hellwig, 'if Communism in its attitude towards the farming community ceased to be Communism...'

'Exactly,' said Ive.

He continued: 'In Russia the proletariat has liberated the farming community; for the impulse to revolution came from the worker. But in Germany the impulse to revolution, as soon as we recognise that it is a national revolution, lies in the farming community, and it is the duty of the farming community to liberate the proletariat. It is the farming community and not the proletariat in Germany that holds the key position of the revolution. And if we recapitulate all the opportunities that Communism offers us, beginning with the destruction of capitalism, the immediate rupture of all associations with the Western world, the tearing up of the Treaty of Versailles, establishment of security in the rear through the East, the break-up and reorganisation of Central Europe, to the destruction of the individualistic point of view, to the winding-up of the period of intellectual history from the Renaissance to the world war, quite apart from the extermination of all those Powers, with whom it is hardly worth speaking except with machine-guns, from the confederation of the Danube to parliamentary democracy, then I cannot but admit that the decision in favour of Communism is not a decision...'

'But?' asked Hellwig.

'A flight,' said Ive.

He continued: 'For in the unique historical vacuum in which the world and we find ourselves today, our task is not to discover the most attractive and most tolerable escape.'

'What then?' asked Hellwig.

'Our task,' said Ive, 'is to attain the fuller development of our own character.'

'Those are mere words,' said Hellwig.

'They are certainly words,' said Ive, 'for which we have to find a meaning. And the way to set about it is, first of all, to leave off talking about all the illuminating examples of the world. We cannot state precisely what is the extent of German national power. Therefore we ascribe to it the greatest extent imaginable. The frontiers of a nation are at the points where it is held in check by opposing Powers. But how can we dare so to enrich foreign Powers as to turn them against ourselves? And if those foreign Powers turn against each other, are we not at the same time fighting against ourselves, here on our own soil, in our own breasts? We have put our own strength into the System, so much so that it seems almost impossible for us to destroy it, and in order to destroy it are we to begin putting as much, and as much again, into some foreign Power? To the devil with this method which allows us to let the centuries roll by while we puzzle our heads and waver, rubbing first one shoulder and then the other, reeling in every direction under the sun, feeding out of every trough; shitting in every corner, rushing, at every attack, into the arms of some newfound philanthropic brother and then, at every well-deserved kick, sitting down in astonishment on our bottoms and venting our anger in intellectual diarrhoea. To the devil with this method which allows more concessions to be granted to National Socialism at its outset than to Social-Democracy at its conclusion; which allows Chancellor Brüning, an industrious, clever and energetic man, to whom we could well give our confidence if he had not already the confidence of those whom we cannot trust, to reorganise the System, not with a view to destroying it but to supporting it; which allows Comrade Thälmann to announce his national programme, with socialism as its centre of gravity or not, as the case may be, at any rate on the basis of the precepts of Moscow, sometimes in favour of the civil war in Russia and sometimes against the imperialistic war in China, and allows Colleague Goebbels to advocate alliance with and support of first Italy, then England, and then America. What have we gained if we have only learned how to live in the shadow of others? If that is so, what difference is there between us and Bohemia, except the extent of our population? Thus, unless we want to exert ourselves for the benefit of others, there is nothing left for us to do except, in calm and modest meditation, to contemplate our navels. Perhaps if we dream the Reich like the Nirvana of the Fakirs, we shall reach consciousness of what the Reich is, and that would be a hypothesis to start from.'

'And meanwhile,' said Hellwig, 'the farmer can go to the devil.'

'Yes,' said Ive, 'he'll probably do that if he does not know where he is going, if he does not know what ought to be done now and in his position. If he still has any existence, it is in the consciousness of his profession. Therefore, he must act in the light of this consciousness. He must not declare for individualism, because his profession has obligations; he must not declare for collectivism, for that would destroy his profession. He must learn to see through every "ism" and recognise it for what it is, vain humbug and jugglery. He must realise that the soil has been given to him, to live on it and to die on it, has been given to him as a heritage which he must pass on, which he and his have to administer, that it has been given to him as the basis of all his labour, in fief, not as a commodity, that he is responsible to his profession and the profession to the whole community. Is that nothing but words? If so, they are comprehensive enough. They comprehend the inexorable and immediate war against the System; they comprehend giving up one's sins and acknowledging one's errors; they comprehend the obligation to put the farmer's house in order, from top to bottom and from bottom to top, from the law of the individual farm to the law of the whole profession. And if the worthy and honourable Herr Itzenplitz wears a top hat because he has given up doing his duty for the benefit and honour of the profession, there is no good reason why the worthy and honourable Herr von Itzenplitz auf Itzensitz should not be deprived of his position of authority and be nominated as chairman of the association of Uckermark beekeepers, since he is no longer fit for his duties as a landowner, or for the profession which he served, or for the nation which the profession serves. And if the profession gave the blood of its sons for the sake of the nation there is no reason why it should not give the property of its masters for the sake of the nation. But the same discipline which the farmer demands of himself he must demand throughout the country in which and for which he lives. He must call upon everyone who wishes to have a voice in Germany's future to take a part in his battle. He must see that the struggle for self-determination is carried on everywhere. He must welcome every independent claim to this same will to nationality, must make alliances now, form associations, give an example of devotion and set the standard of the will to responsibility. He must do all this, for otherwise he would not only be surrendering himself, he would be betraying the revolution, one of whose most essential claims is the liberation of the workers. Is this nothing but words? Is this mere windy enthusiasm? Is not that a new goal? Perhaps it is nothing but words. But those in whom they can touch a chord are the people that matter. Perhaps it is windy enthusiasm. But you, Farmer Hellwig, you, a tenant-farmer, are up to your neck in the seething waters of four dozen conferences, of nine-and-ninety departmental ministers. Your gorge, as well as mine, rises in disgust in front of four hundred thousand dreary saviours. What about the hotch-potch of pamphlets and leaflets and trade-supplements, right, left, and on every side. You, Hellwig, know as well as I do that it is time to be enthusiastic, to be burning with ardour, when everybody's heart is as dry as rotting wood. Perhaps this is no new goal. It is an old goal, an eternal goal that has never been reached. All respect to you, Hellwig, if you feel you cannot embrace any but a new doctrine. But if this is not so, it does not matter at what camp-fire you warm your hands so long as you are prepared, at the given signal, to carry the torch into the old eternal Reich.'

Ive had been speaking loudly, and Hinnerk woke up, blinked his eyes, and asked delightedly:

'Into the Third Reich?'

'You're too fond of saying stupid things lately, Hinnerk,' said Ive, getting up from his seat. 'I liked you better when you were with the farmers.'

And Hinnerk said ruefully: 'I, too, liked you better then.'

XIV

LIEUTENANT BRODERMANN was in the habit of accounting to himself for his feelings and actions. He remembered Ive with an interest compounded of pain, astonishment and warm comradeship. As a young ordnance officer at the Headquarters of the Divisional Commander, it had been his duty to inform Corporal Iversen of the death of his father. Ive had looked at him out of a pale, thin, dirty face with bleared, unseeing eyes, had said: 'Thank you, sir,' and had pushed his way back through the heaps of orderlies sleeping the sleep of the dead.

After this episode Brodermann never missed an opportunity on his rounds of making a detour to visit Ive's company. Unfortunately Ive seemed to find it difficult to make friends with his fellow-officer, though he was only a few years older than himself. Shortly before Ive got his promotion, Brodermann had done him a small service. At a little celebration in the rest camp the chief staff officer found fault with Ive's cap. Ive got up and left the mess without a word. Brodermann had put the matter right, but Ive never referred to the incident again and seemed to be angry with Brodermann because, since the reproof of the staff officer was deserved, he had probably made excuses for Ive on the grounds of his youth and his nerve-racking duties. Nevertheless, even after the shemozzle Brodermann and Ive stuck together in the silent association of the front, which took everything for granted and made the friendship of the men so natural and steady; and at the time of the Kapp-putsch they had been in the same machine-gun corps. Then they both made up their minds to the step which was the turning-point in their lives, leading them, however, in opposite directions.

Ive felt that he could not swear allegiance to the Government, and, in spite of Brodermann's earnest advice to the contrary, he embarked on the settlement adventure. But Brodermann was an officer, not an adventurer, and after mature consideration he decided to adapt himself to the changed conditions. Since he had come to regard his part in the Kapp-putsch as something to be ashamed of, particularly after events had proved how it had been engineered by the leaders, he decided when his troop was demobilised not to enlist in a regiment of the newly formed Defence Corps, but took service in the green-coated police force which was about to be formed at that time and which, it seemed, was to be completely non-political in its activities. He did not make this decision easily. He was, of course, a monarchist, but since by no fault of his own he was now absolved from his military oath, unless he wanted to stand aside from the reorganisation of the Reich, which he realised to be an absolute necessity, an aggrieved and futile grumbler, there was nothing else for him to do but to take the new oath, and to make up his mind to observe it with the same meticulous devotion with which he had observed his allegiance to the flag of the old Army. He did not spare himself. He deliberately strangled all the scruples which were apt to whisper in his ear, and, if he never succeeded in completely conquering the hydra-headed monster of doubts and temptations within him, at any rate, he got used to it and welcomed it, so to speak, as an antidote to his actions, as something essential to preserve the balance which was an indispensable necessity in his difficult calling. He had felt on entering the police force that in working for the good of the whole community he would find the task he wanted, a task that would tax a man's strength to the utmost; he found it to a degree surpassing all his hopes. He had distinct talents as an organiser, and these were made good use of, but, after a few years of exacting office work, Brodermann himself applied for transfer to the outside service, since duties that he had become so familiar with did not give him the complete satisfaction of working at his full capacity, His colleagues probably put him down as a climber; he was merely a man completely absorbed in his work, respected, but not liked, strict with himself, with his subordinates and, indeed, with his superiors; for, even against his own interests, he always said what he thought if he felt that it was right, that is, in accordance with the dictates of duty. So, in spite of his brilliant abilities, his career was slow, and he often observed, though entirely without envy, that when advancement was in question he was passed over in favour of more smooth-tongued colleagues and friends.

With his characteristic doggedness he never lost his interest in Ive. From time to time he gleaned information of his strange doings from the papers in short news paragraphs under the heading of 'Home Politics,' or in the police-court reports. He took the *Iron Front* and *The Peasant*, and read with a very solemn face the articles signed '-v-' or 'Ive.' Once or twice he even wrote to Ive—brief, sincere letters, without a mention of politics—but he never had an answer. Later he read in *The Peasant* the injunction to boycott all representatives of the System, and he realised, without understanding, why it was he had not heard. He spent a good deal of time studying Ive's ideas, with much headshaking. He fully understood the opinions and actions of the rebels, to whichever camp they belonged, and, man of order and duty though he was, he felt no resentment of any kind towards those he had to combat, and he combated them with stern professional zeal, doing everything that duty demanded of him, but no more. This does not mean that there was any point in which he could identify himself with them, or that he was mechanically doing his duty while his heart was on the side of those against whom he was acting. Nothing of the kind. In any case, he ruled everything personal out of his work, but this had only been possible because he was absolutely convinced of the rightness and necessity of his actions and because he identified himself to a hair's breadth with a point of view which he would have represented even if he had not been an officer of the police force. He made no effort to accept the opinions of his superiors in the Service, but he was delighted to find that his own opinions were, in the widest sense, shared by his superiors; if this had not been the case he would have been obliged to take the consequences.

Thus he was saddened rather than incensed by Ive's activities, and, since he knew Ive, he respected his convictions, although he did not for a moment doubt that these convictions were wrong and must be combated. When Ive was arrested, and later, when he had met him on the street that night, it was, of course, impossible for Brodermann to succumb to his first impulse and enter into conversation with him straight away. At the encounter after the Unemployed Trial, however, Brodermann had seen clearly enough the conflict of feelings that Ive had suffered, and he knew that Ive was aware that his behaviour simply denoted incapacity to adopt an attitude or at any rate to adopt the right attitude. Far from being offended, Brodermann sought an opportunity to talk things over with Ive, but when he began to make enquiries, he discovered, to his horror, that Ive was not registered with the police. He was in some doubt as to whether it was his duty to report this; he did not report it, and he made no effort to come to any conclusion about his duty in this respect. But he was all the more eager to follow up the chance that took Dr. Schaffer and himself to the same party. He heard Schaffer mention Ive, and asked him if he could arrange for them to meet. Schaffer agreed to this. He embarked on a long discussion with Brodermann, delighted to have discovered in the flesh an important representative of the 'System,' a rare example of a species practically extinct in either cultured or uncultured circles, and whom he hoped to find stimulating, and he invited him to come to his evenings, which Ive had formed the habit of attending pretty regularly. Brodermann, it is true, had never had much time for what he called intellectual gymnastics, but the prospect of being able to get a serious word with Ive led him to take the very first opportunity of turning up at Schaffer's.

He soon realised that the setting was not exactly suited for a serious, personal conversation, but he comforted himself with the thought that he would probably have to take an unobtrusive part in the discussion and this would ease a situation which, considering the nature of their last meeting, could hardly fail to be painful at first. So he waited for Ive, and sat silently in a corner, very much as Ive had done on his first visit to the circle, examining the guests, and vainly endeavouring to establish the character and political leanings of the circle from the utterances of individual gentlemen. In the first place he could make nothing of Dr. Schaffer, and this very naturally annoyed him. He straightened his back and sat upright and armed as though instead of his hanger, which he had put down in the ante-room, he were pressing an invisible sword into the floor.

A curious assembly, he thought, and as he sat with his chin pulled back into his collar he summed up every single individual as in some degree suspect. Apart from the two Indians, who appeared not to be able to bear the sight of each other—a Hindu and a Mohammedan probably, he thought to himself, but they were only a Northern and a Southern Indian—there was a youngish man who, while airing his opinions on various items of news with wrinkled brow, lapsed into remarkably, shall we say, colloquial phraseology, and whom at first he took to be a Communist Party agitator, and then decided must be the editor of a weekly paper very much of the Right, but who turned out in the end to be a Social-Democratic Trades Union Secretary. Again, Brodermann would never have taken the fair youth, with an old blackened pipe, who flung himself down on the sofa and every now and again gave a grunt, for one of the city editors of the *Berliner Tageblatt*; and he couldn't help thinking it very strange to observe that by far the best dressed person there was a gentleman with amazingly aristocratic features and sensitive, winning manners, whom he recognised as an influential official of the Russian Legation, whereas the name of the sloppily dressed individual with bad manners, who kept interpolating into the discussion a selection of more or less parrot-like Communistic catchphrases, pointed to his being the heir of one of the best known noble families of Germany. Nor could he ever have guessed that the gentleman who spoke so eloquently in favour of the proposed large-scale small holdings policy in the East was an important property owner; nor that the gentleman who defended with such delightful enthusiasm the wages policy of the Trades Unions was an authoritative representative of the engineering industry; and yet it was so. But this curious discrepancy between impression and appearance on the one hand and facts and opinions on the other, aroused, by its persistent obtrusion of paradox, a most violent antagonism in Brodermann, whose mind was always striving for clarity. Anything that could not be verified upset him, and he entrenched himself in a stronghold of opposition as though he were facing a siege.

He might have dismissed all these people, who were making themselves out to be so important, with a shrug of his shoulders, but he had to admit to himself the danger of such an attitude; for there was no getting away from the fact that the subjects and opinions that were being dealt with here were obviously being dealt with seriously; the whole discussion was on a level that allowed of no doubt that this was not a gathering of irresponsible literati, but of men who were perhaps interfering where they had no right, but in doing so were establishing a claim to be heard and heeded when the time was ripe. It was not the general and extremely frank criticism of existing conditions, of which Brodermann would have felt himself to be a representative even if he had not come in uniform, that angered him and made him uneasy; it was the demonstrable fact that this criticism was levelled concentrically so that there was reason for believing that the gentlemen who were carrying on the debate with such an air of reasonableness, when the moment came for them to take over the responsibility for reforming the object of their censure, might disperse eccentrically. Brodermann, quite rightly, had always considered himself to be extremely up-to-date; no one could be more aware than he was of the high degree of disaffection which had seized large sections of the nation, and it would not have surprised him to find this disaffection among those to whom it should have been, not only a matter of interest, but of intelligence, to be in direct opposition to it. But what was he to make of the complete cynicism of a gentleman in his thirties whom he afterwards learned was a Professor of Assyriology, who had just been indulging in reflections on the analogy between a certain epoch in the culture of the ancient Araucassians and the present day, and who, apparently as a sort of protest against some state of affairs or another, seldom had his hair cut, who gave as his reason for joining the Democratic or State Party that people were thankful enough today if anybody joined them? It was this that made him uneasy; to have to take seriously things that weren't worth taking seriously. He was working himself into a state of mind which made him feel that, despite all his self-control, in having to defend the one responsible attitude with the pride of the single combatant, he might have to discard the shield of his personal dignity.

When Ive came in with Pareigat he did not at first notice Brodermann. Following the practice of late-comers to these gatherings, he tiptoed across the room, without greeting anyone, to find himself a chair, so as not to disturb the discussion. Brodermann had half risen, and Schaffer gave him a friendly nod without interrupting what he was saying, Ive now saw Brodermann face to face. He hesitated for a moment, nodded to him almost imperceptibly, turned very red, and sat down exactly opposite him. Schaffer threw an astonished glance at Ive and Brodermann and went on with what he was saying: that, at any rate, it was a mistake to regard the attitude of France, incomprehensible to German intelligence, in regard to the Hoover proposals simply as reactionary stubbornness or as dictated merely by hatred of Germany; nor was it necessary to explain the French theses with benevolent objectivity as psychological, as the result probably of the formal, juristic trend of the French mind, or of the desire for security, arising out of the memory of the devastations of the war in the Eastern departments— Ive thought to himself, Schaffer is surprised that Brodermann and I are not falling on each other's necks as old war-comrades. Old war-comrades! If we had anything in common in the war it was that each of us, uninfluenced by any group egoism, had to find his way and his attitude absolutely alone—For the French struggle for hegemony, which had its counterpart in an at least equally strong and equally natural German struggle for hegemony, was derived from too deep a source to be explained psychologically and to be attributed merely to the political circumstances and the geo-political position. In any case, it was not a question of a political, but of a historical direction of will, which attracts statecraft, whatever views statesmen may represent, into line with itself. Fundamentally, from the very first awakening of German consciousness, the destiny of Germany, and beyond that the destiny of Europe, depended on a single and immutable factor. This was the existence of the Reich, not, of course, just one of the perpetually changing political manifestations in the midst of Central Europe, but the complete content of thoughts and feelings, of dreams and tendencies which are contained in the concept 'The Reich.' Every German attempt to realise the concept must of necessity call into the battlefield all the Powers who are in their essence non-German. Thus it was not surprising that the Reformation in its characteristic political significance, which was expressed at its finest in Luther's hymns, had been far more instrumental in bringing about a movement like the Counter-reformation than Humanism which, as the revolt of an intellectual force, was certainly equally dangerous to the Church. Long after its first historical reaction, if not in any palpable achievement or in any conscious action, certainly in its influence, the Counter-reformation undoubtedly had, and must have even today, a widely operative effect.

As he said this Schaffer looked across at Pareigat, who appeared to agree with him. Now, the first manifest French attempt, of the same character even led to the endeavour of King Francis I to have himself elected as Emperor of Germany, whilst his antagonist Charles V, who, owing to the far-sighted dynastic policy of his grandfather

Maximilian, was also heir to the Spanish throne, was forced, in spite of Turkish wars and Italian decadence, again and again to dig his claws into France. If we could not renounce the pleasure of giving the picture a psychological justification, what had to be said was that obviously the French conception of history was unlike the German; for France the individual epochs of history could be regarded as isolated, self-sufficient manifestations; as historical phenomena they could be used as interesting, but objective examples for comparison and then be laid away among the documents in archives made up of typical examples. Much could be learned by studying Plato and Aristotle, Erasmus and Voltaire, the life of Jeanne d'Arc or even Napoleon, but for the French there was no application which could serve as a lesson for the present day to be drawn from such a study; whereas for us Germans history was not a single process progressing in stages, but to a certain extent the continual crystallisation and solution of one and the same element, and we could still hear today the deep challenging voice of Plato; Meister Eckhart was still thinking today the thoughts that we have perpetually forgotten to think; and with us and today the battle was repeatedly being waged which has been waged from the Hohenstaufen to Bismarck, and every single epoch was a perpetual warning and injunction to fulfil today what has always been desired. It was just this lack of 'restrained' mystic consciousness in the French mind which gave to French politics its amazingly more flexible character. Whereas with us every association led to an eventually disastrous but holy alliance, for the French every alliance from the time of Louis XI to Napoleon and beyond that to the Great War, was always a fine and useful but extremely unholy transaction. But this flexibility gave French politics not only the appearance of, but actual honourableness. What the French wanted they wanted actually, whereas we were forced by historical retrospection always to be wanting something different from that for which we had entered the battle-arena, so carefully prepared and manned. The result was that we always seemed to the world to be the most reactionary and at the same time the most revolutionary nation, for whom it was a necessity to hold itself in readiness for every surprise. With this was closely associated the impossibility of understanding the character of Germany's struggle for power. If we were, as Dostoevsky described us, a Protestant Power, our protest had always been for the sake of the Reich, and at the moment when we were very near to bringing the Reich to complete fulfilment we produced protest and anger in all our neighbours, above all in the French. Thus the conception of the Reich had a far-reaching effect, and whenever it struck root in great individual personalities there was always a strong endeavour to tear them up from German soil, and give them an honourable, but universally palatable, super-national, intellectual origin; and there might even be said to be an effort on our part to drive back to their own sphere any personalities who were in some degree unpleasing, who had in all honour acted against this honour, regarding them with sure instinct as forces antagonistic to the Reich; take for example Charles the Great, whom over there they described, quite as a matter of course, as a Frenchman. In fact, in every incident of German history which, as history, represented the perpetual struggle for the Reich, the world had re-echoed with the accusations hurled by the Germans against the French and by the French against the Germans. Varied as these complaints had been, there was always a germ of similarity to be observed: the complaint had always been that the other was striving for hegemony in Europe. And actually, if we asked ourselves who had the right to this hegemony, then there were abundant reasons for and against, but one thing was certain, that it could only belong to one of the two peoples, one of the two nations, and that the nation to whom it did not belong could no longer exist as a nation, that is as a people with an historical task to fulfil. And however much the odds changed in the game of chance, the winner had always made conditions which were calculated to cut the sinews of the aggressor of the Reich. France knew how great the danger was and so, at the present time, it had had to do something it had never done before, except in the Edict of Nantes, something which was even contrary to the essence of the French method, since it limited its flexibility, that is, to press through a Treaty with the avowed intention of its being permanent and unalterable. Over and above this, but arising out of it none the less, France had organised half the world, and if this had been accomplished in the neutral form of the League of Nations, after all the League of Nations arose out of the Treaty, and though possibly all the Geneva theses of peace and justice had been listened to, read and promulgated by all the nations represented with an enigmatic smile, not so by France, since for her peace was the guarantee of her hegemony, and for her justice really was a slogan uttered from the heart, the highest political virtue to which it applied itself, since everything that France did must—how pleasant—be just, so long as it served the ends of peace. But we saw what it actually meant to us; we saw in the League of Nations a Counter-Reich.

As he said this Schaffer looked at Ive, for it was from a discussion with Ive that he had gleaned the idea. But Ive said nothing. He did not even look at Schaffer. His close-set eyes were fixed on the top buttons of Brodermann's uniform coat. Brodermann, too, said nothing, but he listened with an intent expression on his face. The discussion now took a more lively turn—with interesting disclosures about the Sino-Japanese conflict, and the extraordinary attitude of France, which was not fully understood by the other Powers, nor by the French people, and actually it was a question of interests in Southern China, which only affected a small circle of capitalists, and of the distribution of spheres of interest, which had its explanation in Indo-Chinese affairs—but still neither Ive nor Brodermann took any part in what was being said. Later on, it is true, each one of them in turn ventured on a short remark. This was when Schaffer spoke of the part played by the citizen class —the bourgeoisie—in the form which had crystallised out of its political supremacy, making various attempts to define the word citizen and eventually giving a far-fetched explanation of the supremacy of this class as a manifestation of the idea of the Counter-Reich. Then Brodermann asked politely, and obviously embarrassed, if after all it was not the French Revolution which had created a concept indispensable to the organisation of every state, and which he had been waiting in vain to hear mentioned here: the concept of a citizen of the State? Since Schaffer did not at once realise whether his leg was being pulled or whether this was a serious criticism, and if so, from what angle it was being levelled, he let the observation pass with a few amiable words.

Then Dr. Salamander broke in. He had returned from Paris, since the banks had been closed by an emergency regulation, and he gave the impression of a man who no longer understood the world.

'But in the name of God,' he asked, 'what would become of German intellectualism if the Third Reich was established? Is it conceivable that the intellectual freedom so laboriously won should be suppressed, gagged, and forced to go abroad, into exile—an immeasurable loss to German culture?'

Then Ive said that he could not, of course, tell how the power of the Third Reich would be exercised, but when he reflected that, for at least twelve years, intellectual freedom had been able to put forth what blossoms it liked and had taken full advantage of this and, indeed, had at its disposal a magnificent apparatus which it would be difficult to equal, and that it had made the greatest imaginable use of this apparatus, with the result that those very Powers were now menacing it, which the approved representatives of intellect were steadily endeavouring, with all the weapons of reason, to scare back into their dark lairs, 'then it is easy to imagine, Dr. Salamander, what will happen to you and those on whose behalf you have raised your voice, namely— nothing. Nothing will happen to them, they can go on writing calmly and confidently and peacefully; nobody will read a word of it.'

Schaffer disapproved of this turn in the discussion and, shaking his head playfully, he tactfully led the discussion, which was threatening to go to pieces, into the right lines again.

'Everything we have been saying,' he went on, 'leads to the conclusion that what any German policy needs is an objective point which is a fundamental part of it. What we have to criticise in the present conditions, from whatever point of view we regard them, is their lack of any sort of objective point which would permit of far-sighted action. It is impossible to feel any certainty as to where things are leading. The reason for this impossibility lies in the System.'

Lieutenant Brodermann wheeled round like a hawk, but he said nothing.

Have I got to spend the whole evening gassing away by myself? thought Schaffer. I must say something to rouse that blockhead.

'For,' he continued, 'by reason of its origin and character, the System has no need to do anything but apply the national technique of political theory. That is to say, it is forced always to do exactly what other political Powers prescribe. Once it has assumed hegemony, it cannot conceal by camouflage what it actually is, the tool of Powers which have extranational interests. Whatever policy the System undertakes to follow, it can never be what it professes to be, a national policy.'

'Gentlemen,' said Brodermann, clearing his throat and fingering the air as though he were clasping the hilt of an invisible sword, and, although he was annoyed with Dr. Schaffer, it was apparent to every one that it could not be out of courtesy to his host that he addressed his words directly and exclusively to Ive.

'Gentlemen,' said Brodermann, 'you speak of the System; it is very much the fashion lately to speak of the System; after all, it is a very simple and convenient concept. But I don't know what the reason is, whether I am too stupid, or whether it has to do with the state of public enlightenment —I have tried seriously, but so far I have not been able to understand what you really mean by the word "System," what this "System" you talk about actually is. I might very well imagine what it is by putting together all that I have heard and read for and against the System; but there is nothing here to throw any light on the System; it simply does not exist, if one is to believe all the things that are said and written about it. It would appear to be something which has only a negative existence, that cannot therefore be described as to its qualities, and, although I am far from wishing to assume that it merely lives the ghostly life of the figment of a discontented imagination, you must permit me to fill the gap, which is visible in spite of all the many points of view which have been put forward, by adding my modest contribution to the discussion and telling you what might after all be claimed to be the "System," even if it is not quite what you wish or are able to convey. And you must also permit me to refer to this straight away as the "System" in order to avoid circumlocutions which detract from the necessary clarity.'

'Well, then, the System means something that no movement or idea has to its credit, however great in itself and however imposing a popular success it can claim—in short: an achievement. Moreover, it means an achievement which, according to all I have heard from you here, should be very acceptable to you, and should call for your applause, namely, the preservation of the Reich. That may surprise you, and possibly you have never heard of it before, but real achievement has a quality, which cannot be strange to you, who after all belong to many different professions, without it having been evident in the discussion, namely, the quality of anonymity. You know that Graf Schlieffen, the man who transformed Moltke's heritage, the Prusso-German General Staff, into an instrument of military efficiency such as the world had never seen before, gave his officers a rule of personal conduct: "Be rather than appear." And wherever it is a question of accomplishing real, essential work, detailed work, without which no task with a long end in view is possible, this principle must be observed. It is a Prussian principle, and it is a universal German principle, as soon as we consider the meaning of the State. Now this principle still applies today, or applies again, and it applies where you, and with you all those who know so well how to keep the German public occupied with their claims and problems, would never suspect it to apply, in the System, which does not stand in the public eye at all, and by reason of its sphere of activity, cannot stand in the public eye. I said that the System was an achievement, an anonymous achievement. Maybe, but it is a visible achievement to which you gentlemen, who are gathered here for profitable discussions, are immensely indebted and in which, whether you wish it or not, in a great many of your activities, whether they be of a private or public nature, you co-operate. I do not mean, of course, lest you should misunderstand me, that you are indebted to it because it enables you to organise a protest against the System, although that has become a profitable occupation; what I mean is that it is only by the preservation of the Reich, even if you do not approve of the form it takes, that you are enabled to meet here for this animated discussion and, in spite of your different callings, unanimously to declare that everything must be changed. I tell you the System has preserved the Reich, and without the System it would be today the plaything of foreign Powers, a heap of coloured bricks, from which every political passer-by can take whatever he considers to be his share, but not a building as it actually is today. It is true it is a faulty building, with a leaking roof, and whose stairways and rooms are far too cramped, but in which none the less you can live, have a home, and which, if you want it, can give you an answer to the question of where you belong. As is natural, where people are one on top of another, you can become involved in disputes, fly at one another's throats, in word or action, but if you attempt to knock down the walls of the house itself, your excuse that it had become too cramped for you will not prevent anyone from thinking that you have committed a crime, and surely it is for this contingency that the police exist. For the important thing, which comes before all private interests, is that we should preserve the little that has been left to us, and that from this foundation we should slowly win back, by hard and assiduous labour, what we have lost. And for this purpose it is no use bemoaning a happy past, however near or remote it may be; it is no use indulging in dreams of a glorious future; the one and only thing that is of any use is to realise what has to be done now—immediately—and in this way to provide a precisely calculated basis for what will have to be done in the future. I beg you, gentlemen, do not regard the men whom you consider representative of the System as idiots, do not regard them as self-seekers or party fanatics, do not weaken your own position by an error! And try not to excogitate a thraldom which has no connection with the real issue; in that way you will only be fathering a thraldom whose character, when it is too late, will mightily astonish you and will make you asseverate on your oath that you have no affection and no responsibility for the child.'

'You can imagine that, having served as an officer of the old Imperial Prussian Army, I did not lightly decide to serve the Republic, especially when it bore a very different aspect from what it has become today; that I entered on my duties in a dispassionate and critical frame of mind; and the feeling I had for the men who had taken over the State Government could only be described as one of complete mistrust. What could have led me to take this step but the certainty that it was essential, that all energies should be directed to the performance of the duties which were urgently demanding fulfilment on every side? And I can tell you, gentlemen, if there are any men whom I salute and to whom I say, "All honour to you," they are the men who have saved the Reich by their unflinching attitude, and who have displayed a statesmanship with which I myself would never have credited them. Let me tell you, you may search far and wide through Germany before you will find a statesman who unites such qualities as Otto Braun... And if I may venture to the sphere of analogies in which you are so much at home, then all I can say is that the wonderful relationship on which the foundations of the unity of the Reich were built, the relationship between Emperor William I and his Chancellor Bismarck, has its analogy today between the President of the Reich and Chancellor Brüning. Naturally I cannot fall into the error of thinking that everything that exists today is good and wonderful and beautiful; no one can do that, particularly not anyone in a position of responsibility. The important point is, not to hand out praise, or to paint things black, but to recognise the position for what it is, to consider how it arose and what possibilities for the future it affords. Surely it was not mere chance that out of the struggle between the opposing powers of Right and Left, of West and East, of North and South, of high and low, was developed the Reich in its present form, the System; and if you are searching for a mystic power, I can tell you where to find one. You will find it where out of the unspeakable chaos of endeavours and trends, of opinions and facts, of regulations and emancipations, of clatter of guns and signing of treaties, of hunger and oppression, and hopes and fears, the Reich re-fashioned itself, the Reich that could contain and accomplish all this without falling asunder, and in which today a further step could be taken to consolidate its form and to strengthen its position in foreign politics, if the whole witches' brew had not begun to seethe again, paralysing the energies which had been liberated so laboriously for the great tasks of the future. I do not fail to recognise how serious are the reasons which led to this new revolt; but ask yourselves whether these reasons are of necessity rooted in the System, or whether they do not much rather come from regions where the System itself cannot exercise any direct influence and to reach which it would be necessary that all the interested Powers should act together with a confidence which is lacking at present. To establish the confidence for this task is a part of the foreign policy which is essential today—a task for which, however, the System requires the confidence of those who should have the most direct interest in removing the reasons that are at present leading to an attack against the System. No one should doubt the good faith of the men and the movements who feel that they cannot repose their confidence in the System, but to realise the real state of affairs and to change it for the better, more is needed than overpoweringly strong convictions and the most disinterested and energetic will; an objective knowledge of the material is necessary. But the fact is that it is only where the material is fused that it can be surveyed, and the whole body of public statistics and investigations, of professional and political detailed work, all the knowledge of the mind of the people, of the claims of home and foreign policy, of the technique of government and of economics, are not sufficient to remove the barrier between the study, the party headquarters, the editorial office on the one hand and responsible officialdom on the other. For it is in government offices that the fruit of study are available in essence, the daily changing aspect is automatically recorded, the comprehensive plan is being built up step by step, ratios are adjusted, the matters of first importance are sifted out and decisions made as to how and in what degree they are to be dealt with. This is so, and because it is so, and because it cannot be altered, without immediately making any responsible

course of action impossible and destroying the security of the Reich—
because this is so, no change of authority will bring about a change in
the present state of affairs. What can it matter if one or other responsible leader in German politics goes and gives place to another; what
can it matter even if the whole machinery of government is suddenly
put into the hands of a completely new set of men, the System will
remain because the necessity for perpetual and constant achievement
remains, and, if it is perhaps going too far to say that the laws of this
achievement are categorical and exist independently of human will,
at any rate they possess the organic strength which represents the will
of the people better than any parliament or any form of public opinion. Yes, gentlemen, you cannot escape the facts; however energetically you may advance against them, they remain and must be
moulded and adjusted, and even supposing that a revolution were
carried through unanimously supported by the whole people, if the
System which has built itself up by laborious detailed work were
gradually to disintegrate, the whole organisation to be reorganised,
the same mechanical power would remain and, though the tempo
may be increased at which this mechanical power must be developed
and exploited, its magnitude can never be changed. And to attain this
we do not need a revolution. What we need is that the confidence of
all should be placed in the System, the elimination of all the ridiculous
obstructive ideas based on violence, which set themselves against the
System instead of fulfilling themselves in it in the most economical
way by constructive co-operation, in union with life and for the attainment of the only possible results. For it is not true that the System is a
rigid apparatus, a machine whose fly-wheel runs down when the
driving belts cease working, it is not a motor fed with doctrinal oil,
which stops short when no more of this particular mixture is available; it is a living entity and derives its life from the ideas of its era.
What is the use of talking of rational political technique? Undoubtedly it was the System that made it possible for Germany to enter the
League of Nations, and what else does that mean but to take the battle
for German security into the very territory of the so-called Counter-Reich, a battle which could not be waged anywhere else, because,
even with us actual political exigencies have proved themselves
stronger than ideals, and because the League of Nations has now
become the concentration field on which these political exigencies
meet to do battle. Therefore to cut oneself off from the League of
Nations meant from the outset to renounce the greatest opportunities
of foreign policy, opportunities which it is true can only be tackled
with rational technique, but to what end and with what purpose in
view? Why should it not be possible for us with our political technique to achieve the same national success in the gathering of the

Counter-Reich, to use your term again, as Talleyrand achieved in his day for France in the organ of the Holy Alliance, the Congress of Vienna? The opportunity has been given to us to tackle the opponent with his idealism, and thus to force him to accept us as a partner, although he had hoped to keep us out for ever, and to fight out the battle for the Reich on his own field, where he is most vulnerable. I will gladly, and the System will gladly, give credit to those who are making themselves felt all over the Reich in a serious endeavour to comprehend the essence of politics, and most certainly an important and extensive objective point can be cut out of all this farrago; but, gentlemen, I maintain that there had long since been an objective point, and that it made itself evident, and even you cannot doubt it, at the moment when free economic enterprise, which was more or less necessary for progressive internal development, came to an end, when the State, which was just as much ruled by interests as society, as it were asserted its independence, assumed the initiative in economics and politics, the Chancellor freed the Government to an extent hitherto inconceivable from the Parliament to which you are opposed, in short created a concrete administration which with its tendency to emphasise the authority of the State should be particularly acceptable in nationalist circles. You may deplore, gentlemen, that the great act of reformation, for which the way has been cleared by this fact, is not being fulfilled according to an extensive, clearly expounded and generally illuminating plan; of course you can deplore this, but you should level your complaints at yourselves, at all those who through their opposition to the System are making serious and united action impossible, who stand on one side, armed with mistrust, instead of holding themselves ready to infuse life into the bare bones of the organisation and give it body by their vital and creative impetus. You are forcing the System to progress step by step, giving here and there a consideration to private interests which the generality find hardly tolerable, and only asserting its full power where the wisdom of others has failed. You may point out, gentlemen, that it was not until the hour of greatest need that the System began to intervene, compelled by this need, it is true, but who is to say that the possibility of intervention was not inherent in the System from the very beginning, in the purpose of the System, and that this purpose did not embrace the will to intervene when the time was ripe, no sooner and no later. The time is ripe now, and you may well be dissatisfied when you contemplate the present state of affairs, which is neither flesh nor fish, but who is to say that this state of affairs is not provisional, does not already embrace the will—by supporting the banks, by a far-reaching participation of the State in banking interests, in economics, in society, by the expansion of public economic activity, by intervention in conditions of production and sale, by assuming financial control—to bring about a fundamental reformation of the whole structure of economics, and thereby to attain an integrity of the State which certainly is in our time, and, if I may look back at Prussian history, not only in our time, the essential and only means to force the will to life of the nation to a mighty, overpowering, and in the last resort heroic effort. And you may gaze, my friends of the Left, with enthusiasm towards Russia, and you, my friends of the Right, with delight towards Italy, and you gentlemen, who have not yet decided whether you are Left or Right, towards a glorious kingdom of the future, but here, on every side of you a State is quietly growing which has no need to be looking to every point of the compass for examples; the German State is growing here to fulfil German needs, is being formed, under pressure it is true from the whole world, just as every real life is formed under the pressure of its environment. But it is being formed out of German material, out of the bitter distress of the German situation, and has within it all the objective points for which you are fishing with such praiseworthy zeal, lowering your rods into the fog. It is true that the stupendous process of German reorganisation is proceeding slowly; I can disclose to you that it is sure, that it contains all the germs of German hope, that it is the quiver for all the arrows of German desire, and you can rely on it, all of you, if you do not prefer to draw a bow at random now, that the bow-strings are humming.'

Brodermann drew a deep breath. He continued: 'I know the reproaches that are made against the System: some speak of cold socialisation, for others it is not socialistic enough. Well, you may call it what you like, but one thing is certain, it is seeking for the forms which show the greatest promise of being equal to the important tasks of the future. It was not by chance that the System's will to reorganisation, as soon as it had the necessary freedom, turned first to establishing security in the East, and then to a revival of agriculture, to a revival, not a socialisation, and, if some methods give the impression of being socialistic, other methods give the impression of being far from socialistic, for a revival cannot be based on any one great political theory, to which everything has to give way, or be destroyed; it must be based on the needs of the community as a whole, and if the farmers, if agriculture, consider that their effective existence is essential for the community as a whole, then there is only one way of proving it, namely, by taking an essential part in the task of the System, from a point of view which it is not difficult to comply with when it is really honourable and seriously directed to what is essential. It is said that the State is oppressive, but nothing is being oppressed unless it makes a stand against the security of the Reich, and if it does make such a stand, then there will be no mercy, I assure you. But to want to stir up the storm now, and to cry for "violence," when you have been crying for "violence" all along, is a game I don't understand. Gentlemen, what is it you actually want? Now that the System has at last got private interests and combines under the control of State authority and has put them in the places where they can be useful, do you want, by destroying the System, to let them break loose again and assume command? Do you want to embark once more on the pointless and planless battle, until the opponents are at each other's throats again, without a single political purpose being fulfilled? Do you want a new System? There is no System in Germany, new or not, directed by no matter whom, which will not find itself faced with the same tasks, the same powerful forces, the same tendencies and objective points. Let us preserve what has been created, and work on, work more and more. The System has room for all. You will find all sorts of opportunities—not necessarily in the Reichstag, if that does not appeal to you—it does not appeal to me either and it does not seem to be a sign of outstanding political and revolutionary instinct, when great movements, which are setting about to destroy the System, in order to put themselves and their valuable intelligence in its place, deliberately turn all their strength against the position which is today least representative of the System, the Reichstag, and stare as though hypnotised at all the seats that have to be won there. It would be much better, to begin the work of developing Germany's future in your own proper sphere; to find the best possible and potentially strongest form in your own associations, to bring your idealism into active co-operation with life and thus to contribute to what you and I desire, and with us the System. But to want to stand aside, with your heads perpetually in the clouds, your hearts full of intoxicating dreams, and on your tongues the proclamation of the one right and eternally marvellous salvation by the so-and-so many'th Reich, to agitate for the destruction of the System,'—Brodermann made a violent gesture with the invisible sword—'that is political romanticism,'

'That is political romanticism,' said Ive, standing up. He put his hands on the table, then took them off again, He seemed about to turn away, but then he wheeled round towards Brodermann, and eventually stood leaning against the wall with his arms folded.

'That is political romanticism,' he said. 'It is very much the fashion lately to talk of political romanticism the moment anything occurs in German affairs that cannot be turned to immediate practical use. I don't know whether it is because I am too stupid, or whether it is to be attributed to the state of public enlightenment—I have made enquiries in every direction, but I have always found that the perfectly correct description of a perfectly authentic phenomenon is continually being associated with a point of view, which has no connection whatever with political romanticism in the original and pure sense of the term. I can very well imagine how political romanticism is interpreted, by putting together all that people are thinking and saying and writing about those doctrines and opinions of today which have not yet acquired a conventional status. One has only to turn to the stump orators, party manifestos, or, on a higher level, broadcast discussions, or even to the thick and learned tomes that are filling up the empty spaces on the bookshelves of science. But all these lack something, something which a hundred years of liberal historical study has failed to see, is not capable of seeing, because it is contrary to their hypotheses. The only thing to do, therefore, is no longer to take the hypotheses, assumptions and conclusions of this century as a basis, but to trace back the ideas of romanticism to their source, if I may be permitted to say so. For if we wanted to attack the ideas of the past century on the basis of its own assumptions, we might as well adopt Marxism as our creed, for Marxism by itself is fulfilling this task admirably and with a certain amount of success. Since we do not want to do this, you are quite right to call us romantics. For the ideas of romanticism, which this century is combating, denying and eventually ignoring, and to a degree and in a manner which leads one to suspect that it does not fear that it will be conquered by them, any more than by Marxism, but that it simply does not understand them, lead to something in which neither the Liberal epoch nor the System which, to all appearances, is actually undertaking to liquidate it, have or can have any say, namely, a conception of the State. No doubt this may seem an astonishing statement to those who at the word romanticism immediately picture young men sentimentalising in the moonlight and setting out to search for the blue flower in the maze of politics—although this might well be considered a more praiseworthy undertaking than trying to open an account with the Swiss Bank. But political romanticism is far from being a happy land of tooting horns and vagrant ne'er-dowells. Much rather it is the first comprehensive attempt in German history to sift from its records the elements of the State, to remove from it the flotsam and jetsam of transitory intellectual tides, and from the knowledge thus gained to deduce far-reaching conclusions.'

'Amongst other things the elements of the State,' he went on, 'so that we cannot be surprised that today, wherever a similar effort is being made, it is at least worth while to take every essential idea, and to investigate what has already been thought on the subject in romanticism; for in romanticism is to be found every fundamental argument against the Liberal century; it is impossible for us, once we set about the task seriously, whether or no we have made our own assumptions, not to find useful parallels in romanticism. Actually the intellectual situation today is in essence what it was a hundred years ago.

Today, as then, German claims are defending themselves against the ascendance of far-reaching iconoclastic ideas whose first beacons were lighted in foreign capitals; today, as then, German youth is striving to find the source of these claims not in the existing political situation, not in the laws of evolution, but in an eternal quality of the nation; today, as then, the authoritative political system stands between the two fronts and the reactionary statesmen are ruling not on principles of romanticism or of democracy, but on principles of enlightened individualistic absolutism supported only by the confidence of the dynasts and there is damned little to choose between that method and the methods of the present Chancellor, no matter who he is or by what means he wins the confidence of the President of the Reich. The one thing that differentiates us from the romanticism of those days is the iron infused into our blood by a hundred years' experience and a world war, and the resultant certainty that we need not shrink from ways and means which the young men of those days had not the grit to tackle. So much for romanticism,' said Ive. 'As for the statement that the System has saved the existence of the Reich, that is simply an objective untruth. It is not the Reich that the System has saved, but itself, under the guise of being a State, and we have no intention of co-operating in the tissue of lies with which the System has distorted the act of its birth into an heroic deed, and is seeking today to justify the consolidation of its power in the eyes of history. If the System came into being because the parliamentary democracy succeeded, in the first years following the collapse, in playing off against each other the forces fighting for possession of the Reich, regardless of whether their intention was to destroy it completely or to reconstruct it in new greatness, and then in the most matter-of-fact way annihilating the exhausted combatants, one after the other, with wise precepts and cold judgments, then possibly that was an achievement that leads the System today to hope that it will succeed in playing off the newly formed forces in the same way again, in order to annihilate the parliamentary democracy which has become an embarrassment; and the defective political instinct which vacantly counts the seats in the Reichstag may be very welcome to the System. But what has this achievement to do with the State? What has the sum of achievement of which the System boasts—and even if its value is called into question, the System may still take the credit for it—what has it to do with the State? If an attempt is being made today to eliminate monopolies, what is happening but a shifting of monopolies from one group of shareholders to another, turning the ramp of individuals into a ramp of the System?'

He continued: 'It would be better if the System could not even boast of an achievement, for then what justification would it have?

What justification has a factory-owner but his achievements? But the State cannot be managed like a factory; it would be fundamentally destroyed. That is a conception of romanticism, and to prove the correctness of this conception there is no need to seek proofs in the last century, they are in front of our eyes, and nobody is more aware of them than the System. Otherwise, what need would it have to be appealing in all directions for confidence, and bitterly bewailing that everyone is trying to stand on one side? Why otherwise is the System looking everywhere for its authority and is only able to find it among the men it would like to get rid of? Why the devil is there this anxiety to stand aside, why does German youth consider it a crime to stretch out so much as a little finger to the System, why is there this searching and feeling for distant and unknown and all-embracing and binding principles? Because without them it is not worth making a decision; because in every action it is essential to have an answer to the question of the reason why, and the System has not been able to answer this question any more than the whole of the past century was able to answer it; because at last the certainty has awakened in us again, that every action and every attitude must rest on the unity of a great reason, that every political idea must arise from this unity if it is to be of any value to us, and the State must be nothing else than the willing instrument to fulfil it.

'I do not want to bring God into the debate,' said Ive, and then regretted it, but he continued, 'although it is hardly to be avoided, at least, if we want to investigate the question of the source of any authority. What, for instance, is a marriage if it loses its sacramental character? Happy possibly, but not a marriage, simply a bourgeois arrangement which, after being deprived of all its legal and hereditary rights, can be turned by Communism consistently and frivolously into a proletarian arrangement or repudiated altogether. What is a State if all its members do not serve a higher unity, if it has not arisen from the will to this unity? Comfortable possibly, but no longer a State, merely a bourgeois arrangement for the protection of a privileged society, which Communism is justified in striving to destroy, for Communism has no use for the State and has never pretended to have a conception of the State which justified it in wanting it. I should like to know,' said Ive, 'how the System justifies its existence in the face of Communism, in the face of National Socialism. Merely by its indispensability? Well, it is just this indispensability which is being questioned. By its wonderful devotion to an achievement? Well, it is this very devotion to an achievement that the forces which are opposed to the System are combating. And if it be true that it is the objective power of facts which dictates the tasks of the future, all the more reason why they should be undertaken by anyone, and not only by the representatives of the System. But we want a State and not a System. We want a society which will consciously organise itself into a great national community, and not a heap of individuals thrown together more or less by chance, held together only by the frontiers dictated by foreign Powers and by the political squaring of the circle of a universal reciprocity of interests. We want authority, but not the authority of decaying bank managers and economists, nor the authority of timid government officials, who get cold feet at every measure, nor the authority of putrescent senatorial presidents and ministerial directors, nor that of the bigwigs who attended the last Reinhardt premiere, and make us heave if we merely see their faces in the illustrated papers, but the authority of men whom we know to be at one with our aims. We want a plan, a unified and complete economic plan, not the extension of public economic activity from the most diverse and arbitrary points of view brought about by force of circumstances instead of by spontaneous impulse and excused on the ground of obstructions, which exist only in the System itself—but a fusion of all economic principles by co-related measures, beginning with the soil and covering transport, raw material and eventually man, all of which already contain within themselves the urge to spontaneous cohesion. The System boasts that it has already produced a perfect organisation. It has organised nothing except starvation and itself, and those badly. Wherever natural forms of production and society have been developed, they have been developed in opposition to the System. That is true, and whoever denies it is either a liar or blind. If today German Youth is removing the frontier posts in Innsbruck and the Bavarian forest, it can wait for whatever happens will be bearable, but what will be quite unbearable is that you, Lieutenant Brodermann, will be standing with your detachment not in Wedding but in Innsbruck; or the Bavarian forest, to set up the frontier posts again. For whose benefit? For the benefit of the Reich? For the sake of a principle of State? For the sake of the System which can tolerate no change, and which engenders the mistrust of those by grace of whom and in subservience to whom it alone lives or can live. It is not by chance that for ten years it has acted on the watchwords of others, and the only time it produced a watchword of its own, it dared to do so because it was a question of saving American capital with French money. It is not by chance that it sows tariff unions and reaps the Danube Conference, not by chance that with one hand it guarantees protection of the currency and with the other not only knocks on the head the economy which was moving towards freedom, but the whole economy based on a protected currency. It is true that the System cannot act otherwise, and for the reason that it cannot act otherwise it is not a State, but the thing that it is justly described as, a System, and the greatest of its achievements would be quietly to resign.'

Brodermann shrugged his shoulders. Schaffer was not pleased with Ive, but since he was accustomed to think in centuries, and in the present century he was only concerned with the coming century, the question of the System was no longer a problem for him. He objected to leading articles, and, this being a question which really only lent itself to discussion in leading articles or with armoured cars, he preferred to ignore it altogether. However, he made a few mental notes of subjects of discussion for subsequent evenings arising out of what Ive had been saying—'Nature of the State from the romantic point of view,' 'A Planned Economy —on what form of society should it be based,' 'Autocracy and Decentralisation of Financial Resources and the Position of the Reichsbank'—subjects which seemed to him of sufficient interest to merit discussion within or without the System.

Ive continued: 'Regard us, if you like, as idiots and criminals; regard us, if you like, as people who have nothing else to do but dream dreams, with our heads in the clouds, but you see nothing, and you need to see nothing, of what is going on beneath the surface. What is being accomplished, on principles which are our principles, and in a direction which we realise to be our direction, and in work in which, even when we sit idly talking, we are taking our full share, has a different kind of anonymity from that of the System, from that of a loud-speaker with no electric current. The time is past for attaching any value to profitable results, and those who think they can't get on without them are already in league with the devil. I will tell you why we cannot enter the System, to co-operate with it, because we know that it is impossible to tell lies and compromise oneself for ten years without being corrupted. The whole question is one of order, and it is not we, but the System which has to decide whether it will change itself fundamentally, whether it is prepared to free itself from all its Liberal, parliamentary and Western associations, in order ultimately to become, what it professes to be, a State, or—'

'Or?' asked Brodermann.

'Or,' said Ive, 'when the time is ripe, to be smashed.'

'Well, good luck to you,' said Brodermann.

XV

I've knew that Pareigat was more likely than anybody to challenge him to take up a definite position. He did not avoid him, for after all he had himself with his defence of romanticism deliberately provided the peg on which the explanation must hang. Actually the rather non-committal adherence to romanticism which he professed corresponded to his rather non-committal conception of the idea and was due to his desire not to shirk responsibility, since after all he might have invalidated the reproach by a flat disavowal. He had turned to romanticism much in the same way that the generation ten years behind him had turned to football; he found it in his direct path as a means of distraction, which at first satisfied his intellectual requirements just as sport satisfied the physical requirements of his juniors. He was aware, therefore, that his confession of romanticism had about as much bearing on himself and on the tasks still before him as the official statement that football increases national efficiency. For, just as the pleasant Sunday afternoon exertion could only, by a general concentration of feet on the ball, at most lead to an eventual loudly acclaimed victory for the home team, a representative victory; so too his preoccupation with romanticism, even if he applied himself to it with his characteristic enthusiasm, could only lead in the end to a standpoint comprehensive perhaps and theoretically important, but, regarded all in all, no more than a representative philosophy. For he had sorrowfully to admit that though he might become familiar with the intellectual world of romanticism, with the exciting discoveries it had to offer, he could never live in it as he longed to live. In the bold theses of the Romantic School which revealed a deeper logic than had been possible for the last hundred years, as well as in the suggestions and fragments of romanticism, he discovered references and opinions which had lost none of their force, and was able to formulate maxims for which he had long been seeking, conscious that they must lie hidden somewhere within himself, to follow lines of thought which bore almost directly on the needs of the times; yet there always remained something which he found it difficult to accept. This something lay, however, in a quite different quarter from that in which those who described him and his like as romantics, were wont to seek for arguments.

He was not disturbed by the lack of the hard perception, which the machine age alleged to be necessary, probably to enable it the better to blunt it—this was easily compensated for by a greater sharpness of perception, by a scalpel-like sharpness which made it possible to cut out with accuracy from the chaos of ideas the fertile or unfertile germ; and to attain this attitude again seemed to Ive a task well worth endeavour. What did disturb him, as he admitted to himself, was the attempt of romanticism, which the whole nature of the Movement made inevitable, determinedly to confine all the organic strength which lay at its disposal within limits, within German limits, to create order more or less as an end in itself, whereas Ive preferred to regard perfection of order as a means, not perhaps of snatching from Heaven its ultimate mysteries, but certainly of driving the last non-German Power from the earth. And when he looked around him, he had no reason to despair. The things that were stirring in the times showed him to be right, and anything that did not show him to be right he could easily have proved to be something that was not stirring, or could have attributed it to the influences of another age. He found himself in complete harmony with the present, and he found the present pleasant; both of which facts might have astonished anyone who knew him and knew how he lived.

Ive had really come to love the town, mainly because of its stimulation, which was a purely intellectual stimulation. So he flung himself into the whirlpool of discussions, delighting in their general ineffectualness, discussions that did not enrich him, that did not even lead him to self-knowledge, hardly acted as a cultural education therefore, but rather made him plunge and rear, so that, in the dizzy leaps from postulate to postulate, all his inflammable susceptibilities were kindled. The recognition of the doubtful value of every point of view did not mislead him into voluntarily abandoning his momentary opinions, and he never knew whether this time he would not sink into the abyss. But he did not sink; for his hours of deepest despair were hours of despair of himself, of fear that he was not worthy of what was happening around him, of grief that he had not been called upon to make a complete sacrifice—herein lay his distress, and from it sprang his will to attain the highest degree of self-restraint, in order to become worthy of the infinitude of which he was a part. This seemed to him to be the attitude of the soldier, ready to die for a fatherland that has not even a just cause of war. To know himself meant for him to learn the meaning of his environment; not only learn, understand. So he set about the task of understanding.

He found plenty of opportunities for merely filling up the gaps in his knowledge. When he was driven into a corner, as he had been by Brodermann, and was faced with the responsibility of making concrete statements about concrete things, he was fully aware that it was impossible for him to produce anything but generalities, and though he got no consolation from the realisation that other people, placed in the same position, frequently had the same experience, still this fact led him to the discovery of what was probably the one argument which he ought to have flung at Brodermann, namely, that concrete statements must be based on a concrete proposition, and the injustice of the System precluded any high sense of responsibility, which was a decisive reason for abolishing it.

The longing to have the chance of being prime minister with dictatorial powers was widespread, and anybody who regarded this as childish only showed his complete incapacity to fill the office of prime minister. At that time Germany was made up almost completely of frustrated prime ministers, and we cannot deplore this state of affairs, although we are far from being democrats, since it reminds us of the romantic idea that it is simply a question of economy that there is only one king, and if we were not obliged to be economical we might all be kings. And although we cannot completely identify ourselves with Ive and his views, having long since found an intellectual sanctuary, and, in the consciousness of being useful and worthy members of a commonwealth, which satisfies us and our hopes, can well do without entangling ourselves in such abstruse intellectual adventures, still we can follow with sympathy the path of this young man, which, after he had strayed into every type of misconception and utilised the discovery of his error as a means to knowledge, did at length lead him to that inner forum, which now constitutes the foundation of our existence, and by so doing we find ourselves nearer to Ive's methods than we might have suspected. For all the discussions in which Ive took part so eagerly were more of the nature of soliloquies, in which no opinion was an opinion, but merely a friction-surface to enable the searching mind to ignite. Thus we possibly have reason to be more astonished than Ive, when we consider what an abundance of common conceptions existed silently, and proceeding from these we can affirm that the results obtained did not represent the synthesis of the discussions, but even when as results they had the appearance of compromise, were throughout complementary to a higher ego, and, therefore, only synthetic as the expression of a universally applicable law which, without reference to the discussion, operated auspiciously for each individual. Let us at least try to understand the fascination of novelty which things, that for us have long since been a secure possession, must have had for Ive; do not let us underestimate the significance of the facts which caused the young people of that period to make indiscriminate use of men, books and events as instruments of sensation, on which they were able to harmonise the compositions of their fermenting personalities, fragments from which the music of a whole epoch was derived, and which surely it is worth recording here. And if we turn our attention to those silently existing conceptions, we become aware how great a disparity there is between our own times and the times when they did not exist, and must acknowledge Ive's justification in regarding himself as a part of the future—of our present.

Thus there really have been times—we can establish this fact for ourselves by digging out the documents from the archives—in which, for instance, the Nation not only was not an established and clearly outlined conception, but was even denied as a phenomenon, was regarded as the devilish figment of the imagination of some self-interested Power or another, as an invention to defraud humanity of its most valuable possession. And these were the views of clever, enlightened and influential people, who were able to express them openly in their journals and at their meetings, without immediately being put in their places by a mob, outraged at this terrible insult to the general intelligence, and using the methods customary with an outraged mob. Far from it, they received attention and were believed, and even those to whom we must here give credit for respecting the idea of the Nation, did not do so in the conviction of its actual value, but merely considered it expedient, under the influence of the universal psychosis, to support the 'figment of the imagination' as such, or even their own, conception of the Nation—very different from ours—as a necessary element in the subduing of the covetous masses. If we take all this into account, we cannot despise Ive, when he spoke of the Nation or the Reich, for not being in a position to expound with clarity all the distinctive features so permanently associated with these ideas, down to the least important details which are so familiar to us. For anyone who was fortunate enough to experience, as it were intuitively, the conception Nation, was taxed to the utmost to define this conception, and though we, in the satiety of possession, may be in a position to smile at this, we must guard ourselves against smiling at the seriousness which lay behind it.

Ive was perpetually making new starts in his endeavour to grasp the phenomenon, to pin it down in words. He suffered perpetual setbacks. Again and again he would be stimulated by glorious presentiments, but at every step he was confronted by a new field, full of such an infinite number of possibilities, which were always shifting and re-grouping themselves, complementing each other or even destroying one another, that he might well have despaired instead, as he did, of perpetually deriving new hopes from it. For the fact that there was a purposeful relationship between all things was another conception that he was aware of from the outset, and it was this that held him to his task with such a high sense of responsibility; a single mistake would destroy the divine work of art, and the devil was always at hand to guide the hand of humanity. It was this too that produced the urge to try out every method, and if the empirical method ranked first, at least as a corrective, he did not shrink from regarding his specific experiences as of value; understanding by this not his personal experiences but those things which every one could claim as experience. It is true that in this quest his encounters with people could only be halting-places, and when he found in Novalis the sentence: 'There are Germans everywhere, Germanness is no more limited to any particular state than Romanness, Greekness, or Britishness; they are universal human characteristics, which only here and there have become remarkable in their universality,' he was immediately compelled to strip this idea of its psychological garment—since for him psychology had always meant the contradiction not only of philosophy but of all intellectual processes—and wrap it in the cloak of historical reality. At once the old thought assumed a new meaning for him; Nation, Germanness and culture became one to him, and the world fell into an order which might have satisfied and delighted him, if it had not seemed an even too easy process. The power of the present seemed conceivable to him only as a Western culture, the power of the Church as a nation in itself, as in Judaism; the deceptive frontiers merged and overlapped, and there seemed no harm in ascribing the characteristic figures to their correct environment, to include Dante and Shakespeare in Germanness, and to transport Thomas Mann with one bound into the West, which was his right sphere, even though he might still live in Munich. Suddenly every problem was solved, all sorts of maxims formed themselves into a complete pattern, the ideas of a national Communism and of a social nationalism disclosed their mysterious origin as a protest of Germanness against the West, every duty seemed to spring spontaneously into place, and actually there was nothing left to do but quickly to outline a new programme and step before the public; but, curiously enough, Ive was not yet satisfied. He did not find it difficult to survey the field of political inferences; the claim of Germany was easily sifted out, the unique claim of a German imperialism, the missionary task, as Schaffer called it; but the thing Ive was concerned with remained hidden behind the mountain, a dark premonition of storm. So the bold structure had to remain in his dreams as in the brilliance of the morning sun; stone was laid upon stone, the temple grew up in architectonic majesty, rich altars rose in severe lines, stained-glass windows caught the light, dispersing its rays in all the colours of heaven through the building, a glorious agglomeration surrounding a small empty space, a sanctuary for the unknown God. Actually every consideration faded—whether the Reich was to be regarded as the static and the Nation as the dynamic element of Germanness; what was the relation of the people to the

Reich, that of a biological unity or of a spiritual content; what was the relation of the Nation to the Reich—all faded before the one great question: God.

This was where Pareigat came in, and Ive felt ashamed, not because he would be obliged to give an adequate answer —who could give an adequate answer?—but because even to be silent would be worse than cowardice or lies—a doubt of the meaning of existence.

He found Pareigat in the studio. Helene was out, and the painter was standing completely absorbed before a large sheet of paper. So they retired to a corner, and Pareigat swooped down like a bird of prey on to the fact that the Romantic movement had ended with the acceptance of Catholicism. Ive felt that it would only be a weak objection to say that this did not apply to romanticism as a whole, but only to a section of the Romantics; the profession had not been an essential part of the Romantic movement. Still, he could point to the strong pantheistic attitude, and the relation to mysticism, and then to the fact that the romantic and mystical elements in the Catholic middle ages had been essentially German elements. So Ive went straight to the attack, still uncertain of his position, and in great distress because the urge to speak, to explain himself in some way, was stronger than ever.

Pareigat was a recent convert, but he did not defend his attitude with the ardent zeal which this act of piety usually inspires. He admitted to Ive that it was not so much the means of grace as the Church which offered him the means of grace which had attracted him. Not that he could not have believed with complete surrender, but, and he said, this as though he were speaking to his Confessor, almost imperceptibly within the great unity the principal accent had shifted.

All at once Ive understood why Pareigat, who had recently told him of his wish to enter a monastery, had not been able to follow the step he had taken to its logical conclusion, because an even more important conclusion confronted him. In his case what had been a spiritual urge would have become a flight. Not a flight from the world—oh, thought Ive, if only we could once and for all rid ourselves of all the worn-out ideas—not a flight from the world, but a shameful deceiving of God. Ive would have liked to measure swords with Pareigat, but he saw now that this would only be possible in a quite different field. Just as Pareigat, by his conversion, he, by his questioning resistance, had experienced an enrichment, since every action and every step forced him to new decisions, of which each one was a decision bringing him nearer to unity; but this very fact that he felt to be a perpetual benison, a continual gift of grace, removed him from the actual domain of religion, drove him from direct religious experience to the realisation of an intellectual unity, which for him was the intellectual concept of the Reich, just as for Pareigat it was the intellectual concept of the Church. He had no right to become, as it were, an intellectual, any more than Pareigat had the right to become a monk. For that would have been to deprive of its motive force his painful insistence on being admitted to none but intellectual experience. Pareigat had recognised this. He wanted to be capable of being a saint and a martyr, not to be, but to be capable of being. That is to say, it was an intolerable thought to him that the soil of the Church had become barren and no longer bore saints or martyrs. And the idea came to Ive once more that Pareigat did not want to be more popish than the Pope, but was endeavouring to crystallise all his thoughts and actions into the salt which would once more prepare the soil for abundant fecundity. Like Ive, he could only regard Christianity as an individual culture with an imperialistic bent, which was threatened by the prevailing influence of nineteenth-century intellectualism in just the same way as the Reich. It seemed quite natural to Pareigat to acknowledge that the same enemy was threatening both Christianity and the Reich; and it was the direct menace of this enemy that would mould the intellectual consciousness of the victims.

Pareigat said that he, too, regarded history as a perpetual transformation of immutable matter, the struggle for supremacy between the will to power of the individual, man or State, and the will to power, liberated and alienated from the individual. This meant to say that Liberalism as a Western claim was not a tendency of the times, but a perpetual tendency confined to a particular period. In the end every supremacy was an imposition of foreign elements, and it lay within its scope to complete this process, and it not only lay within its scope but was its right. 'For,' said Pareigat, 'right is the persistent exercise of force, power is the guarantee of right, and supremacy is the authority for power. What we want to discover is from whom the authority comes. For the Church from the revelation of God, and for Liberalism—and since the proclamation of 1789, for the West—from the autocracy of man. And for the Reich?' asked Pareigat. 'For the Reich from the autocracy of the Reich. For myself,' he said, 'my duty is clear, and must be clear. The Church can never forfeit her supremacy, whatever forms it may assume. She can and must attempt to keep the forms pure, to substitute living and pliant forms for those that have become rigid, to combat every incursion of a foreign will to power, and if it is not possible to hold the fortress against the violent onslaught, she must yield elastically, as torn flesh yields, in order that the wound may be healed. The body of the Church is full of scars, but never since the sword-thrust of the Reformation, which aimed directly at her heart, has she been in such deadly danger as she is today, when the poison is creeping into her impoverished veins. In those days Ignatius Loyola arose, fully armed, to do battle for her eternal security with all the weapons of his day, the sharpest and most perfect weapons, whose efficacy has persisted through the ages. He arose as the General of an Order which for four centuries was the pattern for all Societies which "have an organic yearning for infinite expansion and eternal endurance," of a spiritual-worldly society, secret or not. Today again the need is there for the formation of a spiritual-worldly society, once more to save the supremacy of the Church, the organ of a militant Christianity, of the rejuvenated and resuscitated Church, to eliminate by its burning zeal the putrefied and the putrefying humours, to stand at all the fronts where the enemy columns are massed, to take up all the tasks which the secular powers have wrested from the Church in their presumptuous arrogance without being able to fulfil them, and out of it all to build up intellectual power equal to the comprehensive task. For the Church can never forfeit her right to determine the structure of society, from foundations to summit, to keep a watch over every phase of life from the first cry to the last breath, and there is no order in the world for which she is not responsible. Every individual who acknowledges her carries the responsibility for the fulfilment of the divine mandate, and he who shirks the task may be able as a sinner to ask for the absolution of his Confessor, but as a Catholic he can never ask for his own absolution. The Church has left a breach in her strict laws, and it is the duty of those who call themselves Catholics to fill this breach until not a crack is visible. The Church is faced with the whole tremendous responsibility, and it is hers and hers alone, and if she forfeits that responsibility today, then she has forfeited for ever her supremacy. Only in the moment of greatest danger is the hope of victory renewed by a fresh onslaught, and never were hope and danger as great as they are today. Catholicism has got to make a move, but a move in which it no longer needs to compromise because it realises the weakness of the Church's supreme position, but a move in which it can stand as the representative of regeneration, conscious of its strength, just as the Society of Jesus was the representative of regeneration and at the same time the organiser of the attacking powers. And since every individual is faced with the task, this task is for every individual the everyday duty of his life. Every individual has to make a choice and establish his position; and if he is a German it is a German position, that is, it is a position in which the highest duty is of first importance. For this, and this only, is the meaning of the Reich: to fulfil the divine mandate, conveyed by the Church in the past, and to be conveyed again today; to fulfil what has already been demanded of us and which we have failed to fulfil.'

Pareigat said that he could not understand how the Reich could be founded in any other way. Was this mandate a perpetual one or not? And did not its repudiation signify a self-repudiation on the part of the Reich?

'The fact is,' said Pareigat, 'that the first impress of German consciousness and the one that has held good until today, the Reich, did not arise directly from the native German content. It called itself the Holy Roman Empire of the German nation; it was Christian and universal and only handed on to the German nation. It is therefore possible for the German to make use of the Reich if he recognises the direction and magnitude of the task and today is seeking new forms which will make it possible for the Church once more to hand the mandate to the German nation. But it is impossible for the German to make use of the Reich on the basis of the Reich's autocracy, for this has never existed.'

'Has it never existed?' asked Ive. 'Or is it not rather that it has clothed itself, as it were, in the Holy and Roman and Christian and Universal, and the garment has proved to be sometimes too big and sometimes too small for the body of the Reich? If one makes use of the autocracy of the Reich, that means to make use of one's own religious sense; and then you have witnesses cropping up from Eckhardt and Jakob Böhme and Luther to Nietzsche—searchers in whom the divine spark was to be found.

'And the paths they sought and their religious sense was determined in every thought of the omnipotence of Christian thought, that is in Catholicism,' said Pareigat. 'Is protest in itself a sign of autocracy? We must certainly guard ourselves against probing for results, but since Scheler it is impossible to rule out the result as being the ethical importance of the Reformation, and it is from him that we must estimate what was the result of the Reformation. And if God did manifest himself to Luther by a burst of thunder, it was the God of Christianity, and it was Luther who made it possible for Loyola to save the Church and lead her to a new greatness. If Germanness is a culture that fulfils itself in the Reich, it is a Christian culture, and it is Christian values which have determined it. It is impossible to deny this; but it is possible to deny Christian values as such; it is impossible to deny the Christian tradition, the Roman tradition of the Reich, but it is possible to date the beginning of the German Reich from today as the first beginning of German history, and if it cannot do without founding its significance on a divine mandate, then God will have to appear in a burst of thunder again on German soil, and this time a German God. And then the question arises whether he will not have to make use of the Reich again for a new protest.'

'For a national protest, certainly,' said Ive, 'for a protest of German spirituality against Christian spirituality, which has its origins in the spirit of Israel.'

But Pareigat did not take up this challenge, and Ive said that he admitted that it all depended on how far it was possible from the basis of Germanness to attack the antagonistic spirit at its very roots;

that with the unitary philosophy of the Reich, with its syn-philosophy, to borrow a term from Schlegel, the Reich stood or fell; and that it was not permissible to derive and correlate the theses of this philosophy from German intellectual sources alone, since in the end it was only a matter of interpretation. He admitted all this, and it did not even occur to him to seek out paths which led to the religious forms of pagan German antiquity, for the echoes of this period which still rang in our ears had no bearing on the primitive feelings of either religion or history. But since the real history-making power for the German nation was Christianity, the purpose of its content was to be found in the German manifestations of Christianity. And this purpose was in fact united enough in its main features to glean from it an idea of its characteristic manifestation. If it had made a political stand against the supremacy of Rome, intellectually it had made a stand against the ideas of Christian morality.

'Against man's free will, in fact,' said Pareigat. 'No matter how wide an historical survey we make, in the end it is a question of individual choice. It is a tempting idea, to try to attack Christianity at its core, to deny sin, and guilt; to include in grace what the Church has excluded from it: nature; to permit man and nature to be merged in God, so that whatever happens takes place in God, and is therefore perfect; the idea is tempting and not new, I grant you. And if the Reich at one time found itself swamped by Christianity once from the West and once from the East, there is no reason why it should not be possible to exchange Jerusalem for Mecca, the authority of the Pope for the direct communion with God of Mohammedanism.

'And really,' he said, 'it was probably a Western superstition to derive from the fact of Islamite immunity against the means of grace of the Western world the comforting statement that the idea of Kismet led to fatalism; even if it were no longer possible to overcome evil, why should not responsibility to the world be altogether an act of heroic character? But what was impossible with the denial of a moral principle was the participation of the individual in any kind of order; what would disappear in the Reich would be the kingdom of the objective intellect, society. For—'

'Stop,' said Ive, 'that is not right. Responsibility to the world is not the question. That has been imposed upon us and we are answerable. Responsibility means,' he said uneasily, for Helene had come in and slipped quietly past them without greeting them, 'responsibility means to be answerable for one's actions regardless of consequences, for all actions regardless of all consequences.'

What is the matter with Helene? he thought to himself. She disappeared behind a curtain which cut the studio off from a little kitchen, and Ive could hear her washing her hands slowly and thoroughly.

'Responsibility to the world means, therefore,' said Ive, 'that the individual is deprived of none of his influence on the content of his actions.'

'What is the matter with Helene?' he asked.

She flung her hat and coat down in a corner and came towards Ive. But, a little way from him, she turned round with a quick, angry movement and walked right across the studio, her high heels tapping sharply on the floor. The painter barely looked up from his work. Ive followed Helene with his eyes.

'The idea of free will,' he said. 'Helene!'

Suddenly she was standing close in front of him with her hands pressed on the table.

'You talk,' she said, and drew her shoulders up.

'You talk,' she said, and the tone of icy scorn hit Ive in the face like the lash of a whip.

They stared at each other. Helene's forehead was a network of furrows.

'You talk!' she screamed, and her breath beat hot on Ive's mouth.

My God, why this sudden hatred, thought Ive, and he felt the blood draining from his face to meet the upward rush pumped up from his wildly beating heart until it nearly choked him.

'Go on talking,' said Helene, through her clenched teeth, and her words exploded through the studio.

'But I am fed up! I am fed up!' she shrieked at the wall. 'Why do you work?' she hissed at the artist. 'Give me that sheet.'

She snatched it from him, the wet paint coming off on her dress. She seized it quickly by the edge, her hands tightened to tear it across, then she stopped suddenly, cast a glance at the colours, stretched out her arms and returned it to the painter.

'Tear it up,' she said, 'tear it up.'

The painter, white and puzzled, dropped his brush, took the sheet, and tore it slowly across. Pareigat and Ive jumped up. Helene stood in the studio like a slender flame.

'I can't go on,' she said softly, and the piteous, thin voice that came from her contracted throat filled the whole room with its torture. Ive stood motionless. The question leapt into his mind, stabbing like a knife: What do I know of Helene? Her face had puckered up like a child's on the point of crying. But she did not cry; she stood upright with an expression of misunderstood sorrow.

'You talk and you paint,' she said; 'you come to this studio, as you would to a lonely island, to talk and to paint. You talk and you paint on an island, and everything you do is a lie. A lie,' she screamed threateningly at Ive. 'What do you know about all the things you talk about? "This must be and that must be," you say, and "This can't be allowed and that can't be allowed." But what is you do not see. I will tell you what is: Filth!' she screamed, stamping about the studio. 'You and your responsibility to the world! But you have made no attempt to clean up the excrements that fill the whole world with their stink. If it were even a hell in which we are forced to live! But there are no more devils in human form, nothing but petty criminals. What of it if a policeman knocks me down with his truncheon, at least that is brute force, and I am prepared to shoot. But can you shoot slime? Do you call it life to be slowly choked by slime? But you talk. You condone the lie by ignoring it.'

'Helene!' said Ive.

'Be quiet,' she said, turning to him.

Then she said softly and with a great effort: 'You think I am unjust, but I want to be unjust, for to be just is a lie. I want no more lies; I'm fed up with lying. You think I am in despair, but I want to be in despair, for all hope is a lie. Haven't I done my utmost, haven't I even done what I myself should never have thought possible? Who can say that I'm a coward? Do you think I would let myself be conquered by the inevitable? When have I ever given in? Am I daunted by the shoemaker, the baker or the tailor whom I can never pay, and do you care a damn? Do I flinch at my journeys to film studios, to editors, to Jakobsohn? Journeys that you know nothing about, that you probably regard as shameful, bitter, disgusting, but for me just street-walking? And you don't know this? You don't see it, don't realise it? You tolerate a prostitution, because it's legal, because it is so, as though it had to be? But it must not be, my God, it must not be. I am fed up. And you talk. And I put on a short-sleeved dress when I go to see Jakobsohn. And I cross my legs when I am waiting in the newspaper office. And I undress in front of every producer when I want to get a part for three days at twenty-five marks. I don't mind standing naked before the whole world if it is necessary. But it is not necessary, it is vile obscenity. Do you think I'm prudish? Do I jib at realities? But this is not reality, this is low-down disgusting vulgarity. Am I afraid, I, of passion? When I love, I abandon myself. But I won't be dragged into everyone's bed in the interests of business. I won't be pawed by every fat swine, I won't be petted by every perfumed bundle of wadding. I am fed up, fed up, fed up. And you talk. You talk of free will and guilt and answerableness and supremacy and responsibility to the world. That has long since been divided up amongst the filthiest pack that ever existed, who have risen to supremacy from the sewers, and you can't smell their origin? You can't see the dirt in every film they reel off, in every popular tune they thump out, in every column they write, in every word they say? Either you are dense or corrupted. For you talk. You put up with it. You have theories about it. You're so superior, aren't you? Nobody will listen to you; and you are proud of it. But they listen to the others, to these creatures. They sit firmly implanted with their fat bottoms on every seat that's worth sitting on. They sit at every telephone, at every microphone, at every desk. And you may dance to the tune they call. And you do dance. You dance around in a circle with all your talk, to their music, and you are grateful if they praise your clever steps, and are wounded when they laugh at your capers. Respectable people. Swine! And so are you. You talk. Of duty. And you don't see your first and only duty. You talk. And are as independent as is possible for anyone to be today. You are not on a string as we are, who have to tremble if they take it into their heads to cut us down. You have the unique good fortune to be able to talk, but of the things that matter you don't talk—talk, did I say, you don't shriek them out, call them from the house-tops. You are cowards from ignorance. You lie from arrogance. But you are cowards and you lie. Cowardice and lies,' she snapped at Ive, as though she were spitting at him. 'Be silent if you cannot talk of what should be talked of. There is no excuse. For the rest of the world perhaps, but not for you. If you do not stand up to bear witness against pestilence and dung, who is to? But you are too grand to do such a thing as walk the streets. I am a street-walker. I let myself be spat on and besmirched. And I am in damned fine company. In company that has got used to being spat on and besmirched. They think it is the correct thing. And if they didn't think it the correct thing, wouldn't dare to make a stand against it; they have to take part in it, have to spit and besmirch in their turn, to behave as though they were in a brothel, and must not be surprised at being treated as though they were in a brothel. And you tolerate this. You see and talk of other things. And if the filth rises as high as your noses, you too take a mouthful and spit it out again, and behave as though that were the end of it. What heritage are you waiting for, waiting until it has been squandered away and not a rag is left? Waiting is treachery. You are traitors. Petty traitors. Traitors with no character. You're just like the others. You are not even as efficient as they are. You talk of power and the others have it. You talk of decisions and the others make them. You dream of deeds and the others act. Just the same with art. You think they don't understand it, but they understand it better than you do. They know what is dangerous. You don't, and you aren't dangerous yourselves. Leave me alone,' said Helene, pacing up and down.

'You can think I am hysterical if you like. I have a right to be hysterical. But you are worn down. All your corners have been gnawed as though by rats. And you don't know it, you don't see it, you don't realise it. You talk of battle and do nothing but tilt against yourselves. You talk of attitude, and, of course, one shouldn't mention these things, but there are a few people who, before they think of attitude, want to fill their bellies. I am one of them, and I don't care about my attitude. Leave me alone. I'll be quiet. Nothing has happened. Nothing that does not happen every day. I wash my hands every day, and my soul, from the shame that this should be necessary. Nothing has happened. They are making a new film, I am playing a harlot, fifteen yards of her. I have to give a side view of my left breast, naked. My breast was the most beautiful of all those that were in the running. Nothing has happened. The article has to be altered. They said I had a slight anal complex. They said it was only because I was such a charming little woman that they were keeping me on in spite of the general cuts. They said they wanted articles about the spring in Mentone, because of the holiday season. I shall write the articles. I have never been to Mentone and shall never go. And they know it. Nothing has happened. Everything is grand. Better than I thought. No, I am not embittered. Did my voice sound shrill? I have been having a singing audition. I have to go again tomorrow. "The Dream of a Night," from the novel, *War in the Dark*. I do so enjoy dancing in the open air. Perhaps I shall get taken on. If not, thousands of others are in the same boat. I want some paint and canvas. I'm going to the Porza Ball tonight. Why? I promised Jakobsohn I would. Maybe he'll buy the picture after all, if I go. He said he was enchanted. He says he knows a connoisseur of erotic pictures. He knows exactly what I think of him, and that obviously amuses him. You must come with me, Ive. What, am I to go alone? Come on. Put on an old jacket and go as an apache. I'm going as an amazon, with a whip, a short skirt, and high boots. Because I know that's what Jakobsohn likes.'

XVI

HELENE did not say a word in the taxi. She sat upright, one foot forward, and peered through the mirroring windowpane on to the road gleaming in the head-lights. Occasionally, as they passed a street lamp, by its light Ive could see her thin, pale face, bright red lips and motionless metallic green eyes. Over her dress she was wearing a silk cloak, which she had made herself out of some odd pieces, and she held it together at the throat with her slender bare hand. On the corners of her finger-nails Ive could still see a trace of paint, like a dried-up trickle of blood. Ive had a sudden desire to work, to work madly, anything rather than the torture of seeing Helene like this in her wretched, shabby, trumped-up silken finery, in this musty, dirty taxi, smelling of sweat and stale smoke, sitting behind the driver in his brown suit.

He turned to her and said abruptly: 'Let's turn back. Don't let Jakobsohn have the picture, Helene. I'll buy it. Wait a few days, two or three days, there's still some money owing to me for the article on the butter-tax. I have a commission for a series on emigration. I'll begin this very evening. I'll get the money somehow. Do you hear, the picture is mine!'

Helene did not even turn her head. 'You don't understand,' she said, and Ive was silent.

There was a crackle of bare wet branches scraping along the roof of the taxi, the sound of grinding wheels. In the crude yellow light stood the commissionaire. Helene jumped out and went towards the entrance. Ive put his hand in his pocket, stopped short, and at that moment he would gladly have snatched the pistol from the policeman standing stiffly at the corner and made an end of everything. 'Helene!' he called.

'Oh, of course,' she said, turned round and came back. She fumbled in her purse, without looking at Ive.

'I'm thirty pfennigs short,' whispered Ive. 'Don't make me mad,' he said, 'that's mean.'

'You don't understand,' said Helene, and paid the taxi-man.

Cars-rolled up. The policeman made a sign, the commissionaire opened the doors.

He did not open the doors for Helene and Ive. Ive would have gone in, but Helene waited until the commissionaire returned.

'Open the doors,' she said. With a glum face the commissionaire pushed against the doors with his elbow so that they opened just widely enough for them to pass through one at a time. Ive would have gone in, but Helene waited.

'Open them wide,' she said, and looked at the commissionaire. Slowly he pushed the doors wide open.

'Thank you,' said Helene, and went through.

Ladies in fancy costume or in evening-dress were standing in front of long mirrors. Helene threw her wrap on the cloak-room table. Ive stood behind her and noticed how her brownish shoulders were drawn together with every movement she made. He took off his coat, folded it so that the torn lining would not show, and waited. Helene powdered her face. A girl with long, black-stockinged legs, a white frock and a cap with wide-spreading flaps, bent down to pull up her stocking. Mickey Mouse, thought Ive, and at the same moment noticed a hippopotamus in a tail-coat approaching Helene. That's Jakobsohn, thought Ive. He took the cloak-room tickets and felt a sinking in his stomach. Blindly he felt in his pocket; but there was money. Helene must have put some there.

He went up to Jakobsohn like a drunken man, pulling into place his ridiculous coat, sizes too large for him. He took a rather soft hand and smiled, and cursed himself for smiling. Then he trotted after the two of them. Heavens, he thought to himself, since when have I suffered from an inferiority complex? He caught himself trying to look at ease. That's it, he thought, as soon as you can put a name to it, the thing exists, not before. Facts are created, not conquered, by consciousness of them. You don't get classes until you get class-consciousness. The problem doesn't exist till then. What class do I belong to? thought Ive. Certainly not to that one. Certainly not to the Mickey Mouse world. Nothing but shit, Claus Heim would say. Claus Heim. Ive no longer tried to look at ease. I should like to know what Dr. Siegmund Freud would make of Claus Heim, he thought, and smiled with delight at the idea. A waiter pushed a chair out of the way in front of him. Ladies and gentlemen passed by him. The ballroom had been artistically decorated with gay festoons in blue, red, and yellow. Jakobsohn had had two places reserved. Ive seized a chair for himself, expecting that any minute a gentleman would come and say: 'Excuse me.' But no one came. They sat exactly opposite the band of unemployed musicians in dinner-jackets; this was probably one of the usual charity balls that show a deficit. He looked attentively at the cellist. He was an elderly man with rimless glasses and a crushed expression. He was not smiling like the conductor and the man at the percussion instruments, who by knee gyrations and all sorts of contortions of the shoulder joints gave the impression of being in exceedingly high spirits. On the dance floor a number of couples were moving, a dense mass of bodies was circling round the small free space in the centre. But there was no uniformity to be seen in the steps, the couples merely moved to the rhythm of the music. A few of the men only were in fancy costume; most of them wore simple smocks, or white flannel trousers and light shirts with a scarf round their necks; a number of them had blue-and-white striped sailor-jerseys, with short sleeves, which made them look very audacious. The women leant back seriously in the crooked arms of their partners. From time to time, at a particularly long-drawn-out note of the muffled trumpet, one of them would raise her leg, stretch it out stiffly and then bring it gracefully down again. From time to time one of them would smile, throwing back her head, and straining on her narrow shoulder-straps.

Helene was dancing with Jakobsohn. She was slightly taller than he was, and his arm was round her hips. Helene looked down at him, so that she seemed to have her eyes closed. The Mickey Mouse stuck her bottom out well away from her partner, and held the string of a green balloon in her hand. Many of the ladies had balloons, and the swaying of the gay-coloured globes above the monotonous swarm of heads gave the scene its appropriate character of movement and colour.

Ive saw Schaffer in a black Russian blouse and a saucy beret, and he would have thought he was intended for an anarchist if he had not known his lamentable predilection for roller-skating. He was talking to a Communist, whom Ive knew, and who had turned up blatantly in a brilliant red silk shirt. Ive walked across between the dancing couples to greet Schaffer, but half-way across the room he stopped. Why should I? he asked himself, turned round, and pushed his way back through the crowd.

As soon as the music stopped, there were a few seconds' silence; the scraping of feet and hubbub of voices only began again slowly. On nearly all the tables there were a few bottles of wine and plenty of bottles of lemonade. Helene returned on Jakobsohn's arm, flicking her ridiculous little whip in front of his eyes. Ive pushed back the glass that the waiter set in front of him. Helene nodded at him quietly, rested her chin on her hand, and looked silently into the room. Jakobsohn too was silent, smoking a very black cigar. In the adjoining box someone was saying:

'You see, I'm of opinion that the Nazis should be given a chance, to see what they can pull off...'

Jakobsohn looked across furiously. At one of the tables some girls in very daring evening-dress were laughing, and every head was turned in their direction. Now and again men would pass along the gangways behind the boxes, cigarettes held negligently in their hands, scanning the tables with astonishing equanimity, as though they were looking for someone, which, of course, was not so. Occasionally couples met friends, stopped, shook hands and laughed, asked hurried questions about things that didn't interest them, nodded and passed on, turning round to wave good-bye. A gentleman spoke to the waiter, came up to Ive, and tapped him on the shoulder.

'Excuse me,' he said, but Ive did not excuse him, going out of his way to be insolent.

The gentleman seemed to have expected this. He shrugged his shoulders, took another chair, and went away.

The music began again, and Helene rose to dance with Jakobsohn.

'Don't bother me with Communists,' said someone in the adjoining box. 'I tell you there isn't any danger of Communism in Germany now...'

Ive drummed with his fingers on the tablecloth, which was gradually getting soiled from ash and cigarette-ends. He drew a few lines on the cloth with a burnt match, and then looked again at the dancers on the floor. Schaffer too was dancing. The muscles of his face were set as he made his steps and he looked completely idiotic. He looked up and caught sight of Ive. For a moment it seemed as though he was going to leave his partner and come over, but, of course, he went on dancing. One gentleman was attracting attention because he was wearing very elegant brown evening clothes.

'That's the famous criminal advocate Schreivogel,' said someone in the adjoining box, 'he's only famous because he turns up at every ball in brown evening-clothes...'

A Hamburg carpenter, to the accompaniment of much laughter, was trying to drag a girl out to dance with him, but since he did not succeed, he sat down again and rocked backwards and forwards on his chair. Helene passed by. She was looking down at Jakobsohn, so that she seemed to have her eyes closed. What is Jakobsohn getting out of that? thought Ive. But he was dancing with obvious pleasure. Of course, he's not an enemy, thought Ive, nor was the commissionaire an enemy. But is that a reason, he thought... in any case Helene possesses something that I wasn't able to display— discipline.

A lady in a close-fitting silver-lame dress, tall, fair and beautiful, stepped hesitatingly into the box, and gazed across over Ive's head at the dancers. She stood thus for a little while, and then Ive noticed that she was leaning heavily against his chair. He turned round slowly and offered her a cigarette. She said, 'Thank you,' in a soft voice, and smiled at him. He gave her a light without speaking, and turned back towards the room. After a little while she walked away. He was sorry for this and rose, but sat down again thinking: My limbs feel as heavy as lead.

Helene and Jakobsohn returned.

'Enjoyed yourself?' asked Helene.

'Immensely,' said Ive.

'Let's go to the buffet,' suggested Jakobsohn.

Helene thought a moment, and then said: 'Later perhaps.'

In the adjoining box someone said: 'Now Brüning, he's a man. Look how he dealt with the banks?'

'He didn't go far enough, unfortunately,' said someone else. 'If you went and asked for reasonable credit...'

Jakobsohn fondled Helene's hand. Helene withdrew her hand, but slowly. Jakobsohn looked fixedly in front of him. All three of them stared into the empty room. On the broad, sweeping steps that led up to the orchestra-stand some couples were seated, the ladies with their legs stretched out, smoking and laughing.

'In the present crisis,' said someone in the adjoining box.

Jakobsohn lost his temper:

'What do they mean by crisis?' he said. 'It's all a question of confidence. If everybody talks about a crisis, we shall never get on our feet again.'

He looked at Ive.

'The main thing is to get up off one's backside somehow,' said Ive brutally.

Unpleasant fellow, thought Jakobsohn. The music started up a waltz.

'Let's dance,' said Helene to Ive, and Jakobsohn leaned back, taking a very black cigar out of his case.

'Yes,' said Ive, going up behind Helene.

Helene danced well, but she always tried to take the lead. She danced very quickly. Ive looked into her face. She looked down at his shoulder, and it seemed as though her eyes were closed. Ive stopped abruptly in the middle of the room.

'Listen,' he said excitedly, 'this won't do. You came here to sell the picture to Jakobsohn. Please be consistent.'

'Yes,' said Helene softly, and it sounded like a question.

They danced. He could feel her tense muscles through the thin material of her dress. They danced quickly and distractedly. A wave of gaiety seemed to come over the crowd. Faces were flushed, and many were laughing. Jakobsohn was leaning over the side of the box and smiled at Helene. She nodded back to him gaily. They danced away from the other couples until they came to a clear space, where they twirled round wildly. Round and round, first to the left and then to the right. But Helene's muscles retained that strange hardness, not the hardness of metal or bone, but like a frozen towel. When the music stopped, everybody clapped. But Helene went up to Jakobsohn while the others began to dance again. Ive followed her slowly. Jakobsohn was rocking to and fro on his chair, and happily blowing away on a toy trumpet. His cigar was burning away on the earthenware ash-tray. Helene stuffed her ears, laughing.

'Manchuria showed us what the League of Nations is up to,' said someone in the adjoining box. 'What, Herriot, he's a Philistine too...'

Helene did not move her hand. She leant towards Jakobsohn and laughed awkwardly. The rouge on her lips had worn off, and remained only as a reddish shadow at the corners of her mouth. What lovely teeth, thought Ive. Helene fixed a small green cap on Jakobsohn's bald patch, it slipped and sat askew on the back of his head. Jakobsohn made an amused grimace. He edged nearer to Helene, pushed his horn-rimmed glasses down on to the tip of his nose, and peered happily over the top of them.

'Clown,' said Ive very loudly.

But beneath his layers of fat Jakobsohn concealed a first-class character.

'I see,' he said, suddenly serious, to Ive, 'that you're determined to insult me. Good God, I can understand that,' he said. 'It must be difficult nowadays for young men of your stamp. You can't adjust yourselves to life.'

Ive laughed aloud, and rejoiced that his laughter sounded as natural as it was.

'No,' he laughed, 'I certainly can't adjust myself to your life.'

Jakobsohn turned to Helen and said quietly:

'Well, dear lady, I am prepared to buy the picture. You mustn't be offended if I tell you frankly that it doesn't yet seem to me to be absolutely mature work. All the same I see the talent, and I consider it my duty to encourage talent. You've told me the price, and I am prepared to pay it. I think it's a bit high, but everyone should know his own value.'

'Of course,' said Ive, 'after all, art is not a luxury, but a favour towards the artist, from the dealer.'

'Nomen est omen,' said someone in the adjoining box, 'General von Schleicher...'

Jakobsohn wrote a cheque and, covering it with his hand, passed it to Helene. Helene hesitated and held it for a moment folded up in her hand.

'Put it in your stocking,' said Ive out loud.

Helene suddenly looked like a helpless child. Why do I tease her? thought Ive. What a low-down swine I am. But Helene quietly put the cheque in her handbag.

'You're a very naughty boy,' she said almost tenderly, 'Thank you,' she said to Jakobsohn, 'that is a great help to me.'

'I'll talk to your husband about the exhibition later,' said Jakobsohn, smiling at Helene with fatherly kindness. Ive sat back as though dazed.

A group of young men were laughing and making a commotion between the tables. They were trying to burst the ladies' balloons with their cigarettes. A very young girl in wide white trousers and a close-fitting jersey escaped from them and made a dash along the gangways. At last she came to a halt and leant, breathing quickly, against the wall of the box. Five cigarettes took aim at the balloon, which exploded with a weak report. Five young men, with their heads thrust forward, gazed breathlessly at the girl. She stood still a second, looking in front of her with narrowed eyes, then with a deft movement she pushed the cavaliers aside and ran off. A gentleman in a tail coat, with a small white rosette in his buttonhole, bowed to Helene and handed her a card.

'Madam, you are requested,' he said, bending his head, 'to take part in the beauty competition. In ten minutes' time, in the blue room.'

Ive saw that there was an understanding between the gentleman and Jakobsohn.

'Helene,' he said.

'Well,' said Helene, 'I'm only being consistent.' She said 'Thank you,' and took the card, rolling it between her fingers.

Schaffer came into the box.

'How are you?' he asked.

'Splendid, thank you,' said Ive. 'And you? Having a good time? A nice party,' he said.

'Well, I don't know, on the whole I think it's a bit stupid,' said Schaffer, looking fixedly at Helene, obviously wishing to be introduced to her. But the idea never occurred to Ive.

'Of course, your wife isn't here?' he said. 'How is she?'

'Thank you, very well, very well,' said Schaffer. 'Well, till Friday evening,' and he departed.

The Mickey Mouse had given rise to great amusement by losing her tail. Helene went off with Jakobsohn to dance. Ive got up clumsily, and paced through the gangways, his hands thrust into his coat pockets. Couples were camped out all over the stairs. Ive strode over them with wide steps.

'Pardon me,' he said.

'Oh, that's all right,' said a girl, brushing off the patches of dirt that the sole of Ive's shoe had made on her sleeve. The lady in silver lamé was leaning heavily and blissfully against the chest of a very young Argintronian, her blonde head pillowed on his broad shoulder; they both sat motionless looking at the dancers. As Ive passed by he noticed that she was pregnant. He stood behind the bandstand, next to the cellist, and looked into the room. He tried to find Helene among the dancers, but he could not see her. Presently she passed close by him, coming up the steps accompanied by Jakobsohn, and disappeared with some other girls through a door.

Ive leant over the balustrade of the steps and stared into the room... When we were marching back, in the war, he thought, we used to dance nearly every night. The chaps were crazy. Forty kilometres covered in the day and then, at night, instead of flinging themselves down exhausted, started dancing straight away. Sergeant Brückner was furious:

'You can keep on the hop all night, but when it comes to changing guard, all at once you're too tired.'

In Kirchenhain the parish priest had warned the girls on Sunday from the pulpit that the soldiers were all infected; and in the evening what a shindy there was in front of his house. He had had to take back his words. But of course the padre had been right... That was an achievement, he thought, the way the scourge of venereal disease had been stamped out afterwards... He had learned to dance out there. In any old barn, the rain coming in at the roof and the wind blowing through the cracks. When they had had a runt ration, one of them would play on a comb covered with paper, and they caught hold of each other and stamped away in their hob-nailed boots and their dirty, crumpled trousers. Ive caught hold of his comrade's sword buckle and looked at his bronzed, freckled neck emerging broad above his grey tie. One, two, three; one, two, three; it resounded on the floor of the barn... Odd that lately he so often thought about the war. Every night during the last few weeks had been filled with wild dreams about the war. I was never so frightened as I am in my dreams, thought Ive. Wait a bit, old chap, you were even more frightened, you were contemptibly frightened. Or is that a pose? The pose of an old soldier—everything is a pose. But always the feeling—that won't do, the others are looking. But nobody was looking. When the mud used to spurt up in front of your eyes all over the place and you thought— you've got to go through that now... Say not the hardest task's to act, the moment, the emotion gives you strength, the hardest task of all is to decide—something like that. Who was it said that? Grillparzer? Of course. Odd... But once over the top, it was finished, as though it had never been. As completely vanished as dream-terrors on awakening—all you feel is a huge astonishment... Then the fat old innkeeper's wife brought breakfast. Miserable breakfast, two rolls and a lump of butter, and the refreshing beverage. You can only swallow down such loathsome things standing up and in a hurry. Every morning the flabby rolls made you long for the war bread, the dark, bitter hunk, already slimy or going green in the cracks, and turning into hard lumps in your mouth. But how they enjoyed it. Of course, they grumbled and longed for white, flabby rolls. And when they were hopping round in the barn, man with man, sweating like pigs, they probably thought of girls in evening-dress and 'caressing dance music.' God. The Guards may die, but they do not surrender.

Whenever Ive rode on an omnibus, he always chose the seat on top, right in front, exactly over the driver, who was crouched down below in his little cabin stinking of oil and benzine, in an atmosphere of hot dust, in his black leather jacket, like the driver of a tank. And every time he thought of General Gallieni, who saved Paris by scraping up all the men he could find in the town, putting them into every kind of vehicle—taxis, carts, motor-buses—emptying the town of everyone who could fight, and bore down on the front with everything he could find that had wheels. *Sale politique* was written in Gallieni's diary. The town which had come into being by traffic was saved by the instruments of traffic. And by the will of a soldier. And of all those who crouched on the rattling carts, every one knew what the object was. An astounding picture. And now, day after day this pointless riding hither and thither, and you always knew after all; you are only imagining that this is of any importance. Fruitless journeys, all fruitless journeys. Often, when he walked through the streets at night, passing the newsvendors, waiting taxis, the male prostitutes outside the Eldorado, the terrible pictures of the Skala, he dreamed of mine-throwers. If you stuck a knife in the barrel, the bolt always stuck in the breech, the mine fell down into the muzzle and sprang up again. Eight shots into the air, and the ninth in the barrel, until the first burst. Or, if the mine-thrower wasn't constructed for spreading fire, you stood on the gun-carriage behind, took hold of the lanyards and pulled. Bang! The wheels jumped round quicker and quicker at every shot, you were flung back, then forward. Then for the next. If the mine burst in the barrel it was all up. You could see the projectiles flying, like black, shrieking, twittering birds, to the highest point of the trajectory, and then nothing more. But if you stood where they hit the earth, you could only see their fall—queer—why exactly? From Martin-Luther-strasse over the houses to Viktoria-Luise-platz. Berlin has never seen such a thing. From the Pariser-platz to the Kroll. If one of those things were to get to work here. Right in the middle of the crowds; Berlin has never seen such a thing. But we have seen it... Nobody wants to die. Why does nobody want to die? Is this better than dying? ... Hush! Oh, the beauty competition. Everybody stands up, all eyes are turned upwards. First prize—elected as the beauty queen of the Porza Ball, Mrs. So-and-So—a doctor's wife. Not Helene, of course, Mrs. So-and-So. Quite pretty, but bloodless... Where is Helene? ... Second prize, third prize... Dancing. Would you perhaps like to die? Are you any better than anyone else? Where is Helene? What are you doing here? Is it any excuse that you find it revolting? Do you think that nobody else finds it revolting? They are masks and ghosts. And you, aren't you a mask and a ghost? Is that all you learnt from the war, to be a mask and a ghost, and to dissipate your trivial days with trivial dreams? You must know what you're dying for. You need not know anything. Jakobsohn knows. You have lived like a swine, a stupid swine, too grand to wallow in the mire; like an hygienic swine, that produces tasteless ham. Here you stand, and the music is playing, and down below Schaffer is dancing with Mickey Mouse. And you live in the 'consciousness of the Reich,' and Claus Heim lives in the consciousness of the prison cell. And you talk, and he is silent. And he is a man, and you are a weakling... Where is Helene? Why did you come here? Jakobsohn has bought the picture... Curse the picture, where is Helene? The box is empty. Perhaps in the buffet... The lady in silver lamé is still lying on the faithful breast of the Argintronian... Helene is not in the buffet. Helene isn't dancing; Jakobsohn isn't here either...

'I hope you're enjoying yourself, Schaffer; no, I haven't been drinking, not a drop. Make room, man...'

She isn't upstairs either. Perhaps in the blue room? Empty...

'Out of the way. Don't talk rubbish, idiot. I must find Helene, I must...'

The stairs, over there perhaps? You can't see across to the other side. The box is empty. What next, my cloak-room ticket? Waiter, has the bill been paid? Of course... With Jakobsohn. Impossible. Helene wouldn't go with Jakobsohn. Why not? No, you don't understand Helene. He was very polite to her, full of a vulgar, disgusting, slimy politeness. No, Helene with him, that's impossible...

'My coat, yes, that one with the torn lining...'

What next? But if she isn't with Jakobsohn, with the hippopotamus, with the son of a Mickey Mouse fantasy—him and her—ludicrous—if she had gone home, she would surely have said something? What did she say, what did she look like, when I last saw her? Last? What does that mean?...

'Quick, quick,' said Ive out loud, and found himself standing alone in the vestibule.

Without thinking he looked in a long mirror and saw his reflection. He was shocked at his reflection, he looked simply ludicrous, shamefully and humiliatingly ludicrous. He knew he hadn't the money for a taxi, and that made him feel absolutely helpless. He stood, with his coat half-buttoned up, his hat in his hand, in front of the door, and tried to gather his thoughts. But he was completely empty. Nothing would come into his mind but the old, forgotten, military formula: 'Helmets off for prayers.'

He put his hat on. Now Helene is done for, he thought mechanically, without really knowing what he meant by this. He pulled himself together, and walked on aimlessly for a few steps. He walked quicker and quicker, straight in front of him, towards the black trees, seeking out the dark spots, as though he would find Helene there. She is at the studio, he thought, and meditated. Or with Jakobsohn. But this seemed more than he could bear. Not with Jakobsohn, oh God, not with Jakobsohn, anywhere but there; Helene can't do that to me, he thought, and was terrified. He felt a choking fear. Dimly he saw what was possible for Helene, he did not quite grasp it, it came upon him like a thunderbolt. Helene could do this thing to him, knowing that it was necessary for him and for her to be strict and bitter to the very last moment. He stood still, under the trees, and realised that his whole body was covered with a sticky sweat... Until the very last moment: then I must not live any longer, he thought. He thought: now it is decided; I can't live any longer, everything is finished with, including responsibility to the world.

He looked up at the trees. Above his head spread the broad, strong branches... There is no other way out. She washed her hands, her face, her whole body, she took clean linen from the cupboard, the folds must still be visible. The linen smells faintly of soap, her legs stick out of it like a rag-doll's. What can she do after this terrible humiliation? And she has been carrying this about with her for years, and we knew nothing of it, we didn't see it, didn't realise. Of course, we knew. We were cowards, we did not want to see; it was so pleasant not to realise it. Good God, he thought, good God.

'All lies,' Helene had said, 'all lies.' Guilt or responsibility, how we enjoyed juggling with words.

'You do not understand,' Helene had said.

But Helene understood, and she was an abandoned woman, had been for years, as long as she could remember. That is why she was justified, that was why she did not recognise guilt, but was responsible, was above all pettiness, was unassailable, unconquerable in her inmost soul. She was, was... the words kept palpitating in him, and, suddenly taking a short turn towards the town, he began to run. He ran past the entrance of the hall, which he had just left, and heard the sound of the orchestra. The saxophones are sighing in the end of the century, he thought, and began, in the midst of his aimless running, to compose verses, which for a moment seemed to him to be remarkable. At a street-crossing, just as he was about to cross the Damn, the red light went on. This just suited him, he rushed swaying across, between loudly hooting cars; but the next moment he was disgusted with himself, and gave up looking for imaginary dangers. He was surprised at his own theatricality, running like a drunken man, exaggerating his movements, as though he wanted to make it clear to the whole world that here was a man running with the burden of a great sorrow.

If, he thought to himself, it is a question of responsibility, I must not look for Helene, I must let everything go on to the end; be cold, force things on and then bear the consequences. But equally strong was the thought that he would escape the consequences, that he would go on living, without reason, with a wound in his soul, but go on living, that he would be guilty of the most shameful betrayal, a betrayal that could only bear fruit in petty feelings, only be fruitful as the counterpole of his confidence, a useless betrayal, therefore, all things considered, the cause of a wound in his soul. Then he cursed himself for thinking of himself and not of Helene, but he could not help it. Finally, he gave up thinking about anything at all, and from that moment his mind became quite clear. She can't do this, it came to him, she is a Catholic, and he turned into a street which led to the church. If there is no light in the church, if it is locked, he thought... it was locked. He rattled at the door. Through the high windows shone the faint light of the sanctuary lamp. The only thing left was to go to the studio. He ran, his hands on his breast, his elbows pressed to his sides, through the streets, through the eternal, long, dark alleys. He ran along the streets he had so often walked with Helene, past the dimly lighted street-corners, past the waiting taxis, past the shops, all closed now, and the inimical house-fronts. He began to look ahead of him. Breathing heavily, he peered forward to see if there was still a light in the hall. There was no light, but the gate was unlocked. He threw his whole weight against the heavy, creaking doors. As usual he was irritated by the plaster representations of the 'Minstrels' Festival in the Wartburg' and 'The Homecoming of Tannhauser' in the entrance hall. What am I thinking of? He cursed himself, terrified lest all his excitement had been for nothing; and pushed against the door leading into the courtyard and lifted the latch. This door too was open, and with his relief at this was mixed the frightening memory that this door was frequently open. He saw something white in the courtyard. He ran up to it, but half-way there turned back again. It was a piece of paper in the dust-bin. He looked up at the rear of the house. All the windows were in darkness. Then he remembered shamefacedly that the Studio windows, of course, faced the other side. He went up the stairs, taking three steps at a time, opening his coat in order to go more quickly. Stairs, stairs, stairs; at every door, on every landing a fresh odour met him, the dark hole beside the banisters, the deep abyss of the entrance hall had a stupefying odour as he panted upwards. Was there a light in the studio? There was a light. He bumped against the door, he thrust his shoulder against it.

'Open the door,' he cried. 'It is I, Ive, quick,' and fell back, listening.

He heard nothing; he listened, and in the distance he heard the scraping of a chair, slow footsteps. 'Open the door,' he cried, and put his head against the crack, to see if he could recognise the footsteps. They were not her footsteps. The painter pulled the door open, the light struck him in the face.

'Where is Helene?' he cried in a hoarse voice, and rushed into the room. But Helene was sitting silent and in deep absorption in front of her easel. She had on her white smock, on her head her old red cap, and her hand was gently moving as she placed her brush on the canvas.

XVII

Ive was himself astonished to find how one small event was capable of diverting him from one line of action to another. This one movement of the spiritual lever was sufficient to shift the points. It is true that his personal collision with the complications of reality had by no means led to personal consequences. If Ive had had any psychoanalytical training he might have found it possible to have been actually offended with Helene for not committing suicide. He might have been able to dissociate himself from her, not indeed because he was wounded, but for his own peace of mind, and to leave her, with regretful sympathy, to her own fate. Or again, if this kind of spiritual hygiene did not suit him, another course was open to him. He might have frankly admitted his mistake, and have immediately devoted himself to the benevolent service of humanity, beginning with his nearest friends, and thus have entered into the peace of a noble attitude. Unfortunately Ive was not disposed to acquire the necessary knowledge of the psychical mechanism. Not that he would have been daunted by any kind of mechanism, but he attributed very little importance to these things. He was, for instance, happy in the assurance that nobody could excel him in the use of so complicated an apparatus as that presented by a machine-gun. Moreover, he regarded the aforesaid machine-gun as undoubtedly the most suitable means of dealing in the most economical way with a number of problems of the times, including so-called intellectual problems. But he was not interested in the problems of the times but in the times themselves, if one may say so. He was interested in the substructure of power for which the times were struggling.

And his ridiculous adventure in the ballroom and later in the studio had narrowed down for him the field of interest. Narrowed down, that was it.

'What have I learned from the town?' he said to Schaffer, when he went to say good-bye to him. 'I have learned nothing from it except my duty. Rather I should say it has made my duty clearer to me. And after all that's a great deal, it's a very great deal.'

And Schaffer was the first to agree with him there. Schaffer was not in the least astonished at Ive's decision to leave the town. 'That's certainly the best thing you can do,' he said thoughtfully, and from what he went on to say it was clear how well he realised what was impelling Ive, and others besides Ive.

'Everything is a preparation,' said Schaffer with precision, and sighed gently, for he could have wished that the preparation was somewhat pleasanter in his own case.

How else can the Reich be founded, they both thought, except by sixty million spiritual fortresses? But for Ive the process of fortifying his soul had been completed at the moment that he felt the impulse to leave the town—just as this process had begun with the impulse to come to the town. Ive gave no further thought to the matter, he took it for granted. But it would be an exaggeration to say that he took it for granted because he was under the influence of some mysterious urge, because something stronger than himself was driving him. He might as easily have acted otherwise; he might easily have decided to stay with the farmers, and he saw no urgent reason for returning to them now, yet on this occasion, as on that, he made his decision. He realised that this was the zero hour, and he prepared himself to go through with it, although no one, not even he himself, could have reproached him if he had decided to shirk it. 'The time has come,' he said now, as then.

It remains for us to carry out what has for centuries been the recognised task of the chroniclers, without falling into the errors which, for centuries, have been the recognised errors of the chroniclers, namely, in order to make our narrative plausible to resort to means which have nothing to do with the events we are narrating. We cannot, for instance, describe a trial for witchcraft and at the same time deny that witches existed; and we cannot drag in by the hair a mother—or a grandmother—complex or any other contribution of general culture to show why Ive left the town. For even if Ive was aware of these theories, he obviously made no use of them. And as for general culture, he neither tried to make a virtue of necessity, nor to fill in the gaps in his own education. In the first place the value of this culture would have had to be proved to him, and it seemed to him that the possessors of this precious gift were particularly unsuited for this task. He was not educated but trained, and, moreover, trained as a soldier, and, thank God, the traces of this training never left him.

This probably explains why it was that he never joined in the noisy chorus of those who—with the exception of the National Socialists, who had never made any claim to it— regarded it as a reproach to be lacking in what the bankrupts of a whole century, from Jean Jacques Rousseau to Emil Ludwig, leaving out of account their different degrees of eminence, have understood by the term 'intellect.' Ive did not join in, because he could never get away from the question *cui bono*? If he did not join the National Socialists, it was not because he could not discern enough traces of the aforementioned intellect among them. On the contrary, it seemed to him that the wine of the Third Reich savoured too much of the cork of the Second.

'You have not understood anything,' Helene had said to him when he was on the point of taking refuge from a general conclusion in a personal decision, and the outcome of events showed him what she meant by this. Actually she herself was in the same position as Ive, that is she no longer had any tolerance for the prescriptions of Karl Marx, based on socialistic quackery. It never occurred to Helene to wish for any personal vocation; she had character enough to coordinate her own demands with those of her times, and since she herself had character enough for this, she could and was obliged to demand the same of her friends. She had justified herself and she observed with sorrow that Ive was about to renounce any claim to justification. Helene asked him to give an account of himself, and he did so. He discovered that he could say 'Yes' to the town, even a satisfied 'Yes,' almost amounting to a declaration of faith. Ive had come to the town to conquer it, and in his cell in the Moabit Prison he had dreamed of new battalions which would conquer the town—but the new battalions, which were formed without his co-operation, only conquered the streets of the town. Ive would not have objected, by a miracle of energy, preparation and chance, to reaching the responsible position of chief burgomaster—but he was kind enough to admit that even so he would not have been able to accomplish much more than Burgomaster Sahm. Ive was prepared to take from the town anything it had to offer him—but more active conquistadores than he had attempted this in their own sphere, and after a pleasant interlude, which had not lasted so very long, had found themselves landed in a cell of the self-same Moabit Prison. And Ive had gained in the town the only experience the town had to offer him, namely, nothing.

'Just that, and that is an astounding achievement,' he said to Dr. Schaffer, who, while delighted at Ive's laughing confession, could not suppress a sigh. For he had his work cut out to keep on resolutely and rapidly marking time.

'The town has taught me nothing,' said Ive, for all his experience had been in himself, and if the town had any influence it was the influence of pressure. This pressure had shaken his whole being. It seemed to Ive that the real function of the town lay in the fact that it was not in it, but through it, that characteristic sublimation took place, in men, in things, in space, and in time. The town had subjected the whole life of the country to its pressure and Ive realised his duty at the very moment that the town had shown it to be in the country.

'Back to the farmers?' asked Schaffer. But Ive repudiated the word 'back.'

He had set himself the task of worming his way into the inmost core of the town, and in the inmost core he had found the country. He had found the core vegetatively, and he took an animal delight in the realisation that he had reached exactly the same point that he had left when he set out to find it. Exactly the same duty confronted him, only it was more definite. And he recalled that moment in the editorial office of his farmers' paper when he had realised the spiral process to which every life is subject. The town was life, and he was life, and nothing existed in the world that was not life. Every opinion might give rise to ten new opinions, each one exceptional and completely authoritative; but in their oscillations all things tended to meet; all analogues were living; every thought reacted in all directions; the best formulation was always the first, and at the same time the first was the last. For there is no validity that is not derived from ultimate validity. If you thought in terms of epochs, it could not matter in the least, it was even essential, had a deep spiritual meaning, that, in spite of everything, there were six million unemployed, that Helene put on a sleeveless dress when she went to the newspaper office and crossed her legs when she was talking to Jakobsohn. Didn't that matter? Was that even essential? Had that a deeper meaning? Were those validities that were derived from an ultimate validity? Didn't it matter that six million were slowly rotting and decaying, that they were piled one on top of another like lice in a blanket, that they bit and beat each other, scorned and slandered one another, that they cringed and betrayed and did the dirty on one another, that they trampled each other, up and down, and right and left, because each one wanted to snatch the scrap of dry bread from his neighbour's mouth, and to deprive his tired bottom of its tiny resting-place, and yet they were surrounded by plenty? Was it even essential that the farm should be rattling in a death struggle, the wheat withering and the Treasury-office flourishing, that the farmer should be done for and that property should be rehabilitated, and when it was not rehabilitated it should be turned into small-holdings, while the small-holders could neither live nor die, poor wretches, and Claus Heim was squatting in gaol? Was there a deeper meaning in the fact that the painter slapped his paint on to the canvas in mad despair, and Helene rushed off to dance with Jakobsohn and he rubbed his belly against her belly, and bought the picture and sold it, and the painter had an amazing and extraordinary bit of luck as well; that they were marching along all the high roads, young men with brown faces and broad hands, and their hands were open and empty, strength thrown away for nothing, seed sown for nothing, blood flowing away for nothing, and in the cinema they showed Society learning to dance; that some talked of the crisis and emergency regulations, and the curtailing of the powers of the Reichsbank and others talked of nothing; they waited for the stones to speak, but the stones, too, were silent; that all this should be going on, empty streets, and dark desires, the Press frothing at the mouth, saxophones shrieking, some being subsidised and others without a tram fare in their pockets... yes, little man, what now? The Reich buys up bankrupt Gelsenkirchner bonds, not with machine-gun bullets, but with ninety percent profit, and the town takes a deep breath... symphony of work, symphony of the labour bureau, a red glow in the sky over the Memorial Church, cars massed in the Augusta-Viktoria-platz, heaven and hell and illuminated advertisements, Hinnerk calling fresh-baked rolls, empty promises, encouragements, disappointments, joy following fear, ecstasy following despair, well, little man, how d'you like it? Not a bit of it.

Ten thousand go to hear Hitler in the Sport-palace, ten thousand go to hear Thalmann in the Sport-palace, ten thousand go to hear Lobe in the Sport-palace, ten thousand watch the six-day races in the Sport-palace; the horsemen of the Apocalypse gallop through the town; hunger, lies, and treachery; they cackle in Geneva, they cackle in Lausanne, they cackle in the Reichstag, you too have cackled, Ive, but Claus Heim did not cackle; the farmers vote for Nazis, and the proletariat votes for Communists, it's the only way they can vote, and the only thing they can do is to vote; wages are reduced, the enemy is reduced, you yourself are reduced; how can I manage with 150 a month, how can I manage with 100 a month, how can I manage with 50 a month, how can I manage with nothing? It just goes on. They cackle in the Landtag, they cackle in drawing-rooms, they cackle on pay-day, you too have cackled, Schaffer, and you have cackled, Hellwig, and you have cackled, Pareigat. It began with the failure of the Vienna Credit Bank, it began with the stabbing, it began with the world war, it began with the dismissal of Bismarck, it began with the French Revolution, it began with the Reformation, it began with Adam and Eve, when, by all the powers of heaven and hell, is it going to end? Give us back our colonies; we can't pay and we won't pay; the corridor is a disgrace to civilisation; annexation is forbidden; the Russian five-year plan; the American repudiation of debts; events in Manchuria; Memel has given itself to Lithuania, and your wife, brother, will give herself to anyone with money. But Brodermann is still there to preserve peace and order. For, thinking in terms of epochs, all validities are derived from one validity. Well then, it is a validity, that here and there a man should stand up, that you should stand up, Ive; that every one should stand up and say: Finis. And say: here now and with me a new epoch is beginning. And set to work where he feels the need is greatest and knows what he has to do. What has Ive to do?

'What I did, before I came to the town, Schaffer, just that, and with the new knowledge of how necessary it is. Is it the town that taught me that? It was the town that confirmed that. For the town, which has to be, showed what must not be.'

And he realised with gratitude how and why he had lived in the town. And if it was an infinitely tangled and confused web through which he had worked his way, searching and questioning and thinking and talking until he reached the few simple and clear certainties, from these certainties he saw again an infinitely tangled and confused web that he, by his actions, had to create.

'Set to work,' he said, and made a movement with his two hands as though he were lifting a plough from the furrow, although he had no intention of working on the land when he went to the farmers. Ive was not a farmer. Ive was a soldier; not a militiaman engaged for twelve years, of strictly neutral politics, and provided with a ration-ticket; not a storm-trooper, with black tab on his coat and a two-coloured cord on the edge of his collar, presenting colours, and fighting with the Communists, in brown trousers which are stripped off in the police-station; but a soldier in the small, scattered, anonymous, ever-ready army of the Revolution. Was this really so? Certainly, and here we are not making the Revolution, we are the Revolution. Is there never, then, to be peace and quiet in our poor, beloved fatherland? No, by God, there shall not be peace and quiet in our poor, beloved fatherland. Is, then, brute force...? Exactly, and those who wield it must not succumb to it. Then is the Terror, is chaos...? Precisely, and those who exercise the Terror and create chaos must not have it within themselves. Does the nation want this? Nobody knows what the nation wants, or what she will want, but we want the nation. And who are we? We are those who want nothing but the nation, who wanted nothing else in the trenches, or among the workers or with the farmers; wanted nothing else but the nation on the wide stretches of the Marsh, and wanted nothing else in the confusion of the town. We are those who recognise no law and no obligations but the law and obligations of the nation, the will of the people. We are our own will towards the Reich, we are those who are ready to do away with enticement and temptation, with the whole mess of position and consequence and promotion, the whole slime of craft and humiliation, and of filth hidden behind high phrases about duty and responsibility, all the rotten talk of 'live and let live.' Do the people want it? No one knows what the people want, the people themselves do not know what they want, but it is what we want. And if what is to come proves to be bitterer than four years of war and fifteen years of the consequences of war, all honour to us that we have been prepared to face it, and if it should prove to be not bitterer, then once more honour to us that we have been prepared to face it. To hell with the past. Now we are no longer brandishing programmes; now we have no quack cures for sale, but wherever there is strength we will add our strength to it, and where there is none we will take away even that that there is. The farmers still have strength and the workers still have strength, for the former have everything to lose that is worth while, and the latter have nothing to lose that is worth while. But we have nothing to lose but our faith in the Reich and nothing to gain but the nation, and if we are called, it lies with us whether we are chosen also. We live in a period of decisions, of movements which give rise to new decisions every moment, the Reich is as open as a field, ready to receive every seed, and it is for us to see that Satan does not come and sow tares and thistles, it is for us to see that every decision is directed towards the Reich; whatever the world gives to the Reich it will transform and give back to the world. Not that its influence reaches to every corner of the earth, and is of importance, but that every influence finds in us its purifying meaning and we have the will to act within it. This means that we are passing from the sphere of protest into the sphere of construction. Every form of protest, whatever disguise it may assume, be it ballot-paper or a pair of brown trousers, exists outside the actual region of decision; the highest duty of every system can only be to accumulate temporal phenomena, and not to provide a valid objective point. The danger of this lies in the fact that, through systems, a movement that is not yet defined, is transformed into a state of affairs that is not yet equal to its task.

If the Reich is eternal in its power, then history represents the mutation of its forms, and our task today is to seek the form which corresponds best to its intrinsic character. That National Socialism is as little able to provide this form as any other system based on out-of-date or mistaken principles has been proved by the course of its development: the essential thing is to reckon up not the possibilities it has left open, but those it has shut off. No doubt, National Socialism has fulfilled a historical mission, it has led the democracy *ad absurdum*; no doubt, too, with the fulfilment of this mission its power is no longer justified. The positive of the Revolution has not yet been established, which means that the German Revolution has not yet been established. Do not let us fail to realise that in so far as it is aiming at new forms, its elements are to be found in the bourgeoisie. With us, as with the rest of the world, the important thing is to break the supremacy of the bourgeoisie. With us, even more than with the rest of the world, it is plain that the supremacy of the bourgeoisie, in the form it has assumed, is not German, but Western, so that the Revolution against the bourgeoisie is a German Revolution. And this being so, the most urgent task is the abolition of a state of affairs that has become intolerable, since it no longer even rouses the fertile strength of opposition; and because when the moment comes that we are imbued with the necessity of action it can only be the German Revolution for which we should work; the task lies in the hands of the revolutionaries and in no one else's; in the hands of those who have already perfected the revolution in themselves—and not before; for what is the good of being armed to the teeth if we are not armed to the heart? Indeed, it does not matter from what point the advance is made provided it is not situated in a vacuum. The masses have no impetus in themselves, and when, in the consciousness of their position, they decide to organise a revolution, they organise a bureaucracy. It is the few that give them the strength they lack. For these the important thing is not to have a point of view, but to be in a strong position and each one of them must seek the field of action that is ready to support him and from which he can act.

'For me it is with the farmers,' said Ive, 'as I have found before.'

He continued: 'The Reich will not be the farmers' country, but by its daily demands the country transforms the mystic consciousness into a reality. And it is this reality that constitutes society; the farming community contains the only natural form of organised society, and, therefore, so long as we are seeking these forms, it must be a stimulus and a pattern. I know what you are going to say, Schaffer,' said Ive, 'but economic planning alone is not enough, although there is certainly no harm in it, and vital interests do not exist except in the brains of the syndics. We have not yet been cheated out of that which gives a meaning to life, and we are not disposed to let ourselves be cheated out of it as we have been cheated out of everything else we can be cheated out of. The important thing remains, and cannot be argued about, and it is well for us that it cannot be argued about. For our fate does not lie in round-table conferences, nor in the Workers' Committee of the Reichstag, nor in the Governing Board of the General Electrical Company, but in our own breasts, in the breasts of men who not only know what they want, but know how to accomplish it. You want to know what there is to do, for you and for me? You can't see the forest of flags for the flags? Shall I fetch the system and scheme of a Reich out of my dispatch-case? Shall I sketch you a plan straight away, here on the corner of Joachimsthaler and Kurfürstendamm, beginning with the farm, and through community of distress to the Province? Beginning with the Association through the League to the Board of Agriculture? Beginning with the farmer's current account through the accumulations of financial establishments to the State budget? From the economic calculation of trade through the authority of political economy and to the so-to-speak centralised federalisation of economy, of countries and of associations? Shall I enumerate to you the articles of the Constitution, describe the structure of the State organisation, the nature of tariff agreements, of monopolies, of financial policy, of budgetary measures, of reciprocal credits? You know that it is not necessary to do that now, but that it is necessary to remove all obstacles and difficulties inherent in the structure of economy and society and which obstruct any planned economy, and that it is necessary to do that as soon as possible; that it is necessary to go from man to man, and from farm to farm, and prepare them to serve the nation, and to make them proof against the tales of hundreds and thousands of time-servers; that it is necessary for us who are armed to the heart to arm ourselves to the teeth. I am going to the farmers, Schaffer, not because I long for the fresh air of the Marsh, but because I know that the greatest strength of the country is to be found in them; because I know that this is the only strength that can be mobilised now and at once, and that the dunderheads are coming from every direction, with it all worked out in millions of rustling documents, to open the dams carefully and set the idle mills running again; because I know that the town is a function of the country and not its chief shareholder; because I know that if the farmer does not rise up in the country at once, the day will come when we shall not be able to rise up and march together for the sake of the Reich, but will be battering each other's heads for a scrap of land, for a tiny corner of the poor, exhausted, despised soil of the farmers.'

XVIII

THE commissionaire of the *Kadewe* untied the last dog from the railing, a miserable little breathing atom with a wrinkled face and weak legs, and handed him obsequiously to the lady from the grand car.

'Get out of the way there,' he said to Hinnerk, who was standing straddle-legged over his basket right in front of the door of the car.

'Shut your mouth,' said Hinnerk, and the two glared at each other. The commissionaire touched his cap, pocketed his tip and turned his back haughtily on Hinnerk to close the doors.

'Fresh baked rolls,' cried Hinnerk, looking right and left, his basket of hygienically wrapped bread on his arm. The basket was still half full... The big lamp in the entrance of the block of offices went out. The employees came out.

'Fresh baked... Off you go, my girl, to the underground. Fresh baked... Tuppence, sir. Fresh... there's that fellow over there again!'

The fellow was there again, a young man like Hinnerk, in a white apron, cap pulled over his eyes, and a basket of rolls.

'Get out of the way there,' said Hinnerk. 'This is my corner, clear out with all your truck.'

'What am I to do, then?' said the other, 'the comrade over there...'

'Never mind that,' said Hinnerk. 'This is my corner, off you go.'

But the other fellow did not go, and Hinnerk put his rolls in the basket and went over to arrange matters.

'Look out, police,' said a voice behind him.

'What do I care about police,' said Hinnerk turning round. 'Oh, it's you, Ive.'

'Yes,' said Ive, 'leave him alone. Since when have you adopted capitalist methods?'

'You don't understand,' said Hinnerk, 'there must be order, otherwise we might as well all pack up.'

'Leave him alone,' said Ive. 'Listen, Hinnerk,' he continued, laying his hand on his friend's arm, 'I've something to tell you.'

'What have you to tell me?' asked Hinnerk, but Ive only smiled. For a moment they looked at each other seriously.

'There must be order,' said Ive at last, 'that is probably what Warder Seifenstiebel says when he goes to Claus Heim's cell and tells him to clean out his pail with sand.'

'My word,' said Hinnerk. 'My word,' and suddenly he understood, gave Ive a mighty clap on the shoulder and said again, 'My word! Really?'

Ive nodded. Hinnerk took up his basket and put it down again, and pushed his cap on to the back of his head.

'Really?' he said. 'Only think, and I actually believed that it would never happen.'

He was in his element now, and seized his basket and swung it up under his arm.

'Tell us all about it,' he said, digging Ive in the ribs. 'My word, it's taken you two years to think it over? Two years to get to it? My word. Well, we'll forgive and forget. Tell us all about it,' he said.

They ambled along the street and across the square. From time to time Hinnerk set his basket down as though it were too heavy for him, but he did it absent-mindedly, for Hinnerk was in his element.

'When, where, how?' he asked. 'I'm delighted, my word, I'm delighted. D'you know they're doing a lot of cackling again about an amnesty and so on, and it seems as though Hellwig has really got things going. But I've never really liked it as much as I did when you used to go about the country polishing the bumbles' doorknobs for them. And I always used to think: I'll do it, I'll do it alone. But you used to say: he won't, and I thought you knew best, and you thought the time hadn't come. And then I got anxious about you, for you—you were, you know—I thought, I thought Ive is so busy swimming with the stream—don't be annoyed, for you were busy swimming with the stream. Never mind, you're going to get to work now.'

'Don't forget,' said Ive, 'that the Party repudiates individual terrorism.'

'What do I care about the Party?' said Hinnerk. 'What do I care about any party? That was all nothing; Communists or Nazis, a crew. Some of them are dirty dogs and the others are official. Now they are talking about a ban on uniforms. A ban on uniforms, my word, as though that had anything to do with it! And even if they do manage to get an amnesty, it's always stuck in my gullet a bit, for really it's damned sauce that an amnesty should be necessary at all. Anybody can pull off an amnesty. But to get them out— not everyone can do that.'

A girl came round the corner.

'I'm delighted,' said Hinnerk.

'Give me one,' said the girl. She was very thin, very much painted and wore high, red, laced boots up to the knee.

'There,' said Hinnerk, taking two handfuls out of his basket. 'I'm delighted, girl, I'm delighted, off you go.' And he said: 'But this is only the beginning, Ive?'

'Yes, it is only the beginning,' said Ive.

'Of course,' said Hinnerk, 'and I know someone we can take with us. I know a fellow who's been in the cells and knows the lie of the land. No, he's all right, manslaughter over a girl; what do you imagine? He couldn't come with us otherwise, we might get nabbed or something, and we couldn't do that to Claus Heim. Claus Heim, he's the only one of us who's really stuck to his guns. We shall need a car, have you got a car? Never mind, I'll nab one if necessary. D'you think I couldn't?' he asked excitedly,' and put his basket down. 'I'll show you now that I can; wait a bit, there's one over there, an Opel...'

'Don't,' said Ive, catching hold of his sleeve, 'there's plenty of time for that.'

'There isn't plenty of time,' said Hinnerk, walking unhappily beside Ive. 'Soup isn't good when it's cold. This morning when I woke up I thought, it's high time now that we set to work again, and I thought there's no relying on Ive any more; they've got him well in tow. He's joined the lickspittles. Next thing he'll be going to the South of France or the Riviera, and, I thought, if he sews the button on his coat, then that's the last straw. Have you...?'

No, the button on Ive's coat was still dangling.

'Anyway, we are getting to work now,' said Hinnerk. 'The farmers have been swimming with the stream a bit too. Those were the times, eh, Ive, at the beginning. I used to think, we shall never have times like this again. Well, and now! Of course, it won't be easy to get going again.'

'No,' said Ive, 'it won't be easy, but what we haven't done, time has done.'

'Yes,' said Hinnerk, 'the time is ripe. To set to work everywhere, but it's still worth while with the farmers: in the country things grow out of dung, but here it only stinks a bit. What's up over there?'

Something was up over there. Suddenly people were walking more quickly. They were pushing their way in from the side streets. In the shadows, at the corners, in doorways they were standing. There was a commotion in the side streets. Whistles sounded along the fronts of the houses. Isolated shrieks were heard, as though one were calling out courage to the other. Hinnerk stood still and listened.

'Communists,' he said casually, 'come on.'

They went on.

'You know,' said Hinnerk, 'we must talk this all over at once. I can get away from here any time. There's nothing to keep me here, and if there were, it could whistle.'

A flying-squad car dashed round the corner, and then another, and yet another.

'Hullo!' said Hinnerk. 'But that's how things are,' he went on. 'If I have learnt anything here it is that it's up to us, Ive, up to you and me above all. For the others can't do anything. They are tied, they have let themselves be tied. They are clinging to all sorts of things, particularly to their fancy that it had to be and that there was no escape for them. They are hanging, Ive, like flies on a fly-paper. Let them hang. It's up to us who aren't hanging. Who else can it be up to if not to us?'

'Odd,' said Ive.

'What's odd?' asked Hinnerk.

'Oh nothing,' said Ive, 'only somebody else said exactly the same thing to me.'

'That's not at all odd,' said Hinnerk, 'that's how things are, and we should be scoundrels if we didn't act accordingly—Hullo, look at the crowds. Over there.'

Look at the crowds over there. There's a fine bunch of policemen beginning to run all of a sudden. A shot sounds, very faintly, a pistol shot probably, and Hinnerk and Ive are on the spot. The Communists are howling and shrieking.

'Come on,' says Hinnerk, 'the first thing we've got to do is to thrash out a plan.'

'Yes,' says Ive, looking at the dark masses and wondering what is happening. He walks more slowly.

'There's Schweinebacke,' says Hinnerk casually. 'There must be something up.'

'Brodermann?' asks Ive and stops. 'Then I must...'

He peers along the street.

'Nothing, come home,' says Hinnerk.

'Leave me alone,' says Ive, 'Brodermann, I must see this.'

'All right,' says Hinnerk, and they wait.

Everything is in uproar now. The police sweep round in a broad, dense swarm. A shot, and another shot. Shattering window-panes. Shrieks and whistles, one after the other.

'Keep back.'

'Move on.'

The rubber truncheons are whirling. Carbines fly down from their shoulders. Barricades have been set up.

'Just look at them,' says Hinnerk. 'Look how small they are. What's the good of them, they won't stop anyone. Oh no, against the flying-squad! Come on,' he says, and then more urgently 'come on.'

'Leave me alone,' says Ive. 'Heavens, how they're hitting out. And we stand here and look on? It won't do, Hinnerk, it won't do.'

'All right,' says Hinnerk. 'Then I'll just stow my rolls away. Here, in this doorway, but what does it matter about the old rolls now, anyway.'

He flings the basket into a corner, giving it a kick as it rolls over, pushing the contents on one side with his foot. People rush past, young boys with distorted faces, shakos gleam, gaiters flash by. In raging fury the young men blunder on, but there's no escape, the wall of police is approaching. And there is Brodermann. He, too, has a rubber truncheon in his hand. The wall of disciplined, trained, muscular bodies in trim uniforms moves like a machine; here and there the line breaks slightly and closes up again immediately. And Brodermann is there.

Ive sees no one but him. He hears no one but him. He does not know what Hinnerk is doing. He does not notice the fighting. He does not hear the shrieks and whistles and shots. Some one jostles him; he sways for a moment, and then regains his balance, his legs wide spread.

'Get out,' says Brodermann in a loud voice.

Ive is silent and does not stir. Brodermann stands in front of him. Brodermann recognises him. Brodermann says: 'Get out.'

Ive looks into his face: there are the sagging cheeks, the clean-shaven chin. There is the silver-braided collar and the star on his shako; the straight, severe nose and the ice-cold eyes.

'Get out,' says Brodermann, sharp and tense. 'Clear out of it—get out!' and Brodermann raises his rubber truncheon. He raises it high above his head, and Ive sees the muscles in his wide face contract. Then Ive lets out and brings his clenched fist with full force crashing up on his chin and nose.

XIX

Brodermann telephoned at once from the police station to Schaffer. But Schaffer had an important engagement and could not get away. He managed, however, to get into touch with Pareigat. Pareigat came immediately. As he entered the room he saw at once the body stretched out on the floor. But the head was covered with a cloth. Brodermann was very pale. He stood beside the body, and it seemed to Pareigat as though he were trembling, just a little, and on his cheek, above his silver-braided collar, there were still traces of blood.

'How senseless it all is,' he said to Pareigat. 'How senseless it all is.'

But Pareigat did not agree with him. So he said nothing and, as soon as everything that was necessary had been done, he left the room without a word to Brodermann. In the ante-room some police officers were standing round, and one of them was telling his comrades all about it.

'So then I got out my gun,' he said, and added, 'and he stood there.'

And, an East Prussian farmer's son himself, he said, 'He stood there like a farmer. Like a goddamn farmer.'

XX

ANNOUNCEMENT in the *Berliner Tageblatt*:
'We understand that the young man who was killed on the occasion of the disturbances in the Kleiststrasse was the well-known agitator, Hans K. A. Iversen, formerly a Right Radical, and concerned in the struggle of the farmers. In the famous bomb trial in Altona he was acquitted in spite of the more than remarkable part he had played. Afterwards Iversen appears to have adopted democratic opinions. He was even said to have been converted to Catholicism but, to everyone's amazement, he finally espoused the Communist Cause. He was the ringleader in the encounter of the Communist demonstrators with the police, and, since he assaulted a police officer in the exercise of emergency defensive measures, he received a fatal shot.'

The end of a political romantic!

Books published by Arktos:

The Saga of the Aryan Race
by Porus Home Havewala

Against Democracy and Equality: The European New Right
by Tomislav Sunic

The Problem of Democracy
by Alain de Benoist

The Jedi in the Lotus
by Steven J. Rosen

Archeofuturism
by Guillaume Faye

A Handbook of Traditional Living

Tradition & Revolution
by Troy Southgate

Can Life Prevail?
A Revolutionary Approach to the Environmental Crisis
by Pentti Linkola

Metaphysics of War:
Battle, Victory & Death in the World of Tradition
by Julius Evola

The Path of Cinnabar:
An Intellectual Autobiography
by Julius Evola

Journals published by Arktos:

The Initiate: Journal of Traditional Studies

CPSIA information can be obtained at www.ICGtesting.com
Printed in the USA
LVOW06s1105160315

430742LV00001B/51/P